1986

a novel

QuoteStork Media, Inc.

Please follow Morgan Parker on:

Facebook

Twitter @mparkerbooks

www.officialmorganparker.com

ISBN-13 978-0-9950322-2-4

For you... thank you for coming.

1986

by: Morgan Parker

Chapter 1

All of Allana Harrison's stories started with a party. This time, the party happened on a Sunday night, one full week after the big New Year's Eve festivities in the Pripyat town square, better known as Lenin Square by the people crowded inside her and Vasy's two-bedroom, third-floor apartment. Those guests consisted mostly of engineers and their wives, a select, elite group of people that came with reputations, responsibilities, and a pinch of notoriety. There was vodka, the best kind, and the sliding door was kept slightly ajar to keep the air fresh and cool, but also to remind guests that they couldn't smoke at the tables. They could do so outside, on the tiny third-floor balcony.

At one particular point in the night, the small space was jammed with smokers after Allana and three others had gone all-in against Alex Petrokov. Petrokov was an American-born (like Allana) computer engineer (not like Allana), who happened to be the worst bluffer in the world. Except this time, he wasn't bluffing, so out to the balcony they all went, joining a trio of others who had also lost their money earlier and now had little to do but pound back shots and suck on Sobranie heaven.

It was 1986, and the world's attention was focused on their tiny town. Back then, Pripyat was the Eastern world's equivalent of Silicon Valley, or Detroit in the fifties, except they innovated energy here, not technology or automobiles. As something of an outsider, even Allana felt the pressure that came with the rest of the world's watchful eye and at first it felt great, to be a part of something as spectacular as this.

Leaning her head back, drunk and the happiest she'd been since saying farewell to her friends and family in the States seven or so months ago, Allana stared at the clear sky and let the lazy snowflakes melt on her burning cheeks while she inhaled a mouthful of nicotine. She couldn't understand the others around her; their Ukrainian conversations might as well have been Japanese. But she understood their laughter, their spirit, and their insatiable hunger for fun.

"Can you feel that?" Vasy whispered in her ear, sliding in behind her and pressing his crotch against her ass, which he often complained needed more curves. His arms slid around her stomach, his thumbs hooking into the waist of the Levi's jeans that she'd brought with her from home.

Wiggling her hips, she purred, "Yes, I can feel that."

Vasy laughed louder than the other seven people crammed out there on the balcony.

Someone shouted something, raised a half-gone bottle of vodka, and poured shots for everyone, often dumping the liquid straight into their open mouths because not everyone had a shot glass in their hand.

"The energy," he said after swallowing his shot, his lips moist and his breath hot. "Can you feel it? We're in the middle of an arctic hell, yet we've captured the energy of Times Square. Right here in our little home."

She turned around in his big, hard arms and stared into his glassy, drunken eyes. Since the first time she hugged Vasy, Allana fit perfectly against his lean, athletic body, like two Lego blocks coming together at the right height (although he had a few inches on her) and at the right spots (nothing hitching her leg up couldn't fix, anyway). He hadn't shaved today, but the dark growth looked good on him. He swung his head to the side, forcing his thick, black hair, out of his narrow face so she could see his long lashes and the intensity in those eyes that seemed to shine in the moonlight. The only thing she didn't particularly like about her husband was his attachment issues when it came to old, raggedy t-shirts like the one underneath his wool button-down. It had the opacity of waxed paper, and while she enjoyed the sight of his dark chest hair, she questioned why he even bothered with the t-shirt in the first place. It was a waste of a layer and offered no warmth or concealment.

"I love you," she told him.

"I love you more," he answered, leaning in and kissing her on the lips. The others on the balcony witnessed their sappy exchange and started ribbing them. Vasy snapped a smart-ass response, keeping the mood light, then kissed her even harder, deeper. For their benefit, of course. Someone said something else that elicited a roar of laughter, and then the sliding door opened. Still rambling at Vasy's expense, the others left Allana alone in the protective arms of the man that had saved her, scooped her up from the shitty reality of her past, and did what all of the other boys had always promised but could never deliver—he'd given her the fresh start she had always dreamed about and taken her far, far away from the people and life that had hurt her.

# # #

Back inside the humid apartment, a new poker game was beginning. The five players—Allana, Alex the American, Yuri and his wife Svetlana, and Gregor—each threw ten rubles onto the table. A non-drinking engineer, taller than any basketball player Allana had ever seen, sat opposite them. He licked his fingers and dealt the cards with an ease that would excite even the most seasoned poker player.

Vasy retreated to the stereo system and put on a record. She admired how his shoulders swayed, grinning at his inability to stand still on his lean legs while he placed Cyndi Lauper on the turntable. But once he pressed the play button, the music came out rapidly and in reverse. Everyone laughed as Vasy removed the needle and fixed the turntable's direction, and when Cyndi's voice boomed through the speakers, a roar of applause erupted in the apartment.

"You're bluffing," Alex said in plain English. A few of the engineers understood English if you spoke slowly enough, and in his drunken state, Alex Petrokov certainly spoke slowly.

Allana shrugged and tried not to gulp as she watched his eyes wander across her face, down her neck, and between her breasts where they hovered longer than a poker player's gaze should. He licked his lips, closed his eyes and took a sip of Obolon beer—a new and unfamiliar brand in the Ukraine but Vasy hadn't exactly been able to grab a case of Miller Lite at the local supermarket. The worst part was that once Alex opened his eyes, they pointed exactly where they had before he took that sip of beer, and then he licked his lips again.

She hated to admit it, but it felt nice to have a handsome, single man like Alex admiring her chest. She didn't have a whole lot up there—a c-cup if she felt bloated or ambitious, but a b-cup tonight—so finding a man like Alex taking an interest actually felt pretty damn good. Before she could clear her throat to get him to stop staring, his drunk, lazy eyes wandered back up to her face.

"You're bluffing," he repeated with a grin that had his green eyes sparkling again. "All in." He sloppily moved all of his chips to the middle of the table, arousing a roar of laughter from everyone else around them. A few people from the living room stopped dancing to Cyndi Lauper's tune and wandered over for a look at all this excitement.

With the ace and queen of hearts in her hand, Allana took a risk. It was unlikely Alex could beat her, but she played the game. She started with his short, military style hair—light brown but not quite blond—and then shifted to those killer-green eyes, moved down his crooked nose—probably got punched a few times at these poker games—to his wet lips and those perfect white teeth, his muscular neck, and then down the v-neck of his t-shirt. He had a nice chest, chiseled and mostly bare. She wondered how it would feel under her palm, but then she licked her lips and returned her stare to his face and found him grinning back at her.

"You're a jerk," she said, wondering where that insult had come from. *The second grade?* "And you've already forgotten what your cards are."

"Have I?" he taunted.

She didn't even think about it. "All in," she announced, her eyes glued to Alex the American as she shoved her chips to the middle of the table. "You don't even know where you live right now, you're so drunk."

Without breaking his stare from hers, he said, "Two kings," and flipped the cards over.

Okay, not bad.

But, but, but I have an ace and a queen! Both hearts!

The abnormally tall dealer burned a card and flipped the first two cards of the flop. And Allana suddenly felt even better – a two of hearts and a five of hearts. One more and she had him. Except the third card in the flop was a queen… of spades.

The turn revealed another two, this time a club.

What are the odds? Allana wondered, suddenly nervous that she wouldn't have a flush, or a pair of aces, or…

The River—her last chance at victory here—revealed a king.

Diamonds.

"My ass, a girl's best friend, hey?" Alex roared. To Allana, his face looked numb and overconfident.

The others watching the showdown laughed. Some booed Alex and a few really drunk guys called him *piska*, which wasn't a nice thing to call anyone.

Shaking her head, Allana pushed her chair back, mumbling, "Not a girl's best friend."

She left the table while Alex, high from his outrageous stroke of luck, brought his enormous pile of chips closer to his chest. He barely noticed her departure, she realized, and that bothered her because two minutes ago, the way he'd lost himself in a fantasy involving her breasts, she thought she'd meant something more to him.

But no, that had been the same mistake she'd made with all of the boys before Vasy. If her husband hadn't saved her when he had, she'd likely be falling for the same bullshit over and over again.

"That was quick," Vasy said, pulling her into his arms in the living room. He felt sweaty, his t-shirt damp against her chest and his entire face glistening from the heat and vodka. "Come, come, let's dance together. Let's show these uptight engineers how the cool people party." He was so incredibly happy tonight; she loved seeing the smile on his face, the lighthearted tone, the easy way he moved.

And yet she still caught herself glancing back over her shoulder at the poker table, just in time to watch the next round of cards being dealt to the remaining players. They all seemed incredibly intent on beating those ten rubles out of Alex. But from Allana's perspective, Alex didn't notice their eagerness to kick him out of the game because his eyes remained glued to her.

And she liked that.

Yes, even while she and Vasy disappeared into the small group of dancers in the living room, she noticed Alex's hungry stare and she felt good about it.

It was the stupidest thing she'd allowed herself to feel since marrying Vasy.

#

By 3:00am, the last of their guests decided to leave—an older engineer in his mid-forties and his pin-up gorgeous wife in her late twenties that could barely stand without the assistance of her husband or a wall. Vasy winked at Allana as he followed them into the hall. She knew he would make sure they reached their car downstairs before he returned to the apartment and helped her tidy up, at least a little, before getting to bed.

Allana started the tap water, filling the kitchen sink so she could clean the shot glasses and plates. She wet an old dishrag and ran it along the kitchen table, found the big garbage bag and started filling it with the monogramed (A & V) paper napkins the guests had used and left arbitrarily throughout the apartment. The napkins had been left over from their wedding, Vasy had explained to the complimentary guests throughout the night, had been shipped to the Ukraine in a big container from Boston. A couple of times, he'd taken the guests over to the crystal-framed wedding photo on the end table, displaying it to them and then kissing it with his drunk lips before putting it back in place. Allana couldn't help but laugh at his drunken gestures—between his fingerprints and slobber, the frame would need disinfectant once the guests left.

By the time the sink was full, Vasy had returned, breathing hard into his cupped hands to get them warm. She pretended to be lost in the dishes, wiping them clean with the rag and then letting them air dry on the rack on the counter. She hated most chores, but tonight she enjoyed the dishes after their party.

Sneaking up behind her, Vasy slipped his cold hands up the back of her shirt. Allana's heart raced, her legs went weak, and she realized how much she loved that – being *touched.* Quietly, she wished he didn't work so much because she missed him, missed *this* feeling of weakness at those fingertips tracing her spine. She smiled and bent her knee, sliding her ankle up the inside of his leg.

"You like my cold hands on you," he said, whispering with an accent and a slur.

She felt his drunken breath on her collarbone, the hands sliding out from underneath her shirt and moving up to her head. "What are you doing to me?" she asked, her own eyes rolling back and shutting as his fingers traced the sides of her face and grabbed her long, dark hair, moving it aside. "Oh, Jesus."

"You like this?" He pressed his lips against the vein on her neck that acted as a light switch to her arousal. Then he moved his lips upward, along the vein toward her ear.

"Vasy... I want you..." she purred.

He kissed a little longer, released her hair, then stepped back from the sink. When she turned around to face him, she saw the hunger in his eyes, the glassy haze that turned them darker as they swam across her face. His mouth closed and he swallowed. He would take her right there in the kitchen if she allowed it. And although she would enjoy that, she preferred the comfy bed where they could draw the curtains and keep their neighbors' prying eyes out. A history of sneaking around in back seats and pick-up truck cargo beds would do that to anyone, wouldn't it?

She reached down and cupped his groin. "I'll meet you in bed," she promised before hurrying away from the sink, down the hall to the bathroom at the far end.

"Be quick," Vasy called after her, his voice slurred. She wondered whether it came from his drunkenness or sexual desire.

As she eased the bathroom door shut, she glanced back into the hall and watched his silhouette sway toward the master bedroom. Allana was quick, brushing her teeth, stripping out of her pants, and repositioning her breasts to make herself a little more sexual, a little more presentable. She stood at the mirror a little longer, wondering if her shoulder-length hair was still enough, if maybe her flat belly wasn't as sexy here as it was in the States... And then she saw it; her long lashes were stuck together, so she grabbed her nail scissors from the drawer and split the clinging lashes apart with the blade rather than picking them with her fingers. That was better.

She had promised herself to never become complacent in her marriage, never become that woman who stopped shaving her legs in the winter or stopped trying to look sexy for her man. Vasy deserved a perfect wife; he deserved more than what he'd gotten with her and her past, so Allana felt she owed him this. At the very least, she owed him a wife that he'd love screwing for the rest of his life.

But by the time she slipped into the dark bedroom, half-naked with her perky tits and fresh breath, Vasy had already fallen asleep. Snoring, too. He wouldn't wake up now. Even if he could, she realized, sliding her hand down the front of his boxers, it was unlikely that the rest of him would.

This man had partied hard tonight. He was exhausted after six days of twelve-hour shifts.

Knowing that she'd get nothing tonight, she dropped with an uncaring and heavy sigh onto the mattress, slid underneath the thick comforter and reached down to finish herself off before falling asleep.

# # #

Monday morning, Allana woke with a headache and Vasy's stale-drunk breath lapping over her face like the waves at the beach. She rolled over, stifled a groan, and searched the floor for the slippers Vasy had given her on Christmas Eve. When she found them, she slid her feet inside, grabbing her housecoat off the floor on her way out of the room. The apartment seemed messier than she remembered; the cold weather outside left the windows fogged up with condensation. Though Vasy had the day off, many of the people from last night didn't. Their morning would hurt just like hers.

She filled the sink with fresh warm water and finished cleaning the dishes she'd started last night. By then, her head ached and her hands trembled, and she had no choice but to hunt down her Sobranie cigarettes. She found the pack in the living room, tucked between the cushions on the sofa, and then let herself outside onto the balcony.

An inch of snow had already accumulated overnight, and the white flakes continued to fall in shy amounts. But the frigid air was fierce. It took her two attempts with her lighter to get the cigarette going, but after the first long puff, she started to feel better. Her fingers calmed and her head thanked her.

Closing her eyes, she willed herself to ignore the cold as she pictured Alex Petrokov glancing over at her from the poker table, his eyes drunk and wanting. That kicked her heart rate up a notch—made her a little warm, too—and that was also when the sliding balcony door eased open and Vasy appeared.

Perfect timing.

Keeping her eyes closed, she listened to his feet crunching the fresh snow. It wasn't until she could feel his body shielding hers from the wind that she finally opened her eyes and saw that he'd brought a sweater, a kind grin and a soft, bloodshot stare. He offered the sweater to her, he himself wearing only *that* t-shirt. For some stupid and unbelievable reason, he seemed to prefer that horrible t-shirt, nothing else. It had orange-stained armpits. Yes, it was overdue for the garbage. Still, Vasy looked good in a hangover, two-day growth, and red puffy eyes.

"You look cold," she said. "I have my housecoat."

"The sweater's yours. It won't fit me." He nodded at her to put it on.

Once she'd slipped her arms into the sweater, Vasy directed his gaze to her Sobranies.

"I'm almost all out," she complained, tossing the pack to him. He'd smoked a lot last night. *A lot.*

"Sorry." He gave her a guilty wince.

"I thought you wanted to work out?"

He shrugged. "Tomorrow."

"Really?" She raised an eyebrow, even though she knew she'd be heading into the town square this afternoon and could buy another pack

"I'll wake up early and go for a run instead."

Allana decided to play with him a little. "Why wait until tomorrow when today's a perfect day to start achieving your fitness goals and quitting bad habits?"

At last, he laughed, always that deep, throaty sound that reminded her of the country music concerts she'd seen at the Silverdome in her youth. Stepping toward her, he wrapped his heavy arms around her and she swore she could feel the gooseflesh on his muscles pushing through the fabric of the sweater he'd just given her, not to mention the housecoat's fabric.

"You know something?" he asked, giving a stern nod. "You're right." He kissed the top of her head, released her, and reached for the balcony door.

"No, wait," she sighed. She didn't want him to leave—he was *warm!*

When Vasy turned back toward her, she tossed the cigarettes at him. Without much weight left in it, the pack seemed to flutter before he caught it.

"I'm heading into town anyway," she said. "I'll get more at the store."

She sensed his relief as his nicotine-stained fingers fumbled inside and then placed the cigarette on his lips so he could work the lighter. She knew the feeling he experienced as he lit the tip and closed his eyes like it was the first breath of fresh air he'd tasted in a long time.

# # #

Chapter 2

The Pripyat city bus rattled. Each time it hit another bump, it bounced so hard that the hangover pain in Allana's head flared up like a high school punk band. She didn't understand the violent bouncing or chaotic rattling; underneath the snow, the roads were perfectly smooth. In fact, everything about their little town in the northern part of the Soviet Ukraine was perfect. So why was the bus such a piece of garbage? Even the heating system refused to work consistently, coughing up a blast of warm air and then withdrawing into silence like it might be building up a lungful of phlegm.

Despite Pripyat being known across the entire planet as one of the most advanced and prosperous hubs in existence, the fairytale life Vasy had promised, so far, had only been half-delivered. But nobody here knew her language. Plus, this place was located in the middle of an arctic hell. Although Vasy had delivered on taking her far away from the violence and demons of her past, what had happened to the rainbows, unicorns, and eternal sunshine? To Allana, those things were hibernating or never existed at all because while he worked six days a week, she was stuck at home. Alone.

Part of her forgave him for those long hours, but another part resented that he'd been increasingly distracted with work, less attentive with her than he used to be. She couldn't put a finger on what had changed—certainly wasn't her clinging eye lashes or the short hair and flat tummy, how could it be?—but something definitely had.

The bus stopped at a small terminal in Lenin Square, and Allana zipped up her big, heavy jacket, and donned her fur hat. The weather in Pripyat exceeded any kind of cold she'd experienced in the States. Here, the cold legitimately *hurt*.

Allana hurried across the snow-covered town center toward the supermarket, which was the States' equivalent of a general store. Inside, she grabbed a basket and started down the narrow, thinly stocked aisles. The groceries consisted of the basics. Not much in the way of sugary cereals or fancy breads and pastas—at least Pripyat had *some* of those luxuries in a country where a lot of people actually made their own—but the store had all of the ingredients one would need. And it also stocked cigarettes (or the filters, rolling papers and tobacco to do it yourself), a small selection of tasty, local meats (they did *not* sell livestock to make your own meats, interestingly enough) and fresh potatoes. Lots of potatoes.

She grabbed what she needed—flour, eggs, baking soda and cigarettes—and then started toward the checkout when she bumped into a man walking backward into her path, not paying attention.

"Sorry," she mumbled as the corner of her basket jabbed into his hip. That was when she caught a glance at the familiar face.

Alex Petrokov. AKA, Alex the American.

"Hey. Shit, sorry I wasn't paying attention," he said, smirking as those wanting eyes focused on her, surveying and swallowing her entire body, it seemed.

Despite being insulated underneath the jacket and protected by multiple layers of clothing, Allana felt nakedly vulnerable. She squirmed a little, reminded of last night at the kitchen sink with Vasy's cold hand climbing up her spine.

"You clean up well, Allana."

"Same to you." Her heart was pounding, fast. In her throat. "How's your headache?"

He shook his head without blinking. "No headache. That's not how I like to party. Besides, I knew I had to come into town this morning. I just didn't expect my morning to be *this* good." His eyes crawled over her body when he said *good.*

A larger Soviet woman with a square jaw and red cheeks wedged past them in her heavy fur coat, casting a suspicious glare. Two Americans in the same spot in *this* part of the world would cause suspicion in anyone, especially if they looked like a couple of tourists; American couples were rare, it wasn't Disneyland.

"Have you ever been to the café?" Alex asked casually.

"Only in the summer," she gulped. *When Vasy introduced you to me, it was on the beach next to the Café, or the "Dish" as he'd called it.*

His hand latched onto her forearm. Not forcibly or anything, but firm enough to send a message—he wanted her to go with him to the beach-side café that possibly wasn't even open at this time of year. Although a part of her wondered why, another part savored the excitement of sneaking away with him. He was still as beautiful in his sober state as he'd been last night, and his eyes, which were now a brighter shade of green, still made her feel like an object of desire despite the heavy jacket and layers. And he still made her want to take the kinds of all-in risks she'd taken at the poker table. Not because she wanted to lose it all like she had last night, but because she needed more. She needed that weak-knees feeling that had her squirming and feeling human, *alive* again.

Allana shook her head; weak-knees and squirming killed marriages. "Vasy's expecting me. I should get home."

Alex raised an eyebrow, loosening his grip. "You're lying to me."

"No." Maybe Vasy wasn't perfect. Maybe he worked too much and was acting a little more distracted than usual. And maybe Allana needed a little something *more*. But… not this. "I'm not lying."

"You are." Still with that intense stare that made her feel naked. "Vasy likes to exercise on his days off. If he's not in the Energetik's pool right now, he's on his way."

That was true. Vasy didn't get to the pool as much as he liked to. Something about eighty-hour workweeks left little time for exercise.

"So how about we grab a coffee. Or tea," he added, stepping a little closer to her and giving a nod that came across as a touch too persistent. "And I'll drive you home before Vasy's even finished swimming."

As much as she liked the idea of having another American to spend time with, she wasn't sure how Vasy would react. Alex was single, he wasn't like the others with their trophy wives and mediocre looks. Plus, Alex was very clearly American, and Allana didn't trust American men anymore. Not after all that she'd been through. *No thank you, I'll fold this one, all American men ever dealt me were abuse, heartbreak and manipulation. Royal flush my ass.*

Alex leaned even closer to her. "Listen, you're a pretty woman," he confided. "But you're married. I get that. I respect that." The way he said it, she remembered the weekends at home, her father promising to stop drinking after getting a little physical the night before. Alex didn't strike her as genuine, not with those eyes that seemed preoccupied with stripping her out of her clothes. "And, even if you don't believe anything else I've said, Vasy is my *friend*. I wouldn't betray his trust. So, if you're thinking I'm going to try to seduce you at the beach in the middle of winter, you should think again."

Allana pulled free of his grip and continued to the checkout counter.

After paying for her items, she left the store. She hurried across the town square, glancing back in the general direction of the Cultural Centre. She hoped to find Vasy on the front steps, heading out early, or any kind of hint that she wasn't as alone as she felt. But all she saw was a few other people in dark fur coats, a few children playing in the snow, and the upper frame of the

Ferris wheel in the distance.

"Lana," she suddenly heard.

Turning to see a dark Lada sedan idling on the very road she needed to cross, she also noticed the driver leaning across the passenger seat toward the unrolled the window.

It was Alex. "Sorry I spooked you." He seemed a little concerned, or maybe it was the stick-shifter jabbing into his ribs that made his face crunch like that.

"I'm not spooked," she huffed, keeping a safe distance between her and the car. After the words were out in the open, she knew she was lying. Because she was spooked, she just didn't know how to explain it. Not yet. "It's just... like you said... I'm married and... it's always people's perception that causes problems. And I don't want problems."

Alex chuckled. "It's okay. I understand."

"Thank you." She suddenly realized how much her own perceptions were getting blown out of proportion here. Nobody had mentioned an affair; that had all been in *her* head. Besides, very few people knew her in Pripyat. Only the handful of people who had been at the party last night knew of her relationship with Vasy, and even then....

The way Allana saw it, to an untrained eye—which meant the other fifty thousand or so people who hadn't been at the party last night—she and Alex could just as easily be brother and sister. That's right, blood relatives. Cousins at least. Nobody would think they were crossing a line, just from seeing them together at a café, drinking tea and staring at each other's chest. In fact, the café itself would likely be empty at this time of year anyway. Yes, the way Allana saw it, it was probably okay to have coffee or tea.

Inside the small sedan, Alex sat back up. "Great." He waved her toward the car. "Now that we've settled that little matter, hop in."

She laughed.

"Seriously," he said, chuckling. "It's cold."

She stepped toward the car, hesitating a little because she'd often seen things one way. Her track record stunk; in almost all cases, she'd been dead wrong. But she entered the car anyway, and grinned at the excitement.

There was no risk in having tea with this man; she was married.

She loved Vasy. A lot.

"Okay," she agreed, pulling her seatbelt across her and connecting to the latch next to her hip. "Just coffee."

That small decision changed everything, more than she could ever know at the time.

Way more.

# # #

Only half a dozen other people were present at the Pripyat Café when Allana entered ahead of Alex. A couple of men hovered over a table near the large, famous stained glass window like they were coming up with some majestic scheme; a couple of high school kids were holding hands in a corner, staring into each other's eyes—and likely making empty promises about forever and some other soul mate garbage—and, lastly; there were two more men, much older, in bulging snow suits with police badges sewn onto their chests, sitting back and enjoying the warmth. None of those people noticed Allana as she wandered to a table for two in a hidden corner.

Alex followed her, removing his jacket and hanging it over the back of the faux-iron chair. As he unrolled the scarf from around his neck, he said, "Let me guess…latté?"

Grinning, Allana cast a nervous glance at the four people she could see and, again, none of them seemed to even notice her presence. "Yes. That's perfect."

"I'll be right back," Alex promised with a smile that charmed her and made her nervous at the same time. She'd seen smiles like his before, and they always evolved into good times and overstepped boundaries and, ultimately, the heartbreak that followed someone leaving.

As he headed toward the espresso counter, she watched him; his body was similar to Vasy's; lean, flat and hard, except Alex wasn't shy about wearing shirts that hid his biceps, and he let his shirt hang loosely over the waist of his pants so she had to wonder just how flat his tummy might be. Once she couldn't see him anymore, she removed her jacket and tucked her hat into its arm, and then sat down. She checked the time. Vasy would only be getting into the water now, his laps would last forty minutes, then it was a sauna and a shower, and possibly a stop at Gregor's for some music and a cigar. It was unlikely he would touch vodka today, but that was always an option as well.

"You look nervous," Alex said, returning with her latté and a shot of espresso for him. As he settled into the seat across from her, he asked, "What if Vasy walked in right now? Do you think he'd care?"

"He would," she answered with the kind of timid nod that could easily evolve into freaking-out.

Grinning, Alex shook his head. "He trusts you. He trusts me. I'd tell him I invited you out for coffee with my winnings from last night, and that I was going to drive you home rather than send you back on the shitty city bus. And then, do you know what he'd do? He'd hug me and thank me because he knows you haven't made a single friend since you arrived here."

She sipped her latté, noticing a softer, less-sleazy side of Alex, the way his forehead rippled when his big, green eyes just... *noticed* her.

"So, please... stop worrying. We've done nothing wrong."

Yet, she finished quietly in her head.

"Anyway, I'm glad you agreed to chat with me," he went on,

reclining a little in his chair. "I haven't had a good conversation in English since last summer, the barbecue. Do you remember it?"

She nodded. It had been a work function, just outside the power station grounds, and it was also when she'd met Alex for the first time. Vasy had introduced him, a fellow hockey fanatic and conspiracy theorist, and then he'd left the two of them alone to speak English and get to know each other. Even back then, Alex had a charming way about him. It surprised her now that he asked if she remembered the conversation when she'd been the one to bring up the beach barbecue in the first place...

"But even then," he said with an insider's smirk, "it was the regular crap. 'How are you, it's great to be here, where did you go to school' and all of that." He took a miniature sip from his miniature cup. "Maybe we can ask some big person questions now."

Allana had to look down at the latté foam in her cup, the sprinkled cinnamon that looked like the summertime freckles she used to get as a kid. "Like what kind of questions?"

He shrugged. "What's something you've wanted to ask me since you met me?"

"I have no questions," she lied, shaking her head. Because big person questions often led to big person problems. Better not to ask anything.

Her response seemed to surprise him. "Nothing?"

"Nothing."

"Well, I have a question for you." Those green eyes narrowed.

"Ask it," she said, hoping her voice came out with confidence rather than nervousness.

"But you have to answer it with honesty." He frowned at her and took another curt sip.

"Okay. Sure. I believe in honesty." *For the most part, anyway.*

"Okay, good." Another sip and Allana wondered why he looked

nervous all of a sudden.

Alex seemed to study her a little more closely before taking a deep breath and asking the first question. "Why are you here, Lana? And don't give me the standard answer, the one from last summer about marrying Vasy and following him to the opposite end of the world out of love for adventure and matrimonial loyalty."

"But that's the answer," she said as she lifted the cup to her lips and tried to count the cinnamon freckles inside. *Does he think he knows something?*

"Maybe that's the answer, but how about the honest truth?" he asked, coming at her a little harder than she'd expected from him.

"The honest truth, huh?" She watched him over the edge of her cup before taking another sip.

"Please."

"And then I can ask my question?" she narrowed her eyes to match his.

He smiled. "I thought you had none."

"I changed my mind," she snapped.

"Sure," Alex shrugged. He really was laid back. Not a good bluffer, but laid back. "Or if it's going to help you feel better, Lana, you can ask your question now before you forget."

She stared down at the table, the cup, the salt-stained tiled floor. When she finally raised her attention to Alex, she had her answer. The honest truth... *for the most part.* "I'm here because I wanted to get away. And when Vasy proposed, he promised he could make that happen. He promised to get me away, just like I wanted." *He'd also promised kids, a life with lots of friends and a house that matched his pay scale and social prominence as a Gurin.*

Alex seemed to process the honest truth. "So you're running from something..."

"No, not running." She shifted in her seat as she answered, and she wondered if Alex noticed.

He chuckled. "That's not how it sounds to me."

"I've escaped. There's a difference." She took a breath, calming herself. "Now it's my turn," she blurted before he could ask for more truth.

"Let's hear it," he said with that bluffer's stare-down minus the drunken desire. Which was exactly what she wanted to ask about...

"Last night at the party," she started, setting the scene so he would know exactly where she was coming from with her question, "you had this gleam in your eyes, each time you looked at me. And it was... well, it was a little unsettling." *It's the truth, too; it unsettled her that she could respond to something as stupid as a drunken, hungry stare.*

"Unsettling for me or for you?" he asked, and although it sounded like a joke, it wasn't.

"For me!" she chirped, feigning amazement.

He frowned, thinking about it and not at all shaken by her over-reaction, not one bit. "Unsettling how? I mean, did it feel like I was stripping you with my eyes?"

Allana's eyes shot open. "Yes! Why were you looking at me like that, Alex?" *What does he really think about me?*

His Adam's apple bobbed as he swallowed. "Why do you think I was looking at you like that? Like I was trying to get a taste of something I couldn't have?"

Allana noticed that her hands were shaking, and she didn't like that. She placed her half-drunk latté back on the table and stood up. "No. This isn't what this coffee is about, Alex." *Big person questions lead to big person problems, and I'm not a whore, I know what you're trying to do, and I'm done.* "I'm leaving."

"I'm sorry, but..." He clearly looked nervous now, there was no question about it. *And he should, he's a pig! He's gone too far!*

She was already making her way toward the exit.

After downing the rest of his espresso, Alex chased after her.

# # #

Allana sat in the Lada's passenger seat with her legs crossed away from the pervert next to her, her grocery bag in her lap for a quick escape once he pulled up to her apartment. The ride seemed to take forever and she wondered, as they left the town center, how this guy had convinced her to allow him to drive her home, let alone have coffee with him. *Ugh, I knew it, too; he didn't want friendship!*

"Listen," he said from the driver's seat. The wipers worked hard at keeping the windshield clear of accumulation. It was snowing hard, turning the landscape white very quickly. "I didn't mean for any of that to offend you."

She said nothing as she stared out the window at the falling snow turning everything white. She had been right to end their "truthfully honest" conversation at the Pripyat Café. While honest truth was something she believed in, too much of it had a way of clouding everyone's ability to make right decisions.

"Look, you're an attractive woman," he went on.

"You need to stop talking, Alex," she warned him. "Stop. Right now."

They made it a block in silence before Alex piped up again. "Why is it so wrong to talk about these things? You're married, and I work and am good friends with your husband."

"That's why it's wrong," she explained. "Because I'm married and you work with my husband. Jesus, do you even consider him a good friend?"

"Well, yeah. He is." Allana half-expected him to add *duh* to the comment but, instead, the car went silent again.

"Here's the thing," he said, and to Allana's worried ears, it seemed as if he was already convinced they'd have an affair, that it wouldn't be a bad thing if they did, and that he wanted to convince her of it as well. *Perverted pigs work like that*, she rationalized to herself; *they try to convince you of their backwards way of thinking.*

"Alex, you need to let this go. I'm sorry, but coffee was a bad idea. And those questions, they weren't two friends having a coffee and asking about the weather."

"But you're the one who asked about the way I was looking at you," he argued, adding a shrug to keep the conversation moving. "Sure, I could have lied and said I was just drunk, that I didn't find you delicious—"

"It's wrong," she interrupted.

"Honesty is wrong?" he asked, chuckling. "You can't really believe that."

She said nothing. *Delicious?* She crossed her legs.

"Knowing where each of us stands is a good thing. You know why I was looking at you like I was—"

"Stop—"

"Finally," he sighed. "Now I know why you're so insistent on closing your eyes and ears to the truth."

She refused to take the bait. *He wants me to talk about this?* She bit down on her bottom lip, something she should have done at the café.

"At least now we both know the reason for your silence."

Still not taking the bait.

"It's because we're both attracted to each other."

She swung her gloved hand across the console and hit him hard in his face. Really hard. So hard that his crooked nose started to bleed and the car swerved momentarily into the oncoming lane. She regretted her impulsive reaction almost immediately—how would it look to Vasy if she and Alex were killed in a head-on collision?—but then Alex wiped the blood away and started laughing.

"You've proven my point," he said, wiping the blood again. "So with all of that out of the way, we both know the boundaries."

She wanted to ask, with *what* out of the way? The bloody nose or the admission of attraction? Which, she never actually admitted to! She wanted to jump out of the car and put an end to this, because she knew men like Alex, she knew what they were capable of and...

"Because I need your help, Allana," he said, using his tongue to keep the blood from rolling into his mouth.

The sudden shift in conversation shocked her.

"For real," he went on, dabbing at the blood with his sleeve.

"I refuse to help you," she spat back, noticing how her entire demeanor had changed. By taking a swing at Alex, she'd uncrossed her legs and was no longer focused on what passed outside her passenger window. She'd turned her body toward him and deep down—like really, really deep down—she wanted to help him stop the faucet-like bleeding that she'd caused in the first place. "I refuse," she repeated.

He glanced sideways at her, his eyes narrowing. Those fuck-me eyes were gone now, replaced with a mild annoyance. So mild she wanted to hit him again.

"You'll come around," he promised, then glanced into his lap where the blood had pooled. "Look at that. You've ruined my pants."

Allana glanced down at his crotch.

"Stop looking at my package," he said with a grin, but he immediately flung his arm upward to protect his face from another wild swing.

Allana groaned in frustration, simply crossed her arms and her legs, and stared out the window again. "I refuse to help you."

They drove the rest of the way in silence, while she had to keep herself from glancing over at Alex. He could bleed out into the foot well of the Lada for all she cared.

Alex cleared his throat as he steered into the parking lot of the building where Allana and Vasy lived. His demeanor had calmed too, lacking the arrogance and perversion that preceded the bloody nose. "I'm sorry this started off so poorly, Lana. And please trust me when I say my intentions are not to become a wedge in your marriage." His tone seemed genuine, but Allana had her doubts, especially after he'd claimed she was attracted to him. "I love that man, he's one of my closest friends here in Pripyat. But I need your help. I *honestly* need your help."

He stopped the car at the lobby entrance, which had been recently shoveled, allowing a path through the fresh snow. Allana reached for the door handle with her free hand, but then felt Alex's hands on her other wrist, stopping her.

"Allana, please."

Something in his tone—desperation, sincerity, a combination of both?—slowed her down. After a brief hesitation, she released the door handle and sat back in the passenger seat. She stared at the drooping fabric ceiling with moisture stains in it, her wrist still buzzing from where he had grabbed her.

"If I tell you something, I need to know I can trust you," he said, motioning at his nose, the blood, all of it. "It's vital that what I'm about to tell you stays between us."

Allana rolled her eyes. "No thank you, Alex." She reached for the door handle again. "I'm not keeping any secrets for you."

"Just listen, okay? Okay. The Americans want to, um, decommission the power station." The words came out in one long, blurted sentence. And his face turned a sudden shade lighter. And then that lighter shade turned to green. Alex looked ill.

And Allana felt *worse*. Because what did decommission really mean? Of course, she thought of a mushroom cloud, like Hiroshima, or mass contamination like the radiation leak at Three Mile less than a decade ago. She chuckled, a nervous *huh huh* because it couldn't possibly be *that* bad... could it?

"This isn't a joke," he lectured her. He leaned closer, stopping short when Allana made a fist with her gloved hand. "I don't know who else I can tell, Lana. Or who I can turn to. If I go to Anatoly's group, I'll be sent in for questioning by the authorities. They might even torture me for details I don't have."

"No, they wouldn't do that..." she started, but she knew he was right. *What does* decommission *mean?*

"You know they will," he sighed. "And I can't talk to Vasy because he's connected to Nikolai." He shook his head, visibly shaken. As Chief Engineer, Nikolai Fomin wielded tremendous power; Allana knew the name because the Fomin family was extremely close to the Gurin family, Vasy's parents. In fact, Nikolai Fomin had advocated for Vasy's government-paid scholarship to MIT and had promised that, once he graduated, he could come back to a prolific position of authority.

Allana shuddered. What Alex said had merit, it had *honest truth*. The whole world was watching Pripyat, envious of its energy, its innovative power generation techniques. So she had to accept the reasons Alex gave for why he'd come to her instead of her husband, the man he claimed to love as a close friend. Alex was desperate. He needed help. He wanted trust. He believed in honesty.

And now he wanted—no, he *needed* secrecy.

"But what do you think I can possibly do to help, Alex?" she asked. "I'm a stay-at-home wife with a degree in English Literature. I know a few swear words in Ukrainian, I know that the ruble is slightly above par against the dollar, but outside of that I offer nothing of value here. Nothing." *Not even a friend to help pass the hours, which is probably why I need to stay away from handsome, fast-talking men that look at me like you do...* In her mind, she bit back a nervous *huh huh.*

"But you're an American," he said, his wide eyes laced with conspiracy. "Like me."

She reached for that door handle again. "Was. I *was* an American, Alex. So you see, I really can't help."

Alex swallowed hard, and he looked so helpless that she finally softened to his plea. She'd seen his (over) confidence at the café and in the car before she busted his nose. And now she saw this version of him, one that was driven by the same fear she felt about this idea of *decommissioning* the power station. Her stomach rumbled and she felt ill, so she thought about something else, like the Sobranies she'd just purchased, the ones waiting in the grocery bag in her lap. She could really use one of those now.

"I have to go, Alex," she blurted, in a hurry to get away. *The honest truth can do that,* she thought to herself, *it can lead to big person problems that make you want to run away.*

"Lana..." he begged.

"I'm sorry. I just don't think I can help you."

This time she managed to open the Lada's passenger door and get one foot outside before Alex stopped her again, and this time his hand clamped her shoulder. She glanced back, noticing his strong hand, his clean fingernails. She wondered—no, she shifted her attention and he released her.

"Think about this," he asked, the desperation stronger than ever. "If the Americans get their way, it affects all of us."

"Okay," she agreed with a sigh. *What does decommissioning mean?*

"One last thing," he added. "Please talk to me before you go to Vasy.

Or anyone else for that matter."

She studied him. He looked small, vulnerable and that scared her because on a physical level, Alex was anything but those things. "I don't like secrets."

"But this is national security," he insisted. Allana wanted out of the car, wanted away from this conversation. In fact, she'd have taken perverted Alex back in a heartbeat, because that part of him at least warranted a bloody nose; this new, vulnerable, scared, conspiracy preaching version was actually starting to scare her.

"Okay."

"As Americans, we're at risk," he confided. "So if you think about talking about this, call me first."

And there it is: call me first. Call me. It felt like a sham all of a sudden, a way to give her nightmares, create the illusion that they were on the same team, a team of *two*, and when those nightmares woke her in the middle of the night and she needed someone to cuddle up with, *call me first*, wink-wink, bow-chica-wow-wow. *Ugh!*

A brief silence, and then she told him the truth once her disgust thinned out. Because that was what he wanted, wasn't it? "Honestly, Alex? This has nothing to do with me. It doesn't affect me in the least, so I won't be talking or thinking about it after I get back upstairs." *So don't sit by the phone waiting for my desperate phone call looking for someone to rub my back.*

And with that, she stepped out of the passenger seat and walked to the lobby, naively believing the words she'd just spoken about none of it affecting her in the least.

# # #

Chapter 3

The freezing spell that gripped Pripyat at the end of January 1986 forced Allana to quit smoking. Not only did the cold air cause dry skin and eczema, but the moisture inside the apartment seized the balcony door, and she couldn't get outside any longer. She had tried, had even gone as far as scraping the ice and pouring boiling water into the frozen tracks, but with no success. And, on February fourth, exactly one full week as a non-smoker, she broke down.

After locating the last pack of unopened Sobranies in the back of the refrigerator, Allana grabbed a lighter and went for the door. It refused to open.

Outside. She had to get outside because she refused to smoke indoors. She made a fist, but held back from smashing it against the glass. After what she'd done to Alex's nose, she didn't want to break the door and let the warm apartment air escape.

Grabbing her winter boots out of the front closet, she hurried into the hallway, locking the door with a key, and then making her way to the elevator. After pounding the call button, she waited. And waited and waited. An older man with a black fur toque, grey skin, and silver hair bursting from his ears, walked past her and said something in a language she didn't understand. When she stared blankly back, he repeated himself, louder and with hand gestures this time.

At last, he said, "Beh," and made the internationally accepted motion for "I give up on this idiot" before continuing to the emergency stairwell at the other end of the hallway.

Allana assumed the freezing cold had damaged the elevator's motor, and she began to cry as she walked back to the apartment. She cried a little more after pitching the cigarettes at the wall. And then she picked up the phone and called Vasy.

It rang sixteen times before he picked up.

"Sluchaju," he said, *hello* in Ukrainian.

She sobbed into the phone.

"Allana?" he asked. "Is that you?"

"Who else would it be?" she asked, sniffling.

"What's wrong?" Even though he'd let the phone ring sixteen before picking up, the concern in Vasy's voice suggested he had nothing else to do today, like Allana was his sole priority.

"Can you come home?"

It was Tuesday. He'd only been back for one day this week. Sixteen hours into his eighty-hour workweek. Not a chance, she figured. But she had to ask. Because…

"I'll be there," he said, his voice a little worried now.

She wept for ten seconds or so, but it felt like an eternity. "Thank you," she said at last.

"I'll be there," he repeated. "I'm on my way."

The line went dead in her hand, but not right away. Normally, the Soviet version of a dial tone kicked in quicker. Not this time.

Maybe it was the delirious tears that delayed the dial tone. Allana frowned, listening to the emptiness of white noise and figured it had something to do with the week-long freezing spell.

She was wrong.

# # #

Allana woke with Vasy cradling her, her body pulled up against him like a spoon. On the sofa.

With her husband spooning her, and his big arms and warm, muscular chest serving as a blanket, she hadn't noticed just how cold their apartment had become. But the tip of her nose was icy, and she could almost see vapor when she breathed.

The television's power off light (the red one right next to the green one) had gone blank. The red digital clock on the stereo was blank. Their crystal wedding frame had condensation—or frost—on its surface.

"We've lost power," she whispered, sitting up. She noticed the thick manual from the power station on the floor; it had been Vasy's reading material while she slept. It had obviously failed to hold his interest because he'd fallen asleep as well, but when she mentioned the loss of power, he woke up.

"What?"

"There's no heat," she said, a little panicked. "And the TV and clocks and—"

Vasy sat up, wrapped those big arms around her, and kissed the side of her head. "It's okay. Puzzling, but okay."

After a deep breath—in through her nose, out through her pursed lips—Allana felt a little better. Less frightened. Vasy was right, but he would take the loss of power to heart. "I'm sorry," she murmured, regretting making a big deal of the power loss.

He shrugged. "It's not the power station. It's the electrical system in the building."

She considered telling him about her chat with Alex last Monday, not the part where he invited her to call him, but his story about how the Americans didn't like the power station. Probably because it was a nuclear facility, the kind that the entire world wanted, and the Americans hadn't built it. Maybe they also hated how advanced it was, at least from a technological standpoint. This type of facility was being built all across the Soviet Union, in such big numbers that it gave the Soviets a leading edge when it came to harnessing nuclear power generation.

"Allana?" Vasy asked. "You're shaking."

Tell him.

"What's wrong?" he pulled her even closer.

Tell him.

"I… I'm just cold." She smiled and kissed him. A simple, innocent peck on the lips at first, but then a longer, more intimate kiss involving a bit of force and a lot of tongue.

Once Allana finally started to heat up, Vasy broke their kiss. He was breathing heavily, his lips slightly swollen from the passion, his eyes dreamy. "I have to get back to work," he huffed, shaking his head. "I said I'd be gone for an hour."

Allana laughed, grabbed his neck, and playfully strangled him. They hadn't made love in two days.

Vasy smiled, but based on the way that grin fizzled away, it seemed his inability or unwillingness to stay and please her was something that bothered him. So Allana released his neck, kissed him on the forehead the way he often did with her, and then stood up and pulled him out of the sofa. She'd forgotten all about her nicotine breakdown until Vasy mentioned it.

"It's okay to smoke in here," he said, shrugging like it suddenly didn't matter. He'd been more obsessive-compulsive about it than she had. "Just use the second bedroom and open the window."

"It'll make our things smell," she protested, taking his hand and guiding him toward the apartment door where he'd left his jacket and boots. "I'm fine now anyway," she lied. And for the most part, she really was fine; the "decommissioning" had probably been entirely fabricated by Alex, a stupid scare tactic to get her to reach out to him.

"Then we're moving," he told her. "We have state-of-the-art access to power here, and this crappy apartment building can't keep up with it. We're moving."

She smiled to appease him. Almost all of the apartments in Pripyat were the same. Walk in to a tight living space and a small kitchen area, and then turn down a hall that led to a couple of bedrooms and a bathroom at the end. Boston-style, multi-level penthouses didn't exist here. And despite his position at the power station, Vasy wasn't on the list for state-paid housing. He didn't have access to a nice demi-palace in the country with a bit of yard space for kids to ride horses or plant their own food (which would probably be potatoes, though Allana claimed to hate them since coming here).

"We'll get one with a better view of the power station," he said with optimism, pointing to the frozen-shut balcony door and beyond. "So when you have another meltdown, you can look out the windows and I'll look out mine, and I'll reflect the sunlight off of a mirror." He pasted a cute, goofy smile to his lips and nodded with child-like enthusiasm.

Allana laughed. "That's so romantic, Vasy. Barf."

They hugged. "We're moving," he repeated, his face stern. He kissed her one last time before opening the door and stepping into the hallway.

Allana poked her head out after him, watched him head toward the stairwell. "Hey, Vasy?"

He looked back over his shoulder at her, but kept walking.

"Did you ever imagine you'd take a pass on getting laid in favor of going to work?"

Grinning, he shook his head at her and kept moving.

"Hey, Vasy," she called after him again, just as he reached the emergency stairwell door.

He turned around to face her this time. "More humiliation?"

"Nah. I love you," she grinned, staring after him and wondering how she had ever let a man like Alex Petrokov get to her. All she ever needed was Vasy. Period. "I love you," she repeated. "That's all."

His smile got bigger, brighter. "I love you more," he answered before slipping into the stairwell and disappearing.

# # #

Chapter 4

Less than half an hour later, Allana couldn't shake the urge for a cigarette. It started with the shakes, so she stepped off the sofa began pacing. But then the sweats started and she had to wipe her clammy palms down her thighs to keep them dry. Before long, the mind games started, and that was when the real panic set in, so she resorted to her rhythmic breathing exercises. She closed her eyes like she'd been taught in prenatal class, and focused on the inhalations and exhalations. In, in, in… and out… in, in, in… and out.

He, he, he… hooo.

It helped.

After a few minutes, her palms dried, her shaking subsided and she felt her stress levels dropping. The reality of her life felt less cold, less isolated.

"I don't need smokes," she whispered. "Don't need them."

More breathing, and then she collapsed onto the frigid sofa and reached around the work manuals that Vasy had left lying around for the one novel she'd managed to smuggle during the move. *The Great Gatsby*. She'd read it a hundred times already, give or take. Another time wouldn't hurt anyone.

But half a chapter into a party scene and she tossed it onto the faux-wood coffee table. Dammit, she needed a cigarette. Hurrying to the closet, she kicked her feet into a pair of boots, grabbed her jacket and nothing else, and then left the apartment, only to hurry back inside once she reached the stairwell because she realized she'd forgotten the goddamn Sobranies.

Rather than smoke in the second bedroom, which she and Vasy wanted to convert into a baby's room, she took the stairs down to the main floor and slipped out the back exit. The cold felt almost as suffocating as her withdrawal, as the vow she'd made to Vasy after he'd made a single promise to her, to take her away, keep her away, and keep her safe.

Her hands trembled so badly that it took three attempts to get the tobacco burning, and that first pull on the Sobranie felt like her departure day, it felt like salvation. She closed her eyes and savored the taste. No amount of rhythmic breathing could duplicate the calm that settled upon her, even outside in that painful cold of the 1986 freezing spell.

"They say cigarettes are bad for you," she heard from a familiar voice.

The sound stopped her, but she refused to open her eyes to him as his footsteps crunched the dry snow and he approached.

"Like that bacon scare. About how it causes cancer. I bet they find some study that says these cigarettes cause cancer, too."

"I think they already have," she said, her eyes still closed because now she knew that Alex liked to use scare tactics as a way to get women talking to him or *calling* him.

Alex laughed and the sound didn't quite annoy her, but it bothered her. Maybe not the laughter itself, or his approach, but his being here.

Why is he here?

"What are you doing, Alex? Shouldn't you be somewhere? Like at work?"

His hand settled on her shoulder. It wasn't a threatening touch. In fact, she believed it was meant to be reassuring. "Yes, it's very likely that I should be somewhere."

"Then you should go there," she encouraged him, grinning with her eyes still closed because she remembered when he'd touched her shoulder in his car, how she'd glanced back at his long fingers.

"But there's nowhere else I'd rather be than here." The tickled sound of his voice suggested sarcasm.

Allana's eyes shot open, and she found him staring at her, a playful smirk on his lips.

"You've missed me," he continued, his eyes lighting up as his smile deepened.

Although she would never admit it—because he was a perverted pig—she *had* missed him. The playfulness. The lack of seriousness—or what she *hoped* was a lack of seriousness—in his flirtatious behavior. The American voice. The way he unapologetically fantasized about her with those eyes. The way he annoyed her more than the cold. More than anything.

"It's okay," he said, raising a finger and bringing it closer to her mouth. "You don't have to say anything."

She considered biting his finger off. Or at least drawing blood, just like she had when she hit him in the nose, but then she decided to step away instead. "Don't you dare touch me, Alex Petrokov, or I'll scream," she threatened. And she meant it too—*bad enough she was so indecisive about how she felt about him.*

The smile dropped off his face. "That's a little much. You know what they do to screamers here?" Despite his flirtatious choice of words, he blinked. And the glimmer of hope that she had seen in his eyes just two heartbeats ago vanished. Clearing his throat, he pulled down on his jacket, straightening it and his attitude as well.

Allana took another pull from the cigarette, wondering if it made her look as relaxed as it made her feel. She blew the smoke into his face, and once he finished wincing, she asked, "I'll ask one more time, then. Why are you here?"

After a fake cough, Alex told her, "Vasy sent me."

"I don't believe you."

He shrugged. "He asked me to show you my apartment."

She raised an inquiring eyebrow.

"True story," he promised, lifting his hand like he was taking an oath. "Even the bedroom."

Allana swung a closed fist at him, but he seemed to be expecting it, stepping out of her reach and saving himself from another bloody nose.

"Not this time," he taunted, shaking a finger at her.

"Vasy did *not* say that," she hissed at him, then took another, longer pull from the Sobranie.

He winced again as she blew smoke into his face. "Well, maybe I was embellishing about the bedroom part. But it's just not as fun without getting an overreaction from you."

Allana rolled her eyes. *How does he do that? One second, I want to crush my cigarette in those eyes; the next, I want to see that* look *in them from the party…*

"He says you deserve a nicer apartment and knows that mine is a little more… modern."

When Alex nodded back toward his idling Lada and held out his arm in a chivalrous offer, she decided that he was telling the truth. Because Vasy was like that, always wanting the best for her. Besides, how else could he possibly know about Vasy's insistence that they move to another building, one that would not have power failures in the cold?

No doubt about it, Vasy had gone straight to work, found Alex and asked him to spend time with his high-maintenance American wife, who was likely a little homesick during this period of freezing hell. And if Alex had been telling the truth about Vasy, maybe he'd been telling the truth about everything else. Maybe she could trust him, after all.

Right?

#

The drive through Pripyat had a magical feel to it after such a cold, long spell of isolation over the past week. Allana had come close to losing her mind, she realized. The jonesing for smokes, the bite of the cold each time she stepped outside for a Sobranie, her inability to just have a conversation with someone... it had nearly pushed her over the ledge. And now Alex had shown up. *Like magic.*

Except it was Alex. *Not* like magic.

She couldn't help but smile at her own conflicted thoughts!

There were only a few other vehicles on the roads, and as they motored down pr. Lenina, she wondered about Vasy's logic in asking Alex to play real estate broker. Surely, with Alex being an American, Vasy felt she would be more at ease and less stressed with him than, say, some of his more intense, local colleagues like Yuri or Gregor whose broken English would drive her insane. And he probably thought that, if she could be at ease, she might not grow to resent him for bringing her here.

That was how Vasy's head worked...indirectly.

"I didn't have anything else planned today," Alex said, like she might care. "So when he asked if I had lost power, I had no trouble answering him. And telling him about a dozen other things before he finally came right out and asked me to stop by and entertain you."

Entertain her? Had he really said that? It seemed like something he might say. But the timing seemed off, come to think of it. Would Vasy have called Alex if she'd told him about their coffee at the Pripyat Café, or about Alex's insane belief that "someone" was looking to decommission the power station that Vasy loved and where he spent most of his waking days?

Alex glanced over at her, his eyes conveying a message of some sort.

She didn't know him well enough to know what that message was. Not yet. But she would come back to this moment where he glanced at her with that look in his eyes. And then he chuckled, shaking his head and grabbing the steering wheel with both hands. Mr. Serious now. Seriously moronic.

"What's so funny?" she asked.

Still shaking his head, Alex confessed, "He didn't want me to tell you why I was there. Thought you'd be disappointed if you knew he'd put me up to showing you around and entertaining you with apartment shopping for the day."

Allana turned her attention out the window again. She noticed icicles in the corners of the rooftops, hanging from the tree branches and the eaves. The way Alex spoke, even if Vasy hadn't asked him to take her apartment shopping, it seemed he believed it, just as much as he'd believed in the conspiracy to decommission the power station.

He went on, except now his tone came across as a business-like: "Which tells me that you haven't told him about our coffee date."

"It wasn't a date," she reminded him, equally business-like.

"If you say so." Alex shrugged, his hands squeezing the wheel.

Allana refused to humor his twisted way of thinking. "I'm only doing this for Vasy," she explained, her tone firm and inflexible. Because as "cute" as Alex's flirtatious nature could be, and no matter how much she might secretly enjoy the way he touched her and violated her with that hungry gaze of his, she refused to hurt Vasy. "Let's make sure we're clear about that, okay?"

"All clear at my end," he agreed.

Really? Nothing is that *easy.* "Good. Don't want another bloody nose."

The rest of the drive passed with a foreshadowing silence.

# # #

The apartment building where Alex lived was different than many of the others in Pripyat. His building was small, while most of the others were much larger concrete structures like the one where Vasy and Allana lived. Where her building looked exactly like the dozens that surrounded it, Alex's was all on its own, tucked away from the main road behind a bunch of trees so that, in the summer, you didn't have a snowball's chance in hell of seeing it through the foliage. And in the winter, the exterior's white façade looked so much like the snow in the trees that it was practically camouflaged.

"I've never seen this place," she admitted, staring out the windshield as Alex eased the Lada into one of a dozen or so assigned parking spaces.

"It's pretty quiet. Even this close to the road, you don't hear much."

He killed the engine and stepped out of the Lada. Allana followed, walked around the back, and joined Alex. As they headed toward the front entrance, she glanced up at the building again.

"How many units?" she asked. It seemed like a logical question.

Alex shrugged but didn't answer. Either he didn't know or he had never cared enough to think about it; Allana didn't know him well enough at that point to guess which it was.

Unlike the powerless building where she lived, Alex's seemed to have no trouble with the freezing cold; the lights in the main lobby weren't even flickering, and the elevator—newer than the one in her building, with doors that opened so smoothly you barely heard them—moved up the shaft at a reasonably quick speed. It was like being back in the States all of a sudden, with stuff that worked efficiently and smoothly, stuff she'd taken for granted. But that was all she really missed from back home; everything else had a headwind effect on her, had ruined her piece by piece.

"How did you score a unit?" she asked.

"I didn't," Alex answered. He stood against the opposite wall, keeping a healthy distance. Allana appreciated that. The elevator felt confined as it was, and she didn't want to think about him being too close, not after his confession about the way he'd looked at her at the party because now she couldn't help but wonder if his glances still had that same desire in them. "When the power station recruited me, they promised the best accommodations. I guess this was it."

She frowned, glancing over at him. "Nikolai said the same thing to Vasy." How did they end up in such an archaic shit hole when Nikolai had promised to make those arrangements personally? It didn't make sense; Nikolai was the chief engineer at the most prolific power station in the world. You would think he could do better than the apartment building where they lived...

Maintaining his stare—*see, was that a hungry stare, or just a regular stare?*—Alex hesitated long enough that the *ding!* from the elevator afforded him an excuse to avoid her comment altogether. Allana didn't think any more of it. She simply followed him out to the short, fourth-floor hallway. There was just one door to the right and one door to the left, with the emergency stairwell door right in front of them. Two units per floor, five floors... that meant just ten apartments in this five-story building. She liked that, the quiet idea of it, the unlikely possibility that unsupervised kids would be running down the halls early on a rainy Sunday morning when she was trying to sleep in on Vasy's day off.

Alex turned toward the door on the left and reached into his pocket for a set of keys. While he struggled to get the lock open, Allana imagined the type of views this place had. Alex's unit faced the power station, the lake, and river beyond it. The other unit on this floor would face the vast countryside with its beautiful sunsets each night.

Not bad.

She wondered about the other views from this apartment, and then saw that Alex was actually having a *really* tough time with the lock.

He glanced back at her and smiled. "Wrong key," he said, then filed through the six or so others on the key ring until he reached the right one. "Of course," he scoffed. "That was my office key."

Allana grinned. She noticed that Alex's keys all looked the same— standard issue deadbolt keys. Which meant Vasy's office key looked a lot different than Alex's, but that was probably because they worked in different areas of the power station. Most likely, since Vasy worked in such a sensitive department, his office had a bigger lock.

Allana silently hoped that key size was the only comparison she would ever make between the two men.

At last, Alex disengaged the lock and pushed the heavy apartment door open. He waved her inside first. Stepping into the vast, open space, she refused to let Alex see her true reaction. Yes, this apartment impressed her— taller ceilings than the ones in her building, big windows straight ahead, a long balcony that faced the power station and lake just like she'd envisioned. Shiny tile floors in the bright, modern kitchen that overlooked the rest of the freshly carpeted living space. And, also unlike her apartment, the bedrooms here were on opposite ends of the unit. One was to the left, next to the dining area where Alex had positioned six chairs around a large wooden table—which he clearly didn't use because there were books stacked everywhere—and the other bedroom and main bathroom were to the right, down a short hall next to a living space that accommodated two leather sofas and the same kind of floor model television that she and Vasy owned.

"Funny how your eyes went straight to the bedrooms," Alex joked with a flirtatious tone.

Snapping her attention to him, she raised her eyebrows. "I've been meaning to ask, how's your nose?"

The grin dripped off Alex's lips as he massaged the side of his nose.

"The bathroom is pretty big and luxurious, too," he said with a less playful tone, stepping past her and walking toward that short hall on the right.

Removing her boots, Allana followed him as he flicked the light switch in the hall and then the one in the bathroom at the end. He stepped aside, watching her reaction as she entered the large bathroom. She swore she felt his body heat rub up against her, and those eyes—*that damn hunger in them*—ripped away her clothes.

She cleared her throat, more for her own benefit. *Snap out of it.*

Inside the bathroom, she saw a soaker tub, a glass shower large enough for two people, his-and-hers sinks and vanity, and a modern-looking toilet in the corner. An entire family could be in here at the same time and not worry about bumping into one another.

"Wow," she breathed.

Alex eased closer. "Almost makes you want to get naked and test the shower, doesn't it?" His voice was a little too low and seductive to come across as anything but dangerous.

"Alex!" she snapped, swinging at his face again because she needed to send him the right message, one that would get him to grow up and stop flirting with her because she was *not* that girl, not anymore nor ever again, and definitely *not* with him! She'd dated too many guys like Alex to ever make that mistake again, married or not!

Her fist missed its target when Alex leaned back and instinctively reached up with his left hand, seizing her thrown punch like he'd anticipated it all along. He didn't say anything, and that bothered her, made her a little more uncomfortable than she wanted to admit. Because instead of whining like she'd expected him to, Alex simply stared at her.

"Alex," she whispered, her voice mildly submissive, even to her own ears. Like maybe she wanted to get into that shower. Which she didn't, she kept telling herself. No, of course she didn't.

He continued to stare at her, though, and she hated it because she didn't quite know what he was thinking, and yet she feared that *he* could read *her* thoughts, the ones she kept deep down, the ones that she refused to acknowledge. She blinked hard, trying to escape those prying eyes, but every time she looked back, he still had that same hungry look on his face, the kind that said a first kiss between them was imminent.

Unavoidable.

"No, Alex," she begged, shaking her head.

Her legs had begun to quiver. Enough to remind her that this liaison—with the American that paid her a little too much attention and made her feel like the most-desired woman in the Soviet Union—was just plain wrong.

"Let me go," she whispered. "Please, not like this."

He stared at her.

She stared right back.

And as much as Allana loved Vasy, she couldn't help but find this moment between her and Alex intoxicating. She wanted more of this, more confrontation like this, more of his hands locked on hers, restraining her in a way that felt dangerous, and maybe even pinning her down with his body and...

Alex finally released her, and then blinked, breaking his gaze.

He'd read my thoughts, hadn't he? The bad ones, and they scared him off like they're scaring me right now.

Clearing his throat, he left the bathroom without speaking and disappeared into the living area. She watched him go, observing the way his shoulders moved with each step and wondering if he was angry, embarrassed, frustrated, or maybe all three. It took a lot for her to hold back, to not chase after him; she'd done that with other men from her past, so she knew that if she reacted that way with Alex, it would lead to something that would end her marriage.

Taking a few deep breaths, she bit down on her lip and tried to steady the racing in her chest.

Adrenaline, she knew. Pheromones was all it was. She needed to calm down.

As her eyes darted about the bathroom, her finger tracing the edge of the vanity, she did everything in her power to focus on the mundane chore of inspecting the room. It worked, too; her heart rate returned to normal because there was nothing sexy about standing alone in a bachelor's bathroom with a handful of *Soviet Life* magazines stacked on the back of the toilet.

But when she reached the glass shower, she felt her heart speed up again. She saw the shampoo he used—not the kind that Vasy used, thankfully—and the bar of soap that would've travelled across the surface of his nearly hairless chest and the rest of his hard, naked body while he stood under the spray this very morning.

Stop. Just stop.

She glanced back at the bathroom door, fully expecting to find Alex standing there and watching her with the same desire he'd shown her moments ago. But when she saw that he wasn't there, the doorway remaining vacant, she gulped. Incredibly grateful, because she didn't know what would've happened if he had returned.

Allana ambled slowly to the living area. Although she wanted to avoid him—his eyes, his touch, his voice, everything about him in fact—she their interaction was inevitable; he was her ride home to the shitty apartment with no heat, no elevator, no power.

Alex was standing at the balcony doors, staring outside at the four large stacks in the distance. They belonged to the different reactors at the power station. Number four was the newest, the area where Vasy seemed to spend a lot of time because Nikolai had guaranteed he would only work with the best, most up-to-date equipment while they built the fifth and six reactors.

"This apartment is perfect," she said, watching Alex from the edge of the hallway. He had removed his heavy jacket and dropped it on the sofa.

He nodded, and she wondered what he might be thinking. "The view is great, isn't it?" he said with a bit of a quiver to his own voice.

"Yes," she said. Her hands were clammy, so she buried them in her jacket's pockets. "Must be even more impressive in the summer."

Alex pointed at something in the distance, a building at the power station. "That's where Vasy's office is," he explained, and it seemed to Allana that his words were more for his own sanity than to impress her. He chuckled, shook his head. "When the World Junior hockey tournament was on, I called him and reported on the score. Our match against the Czech team was close. Vasy was working. I'd wave and I swear he'd wave back."

Allana started moving closer to him, but stopped. Too close was a bad idea. "Alex?"

He turned around, looking scared for some reason. After letting out a long breath, he confessed, "You're the most attractive woman I've ever seen, Allana. Vasy's lucky."

She took an involuntary step back. "I think I should get going." And then she hurried toward the door, stepped hastily into her boots, and reached for the doorknob. But before she could open the door, she felt his hands on her. One hand stopped hers from twisting the doorknob while the other settled on her lower back, that spot just above her ass. Her legs nearly gave out all at once, and she closed her eyes. *I don't like this man, I don't like him at all, not the way he touches me and puts my wants at ends with what I know is right, because I'm not that girl anymore, and he's an American perv—*

"Don't leave," he ordered, pressing up against her from behind, bringing his lips to the side of her head.

She sucked in a deep breathe. "This won't end well," she warned, her own voice eeking out as a whisper. "People will get hurt."

"Let me kiss you," he begged, brushing the hair away from the side of her face and bringing his mouth even closer to her neck. "Just a kiss."

"No," she answered, pulling her face even farther from his lips. *I've done my part, I can't pull my face any farther away, I'm doing what's right here, I am I am I am I am.*

"Nobody will get hurt," he promised and his hypnotic voice almost convinced her because Allana could tell that he honestly believed his own ridiculousness, just like he'd believed the decommissioning.

He suddenly spun her around and pressed her up against the door.

She gasped underneath his weight.

He had *read my thoughts in the bathroom, hadn't he?*

She liked the way his body settled against hers. A lot. She squirmed, trying to free herself—*I'm doing my part, I'm doing what's right*—or maybe trying to get him into a better position—*no, I'm not that girl*—so she could enjoy the moment a little more. Hell, she wasn't exactly sure anymore.

As Alex edged slightly closer, his dreamy eyes closing, his moist lips opening, Allana realized something—she wanted this. She wanted it no matter what she told herself, no more bullshit about being a changed woman, about honest truth and doing her part to avoid it… she *wanted* this.

But it was wrong. And she hated herself for it. She hated Alex, too. She pulled her face away even farther, a miracle because she hadn't thought she could get any farther from him—*see, you want this!*—but she managed.

"No," she whispered, squinting at the pain in her neck.

"Yes," he responded, rolling his hips against hers as if he knew that it would cause an eruption of want and greed inside her—*but I'm* not *that girl anymore!*

Her hand seized around the doorknob again, and as his hips rolled into her again, and as his lips just barely brushed against hers, and she felt herself giving in a little more, she somehow managed to turn the knob.

But she didn't turn it enough to open the door. Instead, she relaxed against him, moaning lightly as she allowed him to kiss her, as she surrendered to her own desires, her own need to *feel* wanted like this, a half-nostalgic and half-animalistic longing.

# # #

Chapter 5

Allana tried to not return the passion, but she couldn't help it. After a moment, as his tongue slipped into her mouth, she accepted it. Surrendering to her own desires and stepping out of the shadows of denial, she accepted her betrayal and kissed him back as she wrapped her arms around him, pulling him closer but not quite close enough. There were coats and layers of clothing between them, and what she wanted—right now with their lips locked together, their hands wandering and grabbing and groping—she knew she couldn't... *shouldn't* have.

"Allana," Alex choked, pulling back just long enough to unzip her jacket and free her arms from the sleeves. The fur dropped to the floor at her feet, and he kissed her again, pressing his lips to hers harder than before. He blindly thumbed the buttons of her blouse before slipping his hand inside her bra, against her warm, pounding chest.

Gasping at the skin-on-skin contact, she tried not to think about what was happening. She was afraid if she thought about it... no, she couldn't do this.

At last, with Alex's hand cupping her breast, she pulled her lips away, rolled out from underneath him, and rushed down that short hall to the right, buttoning up her blouse.

"What's wrong?" Alex asked, coming after her. He sounded panicked.

She felt his hand on her lower back again, like he knew that was her weakness, that one spot he could touch and turn her into his slave.

"Lana, talk to me," he insisted.

She shook her head fiercely. "I can't do this."

"Hey, it's all good," he assured her.

It surprised her that Alex didn't try to force another kiss out of her. He simply pulled her against his chest and wrapped his arms around her waist, locking his hands so she couldn't escape. At least that was what it felt like to Allana. And she felt safe like that, just like she'd always felt safe in Vasy's arms. Except this was different somehow, and she couldn't quite identify why… and it wasn't that she didn't belong in Alex's arms—she *knew* that the only man who should hold her like this was her husband, Vasy—but more than that she felt safe with him when she knew she shouldn't. Because with Alex, she felt untouchable; with Vasy she felt indestructible. Was that it?

"I'm sorry," Alex told her, still holding on tight. "I didn't mean to complicate things."

She felt her chin quiver. "Vasy is going to divorce me." *And then I'll have the same reputation here that I've worked so hard to leave behind…* The thought terrorized her. "Once I tell him," she went on, "he'll be angry with you too, Alex."

Silence.

"Then don't tell him," he suggested at last, and the way those words slipped off his tongue so easily, it sounded like the best idea in the world. "It's not like we slept together."

Yet, she thought. "You had your hand on my breasts," she argued. But the part that had been the scariest of all was that she'd wanted his hands on her. *All over her.* Not just her breasts, not just her lower back, but everywhere.

"You don't need to tell him that we got lost in a moment. But if you do, if you tell him about the sin, then you also need to tell him about what we did to redeem ourselves and stop from going even farther."

She pulled back a little and stared up at his face. Although she wanted to feel his lips against hers again, feel his tongue inside her mouth, she simply swallowed and hoped the rush of blood to her cheeks wasn't too obvious in the semi-dark hallway outside the bathroom.

"We 'redeemed' ourselves," she said sarcastically. It took all of her inner strength to not laugh at him.

"Yes," he insisted, his eyes wide. It seemed like he really believed his own bullshit. Then she saw that look in his eyes again, the look from the party at the poker table, the look from earlier today before he'd kissed her. "We weren't stupid. We were smart. We stopped before it could go any farther, before we really crossed some lines." She couldn't help but think *no, I was the one that stopped* you. *There's wasn't a* we *in my pulling away.*

"And I can feel your, uh…" She wiggled her hips, pressing her pelvic bone against his erection. That little act did nothing to strip the edge away, but she hoped it proved her point. They'd done nothing to truly stop this. And redemption? Forget about it.

Alex grinned. "You can feel more of it if you want…"

Was Alex for real? "Um, no."

He laughed. Because he was joking… he *had* to be joking, how could he take himself too seriously?

"Alex," she said, taking on the role of the serious adult once again. "I need to leave." *Before we really do something stupid.*

He swallowed and the playful smile washed away. As much as Allana hoped he might take what he wanted, even against her protests, she was also happy when he finally unlocked his hands, released her, and returned to the living area. Her heart was pounding so fast in her chest and her legs had gone so numb that she wondered if she'd collapse just by walking down the hallway after him.

"I need to show you something," Alex said without glancing back.

"Uh, no way," she called after him, following him at a slow and steady pace. When she reached the open living space, Alex kept walking toward the bedroom door on the other side of the apartment.

Before stepping inside that second bedroom, Alex stopped and looked back. His cheeks were flushed, and there were red spots all over his muscular neck. His erection had calmed, leaving only a bulge in the crotch of his pants. She wondered if she'd really felt what she had thought, if maybe she'd imagined his arousal in the first place.

"It's not what you think," he promised with the kind of deviant grin that had her convinced to never trust this man.

Her eyes narrowed. Her distrust of him seemed at odds with how safe he made her feel just a minute ago, and she didn't quite understand how or why that could be…

She raised her eyebrows. "Famous last words?"

He laughed, the kind of raw and unedited laughter that could only be genuine. "I wish," he muttered, then suddenly went quiet and serious. "Allana, do you remember what I said at our coffee date?"

Shrugging, she wanted to remind him that it *wasn't a date*. Or that all she really remembered was his bloody nose.

"The part about Americans wanting to decommission the power station," he added.

At last, Allana nodded.

That was when the mood changed. Quickly and dramatically, the way the scenery could change with the weather in this northern part of the world. They'd moved from happy and horny, to serious and somber in a matter of milliseconds.

"I want to show you how I came to that conclusion, so you don't think I'm some crazy conspiracy theorist," he said, waving her into the bedroom with him, then raising his hand in a gesture of a promise. "Scout's honor."

At last, Allana followed him.

When she stepped into the room, she felt like she'd stepped back in time. There was an old wooden bed frame, tacky pillows and bed sheets, something from the sixties, at best; the kind of good-quality, but old furniture that only belonged in a guest bedroom. A bookshelf with old sepia pictures of Alex, his family, and some sports (football, hockey) he played at schools in the States. Also on the bookshelf were a few pieces of literature that normal people consumed, the kind that nobody in the Soviet Union wanted to get caught with because the authorities would call it capitalist propaganda. Instead of Soviet history, the titles were written by people like Jack Kerouac, Ernest Hemmingway, F. Scott Fitzgerald, and even some modern stuff by celebrities like Stephen King. They definitely weren't titles you'd find on sale at the supermarket.

She noticed the reading chair in the corner of the room, next to a window that faced the north.

"It's over here," he said, opening the closet door and hitting the light switch just inside.

She stepped closer to see that the walk-in closet contained a desk chair and a tower of complicated electronic equipment. Not stereo equipment, but electronics she'd never seen before. He'd stacked it on one of those fold-away tables that most people used at parties.

"Here," he said, taking a seat, and then rummaged through a box on the floor before coming up with a tiny tape reel. It wasn't an 8-track or audio cassette. No, it looked like a miniature film reel, like a smaller 8mm. It wasn't something you'd find in *any* store, not here, and not even in the States... This wasn't commercially available for your everyday audiophile.

"Alex, what is this?" she asked, waving at the boxes on the floor, the equipment, the headphones and wires. Her eyes widened in awe at all of this. *Who is this guy?*

He loaded the reel into one of the complicated machines. "Oh, this? It's just a hobby," he explained nonchalantly.

"Does anyone know about this 'hobby'?" If the authorities knew about this kind of setup...

Alex chuckled. "Only you and I know about this, Allana." The way those green eyes clamped onto hers suggested she keep it that way. "Listen to this."

He pressed the play button and a speaker came to life with the scratchy track, almost like it had come from a vinyl record. She heard voices she didn't recognize, pauses in the conversation that went something like: "...timing is crucial..." scratch-scratch-scratch, "...get the dates and we can take it down..." scratch-scratch, "...complete destruction..."

Her eyes grew so wide she would not have been surprised if she looked down and found them on the floor. She felt sick. *Complete destruction?* She worried about Vasy, wondering what kind of danger he was in.

Alex stopped the playback and glanced at her. "There's more." He reached back into the box and found another miniature reel, affording Allana a bit of time to calm down. Alex loaded the next reel and pressed play again.

The same voice and scratching sounds. "...this level must be deemed a security threat..." scratch-scratch-scratch, "...Soviets have been unresponsive..." scratch-scratch-scratch, "under-calculation will have catastrophic implications, ultimately global annihilation..."

And then another voice, a clearer one said, "Prodovzhyty."

"That means 'proceed,'" Alex said, gulping and hitting the stop button.

Allana wanted to get home. She wanted to tell Vasy about this tape, what she'd heard, because she was afraid for him. His position at the power station was putting him at risk. *But this can't be what I think it means… It's just Alex's paranoid conspiracy theory getting into my head again, just like it had after he dropped me off that day…*

Alex tossed the reel into the box and swiveled in his chair. "So, now you see why I'm so nervous," he said.

"But, how are you coming to your conclusions?" she asked, backing out of the closet and sitting down on the bed to catch her breath and regain her bearings.

He rose out of the chair and moved closer to her, his eyes wide. "They said to 'proceed,' Allana," he repeated, as if that explained everything. "Proceed. They're going to proceed."

She frowned, thoroughly confused. "Proceed and do what?"

"I don't know…" he started, rolling his eyes, "maybe take the power station down? Blow it up? I… I don't know, what else could it mean?" He ran his hands through his hair and shook his head. He looked distraught.

"Allana," he said, lowering his voice to a near-whisper, "I need you to pay attention."

She closed her eyes. "Alex, I… I think this might be a bit of an overreaction." *God, she hoped that was all it was, a stupid overreaction.*

He smiled like she had just proven his point. "Then just pay attention and you'll know if it's all just an overreaction… or if it's the real thing."

Frowning, she shrugged and raised her hands to her head as if she could stop it from all of this spinning. "What are you talking about? This all sounds so insane. All of it. And… and they can lock you up for this."

"At home," Alex insisted, ignoring her warning, "just pay attention to things Vasy mentions at home. Things like *tests*. Pay attention to his *demeanor*. Pay attention to the *names* of new people he talks about. Just… *Pay attention*." By that point, he sounded desperate.

She raised an eyebrow. On any given day, Alex saw Vasy more than she did. Her husband worked a dozen hours a day, spent more time at the power station than he did at home. "Alex—"

"I promise you this," he said, interrupting her. "Once you start paying attention, you'll notice this stuff." He gulped, his neck still blotchy and his eyes still big with fear. "Pay attention and you'll see that something big is going to happen."

"And you think Vasy is a part of it?" she asked, her tone tight with skepticism. *No, not a chance he's involved. He's a victim, he's in danger, he's not one of the voices on the reels. He's innocent.*

Alex seemed to think about her comment. He checked his watch, and his face tightened. "No, not exactly a part of it."

"Then what?" she asked, wondering if Alex could see just how scared she was.

"He'll know something."

"Alex...."

"I have to take you home, Allana," he said, checking his wrist again and shifting his worry from the voices on the reel to the time of day. "I have to get to work. But I don't think Vasy knows what's really going on, or what's really going to happen. I think he's a lot like me. A pawn in their game."

She frowned at him—*who is* they, *the Americans, or the Soviets... or someone else?*—but didn't say anything. Because she couldn't speak, too afraid to open her mouth and get sick or pass out. It didn't make sense to her, none of it did except that maybe she'd allowed a true lunatic to kiss her. But—*oh, how she hated to admit this*—Alex wasn't a lunatic; he was passionate and...

Alex helped her off the bed and led her out of the room. She followed him back to the main entrance where that kiss that changed everything had happened. Allana couldn't help but gulp at the memory of that moment and how quickly the mood had shifted from passion to fear. For an instant, she wondered if Alex was thinking about it too—the passion, the kiss—and when he looked over at her while he slid his feet into his own boots, she knew... That kiss was nagging his memory as much as it was nagging hers, even against the backdrop of what they'd just heard on those reels and what it all could mean.

At last, Alex smirked. "One more kiss for the road?"

Allana couldn't help but chuckle before taking another swing at his nose, which he barely blocked. "Just take me home."

# # #

Chapter 6

Two weeks later, on Valentine's Day, the freezing spell still hadn't let up. Working around a mess of moving boxes piled throughout the apartment, Allana baked a recipe that Alex had translated for her a week prior. She was enjoying her first attempt at baking; plus, the heat from the oven allowed her to forget just how cold it was outside.

A cloud of smoke blew into her face as she opened the oven door. Cursing quietly, she hurried to the sliding balcony door and pulled it open to allow the smoke to escape before the fire alarms started. They'd already had one alarm go off in an apartment downstairs earlier in the week. Even without an understanding of the language, Allana had managed to understand just how angry the other residents had been about having to evacuate the building with temperatures as low as these.

Returning to the kitchen, she grabbed the muffin pan. She finished mixing the *paska* and then poured it into the pan. All she needed to do was let it cook for a bit. Sliding the sheet into the oven, she turned away and set the timer on the battery-powered travel alarm. She preferred it over the oven's timer that she didn't know how to operate.

Retreating to the living room, she found her pack of Sobranies. At the front door, she grabbed her jacket and boots from the nearly empty closet, and started toward the slightly open balcony door when she heard a soft knocking sound behind her. Allana wondered if it might be the kids again; with the cold weather, the younger ones had taken to running the halls and pounding on doors for something to do.

But this knock sounded like more of a grown-up's call.

And it sounded familiar. Too familiar.

Allana returned to the door and glanced through the peephole. Wide-eyed, she watched Alex raise his knuckles and rap on the door once more.

The sound startled her even though she'd seen it coming. *Not on Valentine's Day, a day meant for romance, a day not meant for flirting or working sixteen-hour shifts.*

Alex leaned closer to the door, as if wanting to listen in on what was going on inside. But before he could get too close, she reached down, turned the knob, and yanked it open. She realized a moment later that she should not have done that because he tripped forward and ended up in her arms, just as another apartment resident walked past. The middle-aged woman with the narrow eyebrows glanced over quickly, and then kept walking like she'd seen something she shouldn't have.

Great, now the neighbors will think I'm having an affair.

Allana shoved him back, out of her arms. This time he tripped backward, landing on his ass in the hallway.

Alex chuckled. "Abuse!"

She started to close the door, but he shot his foot out to stop her.

"What are you doing here?" she hissed.

He raised his hands. "Easy, easy. I brought you a gift."

"On *Valentine's Day?*" she demanded. "Are you crazy?"

Alex reached out for her, but when she refused to take his cue, he started making an impatient motion for her hurry up and help him back to his feet.

"Alex, you need to leave," she said before finally taking his hand and pulling him up.

"Did you lose heat again?" he asked, avoiding her question and waving at her jacket and boots. "Good thing you're moving."

She walked away from him, proceeding through the warm kitchen and reached for the sliding door. "Goodbye, Alex."

Before she could draw the door open, she felt his hand on hers. He stepped up against her from behind, and she felt his breath on the side of her neck, just shy of that vein that could melt her into complete submission. She closed her eyes, wondering what it would feel like to just let go. Just this once, just a small notch beyond what she'd allowed at his apartment. *I'm not that girl anymore...*

"Happy Valentine's Day, Allana," he whispered.

"Alex," she said, half panting. "You need to leave." Already, her legs vibrated with the anticipation of what her body wanted but her heart could never give him. *Because my heart belongs to Vasy.* "You need to leave."

"I have something to give you," he said, still pressing into her. His words, their tone, and his position behind her were all so damn suggestive. She wondered if she might be misinterpreting his words about "giving her something," but how could it mean anything else?

"You can't," she whispered, closing her eyes.

Please don't put your hand on my lower back...

At last, Alex backed away from her, letting one of his hands slide down the side of her rib cage, down below her waist where her jacked offered no protection from his touch, then across the outside of her upper thigh. His path left tingling along her skin, through all of those layers of clothes.

Stumbling just slightly, Allana faked a show of struggling with closing the balcony door. *Oh, how she loved it when he touched her, and how he touched her and made her feel.* She hoped it camouflaged her weakness, at least enough to convince Alex she wanted nothing to do with him, his flirting and overt sexual advances. *I'm not that girl anymore.* She refused to step over that line with him. *I'm Vasy Gurin's wife, his wife, and I left my past in the States.* And when she finally turned back toward him and saw that he had indeed walked away, she wondered if maybe he had finally listened to her, if maybe this excitement he injected into her life would finally be gone. Guiltily, she hoped not *because that girl from her past wanted it, more of it, just enough to get her senses buzzing again.*

"It's just a chocolate," Alex said, placing something small on the kitchen counter. "You don't have to share it with Vasy."

Her legs still wobbly and a little numb, she grabbed the back of a kitchen chair for support. *One chocolate?* She watched Alex make his way to the apartment door, her eyes widening. *Don't go, don't leave me like this.* Her days were long while Vasy worked. Too long. She missed having conversations with people, with someone who could speak English, someone who wasn't her reflection in the mirror while she sat alone in this cramped, isolated apartment during the coldest freezing spell she'd ever known. *Give me more, but don't leave.*

"Well, maybe I'll have him feed it to me," she blurted. *You can't touch me like that and then just leave.*

Alex hesitated at the door.

"Naked, in bed," she added for extra punch. *Was that too much?*

Now Alex froze. She watched him stand there at the main door, wondering what thoughts cursed him. Were they torturing him, these images of her naked body in bed, eating his chocolate out of her husband's palms? *I might not be that girl anymore, but I sure hope this drives him as wild as he drives me.*

"That's cruel," he said, slowly shaking his head.

Now she knew she had him. Despite the trembling in her legs, she swallowed the satisfied grin pushing to the surface and realized she had control here, not Alex. "It might be more than the chocolate that I taste on his fingers," she warned, grinning to herself.

"What are you trying to do to me, Allana?" he moaned.

She swallowed, asking herself the same question. *She'd definitely pushed him too far.* Although she wanted him to stay, she wanted it to be on *her* terms. No, she wanted friendship, companionship. Maybe a little flirting, but no kissing and no touching. At least, not like that afternoon in Alex's apartment with his hand on her breast. Not the kind that made her legs go numb, her heart race and… No, none of that.

And definitely no sex.

She wanted him to stay, she wanted him to flirt, she wanted adventure, but without all of the things that he added to it, all of that *tension*…and consequences. *I love Vasy, I'm his wife, I'm married, and married women don't behave like whores.*

Slowly, Alex turned around on that tiny doormat in the tight foyer. He raised an eyebrow, looking a little confused and maybe a little hurt at the image she'd painted for him. "What do you want from me?" he asked, taking a sturdy step toward her.

Allana stared right back into his eyes and watched how they changed from this moment's torture, into the wanting eyes she'd seen at her party. These eyes oozed sexual hunger.

"Alex," she said, shaking her head and maintaining his stare while she took one step back. "Thank you for the chocolate."

The mention of the chocolate seemed to spark an idea in him, the way he returned to the counter where he'd left his gift, grabbed it, and then continued toward her with a grin on his lips.

Before he could do anything either of them would regret, she asked, "Why can't we have a *normal* friendship?" Then she faked a chuckle that didn't even sound convincing to her own ears. She swallowed hard. "Whatever you're thinking of doing…" Her voice trailed off as he reached up and unzipped her jacket.

Licking his lips, Alex slid the back part of his hands right down the middle of her chest, all the way from her collarbone, across her belly, and stopping just short of her pelvic area where the zipper ended. As much as she tried, she couldn't stop her eyes from rolling slightly backwards as her jacket dropped off her shoulders and landed haphazardly at her feet.

"I want to be the one to feed the chocolate to you," Alex whispered, and before she could find the words to protest, he lifted her off her feet and into his arms.

In that moment, suspended like this as he carried her past the moving boxes in the living room and started down the hallway toward the bedrooms, Allana's reality clouded. Her world became dreamlike, hazy, and even a little confusing. Vasy hadn't been this spontaneous in months. He was too caught up in the excitement he found at work. Maybe she hadn't been very spontaneous, either. It wasn't entirely Vasy's fault. He was a good man, a perfect husband. So getting scooped off her feet by a man like Alex—the only other person in this corner of the world that paid any attention to her and made her feel desired, hungered after—she felt it was possibly a little too easy for him to convince her into giving herself up.

"Alex," she slurred. And while she loved the excitement and adventure of this, she reminded herself that the physical part was wrong. *Vasy's wife*. And maybe she didn't have control after all, maybe she couldn't have the friendly fun without matrimonial sin.

"You're nervous," he said, bringing his face close and kissing the underside of her chin. "You're shaking. I can feel you shaking in my arms." He smiled and reassured her with, "It's okay," and then kissed that spot underneath her chin again.

And it was okay, wasn't it? If she followed her heart, if she allowed her actions to be guided by her heart, how could it be wrong? Love wasn't wrong, it never was, and love came from the exact same spot, from her heart.

But this wasn't love.

"Alex, no…" To her own ears, she sounded pretty firm. Determined, even.

But he ignored her and carried her into the secondary bedroom, where Vasy had stacked most of the moving boxes and crap. With a few large steps, Alex deftly navigated around and over the mess. When he reached the bed, he gently lowered her onto the mattress, on her back, and then he climbed next to her, the hand without the chocolate in it sliding up inside her sweater and finding her breasts. He tucked his finger underneath the cup of her bra and circled her sensitive nipples.

The dreamy haze intensified, as did her appetite.

Allana closed her eyes and arced her neck back, allowing a subtle moan to escape. It embarrassed her to make that kind of noise for Alex, but his touch had that effect and she couldn't help it. She felt his weight climb on top of her, felt the pressure of his arousal pressing between her legs. He pumped his hips against hers a couple of times.

She liked that. Too much.

"Open your eyes," Alex whispered. "I want you to look at me."

Slowly, she obeyed. But just as the world came into focus, she felt his lips against hers. He tasted exactly like the last time. And she hated to admit it, but she missed this. All of it. She'd thought about the kiss, the way he turned her on so easily, mostly during those quiet moments alone while she wrestled with boredom and fatigue, and sometimes during those times when it was wrong to think of anything or anyone else except for the man in bed with her.

When Alex pulled his lips away, he shifted his weight and arousal off of her. She wondered why, half-expecting the sound of a chocolate wrapper being opened, followed by the flavor landing on her lips, the taste of chocolate. Instead, she felt his fingertip sliding away from her bulging chest and down her stomach to the waist of her pants. The finger pushed farther south, and she caught her breath.

Suddenly, her eyes popped open. She moaned a *Noooooo*. Because *nooooo* matter how much she wanted the excitement of feeling him inside her, she knew this had to stop. But when she opened her mouth to protest, she moaned another *nooooo* as his hand slid past the elastic of her lace panties and up against the hard and sensitive ledge of her pubic bone.

Her head fell back … *Oh, god, Alex, no…*

And as… *Please, don't bring me back to my past.*

"Noooooo…." She moaned, and that was when Allana made the one decision she knew she would regret later—she opened her legs a little more, just enough to send a message. But before he could cross that line even deeper, or touch her in the way she craved, the timer from the kitchen sounded, instantly slicing through the fairytale fog and her dreamlike haze.

"What's that?" Alex tore his hand out of her pants and jumped out of bed as if Vasy had just walked in and caught them.

Allana laughed at his paranoid reaction, but she was quietly thankful. The way her pulse raced, she knew they had come close—too close—to breaking the kinds of rules that were never meant to be broken.

"Seriously, what *is* that?" he asked, adjusting himself as Allana regained her bearings.

She sat up in bed and then joined him among the boxes. "I'm baking," she told him, stepping toward him because he stood between her and the door to the hallway.

"The recipe I translated last week?" he asked, his eyebrows rising as he put the pieces together.

She pushed herself up onto the tips of her toes and planted a quick kiss on his cheek, one that said *Thank you for not fucking me. You're a good 'friend'.*

After what had happened between them on the guest bed, a kiss like that didn't feel forbidden at all, and she hoped it felt as disarming as she intended. "It's my surprise for Vasy," she whispered with a tinge of guilt before slipping into the hallway and nearly screaming at the sight before her.

Vasy was standing just inside the apartment door, a confused look on his face as their eyes met.

Allana froze. She didn't know what to do. Or say.

"What's that noise?" Vasy asked.

Although her mouth opened, the words refused to come. Instead, she pointed toward the kitchen.

"What's wrong, Allana?" Vasy asked seemingly unaware as he kicked his boots off and started toward her.

She didn't want that, couldn't have him coming toward her and sensing the guilt of what had just happened in that second bedroom. *I almost ruined my marriage, almost returned to the place where Vasy rescued me.*

Instead of backing away, her eyes widened and she rushed forward, meeting him halfway, not letting him get any closer. Opening her arms, she pulled him into a hug and rotated him one hundred and eighty degrees so that he wasn't looking down that hall toward the sin that she'd just committed. *And what she'd* almost *committed.*

"It smells amazing in here," he said, squeezing her. But after a moment, he released her and held her at arm's length. "What's that noise? It's horrible!"

Over Vasy's shoulder in the depth of the hall, she noticed Alex's head peeking out. Their eyes locked for an instant before—

"Are you okay?" Vasy questioned, noticing that her eyes were focused beyond him. "What are you looking at?" he asked, chuckling and turning around to find the hallway empty now that Alex had pulled his head back into the second bedroom.

She blinked hard. "I'm just tired," she said, rolling out of his arms and heading into the kitchen to silence that damn alarm.

Once she struck the snooze button, she opened the oven and pulled out the paska. Consulting the recipe that Alex—still in the secondary bedroom, no less—had translated for her, she reduced the heat and reset the alarm for another thirty minutes.

"Allana!" Vasy called from deeper in the apartment. "What is this?"

She closed her eyes and said a quick prayer. For her and for Alex. "It's not what you think!" she called out. When she spun away from the stove, she noticed her jacket bunched up at the balcony door. "Shit," she cursed under her breath.

Before running into the hall, she draped the jacket over the back of a chair. She wondered if she would have to sleep in it tonight, because surely Vasy would kick her out and kill Alex. She would be left with nobody.

Taking a deep breath, she met Vasy in the bedroom with the messy sheets and boxes.

Vasy noticed her standing in the doorway, her face pale. "The window's wide open," he said. "No wonder you don't look well."

She swallowed the anxiety in her throat, and then it came to her. Just last month, he'd given her the nod to smoke inside the apartment. She reminded him of this. "So I was going to have a smoke," she lied, moving deeper into the room and sitting down on the same messy bed where she'd almost given herself to another man.

As Vasy pulled the window closed, she noticed it—the Dove chocolate on a ripple in the bed sheet, riding it like a surfer rides a wave.

"I came home for a quick lunch," Vasy confessed, wiping the snow and condensation off his hands once the window was shut. "Are you hungry?"

She grabbed the chocolate and buried it inside her pocket.

Later, she thought to herself. *Later, I'll indulge.*

"Allana?" Vasy asked, his voice betraying his curiosity. "Are you okay?"

She smiled and rose from the bed, relieved that whatever Alex had done to escape, Vasy hadn't seen him.

"Let's eat," she said, taking his hand and leading him out of the bedroom.

#

For the duration of Vasy's lunchtime visit, eating the quick meal that she had prepared with hands that trembled noticeably, Allana sat on pins and needles. She could barely eat the soup she'd cooked, or the tomato and cheese sandwiches. Her mind kept hurrying back to the second bedroom, wondering where Alex had hidden, why the bedroom window had been opened up wide, and what would happen next. *Could he have jumped? Why wasn't he dead if he had? Or was he hiding somewhere else?*

"I'm sorry for ruining your Valentine's Day surprise for me," Vasy commented as he finished his soup and reached for a quarter-slice of the sandwich. He shrugged and flashed that grin that she'd initially fallen in love with, the laidback one that betrayed no worry whatsoever. "But I wanted to surprise you, too, especially since I'll be working late tonight."

Her husband occasionally dropped in at lunch, but lately his visits had become scarce. Between heightened demands at the power station and a busier workload thanks to the freezing spell, she wondered if Vasy even took a break at all, forget about taking the time to eat the lunches she packed for him.

All Allana could offer as reply was a faint grin and, "It's okay. I'll probably end up burning the paska anyway."

Vasy's raised eyebrows suggested that he had his doubts about that. "It's about the thought, isn't it?" Okay, maybe he didn't have doubts. "All

I've done for you today is show up for a lunch that you ended up scrambling to prepare for me."

She tried to grin wider, but knew she failed at making it appear heartfelt. "You're right. It's the thought. So blackened paska will have to be good enough for you."

Vasy laughed and reached across the table, tenderly squeezing her hand. She wondered why she hadn't used that same hand to stop Alex from reaching down her pants and into her underwear. As the guilt set in, she started to question more than just that... She started to question this whole matrimonial arrangement, why her husband couldn't come home early on this one night of the year, the night meant for romance and love and the things that were supposed to lead to marriage in the first place. One day, was it too much to ask?

"It's only paska," Vasy told her, squeezing her hand one more time before releasing it and continuing with his lunch.

Only paska, she thought, swallowing the tears that threatened to erupt. *If things could only be so simple.*

# # #

Chapter 7

Once Vasy left for work, Allana barely took a relieved breath before sprinting for that second bedroom. She searched the closet, behind the boxes, underneath the bed, everywhere. But she still couldn't find where Alex had gone.

I know I didn't imagine him! But if I had, things would be so much less complicated...

Peeking into the hallway to make sure Vasy hadn't returned for another kiss goodbye—*because that would be the romantic thing to do on Valentine's Day*—Allana called out, "Alex? Where are you, you sick, crazy jackass?"

Silence.

She stood in the hallway, thinking things through. The bedroom window had been left wide open... Had that been to distract Vasy long enough for him to slip into another room? To escape entirely?

She returned to the foyer area and studied the deadbolt. Vasy would have commented if the lock had been left unlatched during lunch, which meant Alex hadn't escaped.

"I know you're still here, Alex!" she called out. Then, more to herself, "Come out, come out, wherever you are..."

She returned to the hall and entered the bathroom at the end. Grabbing the shower curtain, she ripped it away, fully expecting him to jump out at her. But the tub was empty. Alex hadn't been hiding here—the residue of water in the base of the tub would've trailed out onto the floor if he had so much as stepped behind that shower curtain. She'd have seen footsteps.

Argh.

Next, she searched the master bedroom. Inside the closet, under the bed, in the impossibly tight space behind the few moving boxes.

Still no Alex.

This was starting to feel like a 1980's horror film...She should just leave instead of looking for the beast about to jump out and scare her half to death.

Instead, she crept back into the hallway and started toward the living area. *Where could he be hiding?* She knew she had to find him. She couldn't leave him hiding in her apartment all day.

As if on cue, she heard a rapping at the apartment door. Allana's heart skipped a beat at the thought of Vasy returning, this time clueing in on the fact that something had been horribly wrong during his impromptu Valentine's Day lunch. And what if he didn't leave until he found Alex? Obviously, the American was somewhere inside their apartment...

More knocking.

Then again, if it were Vasy on the other side, why would he bother knocking? He had a key. And if it weren't Vasy, who else could it be but Alex? And if it were Alex, how did he get out of the apartment without killing himself from the fall?

Like last time, Allana brought one eye to the peephole and closed the other so she could focus. And like last time, on the other side of that door, she saw Alex. Except this time, he smiled and waved. Like a goof.

"Let me in," he said in plain English.

"Why should I?"

As if to answer her, he inspected the hand he had just waved at her, then found the finger he'd nearly buried inside her. He placed it in his mouth and sucked it clean, as if he had been munching on salted French fries and wanted the last, final taste of sodium on his tongue.

Watching his suggestive gesture, Allana's breath caught and she felt her knees weaken. "Not a chance," she said, her voice a little hitched as she heard Vasy's dismissive *it's only paska.*

Alex chuckled. "You sound so damn convincing."

"And you sound like... like you're about to turn around and walk back to the elevator and see yourself out," she stammered.

With an arrogance that only Alex could pull off, he shrugged, turned and walked away.

Allana's breathing accelerated. *It's Valentine's Day, a day for romance.* Her hands started trembling again. With Alex en route to the elevators, she glanced back into the kitchen and noticed the paska she'd baked for Vasy. *Only paska, he said before leaving her. Alone.*

Let him go, Alex is going to ruin your marriage and your life.

But she couldn't. *Vasy chose work.* She groaned with the agony of her inability to just let Alex go. *Alex chose her.* For some reason she refused to admit, Allana grabbed the door, yanked it open, and took a step toward the elevator: "Alex, wait—"

"I'm here," he said, stepping up behind her and grabbing her wrist to swivel her back around to face him. To Allana, it felt like a well-rehearsed piece of a dance, where he pulled her back and she spun into his arms, their faces inches apart.

Suddenly, the world around her blurred and all she saw was Alex, his eager grin, the desire in his eyes, the sensation of his breath against her face. Her body seemed to sway against his, left to right, left to right. A sad little dance between two foreigners.

Somewhere down the hall, a door opened.

"Let's get back inside," Alex whispered, leaning forward and brushing his lips against hers. The feeling numbed her faculties; all she could do was nod.

Following Alex's lead, she returned inside the apartment, watched him close the door. That was when Allana reached past him to close the lock. But her hands shook so much, she couldn't manage an effective grip.

Alex's fingers slipped in between hers, curled around her hand and engaged the lock.

"What are you doing to me?" she whimpered as she felt his other hand slide down the front of her pants, finding the exact area that he'd been aiming for earlier on the bed. She closed her eyes and arced her head back, moaning again. "Oh, god."

"Not god," he whispered into her ear before kissing her neck. "Say my name, Lana."

"Alex," she panted, and then nearly collapsed when his finger slid inside her, slowly and softly. "Oh, Alex."

His other hand released hers, clamping onto her jaw, and he brought her mouth to his. Alex kissed her in such a way that she knew she couldn't fend him off. She'd become powerless to him, to his wanting, to his hunger. And while she recognized just how bad this was, how wrong she was to surrender herself to another man, she powerlessly let herself go to him.

I am that girl. Again. Oh, but it feels so good to surrender to temptation, so good to just let go…

He'd seduced her, and with every stroke of his finger between her legs, she felt more and more at peace with her decision to let go. Because as wrong as it was, there was still a loophole in the back of her mind, one that made perfect sense in this very same moment, one she couldn't quite pinpoint right now with his hand where it was.

"Oh, Alex," she moaned. "Please take me. Please…"

# # #

Chapter 8

The guilt struck almost immediately. As the cloud of euphoria dissipated, the guilt struck almost immediately, the reality of her unfaithful act hitting her hard and fast much like the headache that follows a night of drinking vodka and smoking too many Sobranies on the balcony, and losing too much money at poker. For some strange reason, the first thing Allana noticed was the moving boxes all around her. Alex had taken her back to the secondary bedroom, so the guilt would remain there instead of the master bedroom where she slept with Vasy every night. And these boxes, assembled around her like a jury of her closest peers, seemed to stare at her with scorn. A hateful rage for what she'd done.

"What are you thinking about?" Alex asked, his hand sliding across her belly and up to her left breast. When his fingers scraped across her sensitive nipple, she rolled away from him, but he took her motion as an invitation to spoon her from behind, pressing his damp, limp dick against her ass.

"It's nothing," she sighed, both to Alex and the trio of judgmental boxes stacked next to her side of the bed.

"Impossible," his voice was far more triumphant than anything Allana could muster. Made sense; he hadn't been the one to cheat on his spouse. Alex had nothing to lose except his friendship to the man whose wife he'd just seduced. "Even if you tried, you couldn't possibly think of *nothing*. Our minds are always working, formulating stories, drawing conclusions, making stuff up."

He was right. More than anyone else, Allana knew that the projector in her mind could never produce a blank screen. Even as a teen, she could never escape her mind's ongoing analysis of her past mistakes and the perpetual predictions of what would become of her future.

"Tell me," Alex insisted, reaching up with his other hand and brushing the hair away from her face. "I love your face, by the way."

That made her smile. Hearing those words from Alex felt like validation; he wasn't *obligated* to say things like that, especially not now that he got what he wanted. Allana turned her head, looking back at him. His face wasn't too bad, either. She remembered licking it at some point while he thrust himself into her, sometime during their wild and crazy sex on the bed. She also blamed that face for what had led to this afternoon's thrusting in the first place. So she rolled her attention back to the disdainful boxes around her.

"Remember a few weeks ago," Alex whispered to her, seemingly abandoning his curiosity in what she'd been thinking, "when the Challenger space shuttle blew up?"

"Mmhmm," she muttered back as a response. She wondered what the Challenger explosion had to do with her betrayal to Vasy.

"The first thing I thought was that the Soviets stepped over the line. That this was exactly what the Americans needed to finally proceed with their plans to destroy the power station and set the nation back for centuries." He sighed. "Not to mention what would happen to the population. I envision a cross between Hiroshima and the Holocaust, a massive genocide perpetuated by the Americans who would make it look like we made a mistake."

As she lay there with him, Allana couldn't help but wonder if he knew something the rest of the world didn't. *What if he's right about all of his crazy conspiracy theories?*

"If the Soviets had anything to do with that shuttle explosion…" Alex started, but let the thought trail off so she could draw the conclusions herself.

"You're going to drive yourself crazy with these things," she said, rolling out of his arms and finding her clothes on the floor where Alex had dropped them after stripping them off of her. Sliding her legs into her underwear and pants, Allana glanced back at him on the bed. No matter how irresistible he'd been in the hallway, in the foyer inside the door to the apartment, right now he looked like the most destructive sin she'd ever set upon her lips. "Please let it go."

Please let me go.

"I can't," he confessed, sitting up on the bed. His response sounded like determination, and Allana had never heard anything like that from another man. "It's impossible now."

As much as Allana liked to hear those words, they also worried her. Like this relationship between them might never end now.

Allana made a mental note to open the window before Vasy got home; she needed to make sure the scent of her Valentine's Day submission had left the air. She also decided to indulge in a cigarette (or seven) to hide whatever remnants there were of Alex's scent in this room.

"I see all types of data," he went on. "The reactors are built to operate within a specific, optimal range. In theory, it wouldn't take very much to upset the balance between public safety and power. It's a very fine line with this type of reactor. I mean, we've achieved something extreme here. The world is watching. And the Americans… they're just waiting for an opportunity to take it all away from us and feed the rest of the planet the most ludicrous propaganda." Alex moved out of the bed and started stepping into his clothes as well. Allana almost sighed. Although Alex looked as good getting into his clothes right now as he'd appeared getting out of them earlier, she wondered why he didn't share in her guilt. She might have cheated on her husband, but he'd betrayed a friend. It annoyed her that he seemed so guilt-free about this.

After seeing the wrinkles he—and she—left, she reminded herself that she should also flatten out the bed sheets once he left. "Alex, you're starting to worry me with all of this talk."

He froze and stared directly at her. "Lana, you should be worried. Something isn't right here. The world is envious of what we possess in Pripyat." She'd meant the way he talked like nothing had even happened between them, like it was normal for the bed to have these post-sex wrinkles on its sheets. "Right now, right here in this town? There are *teams* of spies, people who have been hired by their government to steal our secrets and destroy our achievements."

"Spies? Really? Alex…" Was that all he could think about? *Spies,* after sleeping with a good friend's wife?

"Listen to me," he urged her, pushing his arms into his sweater and pushing his head through the collar. "This tension between Reagan and Gorbachev, it can't end well. And while these two go on with their pissing contest, what do you think the rest of the world is doing? The Germans are just as capable as the British, the French are just as desperate for an energy solution as the Canadians, and on and on it goes. This cold war crap is a perfect distraction, and we can't let our guard down." He paused. "They're circling like vultures, just waiting to pick off whatever is left of us."

"Uh-huh," she said, nearly yawning as she delicately made her way toward the bedroom door. Playtime had ended with their quick and (almost) simultaneous orgasms, but all of this talk about spies and politics…Okay, this time she yawned.

Alex joined her in the hallway, sliding his hand into hers and walking into the apartment's main living space where she'd danced with Vasy that night of the poker party.

"Here's the thing," Alex continued, his eyes wide with the thrill of telling a story. "I think you're beautiful."

She shrugged. *Maybe we'll have that chat now, the one where we talk about what happens next now that we screwed up?*

"And smart," he went on.

She raised her eyebrows.

"And, there's something else," he said.

"Married?" she asked, groaning.

Alex laughed.

"It's not funny!" She slapped him hard on the shoulder. "And you, you said you love him, too, said he's one of your best friends! Jesus, Alex, don't you feel any kind of remorse over what happened here? All you're talking about is…" she made a rolling motion with her hands, indicating the rambling he'd done so well. "And all I'm thinking is, 'What if Vasy finds out about this?'"

Nodding, Alex frowned. "Yes, I did say that Vasy and I are close friends. And, I'm also sorry that you're married," he went on before looking up with a big smile. "And as guilty as I feel about this, I don't feel like what we did was… I don't know… I don't feel like it was wrong."

"It was *very* wrong," she growled, guiding him away from the sofa and toward the apartment door. "And this… you being here, Alex… it's wrong, too."

Her words seemed to sting him a little, the way his face twisted and how his hand slipped free of hers. He made her feel like she'd just broken his heart. Like she was the heartless one here, like she wasn't the one with a conscience.

"I'm sorry, Alex," she went on, shaking her head. "But this…"

He pulled her into his arms and held her. "It's okay," he promised. "We'll get through the guilt. We'll figure something out."

Allana said nothing. She wanted to figure out a way to never see him again because she never *should* see him again, not after what they'd done and how he didn't seem to care about the feelings of other people. She didn't want to "get through the guilt," she wanted to figure out what happened next. But she knew that never seeing him again would become impossible once she and Vasy moved into the third floor of his building.

At the apartment door, Alex grabbed his jacket off the floor where he'd left it, and then pushed his feet into his boots. "With you and Vasy moving to my building," he said, as if he had just read the fears on her mind, "it won't be too difficult getting all of your stuff into my apartment once you leave him." He took her hands and gave them a squeeze.

Leave him? Allana's jaw dropped open, and she struggled for the right words, but there were none. Not only had she not thought that far ahead, but Alex didn't strike her as someone who was capable of dealing with their sin, let alone a woman like her.

Alex started laughing. "I'm joking," he assured her. Leaning closer, he lowered his voice to a whisper. "I don't think Vasy should find out about this."

Allana managed a grin, leaned in closer, and lowered her voice as well. *Finally, we're talking about this.* "That's probably a good idea because this won't happen ever again."

Alex nodded, gulping. "We'll see."

No, we won't.

As he reached for the door, he turned back to her. "Listen, have you been paying attention?"

"To Vasy?" she asked, remembering the time in Alex's apartment when this crazy talk had surfaced last.

"Yes, to Vasy."

She frowned, thinking about it. "What was I supposed to be paying attention to?"

"This is important," Alex insisted.

"I'm joking," she said, grinning back at him. But the truth was that she hadn't been paying much attention at all. Not because she didn't care or had no interest in what Vasy said about his work. Rather, Vasy hadn't spent more than forty-eight hours with her in the past two weeks. "But the answer is no. There's nothing."

"Nothing?" He didn't believe her; she could see the doubts in his eyes. "Anything about radiation levels?"

She shook her head. "Nothing about radiation."

"Reactor tests?" he pressed, looking more disappointed.

"No, no tests."

Alex raised a hand to his head. "Nothing at all?"

Allana thought about it. "Tests. Yes, he said something about tests."

Motioning for her to keep going, he said, "What kind of tests?"

She shrugged. "I don't know." She didn't know about the type of tests because Vasy had said nothing about tests in the first place. But she felt that if she didn't give Alex *something*, he would never leave her alone.

"Turbine tests?" Alex asked.

Allana shook her head.

"Power tests?"

More head-shaking.

"Coolant tests?"

She snapped her fingers and widened her eyes. "Yes! Yes, that's the one!"

"Coolant tests," he muttered, looking away. "Okay, okay. Now we're getting somewhere." He seemed to think about it some more, but all Allana wanted was for him to leave and let her get on with her guilt and self-hatred.

"That's all he's said," she told him. "I swear."

Alex frowned, unsure.

"I promise I'll keep paying attention," she told him. "*Better* attention."

"Okay, that's a good start." He reached back for the doorknob again. "A really good start. Try to find out when they're going to run the tests. Okay?"

She nodded.

Alex moved quickly. Before turning the knob, he jumped forward and kissed her quickly on the lips, and then he slipped out of the apartment and into the hallway. With his kiss still buzzing on her lips, she locked the door.

And in that moment, she hated herself.

She'd become *that girl* again. The one she'd left behind in the States.

She hated herself for doing what she'd done to Vasy, even though she felt that she had every—or at least a lot of—justification for doing what she'd done.

Alex was using her.

And she'd betrayed Vasy.

Closing her eyes and sliding her back down the wall until she fell into a seated position on the floor, Allana hated herself for what she'd done, justified or not.

# # #

Chapter 9

It was slightly past midnight when Vasy came home. Valentine's Day had expired three or four minutes ago. From the master bedroom, lying under the sheets, Allana heard the apartment door open, followed by the usual routine that involved Vasy hanging his jacket, placing his boots inside the closet before tossing his keys on the counter, and then making a trip to the bathroom for a quick piss, followed by a glance into the bedroom to see if she was awake (and tonight, she pretended to be asleep), a return trip to the kitchen where he opened the refrigerator for the cold water and a snack from the counter (today, he ate the paska, *which turned out surprisingly well, thank you very much*, but other nights he would often reach for a bag of chips or other treats) and, finally, he would retreat to the living room where he turned on the television and sat back to watch whatever propaganda was playing, followed up with passing out on the same sofa while reading his manuals and writing his notes in them.

Allana listened to this routine like she had a hundred of times before, but tonight something nagged at her. She couldn't help but wonder if he somehow knew about what had happened in the apartment earlier with Alex. It seemed he knew, even though he would have surely confronted her by now.

People always know.

Despite her paranoid thoughts, Allana managed to fall asleep. It wasn't a good sleep, though. She tossed and turned, too hot and then too cold. So when the telephone rang at a little past three in the morning, it woke her instantly. What surprised her—other than it being a crazy hour for a telephone call—was just how low the ringer had been.

As if Vasy had been expecting the call.

As if Vasy hadn't wanted her to hear it.

Sitting up in bed, she rubbed her eyes and willed the fogginess from her sleep to disperse, and once it finally did, she questioned whether she'd heard the phone at all. It could have been imagined, part of her tortured dreams. But then she heard Vasy's voice, quieter than the ringer so that she couldn't make out the words.

Curious, she slipped out from the bedroom and crept all the way to the end of the hall. She knew that if she stepped away from the wall, she would see the edge of the television, but not Vasy because the sofa was a little deeper into the room and, besides, if she stepped farther away from that wall, he would probably catch her spying on him.

Spying… maybe Alex wasn't so crazy after all. Maybe there were plenty of suspicious wives like me in Pripyat.

She heard him say, "I want to get away, too…Yes, yes, freedom is important to me, too…But there's a lot that needs to happen at my end…No, you're not understanding me… No, I can't just walk away right now…"

More silence.

Allana felt an immediate pain in her chest, except now it had nothing to do with her own guilt over her infidelity. This pain felt darker. It upset her stomach, because it sounded like Vasy was having an affair. And if she had any doubts about the possibilities of an affair before, that all changed when she heard what he said next.

"If my wife finds out about this? It's not just me. It's you, too. And the whole world will hear about it, you know that, right?" Silence. "Okay. Me too. Chat later."

When he hung up, Allana turned her back to the living area and headed straight to the bedroom, walking as quietly as she could manage despite the loud, panicked ringing in her ears. After what she'd done with Alex, she knew she had no *right* to feel this way.

Vasy is having an affair.

She couldn't help but wonder how long? Who was she? Did she work with him?

Who is this other woman?

By the time she reached the bedroom, the panic had only amplified. She wondered if Vasy had ever taken her in this bed, right here in their bedroom—*at least I had the decency to let Alex take me in the other room!*—before the panicked rage spiraled into heartache.

How was I not enough for him? I'm not the one working seventeen hours on Valentine's Day. I'm not the one who brought him to a country where he can't even speak the language to get by.

She hated her life, wanted to die.

Yes, I cheated. No, I don't deserve Vasy. But that doesn't mean I can't feel broken after finding out about his affair!

She placed her head down on her pillow and couldn't help the tears pouring from her eyes, as the words *Vasy is having an affair* repeated in her ears.

# # #

Chapter 10

The next morning, Vasy's kiss goodbye woke her. Allana didn't recall falling asleep, but she obviously had. Her eyes begrudgingly opened in time to watch Vasy creep out of their bedroom, his stride as confident and eager as she'd always known it to be.

"Vasy," she mumbled from the bed.

He turned around in the hall and faced her, a big smile on his face. "It's okay," he assured her. "Get your sleep."

"I love you," she said, half choking on the words as she pushed herself up on her elbow and watched him for a sign of betrayal.

Although Vasy hesitated only slightly—the way any husband having an affair would —he didn't make it obvious. Like he believed that if his smile brightened, she wouldn't notice. But she did, she noticed alright.

"Vasy?" she asked, her voice quieter with a touch of heartbreak in it.

At last, he responded the way he always did. "I love you more, Allana."

With that, he gave a curt nod and then left their apartment for another excessively long day at the power station.

Allana stared at the doorway where he had stood. Empty. Like all of the hours of her day. And, it seemed like her so-called marriage. Empty.

She thought she might be sick, so she closed her eyes and sat straight up in bed. Just in case she had to make a sprint to the bathroom.

At least today's shift was Vasy's final one for the week; she had him all to herself tomorrow. More time for her to study his behavior, for her to see what kind of signs of betrayal he exhibited. She knew she would find *something*. Vasy was a horrible bluffer.

But for now, he would have a full day at the power station.

Or wherever it was that he spent so much of his time.

# # #

Although Allana didn't fall back asleep like her depression wanted her to, it took her a couple of hours to drag herself out of bed all the same. With noon approaching, she realized she really should get out. Even with the freezing spell going strong for nearly three weeks now, she had to get out of bed. She had plans. She needed to get moving.

Moving...

Allana considered a hot shower, but she knew that if she increased her body temperature too much, stepping outside to catch the bus would be unbearable. So instead of the shower, she headed to the dresser and changed into fresh underwear, a new bra. Then it was off to the closet for a clean pair of pants with the kind of buttons that would make taking them off prohibitive, too time consuming. Even if Alex tried to get into them, by the time he made any progress, she expected she would have come to her senses to stop him.

After brushing her teeth and making sure she had a lot of cigarettes left in her latest pack of Sobranies, Allana reached into the money jar at the kitchen sink and withdrew enough rubles for the two-way fare on the bus.

The moment she stepped into the hallway, she paused. The smells and lighting and silence reminded her of yesterday's moment with Alex, the way he'd held her and how the surroundings had melted away like wax. She remembered his crotch pressing up against her just minutes before they'd retreated inside, his hand slipping into her pants and sealing the fate of their sin.

But as immediately as she recalled those feelings, they turned sour, and she was reminded again of her guilt. Of her husband's possible guilt. Of her whole messed up life.

Alex was no hero. *He's a jackass that turned you into a cheating wife, into that girl you swore you'd never be again, so forget about him!*

Feeling moodier now, Allana didn't have patience for the slow elevator, so she took the stairs and ran out to the freezing cold, catching her breath and wondering, like she always did, whether this weather might actually kill her. It felt like it could, the way her nostrils froze shut and the cold air sucked the moisture out of her throat, spawning the urge to cough. But she didn't cough. Instead, she withdrew a Sobranie from the pack and lit it before making the final trek to the bus stop where she waited.

And waited.

At one point, a couple of men in athletic uniforms stopped their four-door Skoda and asked her something in Ukrainian. She didn't understand and simply shook her head. The man in the driver's seat said something, wiggled his eyebrows as if to display just how classy he really was (there was a booster seat in the back, she noticed) and, after the passenger laughed at the comment, they drove off. She assumed their remarks were not very complimentary, but she didn't get to think about it too much because the rattling bus finally appeared.

Like a good Soviet-Ukrainian wife, she stepped on board, paid her fare, and settled into a seat midway to the back; far enough so the driver wouldn't want to chat her up (she'd made that mistake once before and looked like an idiot when she couldn't understand a single word), but not all the way in the back where she'd find herself unable to escape someone else's attempt at conversation. For Allana, moving here might have resulted in the true escape she'd been seeking, but it also presented her with all types of obstacles and issues…like wondering what her husband was up to at work this morning, which women might have caught his eye, and which one in particular caught his arousal after a 3am phone call.

At the stop closest to Alex's apartment building, she said, "Dyakuyu," to the bus driver and then hurried through the cold, crossing the street and wandering up the winding driveway toward the apartment building buried deep among the cluster of trees.

Nearly halfway there, she noticed another car approaching her from the building. She watched it slow as it came closer, and she quietly feared having to shrug and ignore an attempted conversation from the driver who was like a lot of people here—too friendly to mind his own damn business and carry on with his own life because she was *not* interested.

But once the car was close enough, she recognized it as Alex's Lada.

"Alex," she said as he stopped next to her. She smiled at the sight of him, the friendly and familiar face of the man that hungered for her in ways that her husband likely hungered for another woman. With jealousy pumping through her veins, she felt a little less guilty about the smile she'd given Alex, or the way his eyes made her feel wanted. Again.

"Miss me already, do you?" His eyelids fluttered, sheltering his green irises from her before recovering and offering a wink.

She closed her eyes and gritted her teeth. "Alex—"

"Why are you here?" he asked, interrupting her as if he expected the worst. "Everything okay?"

She nodded toward the building. "It's cold out."

"Hop in," he said, reaching across the console and unlocking the Lada's passenger door. "Let's go for a ride."

She glanced back at the apartment building, considering his offer before realizing that it was probably safer to get into the car because there was no bedroom inside the Lada.

"Okay," she rounded the front of the car and eased into the passenger seat. Once she had her seatbelt buckled and the car still wasn't moving, she glanced over at Alex and found him devouring her with his eyes. She avoided that look, knowing it would only lead to... another mistake. "Let's go."

Her words snapped Alex out of his daytime fantasy. "Right." He swallowed, pushing the shifter into first and hurtling the Lada toward pr. Lenina, where he made a quick right and followed it straight into the town center.

"Have you ever been there?" Alex asked her once he stopped at an intersection, pointing through the fogging windshield at the famous and luxurious Hotel Polissia. She knew that when politicians visited Pripyat from Kiev and Moscow to meet with Nikolai, they stayed at the Polissia. Soviet athletes and movie stars stayed there in the summer. It was the Pripyat version of the Plaza in New York.

"No," she admitted. She couldn't help but stare at the architectural beauty, wondering what the rooms were like, what a weekend away in that hotel would taste and feel like.

"Perfect," he said, steering right and driving straight to the Polissia's parking lot where a handful of cars were already covered in frost and a light dusting of snow. "It's my treat."

She shook her head, eyes wide. "No way!" As wonderful an experience as it seemed, she dreaded committing yesterday's sin again. She couldn't handle more regret, couldn't handle being *that woman* again, no matter how appealing the Polissia might be. No matter what Vasy might be doing at that very moment with the woman who'd called in the middle of the night.

And when she noticed Alex's hand on her thigh, feeling its upward climb, Allana resisted the urge to stop him until she remembered how she'd felt last night, standing at the end of the hall and hearing the whispered tone of Vasy's affair—*if my wife finds out about this?*

"Please, stop," she begged quietly, her stomach gurgling with self-loathing. She grabbed his hand and squeezed it as hard as she could, sending a clear message. "I have no problem with giving you another bloody nose," she warned. "Yesterday was a mistake."

When Alex winced, she released his hand so he could pull it into his own lap. He stared at her. "If I can't touch you, it makes what I'm going to do to you in that hotel room a little difficult…"

Allana gulped, tearing her eyes away. *As nice as that sounds…* "I'm not going with you into the Polissia," she told him, staring into her lap. *As nice as that sounds… the cycle ends here.* "I just wanted to see you and let you know that…" She gulped again. "I need to ask you for a favor."

"I hope it's sexual," Alex said with a smirk.

Allana ignored him, she had to.

"I've been paying attention," she confessed. "And Vasy received a phone call last night."

Alex's eyes changed, just like she'd expected they would. He blinked a couple of times. "What did he say?"

She kept her attention focused on her lap as she shrugged. "I couldn't hear what they were saying. But it was quiet. And late."

"How late?"

"Three in the morning," she admitted.

"Could it have been his family calling from the States?" he asked after a thoughtful delay.

"No. They call on Sunday," she explained with a sigh. "When long distance costs are lower. This was… different."

Alex turned his attention away; Allana watched him from the corner of her eyes. He seemed to be thinking of something, as if calculating the possibilities. She wondered if he came to the same conclusion that she had. Did he know about Vasy's affair? Had he known about it all along? Wait, was that the reason why he didn't seem to feel as guilty about what they'd done yesterday?

Finally, Alex looked up, took her face with his hands, and kissed her on the lips. All of it happened too quickly for her to fend off his surprise advances, and when she finally realized what was going on, he was already stepping out of the car.

"Let's go," he said, pinching his voice with excitement.

"I'm not going into that hotel!" she warned, shaking her head and wiping her lips.

"Sure, sure," he answered, and she wondered if he was just appeasing her. "Just follow me."

Before she could protest—she knew they would end up at the Polissia if Alex had his way—she opened her door and stepped out into the freezing cold with him.

He offered his gloved hand, which she took.

"It's freezing!" she squealed, noticing how others coming and going from the hotel were watching as they ran through the parking lot, toward Lenin Square, holding hands and laughing. "Where are we going?" Her lungs started to burn from how cold and dry it was, but her heart felt liberated after this morning's depression session in bed. She loved how they were acting like *friends*.

They ran through the town center, hurrying past the Palace of Culture, which the locals called the Energetik because it was more than just a place to go and "get cultured"; it was a gymnasium, a large swimming pool (where Vasy liked to swim on Sundays), and the place where most people liked to hang out.

Alex dragged her past the Energetik and brought her to a fenced-in area just behind it. Much of the space on the other side of the fence was vacant, but before the snowfall started, back in October or so, they'd begun building what would ultimately be the town's amusement park, another facility that would draw tourists and dignitaries to Pripyat. Allana had first heard about this project from Vasy, when he'd been trying to convince her that they should have a child. Not that an amusement was a reason to get pregnant, but he'd certainly used the pregnancy talk as an excuse to bring it up.

Even with so much snow on the ground now, she was amazed by the progress since the last time she'd peeked in on the project.

But the biggest structure, quite a distance away, was the large Ferris wheel. In the fall, on those warmer days, there had been tons of children assembled at this very fence, watching the workers piece the big and bright metal beams together. Back then, it hadn't been much. But now, the entire Ferris wheel was assembled; it was only missing the passenger compartments.

"The kids call it the Devil's Wheel," Alex told her.

She rolled her eyes at the name they'd given the ride; it sounded dangerous, but it was a *Ferris wheel*, about as exciting as napping.

"And... I'm going to kiss you on the Devil's Wheel," Alex went on. He leaned over and tried to kiss her again, but she stepped away.

"That's not going to happen."

"It will," he argued, his eyes hungry again.

"I'm not here for this, Alex," she warned, looking away.

"Then why are you here?" He frowned, studying her.

"I gave you what you wanted yesterday," she said, pretending like she hadn't wanted any of it, "and now I need you to give me what I want."

Alex smirked. "Yes, a favor." The way he said it, Allana could only imagine what kind of perverted thoughts were bouncing across his mind. And when he stepped toward her again, she held up her hand.

"No, nothing like that."

Alex's face crumpled as if she'd just hurt his feelings.

"I need your car," she said at last. "Only Sunday."

Studying her, he blinked against the cold. It seemed as if he was deliberating whether or not he could trust her with the piece of crap Lada that he drove around town. "How will I get to work?" Alex asked.

Allana shrugged. "I'll drive you to the power station Saturday night because Vasy will still be at work, but you need to find your own way home on Sunday." She stepped closer to him, reached between his legs, and gave his crotch a gentle massage through the fabric of his pants and the thick material of her mitten. "If you say no," she said in a quiet, whiny voice, "I'll be heartbroken and worried that yesterday wasn't special enough for you."

Alex gulped as his gaze regained its desire for her. "Okay, you can use my car. But you'll bring it back Sunday night?"

Allana shook her head, still massaging his now-rigid crotch. "No. You'll come get it from the building next to mine. I'll leave it in the parking lot, but you can't come until dinner. That way, Vasy will be too busy eating so there's no chance he'll be on the balcony smoking. And if he's not on the balcony, he won't see you."

#

Chapter 11

Sunday morning, Allana woke to Vasy's arms sliding around her shoulders from behind, his midsection pressing into her back. He often woke up aroused, but Sunday mornings he liked to chase that arousal, capture it, and bury it deep inside her. As Allana slowly awakened, she wondered where he buried that arousal during the week during those long hours at the power station.

She felt his face nuzzling her hair, his lips caressing her neck. Once consciousness was fully upon her, her Valentine's Day guilt flared up and an alarm shrieked in her head.

If my wife finds out about this...

Despite the rush of arousal that Vasy managed to stimulate in her, she pushed him off, still upset about that 3am phone call, and rolled away from him, tossing her legs over the edge of the bed. She sat up and covered her face with her hands and, half a second later, she felt Vasy's hand on her back, massaging the space between her shoulders.

"Are you feeling okay?" he asked, sliding into the spot next to her.

"Just a headache," she moaned lightly, raising a half-smile to her lips as she looked over at Vasy. "I'll be okay." *Once you stop screwing whomever is calling you after you spend all day "working" on Valentine's Day.*

Lowering herself onto her back, she winced as Vasy's weight crawled on top of her. He reached down, his fingers sliding inside her underwear.

When the wincing failed to deter him, she raised her hands to her temples and closed her thighs on his hand, stopping him from going any deeper down the path that Alex's fingers had last traveled.

She hated to think about it, but the last time she'd been in this position, it hadn't been with her husband, but a paranoid man who had a curious way of arousing her, making her feel wanted and desired and sexy and...

"But you're so wet all of a sudden," Vasy said, drawing his hand back with a pleading look in his eyes. *Who is she, the woman that gets to feel your arms around her, those fingers inside her while you're* working *all week, Vasy?*

"I'm sorry, but... but my head is killing me," she said, still pressing her temples. "Let me get breakfast started." She sat up again, moaning at the fake pain.

"Do you think we have any Tylenol left?" Vasy asked her while she got dressed.

Glancing over and finding his face crunched up and filled with worry, she felt guilty about lying to him about the headache. A small lie compared to the secret she kept, but still a lie...

"I'll look." They'd brought some supplies from the States when they moved last year, but she didn't know whether anything remained, let alone whether the product had expired.

Without glancing back, she left Vasy in bed and retreated to the kitchen, her breathing fast and anxious because today she planned on meeting his mistress.

# # #

Chapter 12

After breakfast, Vasy retreated to the bedroom while Allana tackled the dishes with her fake headache. In her head, she ran down the bullet points of things she needed to accomplish and visualized how she would achieve them. Although spying on your husband might seem like a simple mission on the surface, once you dig a little deeper into the execution of that task, Allana would argue that it's actually quite complicated.

When Vasy returned from the bedroom in his athletic outfit, he crept up behind her and placed a hand on her forehead, presumably checking for a fever.

"You don't look well," he told her with a compassionate frown.

She tried to smile. "I'm fine," she said.

Physically, she *was* fine, but deep down she was sick. Not only because he might be having an affair, but because of her own infidelity. She wondered how they had ever come to this, how she had allowed that distance to grow between them to the point where the only time she felt valued and wanted by her husband was on Sunday mornings when he wasn't working, when he was actually present.

"Get some rest," he ordered her, leaning forward and kissing her on the side of her face.

She watched him grab his gym bag from the closet, step into his boots, and slide into his jacket. He didn't look like a man heading out to see a mistress, but if she hadn't heard the words—*if my wife finds out about this?*—with her own ears…

It was still cold out—freezing, in fact—so before Vasy left, he also grabbed his fur hat and heavy gloves from the closet shelf. "See you in a few hours," he said with a smile.

If previous weekends were any indication, Vasy liked to swim a few laps at the Energetik's Olympic-sized pool, then work out with the weights, and finally enjoy a sauna. But she knew he also liked to visit with Gregor for a cigar, vodka, and fine music because he often brought record albums with him, which was his excuse for not lifting as many weights or taking as long in the sauna lately. Allana suspected that somewhere in there, he forgot to mention how spending time at his lover's apartment also cut down his exercise time—because when else would he find the time for an affair that resulted in early-morning phone calls?

Allana dried her hands on a dishtowel and started toward the balcony door, tossing the towel over the back of a kitchen chair. She made a fist and used the bottom of her hand to wipe away the condensation on the glass as she stared outside, toward the parking lot entrance.

She spotted their pale blue Zaporozhets, a small car that looked a lot like a Fiat. Vasy stopped before fishtailing and then made his left turn onto the street. With him gone, Allana took a deep breath and headed to the bedroom. She'd buried the keys to Alex's Lada in her shirt drawer, knowing that if even he were extremely suspicious of her, Vasy would never think to look for hints in a shirt drawer. Adrenaline pumping, she grabbed the keys, got dressed, and then hurried out.

She'd parked the Lada in the next parking lot, the one that serviced the building next door. Since Vasy would recognize Alex's car in their building's assigned lot, she thought it might be smart to eliminate, or at least reduce, the chances of him seeing it in the first place, and parking it next door made sense.

Once she got into the car and started the engine, she let it idle for a little while, just like Alex had requested. It was a Lada, after all, and if Vasy's opinion was correct, then the reliability of this vehicle would probably increase if she gave it a few impatient minutes to warm up.

As the temperature gauge on the dashboard edged a small notch away from the C, she lowered the parking brake and shifted into first, following the same tire tracks that her husband had just laid into the fresh snow. Ten minutes later, she arrived in the town square.

Parking in the lot for the Hotel Polissia (Vasy was parked in a lot on the far side of Lenin Square, so she knew she wouldn't run into him by accident), she took her time and strolled into the Energetik. She climbed to the second floor and considered taking a seat on the observation deck where she could "observe" her husband while he swam lengths and did whatever— or whomever—else. But there was nobody else on the deck, which meant she would stand out like a neon sign. So instead, Allana roamed the Energetik, which also doubled as Pripyat's cultural center. Every city and town had one, and this one had paintings and pictures of various Soviet leaders, people that meant nothing to her but were meant to inspire others, be their role models.

Casting little more than a quick glance at the pictures and colors, Allana could barely keep her breakfast down. She was afraid of what she would find today, afraid that she would confirm what she suspected. It suddenly made sense why people back home hired private detectives: it was one thing to hear someone else tell you that your husband is having an affair, but it was quite another to actually confirm it for yourself. No doubt, Allana was out of her element.

After an hour of soaking in the reality of just how much the Soviet people loved (or were forced to love) the historic figures on the walls, Allana slipped outside and got into position behind a delivery truck in the far lot where Vasy had parked their car.

She didn't have to wait long before he appeared, his hair damp and his gym bag flung over his shoulder. Slipping back behind the truck, she held her breath as she watched him open the Lada's trunk, toss his bag inside, and then slip behind the wheel. Once she knew he was on his way, she spun around on her heels and sprinted back to Alex's Lada. This time, she didn't give the engine time to warm up; she shifted into gear, still panting from her run, and navigated to ul. Kurchatova.

On the street, there was no sign of Vasy's blue car, so she held her foot into the gas, slipped a little while making her hard left onto pr. Lenin and, as she safely came out of the turn, the blue car appeared in her sight lines ahead.

She followed it, roaring past the entrance to Alex's building (their next home), then she made a sharp right onto ul. Lesi Ukrainki. As she trailed him, Allana allowed herself to fall a few car lengths back, slowing down as the heater coughed to life. Unless Vasy's lover lived in the same district as Gregor, it seemed he was sticking to his typical Sunday plan, just like he'd promised he would. He might have spotted her by now, but she didn't truly believe she'd been wrong about the suspicious call, so she followed him to the high-density apartment complex at the corner of ul. Sportivnaya. She knew which apartment building Gregor lived at, so she wasn't worried about losing sight of Vasy by giving him some extra distance.

By the time she turned onto the street-like driveway and followed it to the large lot outside the quad buildings at the far back, her husband had already vacated the light blue Zaporozhets. He was most likely lighting up a foreign cigar on the Gregor's fifth-floor balcony on the other side of the building.

After parking Alex's Lada a little deeper into the complex, she walked around to the opposite side of the quad and surveyed those fifth-floor balconies for signs of her husband. When she saw none, she walked back around to the front of the building, and that was when she saw him leaving Gregor's building.

She frowned. *Already?*

She noticed that he was carrying his gym bag, too. Allana didn't quite understand why he would have brought his bag to Gregor's apartment. Something wasn't adding up. Stepping back behind the corner of the building, she discreetly watched her husband replace the bag in the trunk of the car and then retreat back to the building.

Was he headed back to Gregor's unit?

Or someone else's?

Allana's breath caught in her throat as that same hurt from earlier rose up inside of her again.

Do I really need more *evidence?* She felt like she might get sick.

She decided to follow him, hoping he would go straight back to Gregor's unit despite her womanly sixth sense suggesting that he wouldn't. Rushing to catch up, Allana realized that she was already walking on her tip-toes.

Silently cursing herself for the over-prudence, she entered the lobby. She was so convinced she'd catch him with another woman that she told herself it would exonerate her from her own marital slip with Alex. *But that's wrong, it's so damn wrong!*

Directly before her in the lobby, there were two elevators, which she hadn't expected. And the doors to one of those elevators were in the process of closing, affording her just a glimpse of the shoulder of Vasy's heavy jacket.

"Nice," she muttered, a little disappointed that her husband wasn't enough of a gentleman to reach out and hold the elevator for her.

Lucky for Allana, the stairwell door was next to the small enclave that housed the two elevators. Hurtling through the doorway and up the stairs, she stopped at the second floor and peeked into the elevator enclave. When she saw that neither compartment had stopped, she raced to the third floor. Same thing. She repeated this tiring race-stop-look-repeat routine all the way up to the fifth and top floor, breaking a sweat in the process; her boots and jacket were warm and heavy!

On the fifth floor, she stayed in the stairwell so that Vasy wouldn't see her. She hoped he was heading to Gregor's anyway. Besides, she needed to catch her breath and wipe the perspiration off her forehead. Once she knew he would be too far into the hall to see her, she carefully opened the stairwell door and crept into the shallow elevator lobby. *Please be headed to Gregor's.* The loudest sound on the fifth floor was the blood pumping through her veins, which told her something: She was afraid of the truth.

At the corner where the hallway met the elevator lobby, she poked her head out and glanced left—nothing—and then right. She saw Vasy strutting toward Gregor's unit at the very end.

So she watched him, just to be sure. *Go to Gregor's.* A spark of hope flashed across her mind, but it was brief.

Because Vasy didn't quite make it all the way to the door at the end of the hall. He stopped two units short of it.

I knew it.

Allana frowned, watching. The chaotic pumping in her veins amplified as he removed his gloves. Then, almost as if he could sense her presence, his head turned toward her. Hastily, she retreated behind the corner and pressed her back against the wall, listening to him knock on the door—*tap-tap,* pause, *tap.*

When the door didn't open and wasn't followed by the sound of a woman welcoming him with a slutty, overly flirty tone, she wondered if maybe Vasy were walking back toward the elevator, disappointed that he wouldn't get any loving from his mistress today before heading home. And that thought relieved her, no matter how much it would amplify her own guilt.

To be sure, she considered peeking into the hall again, but decided against it. Too risky. She'd get caught.

She also didn't want to risk slipping into the stairwell, so she reached for the elevator's call button. But that was when she heard something else, something that stopped her.

The sound of a key slipping into its counterpoint, followed by the lock being disengaged and then the creaking sound of a door opening.

At first, she denied that it could have been Vasy that unlocked and opened the door—how could she hear the creaking from all this way? But she realized that her senses were heightened by the adrenaline. Plus, when she chanced a glance back into the hallway, she saw that Vasy was the only other person there.

Her heart sank as she watched Vasy nudge the door open and remove his key before stepping inside.

He has a key?

She moved back into the safety of the elevator alcove. "Oh, god," she groaned, pressing her back to the wall and allowing her trembling legs to gradually lower the rest of her body to the floor. She buried her face in her hands, wanting to cry but still too confused about confirming what she'd suspected since that 3am phone call.

Why would he have a key? Was there a secret family on the other side of that door? A wife and... and the one thing she hadn't been able to provide: kids!?

It had to be a secret family, why else would Vasy have keys to another apartment? Why hadn't Allana known about this until now?

Yes. Obviously it was more than just a fling, a Sunday afternoon sexercise session with a coworker.

It's serious... Serious enough that he has a key to her apartment!

Her stomach sank again. She felt sick. Lifting her head out of her hands, she stared at the ceiling and practiced her breathing exercises. *He-he-he-HOOOOOO.*

Vasy… is having more… than an affair…
He-he-he-HOOOOOO.

She realized and accepted that she'd cheated on him, too—*just once, and chalk that up to a momentary lapse of judgment*—but Vasy had a *key*, possibly a whole secret family—*no, that's just stupid, it wasn't like there'd been baby cries*—and that was serious, not something you could dismiss as a single momentary lapse of judgment that would never happen again!

At last, she couldn't help herself. The tears poured from her eyes, and they burned, her eyes stinging from the madness that could be expected from discovering a betrayal like this one.

When she heard another door opening down the hall, she came back to reality. Whether it was Vasy or not, she didn't want to get caught in this building by anyone.

But if it were Vasy…It would have been a quick visit, which meant either his lover had left him more frustrated than Allana had when she'd turned him away this morning, or it meant that he hadn't been able to last more than a few seconds once his mistress took him in her mouth (or wherever she took him).

Or maybe it meant he wasn't having an affair after all. She wiped the tears away, a sloppy motion of her sleeve across her cheeks and in the end, the door opening down the hall wasn't even Vasy's doing. She knew this because a second later, she heard more knocking.

Rising to her feet, Allana considered taking a peek into the hall, but she would have been too late. Plus, it didn't matter because a couple of seconds after the knocking, she heard Vasy's voice.

He gave a laid back chuckle and said, "Hey, I've missed you," followed by another chuckle and the sound of the door closing and its lock latching.

What the...?

# # #

Chapter 13

Allana didn't drive straight home. She drove out of town and sped through the frozen countryside. The snow and ice-covered trees didn't exactly blur while she held the gas pedal to the floor (she was driving a Lada, not a Porsche), but it felt nice to reach the higher speeds. Like she had achieved some form of escape. An escape from her big escape, she thought cynically, and then she opened her mouth and let out a wild scream that went nowhere beyond the car's doors and windows, but it felt good to get it all out and make her vocal chords burn.

It didn't take Allana long to remember that she wasn't familiar with these rural roads; the farms she passed were completely foreign to her. Kicking down on the brake, she skidded to a stop at the entrance to one of the unfamiliar farms. A potato farm, with cattle that produced thick vapor in the sharp, cold air with each breath.

She knew that most of the farmers here were extremely friendly. Vasy would always speak with the farmers in town on Sundays. That is, back before he started working out and carrying on with secret women in secret apartments.

He has a key!

Gritting her teeth, she turned into a driveway, then shifted into reverse and backed back onto the rural road, heading back in the direction she had come. Just as quickly as she'd left the town of Pripyat, she returned to it, an exercise with which she'd been extremely familiar back home in the States.

But instead of driving back to the old apartment where she still lived, she drove to the new one where they'd be moving.

The same apartment building as Alex's.

She needed someone to talk to, and even though Alex was supposed to be at work for another couple of hours, she decided she would use the keys he'd given her for the car, let herself into his apartment, and wait for him. Maybe snoop around a little. But ultimately, she would wait for him.

And as for Vasy, he would come home and find the apartment empty, she realized. She wondered if he would know that she'd followed him and uncovered his love affair. And even if he did eventually figure it all out, would he care? He was so deeply in love with this other woman that he kept her apartment key on his key ring!

Coasting up the driveway to the new apartment, Allana felt her anxiety levels creeping up. She knew just how aggressive Alex could be with her, how hard he always seemed to push to get into her pants. He'd already accomplished that once. But the way Allana saw it, he'd seduced her and taken advantage of her loneliness. Giving herself to him was still wrong, but doing it once was less wrong, in her mind, than sleeping with him willingly and chronically. No matter how much she could justify it because of Vasy's own affair, Allana refused to let it happen again.

Suddenly, in her state of vulnerability, she began to second guess her decision to go there and wait for Alex. But she decided to stay anyway. Firstly, she didn't want to go home. She needed to be somewhere else and, without knowing and understanding the language and without a bankroll of rubles in her coat pocket, it wasn't like she could go rent herself a room at the Hotel Polissia. She needed to stay at a friend's place. And, as pathetic as it sounded, Alex was the only friend she had here. He won by default.

Parking the Lada in Alex's designated spot, she locked the doors and took the elevator to the fourth floor. With just two units per floor in the building, it was easy to remember which one belonged to Alex, even in her current emotional state. At his door, she located the right key on his key ring. There were only two keys there, one for the Lada, the other for the apartment, even though she remembered how he'd inserted the wrong key into the lock when she had been here with him the last time.

Where have all of the other keys gone?

Allana let the thought pass. She didn't have much of a choice because the moment she unlocked the door and pushed it open, she found Alex leaning against the foyer's closet frame. He had his arms crossed and a big grin on his face. "Welcome home, honey."

"You're here," she said, her chest pounding hard at the sight of him. Part of her had counted on having a couple of hours to plan out their conversation, what she'd tell him, how she would fight off his advances.

Alex stepped toward her, holding out his hand. When she relinquished the car keys, he tossed them blindly behind his back, and then offered the same hand to her.

He wants something else, Allana realized.

"Let me help you out of your jacket." He took her hand, but the moment their fingers touched, Alex's cocky little grin softened. "What's wrong?"

"It's nothing," she sighed, allowing him to pull her out of her jacket. "Why are you home so early?"

"System upgrades," he explained, taking her jacket and finding a hanger inside the closet. "They let us go home early. It just means I'll have a few extra hours to make up next week."

When he came back to her, this time he offered his open arms. Allana found the gesture welcoming, so, still in her wet boots, she accepted the hug. As his arms constricted around her, she half-expected him to make an advance, but he didn't. This time, he played the role of a friend. Too well... *which isn't like Alex.*

"So what did you discover?" he whispered into her ear, and the sensation of his breath against her skin reminded her of Valentine's Day, that moment they'd shared in her second bedroom. The good parts, though, not the parts involving guilt and regret. Except this time, Alex was all business.

"What are you talking about?" she asked, feeling a little dizzy from being in his arms.

"That's why you wanted my car," he explained, pulling back so he could stare into her eyes. "Today is Vasy's day off. We both know he goes to the Energetik. We both know he works insane hours."

"And so what?" she asked, giving him a shove. "What are you implying?"

Alex shrugged, his regular, cocky attitude returning. "And then there's the late phone call after Valentine's Day. The day we made love," he reminded her with a smirk and, at the mention of their sexual encounter, his eyes bore so hard into hers that she felt her head beginning to spin.

"Alex," she warned, shaking her head. "It won't happen again."

He didn't want to hear it. In one fluid motion, he bent forward and lifted her up onto his shoulder like a potato sack. Before she could protest, he eased her feet out of her boots. Allana couldn't help but laugh, even though one of her socks had come off inside the boot.

Alex carried her into the living area (*at least he isn't delusional enough to bring me to the bedroom!*) and she squealed, "My sock! My sock fell off!"

"One less thing to strip off of you." He tossed her onto the sofa.

Allana shook her head. "No. *That* is *not* going to happen again. Not a chance."

Ignoring her again, he asked, "What did you discover?"

For the first time in, well, forever, Allana actually wanted Alex's playfulness. She had come here because she needed a friend, someone to talk to, to lean on and cry with (and eat Ben and Jerry's, except they were in the Soviet Union and nobody had Ben and Jerry's). But now, she didn't want to put the reality of what she'd discovered into words. In fact, she would've rather slept with Alex again and felt his naked chest against hers, brushing against her as he thrust—

"Allana," he asked, sitting next to her and taking her face with his hands. The way he looked at her, she could tell his interest was more than just sexual. It was genuine. Alex cared for her, no matter how much she wanted to deny that. He cared. "What's going on?"

She looked away, and then the tears started.

"I'm going to kill him," Alex growled, standing up. But before he could get away from her, she snapped her arm out and grabbed his hand. When he tried to snap free from her, she yanked him back as hard as she could.

"Alex," she begged, and the sound of her plea—the vulnerability and fear and sadness all rolled into one—stopped him.

Lowering onto his knees before her, eyes wide, he waited for her direction. "How *dare* he—"

"Kiss me," she begged, the tears dripping down her face. She didn't want to talk about this, didn't want to face the reality of what she'd discovered. She wanted Alex to take her away, drown out the betrayal by seducing her into committing more of her own. "Kiss me and make this all go away."

Alex hesitated, but when Allana reached underneath his arms and pulled him up against her on the sofa, he finally did as he was told.

With a voracious determination, he closed his eyes, puckered his lips, and kissed the sadness off of her cheeks. Then he brought his mouth to hers and, eventually, stripped her out of her clothes, kissing every inch of her body before taking her in the middle of his living room.

# # #

Chapter 14

There was no guilt this time.

None.

Not even with the brush of her wrist across the sweat-dampened back of her neck. And not even when she sat up on the carpet, her body still buzzing from Alex being inside her. All Allana felt was numbness and euphoria, which was odd that those two feelings could even work together.

With a deep inhalation, she saw the digital clock on the VCR above Alex's television. Frowning, she realized it was getting to that time of the day when Vasy would arrive at home and find that she'd left, their place was empty, and he would probably question why. Since their arrival in Pripyat, she'd always been there to welcome him home.

Or would he even care?

How could he care when she stood between him and the mistress whose key dangled from his key ring?

So… No guilt. Not from Allana.

If she felt anything at all, it was rage.

"I'm sorry," Alex panted. He remained on the floor, lying on his side and propping himself up with his elbow. His face was flushed, his neck blotchy with red spots from where she'd kissed him, and his chest heaved as he worked at coming down from his own high. At last, he reached out, the backs of his fingers tracing the inside of her thigh, still as hungry as the gaze in his green eyes. "I couldn't control myself."

Allana glanced down at his hand on her thigh and smiled. Pulling his wandering fingers off her skin, she kissed his palm.

Alex offered a cute but innocent grimace. "My endurance normally gets better with time…"

"It's okay," she assured him with a chuckle. "You haven't left me dissatisfied." And he hadn't, because with Alex, she knew she was the only woman.

The same could not be said for her own husband, a man that barely acknowledged her existence… and now she knew why.

Lowering Alex's hand, Allana stood and started gathering the clothes he'd torn off her. She felt his eyes watching her, as if they had a way of physically touching her when she bent over for her bra, or when she squatted down to disentangle her pant legs from his. She enjoyed that feeling, the imagined sensation of his eyes groping her body, looking for a way to taste her and drive her wild all over again. Just *knowing* how badly he craved her was enough to reinvigorate Allana's own appetite. Because to hell with Vasy. He didn't deserve her, especially not after she'd witnessed him entering that unknown apartment this very afternoon.

"I wonder how any other woman could ever compete with this view," Alex said.

Allana glanced back at him. "Thank you." She wiped at the corner of her lips, having noticed that his arousal had returned as well. After finding the last of her clothing, she placed the pile in a tidy lump on the sofa before lowering herself on top of him, straddling his lap and allowing her head to tilt back as she took in the sensation of him filling her once again.

He smiled up at her, moving his hands around to her backside. "You're not a choice, Allana," he whispered. "For me, you could never be a choice. You…"

I don't deserve to be a choice, she thought as she kissed him, hard. "Then what am I?" she asked.

"You just… are," he said.

And that was all she needed to hear before taking what she wanted. She threw her head back again as Alex's movements accelerated.

###

Chapter 15

Something happened that day at Alex's apartment. It wasn't just the sex, Allana concluded. It was something deeper, something she had felt with Vasy when she first met him in her senior year at Wellesley. When Vasy was an MIT student with no knowledge of her past. And she—an English Literature major with no clue how her future looked—found inspiration in his promises of faraway seclusion.

"Maybe I was a little too eager to get away," she told Alex.

They lay tangled on the floor, still naked. Outside the southeast-facing windows, the sky began to darken. Part of her wondered why Vasy hadn't called Alex, looking for her. Because where else would she be?

"What were you so eager to get away from?"

She shrugged, reaching back over her shoulder, her hand swiping across the sofa's cushions for her clothes. When she found the mound, she pulled it down and started getting dressed. "I grew up in Detroit. My parents drank too much, couldn't hold down jobs. And I..." She shook her head, shaking away the nostalgia and hoping to shun her own disappointment at the same time.

Alex's hand rubbed her back. "It's okay. It's in your past."

Glancing out the windows, she realized that, as far as she'd run from her past, it had finally caught up to her. "I got pregnant in high school," she admitted. "I was sixteen. Junior year. The guy, James Brentwood, he came up with a plan to keep the baby. It was our secret. We'd finish the year off at school, then we'd run off and raise our baby."

"You were sixteen," Alex pointed out. "What was Jimmy going to do to support you?"

Allana couldn't help but grin. Jimmy—she liked that better than James, seemed more suitable—had a lot of big ideas. He was a smart guy, the smartest she'd ever known until she met Vasy. "He was a business student at Michigan State, but he also invented things. Lots of things. He'd already registered a few patents while at school. And his father was an exec at one of the automakers, I can't remember which one. James—"

"Jimmy," Alex corrected.

Allana chuckled. "Yes, *Jimmy* said he knew of a way to make cars safer."

Alex raised an eyebrow. "Like with seatbelts?"

"No, with radar," she elaborated, trying to remember exactly how he'd explained it to her. "He figured that if you could shoot radar out of each corner of a vehicle, you could apply brake pressure if another car was detected as approaching too quickly. No more need for seatbelts because the cars would be smart enough to avoid the bad accidents. James—*Jimmy*—said the worst were side-impact accidents. They happen so fast that a second or two difference is all it takes to avoid them. And his radar system would give you that time, slow you down just enough to save your life."

Alex's eyebrows rose. "That's actually pretty smart. Did he make any money at it?"

Shrugging, Allana admitted: "No. The technology was too expensive. But even if they'd gone along with it, it didn't matter." She shook her head because she hadn't told him the worst of it yet. "When I started to show and our parents found out, James disappeared."

"How?" he asked, surprised.

"My parents suddenly started insisting on an abortion that they couldn't afford. My dad knew someone who had a daughter who 'fucked up' like I had," she said, her tone bitter. But she wasn't bitter, not anymore. Now she was just sad, because she'd had no support from the people who were meant to support their child. "Even if my dad really knew where to find a cheap abortionist, I don't know where he thought he'd find the money to pay for it."

After a silent spell, she felt Alex's hand on her back again. "That's quite the past...."

She blinked back her tears. "I should have known I was being manipulated. After that argument with my dad, I ran straight to Jimmy's house looking for him, but his parents said he'd left and he wasn't coming back. Like I was an idiot, like their son played no role in any of this." She shook her head again, feeling the anger boiling inside her at the memory of how everyone had treated her. "They told me Jimmy was going to a new school, and when they reminded me for the millionth time that I would never see him again, they offered to pay for the abortion." Allana closed her eyes.

"And that's when you knew?" he asked.

She nodded, staring down into her lap. "Yes. That's when I knew where my parents had come up with their own abortion ideas. It was Jimmy's parents' idea, and my parents were more than happy to jump on board."

"Nice," he whispered.

"It gets better," she groaned, disgusted. "Because Jimmy's parents offered to get me 'proper' care. See, his parents wanted to look like the good guys, like they weren't being selfish like my father and his 'cheap doctor' solution."

"Jerks."

"But I refused it all. I wasn't an idiot. I thought I'd keep the baby and play their game. And so I decided to go after their son for support." She shrugged and felt the disgust boiling in the pit of her gut again. "Jimmy had promised to take care of me, and that was what I wanted—Jimmy. I figured if I could find a way to sue for support, I'd see him again, and he'd see me and our baby, and we'd be together again."

"So what happened when he saw you again?" he asked.

She bit down on her lower lip, almost enough to break the skin because this was where she normally fell apart. "He didn't," she whispered, closing her eyes and counting to three in her head. "I had the baby." With that admission, Allana's voice hitched and her chin trembled. But she didn't allow much silence to build up this time because the longer she waited, the more choked up she'd get. "But it was stillborn."

And that was it. Alex sat up, stunned. He watched her for a moment before wrapping his arms around her. Nobody ever knew what to say about her loss.

"I loved James," she admitted, her voice quiet, and this time Alex didn't correct her when she called James by his real name. "He was my first everything. And then one day, he was gone. All I wanted was our child, some kind of reminder of what that was like, what James was like, and to know that if I found love once, I could find it again."

Still nothing from Alex. So she kept talking, because doing so would soften the edges of that lump in her throat.

"Allana…" Alex started, brushing the hair out of her face.

"He'd convinced me that our love was strong, unique, nothing else like it. He'd convinced me that nobody could ever stand between us. So of course I thought he'd love me again."

She felt Alex breathing against her shoulder.

"It wasn't that he'd convinced me that he loved me, but that love like that ever existed at all," she went on, surprised by her own willingness to open up. She refused to admit it, but she trusted Alex. A lot. He meant more to her than she wanted to acknowledge. "I believed him. I believed all of it. Until I gave birth to our stillborn baby. And that was when everything I had in me, it all died." And it had; she'd been a lost teenager, agonizing over every fine little detail.

"He should have come for you," Alex said with conviction.

She shook her head. "I was the girl that put out, the one that slept with him whenever he wanted it. Some of the guys at my school found out about the pregnancy and they took advantage of that vulnerability. They made promises, each of them. Big cars, big houses, big money. And after a couple of weeks, they all disappeared." At first, that reality hurt.

Alex shifted, a little uncomfortable with her admission. "What does Vasy think about all of this?"

Allana sighed. Vasy had been the first man to see her, to appreciate her and ignore those scars. "Vasy was the only one that ever delivered on his promises. He brought me away from the past. He saw me for who I was, and allowed me to heal without breaking me even more."

Alex allowed a half smile. "And the baby?"

"A girl," she admitted, feeling her nostrils flare as she inhaled a deep, soothing breath. She'd even named her daughter, but didn't want to talk about it.

Alex frowned, shaking his head. "I meant, does Vasy know you had a baby? And what does he think about that?"

"He knows," Allana admitted, allowing a smile to surface. The only secrets she kept from Vasy involved... well, they involved Alex. "Vasy wants a baby. Someday. Obviously not with me," she pointed out with a bite to her words, "but he likes the idea of a baby, a big family like the one his parents have." The truth was, Allana didn't think she could conceive. Since arriving last summer, she'd started flushing her birth control pills each morning. At first, she and Vasy had made love frequently. But as conception evaded them, she'd lost interest. And then Vasy started working more hours and he'd lost interest as well. Before long, they were doing it less than three times per week, then once a week, then once every other week. Almost like Vasy had known she'd become infertile…until recently when he started taking a little more interest, at least on Sundays, but by then she'd begun faking headaches and her own disinterest…

At last, Alex's hand returned to her back. He was quiet for a moment, probably mulling everything over. Then he said, "I think you're an amazing woman, Allana."

That's original.

"And," he continued, taking a deep breath, "I think I'm falling in love with you."

Allana laughed. Loud. But when she saw that maybe Alex hadn't been joking around, she stopped abruptly and frowned, trying to find her way back to the tender moment they'd just shared. "Um, well, that's just my shitty past."

"It's unique," he said.

She sighed. "I broke apart and Vasy helped to rebuild me."

"And now here you are," he went on.

She nodded and smiled. "And now here I am with you. But what we've done, Alex? It's bad. It's the type of thing I thought belonged in my past. It's not me, Alex. Not anymore." She meant it, too. She'd left those mistakes, that behavior back in the States. For saving her and giving her this second chance in this new part of the world, she should not have given herself to Alex. She knew that. Yet… for some reason, she didn't feel as guilty as she should…

"But this *is* you, and you're perfect," he insisted, taking her face with his hands and kissing her on the lips. When he pulled back, his green eyes looked glassy like they often did when they were together. Like that day in the hallway outside her apartment, or that night at the poker party. "You feel it too, Allana. I know you do. I can see it in your smile—" and she realized she was smiling, nobody had ever called her perfect before "—and your eyes. This wasn't revenge sex. It's more than that. It's a connection that cannot be described."

Swallowing, she shook her head before standing up and grabbing her clothes off the sofa. "I have to get home. I have to confront Vasy." She didn't have time for this, not after he'd convinced her to talk about her past. She disappeared down the short hall to the large, luxurious bathroom, denying everything he'd just suggested. Once inside, she locked the door and pressed her back against it, clamping her eyes shut and grabbing at her hair before shaking her head.

She needed to get dressed; she needed to get home and forget about this.

After regaining her bearings, she started pulling her clothes on.

When she opened the bathroom door, Alex was standing in the hallway, waiting for her. He smiled and waved her into his arms. She didn't move toward him, though. So he came to her and wrapped his arms around her.

"Alex, I don't think this is a good idea," she told him, wincing.

"Probably isn't," he admitted. "But like I said earlier, you're not a choice. This isn't a choice. It just happened. It just *is*. So let's go with that, okay? Let's see where it leads."

As she considered his words, Allana realized he was right. And even if he wasn't, what option did she have? Where could she run off to in this Godforsaken armpit of isolation if she didn't have Alex in her life?

She took a deep, emotional breath then asked him, "Can you take me home?"

# # #

Chapter 16

Allana opened the apartment door with hesitation, holding her breath. She figured Vasy would jump out at her, demand to know where she'd been and then, at the height of his rage, he would catch a whiff of Alex on her and know. He would just know, she assumed, believing that some part of our human intuition always did know. As if by some unspoken and unidentified intuition, we could detect the adulterous behavior of a spouse or loved one.

Except nobody welcomed her home. Nobody except the darkness and the echoes of her own disloyal secrets.

"Vasy?" she called out, flicking the light switch and then locking the door behind her. "Vasy, are you here?"

Allana walked through each room—the kitchen, the eating area, the living room, the hallway, the secondary bedroom, the master bedroom, and finally, the bathroom. She turned on the lights in each.

Empty.

She walked through each room one more time, just to be sure.

Still empty.

Slightly deflated, she decided on a shower and saved her clandestine confession for another day.

# # #

Around midnight, Allana settled into bed and Vasy still hadn't returned home. By now, she was starting to worry, just enough to wonder whether she should call Alex and ask him to bring her to Gregor's building. Because where else would Vasy be but that apartment two doors down from Gregor's?

Allana rolled over, clenching her eyes shut and bringing an image of Alex into her mind, his smile, the way his eyes were so obsessed with her. Perhaps it was the guilt from sleeping with him, or something else entirely, but thinking about him left Allana feeling paralyzed. She didn't call anyone. She remained in bed, her knees pulled up under the heavy sheets so she could stay warm, and somehow she drifted into sleep.

But without Vasy at home in bed with her, Allana's sleep always had a delicate shell and the slightest noises would crack it open and awaken her. Tonight was no different, even though she'd fallen asleep thinking of another man. Sometime after 3am, she awoke to a noise. She didn't recognize it at first, but as the sleep-fog dissipated, she identified it as the telephone's intrusive ring.

The mistress.

Except Vasy wasn't home to answer it.

Snapping the blankets away, she hurried out of bed, the cold hitting her feet like needles as she hurried to the living room and grabbed the phone.

What will I say?

"Sluchaju," she mumbled, keeping her voice quiet as if that might get the woman on the other end to start talking. But when there was no answer, she reverted to the only language she knew: "Who the hell is calling my husband at three in the morning!"

"Allana?" Surprised, maybe even a little scared of the aggression in her tone.

"Vasy?" she asked, fully awake now. She heard people talking in the background, heard the adrenaline on the other end, their wide-awake conversation out of place at this time day. "What's going on?"

Vasy hesitated, and she didn't know why.

"Vasy?" Now it was her turn to sound surprised and maybe even a little scared.

"It's the cold weather," he answered at last.

"Vasy?" she asked again, the third time by her count and each time she'd asked with a different tone. She expected the worst now. "What's going on over there?"

He sighed. "I'm sorry. I'm not making sense."

She swallowed the lump in her throat. "When are you coming home?"

Another sigh. "Not tonight, I'm afraid." At this point, she could tell from the sound that he had cupped his hands around the telephone's mouthpiece. His volume dropped, too, and he seemed worried. Why else would he cup his hands around the phone? "We're running some tests. Routine tests. This new reactor, sometimes… sometimes, it acts up."

Allana's heart lurched. *Could Alex have been telling the truth?* She wiped her palms along the thighs of her pajama pants. Alex had asked her to pay attention to things like this. And no matter how "normal" and "routine" Vasy made it sound, she couldn't help but wonder if Alex's paranoid warning or request or whatever it had been had some kind of sane legitimacy to it. He'd told her about these things, and now they were happening… was tonight going to mark the end of the power station?

"Allana?" Silence. "Are you still there?"

"Tests?" she asked, noticing how her voice had taken on a higher pitch. "What kind of tests, Vasy?"

"Routine capacity tests," he said, and now she could sense his curiosity in why she asked the question.

"I see." Another lump. Another swallow. Despite everything, Vasy would always be the man who had saved her. She felt loyal to him for that, but she couldn't help but entertain a few questions about Alex. Especially the questions about his conspiracy theories. "Vasy, please be careful."

"I will," he promised, and the caring tone of his words made her uncomfortable. Like she'd just revealed all of her secrets to him when she'd asked those questions, and now he knew just how close she and Alex had become.

"When will you be home?"

"I'm working an all-nighter," he confessed. "I'm sorry, but they need someone with seniority here."

"Okay." She felt her throat constricting. Where was Nikolai? Why wasn't Vasy sitting safely at home?

More silence and it felt like their conversation was coming to an end. But then Vasy added: "One last thing, Allana."

"Of course," she gulped, second-guessing what she'd seen earlier. *Maybe it wasn't a mistress's apartment, maybe I thought I saw that?*

"Where were you today?" he asked.

Instantly, Allana's ears rang and her legs gave out, but she reached back and gracefully eased herself onto the sofa. She remembered what it had felt like when Vasy hesitated after she'd asked what was going on. Was her husband *paying attention* to her, the same way Alex had asked her to pay attention to him?

Before she could reply, he said, "I need to get going," as if giving up.

"Wait." Deep breath. "I was with Alex. We got to... talking," she said, pressing her eyes shut. A hot tear dripped down her cheek, and she shook her head. *Not now*, she told herself. *For now, this is my weight to bear. Mine alone.* "He drove me home."

Without missing a beat, Vasy said casually, "So you were in good hands."

His hands were all over me.

She squeezed her eyes harder and now her nose started to drip.

"I need to get back to the panel," Vasy told her. "Make sure the door's locked."

"I will," she whispered, wiping her face and holding back her sobs. "I will."

"Love you."

"I love you…" she said as Vasy hung up the phone the on the other end. She took a deep breath and clenched her eyes shut before adding, "more."

# # #

Chapter 17

By Wednesday, the temperature showed promise of breaking away from its incredible freezing spell. Having spent so much time alone while Vasy worked and worked, Allana began questioning her sanity. She'd wished for Alex to swing by, but it had been silent… crazy silent.

The cold and isolation had that effect on a lot of people. But she was used loneliness. Her parents had raised her in one of the most prosperous and industrious cities in the United States, and she'd often felt all alone there too, especially after James disappeared forever and she'd leaped from the arms of one douchebag into the arms of another.

Alone. Isolated. Unloved.

Alone, isolated and unloved is what I deserve after what I've done to Vasy.

Slipping out to the snow-covered balcony—now that the door was no longer frozen shut—Allana lit up her Sobranie, closed her eyes, and remembered the view from Alex's apartment. Next weekend, she could indulge in her nicotine habit and see Vasy's office during her cigarette breaks and could imagine him staring her down with hatred and an accusatory disappointment. Her stomach rumbled at the prospect—*I might have to quit smoking altogether*—and she reveled in the fact that today, all she stared across was the vast countryside, the frozen treetops, and the sun over the horizon. No guilt or damnation in that.

But the relief didn't last long, because her mind returned to what

Vasy had said earlier about the tests.

Tests. Routine capacity tests.

She'd struggled with Vasy's admission of the tests. Not his admission of infidelity, but tests.

Capacity tests, he'd said. As much as she'd wanted to reach out to Alex and tell him all about these tests, she'd exercised some good restraint. She didn't know what would happen once she saw her American friend. The way she'd ended up crying herself to sleep after her early morning conversation with Vasy, she knew that this relationship with Alex would not end happily.

Never wanted anyone to get hurt, she thought, but even in her head the statement felt empty. Her entire soul felt empty.

Down in the parking lot, the Soviet version of a mail delivery van roared toward the building's front entrance. Its blue paint and red and white lines with the ever-foreign Soviet lettering offered Allana a breath of hope. She hadn't heard from her friends and family since Christmas, and while part of her wondered if the Soviet authorities held back some of her mail, another part wondered if maybe something might slip through this time. She needed something from her parents because as poor at parenting as they'd been, they were also simple. They rarely tried to manipulate her; they couldn't be bothered with the complexity of it. She needed to read their words, to hear their voices in their handwriting, to feel less insane and isolated.

Allana took her time with the Sobranie, not wanting to make the trip downstairs to the mail slot while the mailman was still sorting. Conversations with the locals never went well, especially without Vasy around to bail her out with his translation skills.

But after fifteen quick minutes, she heard an engine start up below and leaned over the railing to watch the blue van drive off. Finishing off the last bit of the cigarette, she hurried into the house, found her boots and mail key, and then took the stairs to the lobby.

The place was empty. She slipped the key into the lock and opened the box. Indeed, there was mail from home (she smiled), but she could tell from the envelope that someone had read the contents (her heart sank).

There was also a magazine, the latest *Soviet Life*, which Vasy received because, thanks to his family and their connections, he knew many of the powerful people featured within its pages. When it fell open on the wet lobby floor, she bent forward to pick it up when she recognized the face of the Minister of Energy on the cover. The picture was of him standing outside the power station, his arms crossed over his chest with his pose set in the traditional, Soviet, non-smiling firmness. The grey, overcast sky and big, yellow letters in the title added to the seriousness of the piece, but she couldn't understand the words.

All she knew was that last weekend there had been a test at one of the reactors that had called Vasy away on his day off. And now Vitali Sklyarov's picture occupied a full page of *Soviet Life*'s February issue, a serious-as-a-tumor glean to his eyes and equally frightening printing on the next page. What convenient timing for this article, she thought, almost as if the entire Soviet Union had expected problems at the station this past weekend.

Pay attention, Alex had asked her. And now she wondered if there *had been* problems. If she could read Ukrainian, she'd surely know.

"Hey, beautiful," someone said behind her with a fake accent.

Snapping upright, Allana bit back a scream and she spun around and was suddenly staring into Alex's mocking eyes. A smile spread across his lips.

"Did I scare you?" he asked, taking her wrist and unapologetically pulling her against him.

She gasped, yanking away from him. "Alex, not here."

"Then kiss me." He closed his eyes and leaned toward her.

Although she could no longer deny that *something* existed between them, Allana didn't feel like kissing Alex in public. She raised her hand, as if ready to slap him, but she couldn't swing. She blamed it on the fact that his eyes were closed—it would have been a cheap shot. It had nothing to do with the fact that maybe she was growing fond of the man. *No, nothing like that at all.* Sighing, she nudged him aside and headed to the elevator.

"Where's Vasy?" Alex asked, opening his eyes and following her. He didn't sound disappointed that she hadn't kissed him like he wanted.

"Where else would he be but at work," she snapped. She handed Alex the *Soviet Life* magazine. "What is this?"

"*Soviet Life?*" He shrugged, hitting the call button. "It's our national magazine. Like *USA Today*, except a magazine instead of a newspaper."

"The Minister of Energy?" Allana asked. She felt her chest pounding at the coincidence of the article appearing so soon after the past weekend's tests. Of course the publication had been scheduled long ago, but Alex had mentioned that she should pay attention long ago as well. Something didn't feel right. "There's an article about him inside. And pictures of the power station."

Once the doors opened and they were on board, Allana hit the number three and Alex flipped to the article. She glanced over at him while he read during the slow rise to the third floor. Whatever the words said, they captured Alex's attention.

"What does it say?" she asked as the elevator stopped and the doors opened.

Alex kept reading while he followed her to the apartment, but she didn't unlock the door and let him in.

"Alex, you can't come inside."

He looked up from reading, a little confused. Allana couldn't tell if that was because of her refusal to let him in, or what he'd read in the *Soviet Life* article.

"Why not?" he asked "You already told me Vasy's at work. What's changed between us since last weekend?"

She raised her eyebrows. "What if Vasy comes home?" Seemed like a reasonable worry to Allana. Did Alex really want to get in the middle of her failing relationship with Vasy?

He shrugged. "Then I'll jump out the window and slide down the wall like I did last week."

Allana chuckled before realizing that he wasn't joking. Shaking her head because she couldn't quite understand what he was saying—*did he really jump out the third-floor window without getting hurt?*—she let it slide. "I'm sorry, but even if you're Batman, you're not coming in."

"I think that's a bad decision on your part," he told her, his face unflinching as he raised his eyebrows. "After all, I know that you love my company and how I make you feel."

Crossing her arms, Allana leaned back against the apartment door. "How so?" No, she refused to admit that he could be right.

Alex waved the *Soviet Life* magazine at her. "Besides, you'll want to know what this says about Vitali Sklyarov and the nuclear power station where your husband and I work. It's under his supervision after all, and he's being asked about the safety of the facility." He wiggled his eyebrows at her.

Pretending like she didn't care, she suggested, "I'll be fine waiting for Vasy to get home. I'll ask him to translate it for me then."

"Home from work?"

"Of course from work!" she snapped back, but it spooked her that he'd semi-read her mind. It was why she'd said *I'll be fine waiting for Vasy to get home*, without qualifying where he would be coming *from*. "Where else?" Despite the guilt from her own affair, it still hurt to think that Vasy might be seeing another woman, might be sharing an apartment and a life with her.

Frowning like he could read the disappointment in her heart, Alex nodded past her, at the door. "And… that's the second reason why you might want me to come inside."

"I hate you," she whispered, but it was a complete lie. As much as she tried to act like his suggestion had no impact on her, Allana knew that Alex spotted it, the same way he'd known to go all-in that night in January, during their poker game. He'd seen it then and she knew he saw it now, and maybe her transparency wasn't such a bad thing.

"Just let me in, Allana," he begged. "I won't try anything this time. I'll behave."

She considered him for a moment before finally nodding and opening the door to let him in. As much as she refused to admit it, she realized that she could trust Alex. He was not only harmless, but he seemed to care for her.

Famous last thoughts.

# # #

Chapter 18

With the balcony door open an inch behind her, Allana felt the occasional breath of freezing air on the back of her neck. Seated across from Alex, she felt her leg bouncing underneath the kitchen table. It all kept her grounded—the cold air, the bouncing leg, the table separating them—and she realized that if they were to leave this table, the same one where Alex had taken her rubles over a game of poker, things would get out of hand.

They already have. He shouldn't be here.

Swallowing the anxiety, she nodded at him. "So? Tell me." If they started talking, she would stop staring into those eyes, would stop feeling lonely, would stop feeling drawn to him in ways she refused to acknowledge. And that meant no more guilt.

Alex brought his hands together, as if in prayer. "They're being told about safety concerns. People have raised issues about the design of our RBMK reactors."

She frowned, not quite following.

"It's the type of reactor core we have here," he explained, sensing her confusion. She hated that he was so good at reading her. "It's Soviet-designed and developed, but apparently some so-called experts think there isn't enough of a safety buffer in the system. So in the article, the Minister says the odds of a meltdown are one in ten thousand."

Allana swallowed, a little relieved to hear that. "Those are good odds."

"Yeah, they're excellent," he agreed with a dismissive shrug. "Unless they're bullshit and someone's working hard at sabotaging our nuclear program."

The cold air flicked across her neck again, and she had to wrestle the urge to shudder against it. "What was the second thing?" she asked, trying to keep their conversation on point.

Alex reached across the table for her hand, but Allana withdrew from his reach and placed both hands in her lap. She shook her head at him.

"Vasy likes to come home for lunch," she said, which was only a partial lie and her leg started bouncing faster. "You'll have to leave before he gets here."

Rolling his hands down his face, he stared at her with the same eyes that had stared into her soul while he'd made love to her. Each time. Whether she happened to be on top, or he happened to be, those eyes had a way of squeezing in and latching onto her. Or maybe she'd imagined that; either way, she knew her track record with men and continued to deny that she and Alex had more than a physical attraction uniting them.

"Alex," she begged, hoping for another burst of ice-cold air from the door. "Don't look at me like that. Please, just tell me the second reason you're here." She felt the breeze at last, but it didn't stop her leg from bouncing or her hands from shaking.

Without shifting his attention, he told her, "I've done some digging, Allana. Like Vasy, I know people. I have connections. I can access certain things that a lot of other people can't."

She narrowed her gaze. "What kind of things?"

He angled his chin downward so that, if he wore glasses, he would have been staring across the upper rim at her. Like a condescending teacher.

"There's no record of your marriage to Vasy. Which means what we've done—"

"We were married in the States," Allana blurted, possibly too quickly but she hadn't expected him to creep on her like that. She pointed toward the living room, to the photo on the television. "I have a photo…"

Smirking, Alex shifted his weight in his chair. "Yes, I remember the photo. But remember what you told me that night at the poker party? About how I'm an awful bluffer?"

Allana pushed her chair out, defensively. "If you're here to argue with me about whether or not I'm married, I think you should just leave. This is crazy. Disputing my marriage like that. And ridiculous. After the sin I've committed with you, I *wish*, for my soul's sake, that I weren't married." She allowed her chin to tremble before biting down on her lower lip to stop it.

Alex kept watching her, studying her like they were seated at a poker table again. She hated this. To Allana's eyes, he didn't appear all that convinced with her message.

"Alex," she added as if her entire life might be unraveling right here in her kitchen, "I can assure you that regardless of what you think Vasy will react like any husband would if he finds you here alone with me." She gave an exaggerated nod that didn't fool her, let alone Alex. "You need to leave."

At last, Alex sighed and stood. "Then I should get out of here."

"Yes." She nodded some more, knowing how foolish she appeared to him. "Yes, yes, you do."

He started toward the door, but stopped and turned around with a thoughtful frown on his face. "They terminated Gregor's employment at the power station," he explained to her. "Did Vasy mention that to you?"

Allana shook her head, holding her trembling hands behind her back so he couldn't see them. "No. When?" *Why hadn't Vasy said anything?*

"Three weeks ago, it turns out," he said, watching her for a reaction.

"It's interesting that Vasy didn't mention anything, especially since he like to spend so much time at Gregor's building on Sundays after swimming his lengths."

Yes, that's what I was thinking, except maybe he wasn't spending as much with Gregor as he wants me to believe....

Alex's frown deepened. "There was talk at the power station about corporate espionage. Like Gregor might've been copying sensitive documents and bringing them home."

"Wow." Allana couldn't believe it, but her mind was elsewhere, back to the part where Vasy snuck into his lover's apartment. Something wasn't adding up.

"Do you think Gregor is a spy?" Alex asked, still watching for her reaction.

Finally, Allana caught up to the conversation. Vasy routinely brought binders and manuals home. "Gregor, a spy? Are you serious?"

"Very." At last, Alex shrugged and continued toward the door. Before he turned the doorknob, he reached for Allana's hand.

She didn't pull away this time, mostly because his touch calmed her. And also because with everything she'd heard today she knew she wouldn't give herself to him. *I need to put an end to this.* "Alex, no matter what your Soviet search revealed, we can't keep doing this. I'm married." She closed her eyes as his hand crept up her arm, along the side of her neck, and settled in a cupped formation at the side of her face. She remembered Vasy entering that apartment in Gregor's building and wondered if his hands had crept over his lover like this. "Alex, no."

"Let me in," he whispered, bringing his lips to hers. "Let me love you."

Still with her eyes closed, she allowed her mouth to open to his tongue. She didn't fight the passion—*how could she?*—but she made sure to keep a couple of inches' distance between them, to keep her walls erect.

"Listen," Alex whispered, pulling away. "I'm worried about you, Allana. I can't help it. And... I..." he shook his head, but she wanted to hear the rest. "I love you," he admitted. Again.

And I care for you, too, but no matter how much Vasy might be in love with a woman that lives in Gregor's building, he will kill you, and this will destroy him, and as his wife, I've made a promise to him, a promise I've broken but now I have to try my hardest to make things right, no matter what feelings I have or refuse to admit that I have. "This," she choked out, pulling her hand out of his, "has to stop before someone gets hurt."

Taking a step back, Alex turned the doorknob with the same hand that had held hers. He didn't appear to like her response to his confession. She ignored it—*I love you*—twice.

"I'm glad you mentioned that," Alex said, his voice firm. "The part about people getting hurt. Because—and this is important, Allana—I really need you to pay attention."

Those words—*pay attention*—echoed in her ears. "To what?" she asked, a little dizzy from how he'd just spun a 180-degree turn from *I love you, I love you* to *pay attention to my conspiracy theories.*

"Papers. Conversations. Late hours. Anything about reactor tests. Or problems. Or employment terminations." He sighed, but the weight and severity of his words were unmistakable—Alex was back to business. "It's extremely important, or people will get hurt."

There was something in what he said, or maybe it was *how* he said it, but it clicked for Allana. For the first time in, well, *forever*, she grabbed Alex's shoulders. She shook him, harder than she thought she could. "You're still an awful bluffer, Alex! Goddammit, what aren't you telling me?"

After considering her request, he simply shook his head and looked down. "I can't."

"You can!" she argued, shoving him back.

Alex's eyes widened at her strength, but he kept his balance and shook his head. She knew from the softness in his eyes that he had been telling the truth earlier; he truly was worried about her. "No. I'm sorry, but I can't."

Allana deflated; she felt her shoulders sag. "Why, Alex? I've given myself to you. I trusted you with… with everything, my past secrets and my present secrets, and you can't tell me?"

His eyes latched onto hers again, but she could tell he wasn't reaching into her soul like he previously had. The look she found in him was tortured. Frightened. Disturbed. The face of a man who had witnessed real-life horror.

He knows something. "Alex…"

"I can't. If I told you, you wouldn't be able to sleep, Allana. And I need you to be well rested. I need *you* to pay attention. Please. So nobody gets hurt and we all get out of this alive."

#

Chapter 19

Sunday, February 23, 1986. Although the freezing spell had ended, Vasy promised over breakfast that the coldest days of the year were behind them. Allana half-listened, too worried about *paying attention so nobody would get hurt* and trying to pick up on some key detail. Maybe it was nothing. Maybe it was everything. Who knew? She was so confused these days, caught up in the chaos of her life—the cold weather, the isolation, the move next weekend, the boxes, the disorganization... And forget about her affair with Alex or Vasy's affair with some unknown woman, probably someone who was not only willing to have his babies, but someone who could conceive in the first place.

She felt her impatience come to a boil.

Still in his pajamas (translation: his see-through t-shirt and plaid cotton pants) Vasy sat across from her at the kitchen table, in the same seat that Alex had occupied just a few days earlier. And when Vasy reached across the table to take her free hand, she snapped it back, nearly knocking her plate into her lap.

"What's wrong?" Vasy asked, tilting his head and studying her with a tone of worry.

"Your t-shirt's wrong," she blurted back. *Oh boy, here it comes.* But she couldn't swallow the words back into her mouth, they just dropped out like angry little bombs. "Your eighty hours of work every week is wrong. Your one day off every week is wrong. Your thoughts are wrong. Your…" *Stop now before you say too much.* "Your… keeping secrets from me is wrong. It's *all* wrong." She took a deep breath and tried again to regain control of her mouth.

Vasy's jaw muscles flexed as he studied her, but then he softened. He didn't reach for her hand again; that was something Alex would've tried, and she'd have broken his nose for it, too. Instead, Vasy leaned back in his chair, probably trying to add a buffer of safety between them. And then he stared at her, still chewing the scrambled eggs and hash browns.

The silence felt like an eternity, but she stared back, feeling the quiver in her lips and the tears pooling in her eyes. At last, she'd had enough of the stupid silence.

"You didn't tell me about Gregor," she hissed. "And if he's not working with you, then why are you still going to his apartment after your laps at the pool?" She barely gave him an opportunity to answer. "Because you're not, are you?"

Vasy frowned, still studying her, still chewing, still the most patient man in the world.

"Then it's true?" she demanded, fed up with the silence. *He has secrets.* She felt her chest bulging, because she knew she was right. "So is he also bringing things home that got him accused of stealing?"

By the time Vasy swallowed the well-chewed breakfast in his mouth, he seemed to have his answer. And he did, because his face had a dead serious numbness to it. "Alex."

Allana felt the color drain from her face, and she quickly regretted saying everything that she had. As much as she wanted to ask him about his 3am phone call—*if my wife finds out about this*—or his key to the mistress's apartment in Gregor's building and whatever it was that kept him "at work" until the craziest hours of the morning, she bit her tongue and played his game of silence. And when she couldn't take it any longer, she asked him, "Are you allowed to have work documents at home, Vasy?"

At last, he raised his attention and stared straight into her eyes. "How often does Alex visit you while I'm at work, Allana?" She wished she had his calmness.

Although she could barely breathe now, she didn't want him to see that. Something she both loved and hated about Vasy was his exceptional perception. So she lowered her utensils and stared straight back at him. "He's my only friend, Vasy."

He rolled his eyes at her. "Do you mean 'close friend'?'"

Glancing down at his plate, he took a bite of food. It almost seemed to Allana that Vasy wanted to avoid the truth as much as she did when it came to Alex. Because, yes. Yes, Alex was close. More than close.

But wait, this isn't about Alex. This is about Vasy and his secrets.

"About as close as yours from last Sunday at Gregor's building," she snapped back at him. "Except I'm not sneaking in and out of apartments."

Allana watched him while he chewed again, and she swore she noticed him flinch at her accusation. She expected something in return, a defense or possibly even another accusation about her and Alex. But Vasy didn't say a thing. The way his eyes shifted back to her, she knew what he was thinking.

"Is that what you're all worked up about?" he asked. "You think I'm sneaking around behind your back?"

She gave an aggressive and affirmative shrug, noticing how tightly she gripped the bread knife in her hand. Placing it down on the table, she asked, "You spent all day with someone who no longer works with you? I don't know, Vasy…" She wanted to mention how she'd seen him—*with her own damn eyes!*—sneak into the other apartment on Gregor's floor, so she knew—she *knew!*—that he hadn't spent all of that time with a former colleague. But she kept her mouth shut and tucked that knowledge away. Not only to see if he would volunteer a confession, but because if he kept that secret to himself, she might feel less guilty about her own.

"Gregor's a friend and a professional ally who knows a lot about the power station," Vasy explained, locking his emotionless eyes onto hers so that she could see he allegedly had nothing to hide. She matched his stare and searched for signs of a lie, a crack in his story. "He's a genius, just like all of the engineers, and I need to know what he knows. After I left his apartment, I stopped by the power station and they kept me there, gave me a lot of work to do until I was able to call you."

And there it was, that crack in his story. She heard it in his words. It was a lie because after he'd left Gregor's, he'd gone straight to his mistress's apartment!

She felt her chin quiver and noticed how her hand had returned to the bread knife. "You're lying," she whispered, wanting to stab him in the neck for that lie. Not just for the lie, but because his own infidelity meant he wouldn't even care about what she'd been doing with Alex. She was angry and sad at the same time.

"And you're holding back," he accused, still calm but with a newly formed creepy glare. "I see it in your face. I notice it in how you behave around me. It's been over a week since we made love, and you think I don't notice that?" His voice started to get louder, but Vasy was a master at reigning himself in.

Shaking her head, Allana admitted, "I'm afraid of what you're doing, Vasy. All of this secrecy. The time at Gregor's...*building*." She bit down on her lip, took a sip of juice to swallow down her emotion threatening to erupt from her. "And all those hours you spend 'working'. Something doesn't add up, and I swear—"

Vasy laughed, a crazy sound that lacked any sincerity at all, but it sure silenced her quickly. "What else has Alex been telling you?"

At last, Allana stood and brought her plate with the half-eaten meal to the kitchen sink. She needed to calm down or she really would stab him in the neck. Besides, they were coming at this conversation from two different angles—hers involved cheating and Vasy's, she was starting to believe, involved something graver. Something along the lines of domestic terrorism. What they were both doing could get them in trouble. Except in Vasy's case, it meant more serious trouble.

In her husband's case, it meant death.

"Jesus, Vasy. I don't think the Soviets look at treason very lightly."

"What else has Alex been telling you?" he repeated from the table, more sternly this time as his eyes narrowed and his forehead tightened. He hadn't asked *what has Alex been* doing *to you*, which made Vasy sound like he was as much of a conspiracy theorist as her lover.

"Does it matter?" she asked, her tone as defiant as the look he shot her. "If they did this to Gregor, what's to stop them from going after you? And…" she paused before adding, "And me?"

Vasy stayed quiet and continued to eat his breakfast. "You realize that I'm a native in the Soviet Ukraine." There was a hint of insolence in his voice. "The Chief Engineer, Nikolai Fomin, personally arranged for the Minister of Energy to cover my tuition at MIT, Allana. So what happened to Gregor will *not* happen to me. Or you." He shook his head like she was an idiot, like she didn't know the first thing about how things worked here, but Allana knew too much. She wished she didn't, but she did. "I've got some powerful and politically connected friends on my side that will make sure that we're both safe."

She studied him a little closer, her attention jumping all over his face for signs of another crack in his story. At last, she shook her head at him because he was so very mistaken, and it was sad to see in a man of Vasy's intelligence. "You're wrong."

Another insincere, wild laugh from Vasy. "Tell me how it works, then, Allana? What kind of stories has Alex dropped into your impressionable head?"

She ignored that. "What if Nikolai finds out about you bringing documents home? You just finished telling me how powerful and politically connected he is. So do you think he'll be as forgiving with us—I mean with *you* as his minions were with *Gregor*?" she asked, her voice shaky. She knew that whatever they would do to Vasy, they would do ten times worse to his pretty, American wife who couldn't even speak their language.

"I probably don't need to point this out," Vasy went on with an undertone of disgust in his voice, "but Alex is an *American*. As much as he's one of us, he's also one of *them*. He's an outsider whose looks alone will get him shot in the wrong city, wrong neighborhood, and at the wrong hour. What do you think his behavior will earn him?"

Allana crept up behind Vasy. When she placed her hands on his shoulders, he flinched at her touch—*a guilty flinch*. Allana started to wonder whether his conversation truly concerned espionage, or whether it reached deeper. *What is Vasy really involved in?*

"What I'm doing is acceptable work," he told her, but it sounded like he was trying to convince himself more than her. "They would convict Alex of being an American spy before they ever think to ask me about why I study my technical specs at home."

Why do you study at home, Vasy? Is something else cutting into your study time at work? Or, rather than something, is it someone? She couldn't help but remember him standing at the apartment door in Gregor's building before knocking—*tap, tap* pause *tap*—and then pulling out his own keys and letting himself in.

"And Gregor?" he asked, turning his head and looking upward at her.

"He's my friend. My close friend. So before you start wondering why I continue to spend time with him, consider the friendship I share with him and the professional necessity of my spending time with him. He's a good man, just like Yuri and the others."

She pulled her hands away from his shoulders, a little exasperated. It wasn't his matter-of-fact explanation of his friendship with Gregor but more that he'd mentioned Yuri and the others, almost as if he wanted to distract her from her true issues. "What's really going on, Vasy? Because these good people are being accused of crimes that can cost their lives. And if it can happen to them, it can happen to you. And if it happens to you, I don't know what would happen to me…"

At last, Vasy abandoned his breakfast and wrapped his big, solid arms around her. "I won't let anything happen to you," he promised, but it didn't feel genuine to Allana.

She let it go, though, and held him close. "I love you," she whispered, just like she knew he expected.

And, as if on cue, he replied with: "I love you more."

So it was settled.

# # #

Chapter 20

With Vasy at the Energetik for his weekly workout, Allana spent a small amount of time on the sofa, staring at the blank television screen across the room, flanked by moving boxes and secrets and all kinds of potentially horrible things. She chewed at the corners of her nails—the nails had taken too long to grow out, so she gnawed at the edges instead—and couldn't help but feel nervous about everything that was going on. Most of all, she worried about what would happen if he ever found out…

She considered going outside and lighting another cigarette to take the edge off, as if a puff of Sobranie could make the silence go away or make Vasy's post-workout affair not happen.

Maybe I should have said something. Maybe I should surprise him at Gregor's building. Maybe I should…

It didn't pass beyond her, this apparent double standard of hers. She was a hypocrite. But at the same time, she knew that Alex meant more to her than she wanted to admit. And she figured Vasy's lover meant a lot more to him, too. In Allana's defense, she could argue that Vasy had a busy career, activities at the Energetik, a lot of friends. And, in this isolated armpit of the world, he was at home, entirely in *his* element; but for Allana, she had *nothing*, just a blank television screen and hours and hours to fill while her husband did whatever it was that required all of his time.

And now, knowing what Alex had told her earlier in the week about

Gregor, she wondered how dangerous the threat of her husband's activities truly were. If Gregor could get dismissed, what would happen to Vasy?

Snapping out of the sofa, she retreated to the secondary bedroom where she'd first made love to Alex. Making sure that her glance avoided the bed, she began searching through the moving boxes. The first two boxes offered clothes, immigration documents from when Vasy entered the States and when they both left together, academic transcripts, bills, and receipts.

But the third one, buried roughly midway through that first tower next to the bed where she'd committed her sin, was the winner. She bent open the top flap and found exactly what she wanted—the documents, manuals and binders that Vasy had brought home from the power station. Without thinking about it, she sat on the edge of the bed and pulled the treasure out of the box.

The first batch of papers was a dot-matrix printout of readings. It looked like time and date, followed by readings. Not a lot of value unless you understood their relevance. Or the language of spreadsheets.

She opened the manual next and noticed some computer drawings. It looked like plumbing—a *lot* of plumbing—with arrows and Ukrainian descriptions and numbers for cross-referencing next to them. In the pages that followed, she found a lot of those descriptions and numbers, followed by paragraphs of more descriptions. She wondered if they were technical in nature. On some pages, she discovered handwritten notes in pencil. Some were in English, always on the dog-eared pages. And based on the size and condensed loops of the L's and G's, she believed that the notes had been written by her husband.

"What are you involved with, Vasy?" she whispered as she read the first note: *moderation material—graphite enhanced by release of helium and nitrogen, enabling fission chain to continue in a safe environment.* It meant nothing to her. Many of the other notes, like *fuel rod replenishment possible at safe levels during reactor operation*, were just as foreign and would require a translator to make any kind of sense to her untrained eye.

But then she reached something that finally seemed to stand out. Maybe it was the hand-drawn asterisk next to the personal note. *Reinforced concrete required = 45.5K m2... received = 42.3K m2... shortfall = 3.2K m2... structural integrity questionable with 6k m2 reported as defective, or approx. 20% of structure.*

The following comment was underlined twice: *reactor 4.* The hair on the back of her neck stood up and she couldn't help but shudder.

This is where Vasy works...

Closing the manual, she moved on to the big binder. Like everything else so far, she didn't understand any of the printed material, but there was another handful of notes that Vasy had seemingly written in English. Some of the notes had even been erased, impossible to make out now.

It all seemed extremely technical in nature, the comments and numerical references that her husband had made in the margins. But what confused Allana the most was why Vasy would have bothered with all of it in the first place? Vasy already had his position at the power station. He had the chief engineer as his mentor, not to mention a vast, talented team of experts surrounding him.

Who is really reading these notes?

When the telephone rang in the main living room, it startled her and the heavy binder slipped off her knees and fell onto her toe. It hurt but she rushed to answer the line.

"Hello?"

"Just me," Vasy said. "I'm finished here and Gregor has some other business to attend to. So I was going to surprise you with a treat."

She grinned in spite of the throbbing in her toe. "Not much of a surprise if you're telling me about it."

Vasy laughed. "No, that's not why I'm calling. Do we need anything from the supermarket before I drive back?"

"Eggs, flour and butter," she rhymed off, clamping her eyes shut because the pain flared up. "See you soon?"

"Not soon enough," he said before hanging up.

Before Vasy returned home, she hobbled back to the bedroom and packed the incriminating material back into the moving boxes, exactly as she'd found it.

No need to surprise him at Gregor's building after all…

# # #

Chapter 21

Vasy's surprise consisted of fresh flowers that he'd picked up at one of those friendly farms just outside of town, and super-rich fudge that he'd picked up at the same farm; the fudge probably cost more than the flowers. Both of those gifts turned her day around, though. And when Vasy scooped her up off her feet and carried her to the bedroom to make love to her, it took every ounce of willpower for Allana to bury her guilt and pretend like Alex hadn't happened.

It's in the past.

Lying in bed, Allana ran her fingers through Vasy's dark chest hair. She wanted to suggest he forego his t-shirts, but she knew better than to bring that up. The problem was that the only other thing on her mind was Alex…the way he made love differently, the way he grunted (Vasy's breathing accelerated to a climax, no grunts), the way he always liked to be close to her once they finished (Vasy preferred a bit of distance, but never pushed her away), the way Alex liked to make sure he made her come (Vasy just took what he wanted, like a freight train and if she wasn't on it, he would just keep going until the end of the line).

She swallowed her guilt.

"You're different," Vasy admitted like he could read her thoughts. He reached across his chest and slid his hand into hers. "I noticed it."

"Noticed what?" Could he seriously detect a difference in how she felt now that she'd decided to put an end to her affair with Alex? She withdrew her hand and faked an itch on her shoulder so he wouldn't notice her clammy palm and trembling fingers.

Vasy stayed quiet, his eyes locked on her while she tried to act calm, collected, cool.

"Will we ever make it back to the States?" she asked, changing the subject. "Because I don't know if I want to go back." And that was the truth. Before she'd met Vasy, she'd made a lot of bad choices. Starting with her teenaged pregnancy, of course. But the bulk of the damage had happened after all of that. After she'd delivered a stillborn child, after she'd returned to school, and even after she'd moved to Massachusetts on her scholarship to Wellesley. And then she met Vasy, and now she was safe. She felt safe in Pripyat, but then the greatest damage of all: Alex.

Her husband remained so quiet that she wondered if he'd fallen asleep. Glancing over, she saw that he was staring at the ceiling now, lost in his thoughts. She wondered if he was imagining his own lover, the one he still hadn't confessed to having, even after she'd seen him go into that apartment. Was he dreaming about the way she moved and comparing the way she felt, tasted, and sounded?

"I'm looking forward to moving to the new apartment next weekend," she said, hoping to banish the thoughts of infidelity once and for all.

Still nothing from Vasy, and by now his silence unsettled her. So she withdrew her hand and propped herself up on her elbow.

"There's an article in the *Soviet Life* magazine. The Minister of Energy was in it, and Alex told me that he said the power station is safe and that the odds of an accident are one in ten million or something."

That caught Vasy's attention—was it the mention of the Minister or Alex?

Vasy turned his eyes to her and swallowed. *Probably the mention of the Minister.*

She pasted a smile to her face, hoping to encourage him into having a conversation.

"I'll be able to see where you work from the new apartment's balcony," she explained.

"The Minister is a con, Allana," he admitted in a voice so quiet it sounded more like a half-mumbled curse. At least now she knew that her mentioning the Minister was what had caught his attention, rather than her mentioning Alex's name. "He's corrupt and self-serving. Like a lot of them."

Frowning, she edged a little closer to him. After a moment's hesitation, Vasy repositioned himself so he could wrap an arm around her shoulders and draw her even closer to him.

"And I don't think there's a long-term future for us here," he admitted out of nowhere. He sounded sad about it, too.

"Why not?" She asked, a little shocked. It didn't make sense, this was Vasy's homeland, why the sudden change in heart, why the lack of a long-term future here?

He shrugged and was quiet again. She felt like she'd lost him, but after a minute or so of silence, he continued. "They blamed Gregor for missing documents. And there's talk about more and more thefts happening at the power station. What you said at breakfast was true, these people are powerful. And I think they've got their own agendas, from things as simple as kickbacks on the construction contracts to the multi-dimensional cons of ensuring an ideal is presented to the public rather than a reality."

"What does that mean?" she asked.

"Nuclear is complicated," he explained like he spoke with a child. But then he frowned as if lost in a difficult question. "But something still doesn't feel right."

"Then you need to bring those documents back," she blurted, a little worried now that Vasy had just confirmed that Alex's paranoid conspiracy theories seemed to have merit. "You still have them, right?"

Vasy nodded, but he seemed to be half asleep now. "And you know what? There's been talk about Alex. I don't think it helps that he spent so much of his life in the States. With the politics and tensions…"

Allana gulped, her worry levels increasing a nudge higher. She needed a cigarette.

"What kind of talk?" she asked. Her mind turned to the first time she'd gone to his apartment and he showed her the fancy electronic equipment in his closet. She'd never seen electronics like that before, let alone the small audio reel that captured seemingly random conversations. And those voices he'd recorded, she knew they belonged to the kinds of powerful and connected people that could hurt them. All of them. "Are these people suggesting he's involved in espionage, like they did with Gregor?"

Silence.

She considered confessing what she'd seen that day, but she feared it would lead to assumptions about what she might have been doing in his bedroom in the first place. She wasn't ready for that conversation, not now.

"You asked me about the time I spend with Gregor," Vasy said, glancing over with an innocence in his expression as tiny wrinkles formed at the corners of his eyes.

"And you told me it was a mixture of friendship and professional necessity."

Vasy lapsed back into contemplative silence before continuing. "The accusations against him mean he'll be dead before the May Day celebrations," Vasy explained with a sad yet cold sigh.

Allana snapped into a sitting position, her back straight. "What?"

Frowning, Vasy put a finger to his mouth. "It's alright. We've been planning a way for him to escape before they link the reports to Gregor's role at the power station."

Link what reports? Escape to where?

"Allana," he said, a calming urgency to the way he raised his eyebrows, "there was a lot of material that should've been used in the construction of the newest reactor, but it was never received. And a lot of what *was* received turned out to be defective."

She remembered the binder and manual that she discovered in one of the moving boxes, along with Vasy's handwritten notes in the margins. She knew this already, she knew because *he* had written about it in the margins.

He went on. "Gregor knows a lot of people, and the company that built the concrete molds was instructed to produce less than the order forms showed. And what they did produce, they were ordered to keep it cheap. Really cheap," he added for emphasis.

Her nostrils flared at just how dangerous that seemed. "Why would anyone ask them to do that?"

"Let me finish," he said, closing his eyes as he explained the rest. "A payment was cut to the contractor. That payment was for the full amount, but only a portion of the goods was ever delivered. So the contractor redirected the excess payment to a Soviet-Ukrainian official. Not the government, but an individual."

"Like a kickback," she whispered, her arms crawling with goose bumps.

He nodded with confidence. "The reports that Gregor was accused of stealing were located in the apartment that belongs to a reporter in Kiev. That reporter's gone missing."

Allana couldn't believe what she was hearing and her nostrils flared once again while she tried to calm her breathing. But then Alex's words came back to her—*Pay attention before someone gets hurt*. Well, it seemed someone was missing, did that count?

"Gregor believes she's been executed," he explained without any emotion, any worry in his voice. "Which means they'll track the reports back to the power station, and eventually fingers will point to Gregor."

"Wait," she said, her stomach tight and her pulse racing. She felt ill. "The *Soviet Life* article... How truly safe is the power station if those reports are true?"

He sighed. "The reports are definitely true, but even with the deficient construction materials, the power station still seems relatively safe," he admitted, rubbing his hands down the length of his face. He looked tired. "I've researched it myself. The radiation levels are within range, there's no excessive exposure to the public. But with everything that's happened to Gregor and this reporter, there's something bigger at play, Allana. There's missing money, a defective nuclear power station, and a lot of opportunistic officials that need to cover their tracks. If anything goes wrong..."

If *what* went wrong?

"You need to be careful around Alex," Vasy warned, his eyes glued to hers in a way that underlined the seriousness of his message. "If he's an American spy, people will identify you as his 'close friend'," he said, using the international signal for air quotes. "And that's when things will get nasty if the authorities ever get interested in what's going on here."

She took a deep swallow before nodding her understanding.

Vasy maintained his stare, as if making sure she understood him completely.

"I can't trust him anymore," he went on. "So when you're with him—and I'm fine if you spend time with him, he's your friend and was very welcoming to us when we arrived—I just need you to pay attention."

There it was again: *Pay attention.*

"You understand what I mean by that, don't you?"

The way he stared at her with big, bulging eyes, she didn't really understand but she nodded anyway. "Yes. Of course. Pay attention. But... to what?"

"The questions he asks. About me, about us, about my work. Like if he starts asking about testing schedules, or output rates, or radiation levels. Anything that has to do with the power station, I need to know."

She nodded some more, and couldn't help but wonder whether Vasy already knew that Alex had asked her to *pay attention before anyone gets hurt* to those very same things. Was this a sick test? Who was the true paranoid here, Alex the conspiracy theorist, or Vasy the man who'd saved her?

Vasy's attentive gaze lingered, but then he reached out with both of his hands and took her face. He eased his lips to hers and kissed her like old times, the kind of kiss that felt like goodbye to her past.

Allana felt the heat crawl up her spine and warm her cheeks during that kiss, but it wasn't all good. She feared for the men in her life, not just for Alex. She feared for Vasy as well.

When he eased away from her, he allowed a smile before rolling over and pulling the blankets over his naked shoulder. Still a little shocked, Allana rolled over as well, giving Vasy the space he preferred even though she wanted nothing but to wrap herself in the safety of his arms. Or Alex's arms, but she quickly dismissed that thought.

It took Allana a long time to fall asleep that Sunday night. And even once she did, her sleep wasn't restful. It was the kind of light, twitchy sleep where she kept snapping awake. And somewhere around two in the morning, when a nightmare of some sort jabbed at her and startled her awake, she rolled over and found Vasy's side of the bed vacant.

"Vasy?" She listened, but the ringing in her ears kept her from hearing anything, including the silence. So she stepped out of bed and into her slippers, walked into the hallway and noticed that the living space at the end was dark and quiet. "Vasy?" she asked again, a little louder this time.

Silence.

She fully expected to creep into the living area and find him hunched over the telephone table, his ear pressed to the receiver and an unfaithful smirk on his lips. But the living area was vacant; there was only the moonlight pouring in through the frost in the windows, allowing a faint amount of illumination so she could not only see her way, but see that Vasy wasn't here.

She walked through the kitchen—not that she expected him to be hiding under the sink or anything—and then stopped at the foyer. Opening the closet, she discovered an empty hanger where he would've normally hung his jacket. His big, heavy boots were gone, too.

Blinking back the fear that kept ringing in her ears, she questioned why she was afraid in the first place.

Where could he have gone at this time of night?

# # #

Chapter 22

As the city bus neared its stop at Lenin Square the following Monday afternoon, Allana stared out the window. The town center was bustling now that the freezing spell had finally broken. She hadn't seen it this crowded it in a long time, as if it were already Spring even though the snow was still falling and she had to wear her fur hat.

Taking a deep breath, Allana grabbed her athletic bag and stepped off the bus behind a mother and her young son, and started toward the Energetik. It was where Vasy worked out, where he got into his swim trunks every Sunday after she cooked him a healthy breakfast, and where he would swim for nearly an hour without taking a break.

Allana made it to the front steps, climbing a few before she felt that familiar touch on her lower back. She had hoped to not run into anyone she knew.

"What are you doing here?" she said without turning to look at Alex. She particularly didn't want to run into him, especially after her conversation with Vasy last night.

He shrugged. "Thought I would go for a swim," he said, grinning. "Looks like great minds really do think alike."

She picked up the pace, putting a couple of steps' distance between them.

"How will you pay your admission if you can't speak the language?"

Alex asked. He sounded cocky, arrogant.

She ignored him, reached the doors, and opened them to the large beautiful lobby. There were photos of key political figures on the wall with a bright and colorful mural up above. A team of young men in shorts and tank tops walked past her, presumably to the gymnasium.

"I'd love to see you in a bathing suit," Alex whispered into her ear.

Allana swung around and showed him her balled fist. "I'm not supposed to talk to you."

Alex raised his hands. "Easy with the violence." Once she lowered her hand, he asked, "Why doesn't Vasy want you talking to me? He didn't mention anything to me this morning in the cafeteria."

Frowning, Allana tried to compute this new piece of data. At least she knew that Vasy had gone to work in the middle of the night. She'd thought he'd disappeared to his mistress's apartment, especially after the comments about how she was *different*. She'd assumed the worst, but was quietly pleased that he'd gone to the power station instead.

Alex matched her contemplative frown. "Oh, I see."

"What?" she demanded, her voice a panicked whisper. "What do you see? Because I don't understand any of this!"

"He doesn't trust me now," Alex explained, his face hardening with contemplation. "After what happened to Gregor, he's nervous. And he thinks I might be involved. But in what capacity, I don't know."

"Is that it?" she asked, keeping her voice quiet and taking a step back from him. "Are you an American spy, Alex?"

He laughed loud enough to attract attention, which meant it sounded fake. "I'm as much a spy as your husband," he confided, then nodded toward the entrance to the pool. His words barely reached her ears. "Come on, let's get changed and get into the water."

Alex winked, and the change of subject annoyed her. She couldn't help but look at him in a new light. He'd barely refuted Vasy's damning claim that he was an American spy, something that could make anyone disappear for a long, long time if anyone of importance overheard the accusation. Worse yet, Alex *looked* the part. He surely still owned a navy passport somewhere, alongside the burgundy one he kept closer. Allana considered asking him that very question, but bit her tongue.

Alex motioned for her to follow him, an over-eager gesture that made her nervous. She promised herself that she needed to end this relationship, just like Vasy had suggested. And yet, here she found herself willing to follow him into some unknown corner of the Energetik and... *No, this needs to end. Right now.*

"Fine," Alex said, starting toward the pool area by himself. "I'll see you in the water."

Except he wouldn't. Because after he disappeared into the men's change room, she knew she couldn't follow through with her initial plans to exercise and fill her boring days. Not with Alex there, anyway. So she pivoted on her heels and left the Energetik; it wasn't worth the risk.

# # #

Chapter 23

The movers—teen sons of a few men that worked with Vasy—carried boxes into Allana's new third-floor apartment. Having taken the Saturday off as a personal day, Vasy directed them to the right rooms and helped with the heavy lifting whenever the kids needed it, or whenever they touched something valuable or fragile. Allana watched closely, noticing how he carried a handful of boxes all on his own. One of those boxes contained the binders and manual and notes from the power station, but there were two other boxes that she hadn't known about. All three of them had been placed somewhere in the second bedroom, similar to the one where Alex was keeping his fancy equipment upstairs.

By three o'clock, all of their belongings had been moved in. Once the kids assembled the kitchen table, Vasy broke out the vodka. Back home, these kids needed a fake ID if they wanted to get served at a nightclub, but here they were always allowed a few sips of vodka. So Vasy poured them each enough as a way to say thank you before driving them home in the moving truck.

All alone, Allana had to decide between making a trip upstairs to say hello to Alex (if he was even home) or locating those three other boxes in the second bedroom, the ones that her husband had been careful about handling himself.

She chose the second option, not only because she recognized just how dangerous it could be if anyone spotted her with Alex—*was he really an American spy?*—but because she wanted to know what else Vasy might be hiding from her.

Before locking the main door, Allana took a quick inventory and saw that Vasy had left his key behind. Her face crunched with curiosity at this, but she dismissed it as Vasy being too busy with the move to be bothered with inserting it on his key ring. Because he'd left it behind, it meant that if he wanted inside, he would have to knock on the door once he arrived back at the apartment.

Confident with her odds of not getting caught snooping, Allana disappeared into the second bedroom. The room looked exactly the same as Alex's upstairs, with the exception of the furniture. Maybe the tree line outside her window was a little higher, but when she entered the room and saw the closet, the bed frame, and the big window, she was reminded of her visit upstairs.

Alex was so close and accessible that it turned her stomach. Now that she'd decided against making a visit upstairs, she wondered how long it would be before he would come down to welcome them to the building.

Ignoring that dreadful thought, Allana searched through the boxes. One of the first ones contained the materials Vasy had taken from the power station. Having already seen the contents of that box, she set it aside and searched for the others. But it wasn't until she opened a dozen or so boxes that she found what was likely one of the other boxes Vasy had handled himself.

It was the box with their record collection. Cyndi Lauper was on the top. It was the kind of thing that probably wouldn't be punishable unless the authorities really wanted to make a case against you.

She frowned. *Is Vasy this worried about the American music getting him into trouble? If he is, why?*

She searched the rest of the boxes but found nothing that stood out. So she went back to the box with the albums in it—Cyndi Lauper, the Beatles, Bruce Springstein, AC DC, Pink Floyd, Billy Joel, Supertramp, and a handful of other popular albums they'd enjoyed as students and even here in Pripyat. They weren't all American artists, either, which meant it wasn't the kind of music that made your ears bleed. Even the Soviets enjoyed this kind of music, even if it meant they couldn't openly admit to it in public.

So why was he so insistent on handling this box himself?

Allana jumped when she heard the door handle, followed by the expected knocking.

Vasy.

Half of the records spilled out of the box and onto the floor. Cursing, she dropped to her knees and started gathering them and their cases when she noticed something strange. The Billy Joel album—*Glass Houses,* the one with someone hitching his arm back like he was ready to throw a rock through the window—had slipped out of its sleeve. It was just Allana's luck that she'd probably scratched the vinyl surface and ruined *It's Still Rock and Roll to Me.* She cursed and reached for the album, but she noticed that it didn't have a label at its center.

More knocking. *Vasy.*

The missing label was odd to her because all of their albums had labels. And she specifically remembered this one having a label because it had been hers before she ever met Vasy. In fact, it was one of the few albums she'd contributed to their collection, and it happened to be the one that Vasy despised the most. *Would he have ripped the label off to annoy her?*

He knocked again at the apartment door, so she worked quicker, got the box replaced where she'd found it, and then hurried to let him in.

"Where were you?" he asked with an irritated hiss, stepping past her and into the apartment.

"Bathroom," she lied. "Might want to steer clear."

He didn't bother with any other questions or think to ask whether she was feeling alright. "I'm going to start unpacking," he said instead, more annoyed with having to knock three times than she would have expected.

And then he disappeared into that second bedroom, closing the door and making his point clear—he wanted to be left alone.

# # #

Chapter 24

On Sunday, after their breakfast in the new apartment, Allana surprised Vasy when she asked if she could join him at the Energetik. She wanted to swim with him, she said as she gathered the plates from the table and brought them to sink. It took all of her strength to calm her clattering hands.

"But we still have so much to unpack," he protested.

"I'm home all day. It'll give me something to do while you're at work," she answered. Yes, she'd prepared for his objections because she knew he'd have some. Any man who continued to have a love affair behind his wife's back would, even after she'd resolved to end her own relationship with Alex, who still hadn't stopped by to welcome them, oddly enough.

At last, Vasy shrugged. "Sure, I'd like your company," he said, and she blamed his early acceptance on the fact that he was probably lying.

So after tidying up the kitchen table, she hurried to the bedroom and packed the same gym bag she'd packed when she last attempted to get to the Energetik, the day Alex had snuck up on her and tried to seduce her by saying how much he wanted to see her in a bathing suit. In fact, that had been the last time she'd seen Alex and, while she refused to admit it, she missed him a little and worried a little more because of what Vasy had said about Alex being an American.

"Are you just about ready?" Vasy asked from the other side of the bed.

She dismissed her thoughts about Alex and put on a big, happy smile for her husband. "Can't wait to see you in your Speedo."

Vasy laughed, jumped across the bed, and wrestled her on top of him. She played along for a moment, humoring him and wondering if this was just some crazy delay tactic. *Will he suggest missing his swimming session now?*

Straddling Vasy, she moved in for a kiss, but he turned his head. "No way," he said. "If we start with that, I'll miss my workout." With the same ease that he'd managed in getting her on top of him, he rolled her off and then helped her out of bed. "Let's go."

I know you're hiding something, because it's been too long since we last made love and you're acting like it's not a big deal.

Dismissing her doubts, she grabbed his hand and her gym bag.

I have a suspicion that I'm about the find out why that is.

After locking up the apartment, she followed Vasy to the elevator. The call button stimulated a *whoosh* of air from the narrow crack in the doors before them. This was a pleasant change. Their old elevator barely responded at all, forget about feeling the gust of air from its ascent inside the shaft.

Glancing over at Vasy, she noticed how he stood in silence, watching those doors with the wind breathing out from that little crack. She wanted to ask him about Gregor because she knew he was dealing with that little detail in his head. *If you normally spend hours away on a Sunday, apparently smoking cigars and listening to illicit music, how will you fill the time with me tagging along today?*

The elevator doors opened and they boarded.

"Gregor will be happy to see you," Vasy admitted, as if he could read her mind.

"I'm looking forward to seeing him, too."

"You still like cigars, don't you?"

She shrugged.

The doors opened and Allana blinked. They were already at the lobby.

She noticed how quickly Vasy walked now, his long strides swallowing up the distance between the apartment lobby and their assigned parking spot. She glanced across the lot to the spot where Alex normally parked his Lada, but noticed that it was vacant. The fresh snow and missing tire tracks suggested he hadn't been home in a few days. She frowned. *When was the last time it snowed?* This worried her a little more.

Stop worrying, it's not like you love the guy.

"Allana," Vasy barked, and she snapped back to reality. Shaking her head, she stopped and looked around; she'd walked right past their car.

"Sorry."

"Are you alright?" He seemed genuinely concerned, the way he tilted his head and glared at her like something was wrong. She'd have been equally concerned if he'd been the one to walk right past their car. "If you don't feel focused enough, I'd hate for you to get into the water with me and struggle with these laps."

She smirked. *Like it's going to be that easy to blow me off.* "Like I said, I can't wait to see you in your Speedo."

Rolling his eyes, Vasy tossed his gym bag into the back seat. Not the trunk like every other time he went to the Energetik.

"Get in, we're going to be late."

The trip to Lenin Square started in relative silence. The temperature was a lot kinder these days, so after the equivalent of an American city block, she mentioned the warmer climate to Vasy. He grunted his acknowledgement and said something about May Day, which was a big celebration that happened on May first.

"They're opening the Devil's Wheel for May Day," he went on.

The Devils Wheel…Allana's stomach tightened as she remembered Alex pointing through the temporary fence and promising to take her on the new Ferris wheel and kissing her up at the top.

"Yeah," she mumbled, suddenly regretting the conversation and hoping her quiet response would get him talking about something else.

"They'll make the junior engineers work that day," Vasy said, allowing a lighthearted smile. "We'll have completed most of our scheduled tests by then, so the day is ours."

She glanced down, feeling his hand reach into hers. When she raised her attention to him, she found him grinning wider. But it seemed forced, too big a smile for a husband like Vasy to flash at a wife like her. How long would it take before he slipped up and something stupid fell out of his mouth about some woman he'd met at the pool, or at Gregor's apartment, or whatever the hell was really going on here? Because by now, Allana was wondering just how reliable her suspicions were.

Vasy parked in the same area as always, behind the Hotel Polissia and closer to the Energetik where it was easier to get in and out of one of the back entrances. Following his lead, she slipped out of the car, grabbed her bag from the back seat and struggled to match his pace.

"Are you anxious?" she asked as they climbed the concrete stairs to the building's back entrance. "I'm breaking a sweat just trying to keep up with you."

Vasy chuckled. "Sorry. There's only ninety minutes before they clear the pool for the public swim." He held the door for her and pointed her down the hall. "That's the women's change room."

"Be quick," she said, mostly because she figured it was what he wanted to hear from her. "We only have ninety minutes."

# # #

Chapter 25

In the quiet women's change room, Allana took mental notes of the other female swimmers. *Where's the mistress?* There weren't many other women in the change room; just four others and two of them had hair so gray that it looked blue under these lights. Of the remaining two, one was a teenager pulling a swimming cap over her short black hair—too young for Vasy. But the other was a possible candidate.

That woman had a gorgeous body, shoulder-length black hair, and a naturally pretty face, which meant Vasy had likely met her at the pool. Allana estimated that Mrs. Perfect was somewhere in her late twenties, a couple of years older than Vasy. And also like her husband, she wore a ring on her left hand, which didn't surprise Allana; women in the Soviet Union tended to get married while they were still young, fertile and lively. Which meant Mrs. Perfect had more time than Vasy to get bored with her marriage—*leave it to a bored housewife to take advantage of her husband's genuine and innocent kindness*— which also meant she'd probably been the predator in the affair.

Yes, if Mrs. Perfect was the reason why her husband missed less exercise than church, then she'd been the one who approached Vasy. She'd encouraged him into her apartment. She'd convinced him it was okay to love two women—one like a wife, and the other like the love of his life. And that, Allana deduced, was what allowed her to seduce him.

Before Allana could dig too deep into the possibility that Mrs. Perfect was her husband's mistress, she snapped back to reality as the other woman stepped into her one-piece swimsuit; Allana had barely stripped out of her underwear. She needed to hurry up if she wanted to watch how this woman interacted with Vasy in the pool.

Picking up the pace, Allana raced into her own black swimsuit, glancing over her shoulder to watch her possible enemy slip into one of the bathroom stalls. This afforded her a little more time, but she was too hurried and almost failed to cover herself properly. As she rushed toward the showers, she took a look at herself in the mirror. She was maybe a few pounds more, but not a whole lot separated her weight from Mrs. Perfect.

As Allana finished in the shower, Mrs. Perfect appeared and got the spray working. Armed with her marginal lead, Allana punched the faucet to stop the water and then slipped out to the pool area. A few people were already heavy into their lengths, but not Vasy.

In fact, she couldn't spot Vasy at all. *There's no way it would take him longer to get ready than it takes me.*

Easing herself into the water, Allana watched the men's change room door as a younger blonde woman swam past. As she began to assess the blonde swimmer, she wondered why Mrs. Perfect still hadn't emerged from the women's change room either. *How in the...?*

And then she noticed that the women's change room door opened. She watched her competition emerge, even more sexually appealing now that she was all wet and slippery. Glancing back down the lane at the blonde, she couldn't decide which woman would be of greater interest to Vasy.

Less than a couple of seconds later, Vasy emerged from the men's change room.

As if that wasn't odd enough on its own, she noticed how neither of the swimmers took note of her husband in his Speedo. And as for Vasy, all he did was look straight at Allana and, once he was close enough, he jumped feet-first into the water.

"Did you get lost?" she hissed at him. *Why hadn't he noticed either of those women? Or, more surprising, why hadn't they noticed* him?

And that was when she saw it. At last, Vasy's eyes shifted toward Mrs. Perfect, just for a moment as she looked this way and climbed down the ladder into the deep end at the other side of the pool.

"She's pretty," Allana said.

"Who are you talking about?" he asked, seemingly faking surprise at her comment. "The one in the black?"

They *all* wore black swimsuits, like it was part of some unspoken dress code among those who frequented this pool over the two others in town. Black swimsuits for the women so they could appear more athletically tuned, slimmer to the eyes of husbands who worked too many hours.

"She's here every week," Vasy said at last, shrugging like it was no big deal.

Allana narrowed her eyes and watched him glance at her again as she dunked her head and swam underwater across a couple of lanes to a less busy one. The one next to the blonde's.

"Does she have a name?"

Vasy rolled his eyes. "Let's swim."

And so they did. They swam for an hour, and even though Allana's arms hummed with fatigue and she could barely see straight by the end of it, she patted herself on the back for keeping up. Plus she'd outlasted the blonde *and* Mrs. Perfect, who were both applying makeup in front of the mirror inside the women's change room when she finally finished in the shower and stripped out of her black bathing suit

Bitches.

# # #

Chapter 26

As Vasy drove away from Lenin Square, Allana reclined in her seat and studied the passenger-side mirror outside her door. She watched for signs of another vehicle, one that might belong to Mrs. Perfect's husband or the blonde. After all, Allana fully expected some other car to pop into sight and follow them all the way to Gregor's building… and, she was willing to bet—*all in, at that*—that Mrs. Perfect or the blonde would follow them up to Gregor's floor…toward the door at the same end of the hall, but then stop just two doors short.

"It feels amazing to swim that hard for an hour, doesn't it?" Vasy asked from the driver's seat. He reached across the console and placed a hand on her pulsating forearm. She glanced over at him and wondered: *Blonde or brunette?*

"Absolutely amazing." Her smile was nothing but a lie, one that curled her lips upward and curdled her stomach inward.

"And nothing feels better to your lungs than a good cigarette after a swim like that," Vasy said, nodding toward her jacket pocket where she kept the Sobranies.

Allowing a faint chuckle, she ignored his implied request and stared out the window at the mirror again, resolving to try a little harder at quitting her smoking habit because it would improve her cardiovascular performance. Plus, she felt a little sick and didn't think she could stomach the odor of stale cigarette smoke in their car.

Still no other vehicle appeared to follow them. Not then, and not once during their commute to Gregor's building, where Vasy claimed an empty spot where last night's snowfall had already melted away.

"It's supposed to get warm," he promised as they walked to the lobby.

"I can't imagine what life without snow would be like," she confessed, sliding her hand into Vasy's as she heard an approaching vehicle behind them. When she glanced back toward the sound, she noticed a heavy, bearded man behind the wheel of a Lada…like Alex's, except this one was green and older.

"Piece of shit," Vasy muttered under his breath, and then opened the lobby door for her.

They rode the elevator up to the fifth floor. Making sure to remain a couple of respective steps behind her husband, Allana tuned her hearing to the unit two doors away from Gregor's, the door where her husband had gone. She hoped to hear something, a hint of some sort. A woman's laugh, a voice, anything.

But she heard nothing, except for Gregor's booming voice as he opened the door at the end and welcomed *Piska* to his unit. His insulting tone quickly changed when he spotted Allana.

"You weren't kidding!" he said with his thick and deep Soviet accent, a big smile on his face as he motioned Allana to enter with them. "Always a pleasure, Mrs. Allana."

She smiled, noticing the growth on his face and the cutting scent of cigar smoke on his clothes and in his unkempt hair. She felt sorry for him, as if he were already gone. Or dead. "Likewise, Gregor."

He chuckled like a lumberjack and locked the door behind them. "This is what a dead man's apartment looks like, Allana."

Allana stared at her husband, her eyes wide with fear.

"Now, now," Vasy said, noticing her response and chuckling. He removed his shoes and stepped around the tower of moving boxes that had been stacked four-high. He opened the flap on the top box and looked inside. "Nobody's going to die," he added absently.

Allana glanced inside as well, surprised by all of the paperwork. It was packed to the box's lip. And from what she caught, she spotted Soviet characters and words and gibberish.

"So melodramatic," Vasy went on, his voice trailing off as he became interested in the top sheet of paper. He withdrew it from the box and asked Gregor something in Ukrainian, something Allana couldn't understand outside of the seriousness in his tone.

Pay attention before someone gets hurt.

"*Tak*," Gergor answered, which was something Allana *did* understand. It meant *yes* in Ukrainian. "*Tak*," Gregor repeated, sighing and moving past Vasy and into the kitchen. Then in plain but crappy and broken English, he asked Allana, "Can I make you tea? I might even have some coffee somewhere in here, straight from the America States."

Allana grinned at his effort. "I'm fine, Gregor. But thank you for the offer."

"Vodka?" he asked, poking his head out from the kitchen and forcing the biggest smile she'd ever seen onto his face.

Still grinning, Allana shook her head. "I'll pass. I'm fine, really." *I feel like I might vomit after that workout, I don't need vodka to accelerate that... or to blur my attention should Vasy say something important.*

Glancing back, she watched Vasy flip through more of the papers inside that box before he asked something else in Ukrainian, another serious question that pre-empted a bout of silence from the kitchen. And just when Allana wondered if Gregor had heard Vasy at all, he came out of the room with two cups of water or vodka, and an unlit cigar in his lips.

"Let's not talk about these serious *work* matters," he said to Vasy. "We are in the presence of beautiful wife. Please, let's sit and enjoy our cigar and company, shall we all?" He didn't seem to care about a response as he moved past Vasy and Allana, using a foot to kick out a chair from the table.

Allana shrugged at Vasy, who shrugged at Gregor's suggestion and eventually stuffed the paper back into the box. She watched her husband settle at the table and help himself to the humidor. After wetting the cigar's exterior layer, Vasy snapped his fingers for the book of matches.

"*Kukhnya,*" Gregor responded, and once Vasy disappeared into the kitchen, she remembered what that word meant: Kitchen. With Vasy in another room, Gregor reached across the table and patted her hand. "Thank you for being here, Allana. You are true friend." His eyes lit up—or maybe those were tears?—and he gave her that big smile again.

"I'm happy to be here," she answered and her stomach suddenly gurgled. She blamed it on feeling frightened for him, afraid that she truly might be looking into a dead man's eyes. Her stomach made another funny noise, and she shifted in her seat and faked a smile.

When Vasy returned with a lit cigar, he tossed the matches to Gregor, who lit up as well. After the men exhaled their first big puffs of smoke, it hit Allana with the intensity of a baby's dirty diaper.

Her stomach gurgled again, and she asked, "Where's the bathroom?"

Gregor pointed down a short hall.

Walking slowly to give the impression that she wasn't as close to getting sick as she truly was, she reached the bathroom and had just enough time to close the door before she vomited into the toilet.

Despite the possibility of pregnancy, she blamed this on the workout and, as her stomach tightened again, she wondered if maybe it wasn't such a big deal if Vasy exercised all by himself on Sunday from now on.

# # #

Chapter 27

As Allana's stomach calmed and she realized just how silly it was to jump into the pool with a former college swimmer like Vasy, she started to piece together some of the things she'd seen recently. Starting with the documents in the box that he refused to let anyone else touch, the clandestine phone calls in the middle of the night—*if my wife finds out about this*—the extra hours at work, the Billy Joel album, the interest in the documents he found here in Gregor's own moving boxes...

Was it possible? Could it be that Vasy was the very thing he had accused Alex of being—a spy.

As the realization set in—she just couldn't believe it—she leaned forward and vomited one last time into the toilet. But... it made perfect sense. After all, Vasy had been educated in the States at the kind of Ivy League school where spy organizations would recruit, he'd married an American, and now he was fighting for the safety and security of the American people by learning as much about the Soviet nuclear program as he possibly could.

Would he end that program the way Alex suggested the Americans wanted to?

When she heard a knock at the bathroom door, Allana slapped a hand to her to mouth.

"Are you okay in there?" Vasy asked.

She had to close her eyes and ignore the pounding in her chest before giving him a quick: "I'm good, just nauseous after all that exercise."

"I'm sorry," he said, a new softness in his voice. "I'll take you home once we're done."

Nodding to herself, she thanked him and wondered what it meant to be married to a spy. And she also questioned what it meant for Vasy and Alex to be working *against* one another. *Did they want to kill one another? What impact would the affair have on that animosity?*

After splashing water on her face and staring at her ashen reflection in the bathroom mirror—her big eyes looked worn and tired, her brown hair messy and haggard, like she'd gone to war rather than vomited into a friend's toilet—she began to wonder if maybe she was wrong about her husband. If maybe she was reading too much into these mild subtleties. Earlier this morning, she only suspected Vasy of being a cheating spouse. Now he was a full-on spy?

On a logical level, it really didn't make any sense. She blamed the cold weather, her upset stomach, the everyday boredom at home for her suspicions. Shaking her head, Allana tried to laugh at her reflection in the mirror before turning away and opening the bathroom door.

They dry, biting scent of cigar smoke bit her as she headed down the hall toward the sound of Vasy and Gregor's Ukrainian conversation, yet another example of why her suspicions could not be true. *Spies that spoke so freely at a kitchen table with an American woman in the next room?*

Unless... unless Vasy was an American *spy!*

She couldn't help but chuckle at herself—this is *ridiculous*—as she cast a sideways glance into the single bedroom—the place where Gregor slept.

And that was when all lightheartedness dropped off her face.

It wasn't so much the stack of unmatched socks on the dresser that surprised her. Outside of those socks, the dresser was relatively tidy. She almost wanted to take a full step into the room to be completely sure that she recognized what she'd spotted.

Glancing toward the end of the hall, Allana gulped and started to take a step deeper into the bedroom, but she didn't need. She'd been correct: it was the same type of audio reel that she'd seen Alex use.

"Allana," Gregor called out as he peered into the hallway.

Startled, she glanced over at him and noticed that, in spite of the smile on his face, his eyes had a dark curiosity about them. The way he watched her with those big eyes sent a chill up her spine.

Gregor took a cautious step forward, tilting his head to the side as he studied her a little closer. "Ah, curious about the magic of bedroom," he said with a sleazy wink, "but a good magician never reveals his tricks."

Allana forced a chuckle, got a final look at the reel on his dresser, and then shook her head. "Actually, I was afraid my stomach might act up again." She rubbed her tummy to illustrate and noticed the slight bulge there. Maybe she *was* letting herself go a little. Maybe that explained her feelings of insecurity at the sight of Mrs. Perfect and, less so, the blonde. "I didn't want to stray too far from the bathroom."

"Ah, yes." Gregor waved her over. "We go back to kitchen now, yes?"

She joined Gregor for the final few steps to the end of the hallway, and veered into the kitchen where Vasy sat, still smoking his cigar. He didn't notice her return right away, obviously caught up in his own thoughts—*where are you in your head, the pool or the apartment two doors down?* It was the same pensive look he had on his face those earlier nights when they'd first arrived, those nights when he would peer into the power station's binders and manuals and other documents. The same look she'd found on his face as a student at MIT, those nights when she would sneak over for a romantic weekend and she would catch him slipping out of bed to labor over his textbooks or typewriter.

That look belonged to calculating, deep thoughts.

"Your wife has an interest in my bedroom," Gregor joked, smacking Vasy on the back as they all sat down at the table.

Vasy snapped back to reality and pasted a smile to his face. "Hmm? Oh, right. Yes, Allana has a perpetual curiosity about her." He reached across the table and squeezed her hand, but it lacked any kind of conviction. "It's what brought us together, isn't it?" He wiggled his eyes at her.

She nodded, wondering what it meant—the *perpetual curiosity* part as well as the wiggling eyes.

"You look unwell," Vasy said, frowning.

She glanced at Gregor and found him taking a long pull from his cigar, his eyes a little glassy as he watched her..

Sighing, Allana pushed her chair back and walked behind Vasy. She whispered into his ear, "Don't rush on my account." Her hand slipped into his pocket, slowly and gently and with a 'perpetual curiosity,' which Allana wasn't sure was offensive or just plain curious. Once her fingers hooked into his key ring, she kissed the side of his face. "I'll wait in the car while you finish your cigar."

Drawing the keys out of his pocket, she felt his hands latch onto her wrist. He held onto her with the same intensity that he exhibited while studying. And for a heartbeat or two, Allana feared she had been caught. Caught cheating, caught solving his mysteries, caught stealing the key to his mistress's apartment. Caught. She took a deep breath.

"I might be five minutes," he said finally, pulling on her arm so that her lips got close enough for him to give her a proper kiss. The kind of kiss that Vasy liked to give—a passionate one.

Once he let her go, she slipped into the foyer and stepped into her boots, relieved that he hadn't seemed to notice her ulterior motive with the keys. Her chest pounded and she felt her breathing accelerate, as if panicked. She needed out of there, away from the cigar smoke, away from Gregor's intimidating eyes.

She needed to know who lived two doors down.

Hearing the scrape of cardboard, she snapped her attention around to discover that Gregor joined her. He'd placed a hand on the stack of four moving boxes. Acknowledging him with a quick nod, she reached for her jacket, and he stepped forward to help her slide into the long sleeves.

"A pleasure seeing you again, Lana," Gregor said, pleasantly enough, but the way he said her name sounded oddly like *Layna*, and that reminded her of another song from Billy Joel's *Glass Houses* album: *All for Layna*.

"Likewise," she admitted with a tone that sounded like goodbye. "Take care of yourself, Gregor."

Smiling, he nodded his promise to do just that.

Aware of his suspicious eyes following her, Allana let herself out of his unit and started straight down the hall. As she reached the second door to her left, the one that Vasy had disappeared into, she gripped the key ring she'd lifted from her husband's pocket and felt her heart racing. But glancing back at the Gregor's door, she noticed that the peephole wasn't bright with light. It was dark, closed off.

Like Gregor was making sure she kept walking, all the way to the elevators.

Like he knew that she knew about her husband's affair with Gregor's neighbor, and he wanted to make sure she didn't pose a threat.

Rather than stopping and trying the unfamiliar keys in that lock, Allana kept walking.

Just like Gregor wanted, no doubt.

# # #

Chapter 28

Seated in the Zaporozhets' driver's seat, Allana hesitated. Her eyes focused on Vasy's key ring in her hand. There was the ignition key between her thumb and forefinger, and half a dozen others on the silver ring. Including the one that belonged to his mistress's apartment.

Two of them looked like regular deadbolt locks, and the other four belonged to heavy-duty locks, probably from the power station. She could easily identify the new apartment's key, but there was one other that looked completely unfamiliar. This one *had* to be the one that opened the mistress's door.

Wide-eyed, Allana looked up through the windshield toward the lobby's front door and when she saw that Vasy wasn't walking toward her, she deliberated heading back into the building, up to the fifth floor, and letting herself into that apartment. Yes, it was risky. And yes, she didn't exactly know what kind of trouble she could get herself into.

But she also knew that if his lover had been at the pool, the most likely candidates were Mrs. Perfect or the blonde. And neither of those women had followed them because she'd been watching the rearview mirror the entire time. Knowing that the lover's apartment was most likely empty, Allana pulled on the door handle and sprinted into the front lobby. She didn't have a lot of time because Vasy wouldn't want to keep her waiting in the car—*he'd said five minutes.* Two minutes had already passed...

At the elevator enclave, she pressed the buttons multiple times, but when she saw that the neither of them stood waiting on the main floor for her, she opted for the stairs instead. Leaping up those five flights in her winter gear, with her body still buzzing from the hour of swimming, would have nearly killed her if not for the adrenaline.

Two more minutes gone… I'm on borrowed time now.

As she reached that second-last unit before Gregor's, she looked up at the peephole again and when she spotted the light in the little circle and knew nobody was watching, she felt like luck was finally on her side. So she flipped through Vasy's key ring to the unfamiliar one—the one that looked like a deadbolt key, not the big *work* keys—and was just about to slide it into the mistress's lock when she heard Gregor's deep laughter.

Allana had just enough time to bury the keys into her pocket before Gregor opened the door and both he and Vasy stepped out of the apartment. As she walked toward them, Allana prepared herself for a potential confrontation.

Gregor saw her first, then elbowed Vasy to look up. Allana could hear him bragging, likely trash-talking someone at work.

When Vasy turned around and saw her, his eyes widened and he hurried over. "What are you doing? Are you okay?" He seemed genuine with his concern.

"I… I came to get you," she said with a smile, her breathing still heavy from having sprinted up the stairs. And that was when she realized she was sweating a little, too. No wonder Vasy seemed concerned.

"You look like hell, Allana," he said, wiping the sleeve of his jacket across her glistening forehead. "Like you've got a fever or you've just run a marathon."

"I'm fine," she mumbled, raising a hand to her mouth to suggest she might be sick again, while, inwardly, she smirked at just how right he was about the running, except it had been a mad sprint, not a marathon. "Should get home, though."

Gregor piped up next, joining them for the trek back down the hall to the elevators. "Vasy, take her to see Dr. Miroslov. She had sickness at apartment, now this…" He placed a hand on her back, right between her shoulders. "Maybe you have virus?"

"I'm fine," she repeated dismissively, glaring at him because she was *not* sick, she was just too far out of shape.

"Then maybe you have baby?" he asked with a wild shrug.

Chuckling, Allana narrowed her eyes and shook her head, no, not a chance. But now she wondered… "I'm fine. Just a little exhausted."

When the elevator arrived, Vasy and Gregor shook hands and then exchanged a few words in Ukrainian before Vasy stepped aboard with Allana. Gregor glanced at Allana and asked her to get well soon.

"Feel better soon, Lana." Again, the way Gregor pronounced her name as *Layna*, she wondered whether he was telling her something.

"I will. You take care of yourself, too, Gregor," swallowing back the anxiety, she smiled and watched him disappear behind the closing doors of the elevator.

It was the last time she would ever see Gregor.

# # #

Chapter 29

It was Thursday, March 6, 1986, four full days later, when Allana finally found where Vasy had packed the records albums, specifically the Billy Joel one that she'd been searching for all week. She'd been stacking some of those lingering boxes that seemed to clutter the second bedroom's walk-in closet when she came across it, packed two-high on the shelf. Because she couldn't reach it— and they didn't have a stepladder—she had to rely on a kitchen chair, banging a wall in the process and leaving a dent.

Climbing up on the chair, she pulled the box down and set it on the floor. But when she opened it up and dug the Billy Joel album out, she noticed something even stranger than when she'd discovered the missing-label vinyl the first time around: this one *had* its label intact. It said *Billy Joel*, and *Glass Houses*, followed by a list of songs.

She flipped the album over and noticed the same label in the middle, except the list of songs on this side was different.

"No," she muttered under her breath. *What happened to the mysterious vinyl with the missing label!?*

Before she could let herself get too worked up about it, she heard a knock at the door and left the box open on the floor, the Billy Joel album on the chair that she'd used as a stepladder. She didn't expect to be long at the door anyway, but a quick peek into the peephole revealed Alex.

She groaned quietly. She just didn't have the time or patience for whatever it was he wanted.

"I'm sorry," she said, easing the door open, "but I'm busy, Alex."

He didn't seem to listen, or hear her, or even care, because he stepped past her and let himself into her new apartment, like he'd been there a million times before when, in reality, he hadn't even stopped by once. "It's like mine," he said, impressed.

And it was, too. Not just the floor plan, which was identical, but the furniture arrangement as well—there were only so many combinations when it came to arranging a sofa and a loveseat around a floor-model television.

Grinning, Alex gave a confident nod. "You'd almost think you missed me so much that you wanted to recreate the magic you've experienced upstairs." He winked at her.

Allana rolled her eyes. "Nice of you to finally show up, Alex. But I'm still unpacking and I'm just too busy." *And, Vasy says you're bad news.*

Alex walked to the sliding door that led to the balcony and slid it open. "It's supposed to get into the forties today," he explained. "The snow's melting more and more every day." He glanced back at her and winked, like old times. "We should be enjoying this weather, Lana."

She shook her head. "I can't."

"Just a walk to the town square," he suggested, then started toward the second bedroom. "Or we can hang out in bed all day, and I can help you christen your new apartment."

Groaning at his incredible arrogance, Allana raced over and stopped him before he reached the second bedroom. She'd left the box open and the album on the chair, and couldn't allow Alex to see what she'd discovered in the closet. Because then he might ask more questions about the label-free albums, things that he probably shouldn't know about if she was to believe Vasy.

"A walk," she said, grabbing his wrist and steering him back toward the foyer, away from the bedroom; even if he didn't care about the albums, it was best to avoid bedrooms with him. "Just a walk."

He smiled, looking down at her hand clamped around his wrist before opening his arms and pulling her against his chest, squeezing her tightly. "Ah," he moaned, breathing her in. "I've missed you too."

She closed her eyes for the smallest of seconds, enjoying the feeling of his arms around her a little too much. She didn't quite understand why, but she did, so she pushed herself out of his embrace. "Um, yeah, let's go for a walk. I could use the fresh air."

Nodding, Alex cleared his throat, and then they walked back to the front door. Allana slipped into her boots and jacket, grabbed her Sobranies and house keys with a trembling hand before leaving the apartment. Best to be out in public where nothing can happen.

But inside the elevator, he moved closer to her and took her face with his hands. He didn't say anything; he just looked at her with those killer-green eyes in that seductive way that left her wanting him when she knew she shouldn't. *There's no reason for this!*

She stepped back, trying to get away from him, but he matched her, move-by-move. *Shit.* As the elevator doors opened in the lobby, he released her face but kept staring at her.

Thank goodness!

"I missed you, Lana," he admitted with a guilty tone.

"Let's walk," she said, tearing her eyes from his and focusing on getting through the lobby, outside where she highly doubted that Alex would try to seduce her. Which was what she needed—for him to leave her be.

"How do you like the new apartment?" he asked, catching up to her.

"It's gorgeous outside," she said, ignoring him and reaching for the Sobranies. Withdrawing a cigarette, she stopped walking, cupped her hands around the lighter, and got the thing lit. She hoped Alex didn't see the trembling in her hands. After that first puff, she began to imagine what Spring would be like, just around the corner.

"Let's take a shortcut," Alex said as she started toward the road.

"That sounds risky," she admitted with a timid voice.

He pointed toward the forest behind the building. "It's a little more scenic."

She raised an eyebrow. "I don't think I can trust you in a forest, Alex."

He laughed. "I don't think you can trust *you* in a forest. Not with me, anyway."

Although she admitted that there was a bit of truth to what he'd just said, Allana formed a fist and asked, "Has your nose ever recovered properly?"

Alex stopped laughing. "Actually, walking along the city streets is probably a little more convenient. Less muddy, too."

Settled.

They passed Alex's Lada on their way to the road at the end of the apartment's driveway. Allana glanced at it for clues, for anything because Vasy had suggested she not trust this man. *Could there be anything in his car that should interest me? Like a gym bag in the trunk?*

"Have you spoken to your 'husband' about Gregor?" Alex asked as they started down the street.

She shrugged. "Those documents from the power station were found at a missing reporter's apartment."

"And yet, that report is still missing," Alex informed her gravely. "Which is better than her body floating onto the shore in the Dnieper." They walked half a block in contemplative silence. "All those reports showed deficiencies in the construction of the newest reactor," he explained. "Some people are also worried that the documents might link a handful of government officials to bribes and kickbacks." He glanced over at her, his eyes studious like he wanted to see if she knew this already.

"So there's a political motivation to make sure these reports never surface," Allana said, as if coming to that conclusion all on her own. She decided to take it one step farther, to play his game, so she added: "But I'm still not sure what Gregor's involvement is." She watched him with her own studious eyes to see if he might tell her something new, something Vasy didn't know or hadn't shared.

After a moment of hesitation, Alex shrugged. "My guess is that the officials will accuse him of treason or conspiracy. Gregor's timing was bad, especially after the Minister of Energy went on the record saying the power station is safe, and here Gregor appears to be trying to discredit him. But there's more," Alex said, stopping at an intersection to let a few cars and a city bus pass. He grabbed her hand and they ran across the busy street. "I really missed you, Lana," he said. She could tell that he meant it, but after all of that talk about Gregor, she started to wonder whether he missed her for some other reason than her good company.

"What else is there?" Allana asked, pulling her hand out of his grip and sliding it into her pocket where he couldn't reach it. She didn't want him touching her, didn't want to *feel* whatever it was that existed between them. She was married, she was trying to get back to her marriage (this time, she really meant it), and she refused to let Alex or anyone else distract her from that. *Besides, what's really going with Gregor that nobody wants to tell me, and how does it relate to the rumored sabotage of the reactor?* "You said there was more."

Alex buried his hands in his own pockets and kicked at a chunk of melting ice on the sidewalk. "If there were bribes and kickback figures listed on the reports, it would suggest that Gregor accessed documents outside of his working area. In other words, it shows that he was actively searching for information to tarnish the government's reputation, because you don't just come across documents like that."

"I'm not sure I'm following."

Nodding, Alex gulped. "All I'm saying is that if Gregor went searching for those documents or figures, or whatever it is that he gave the missing report? It suggests espionage."

Allana whistled. "Maybe someone left the documents on a photocopier."

"You're joking," Alex scoffed, glancing over with narrowed, curious eyes.

Allana shrugged. She didn't feel like he was telling her anything new, or important.

"There's been a lot of talk about increased thefts at the power station, but it pales against this. If the Minister of Energy said one thing and there are documents that refute it, it shows he had no control over the construction of the reactor. And that he also gained financially from it, off the backs of the hardworking Soviet people who trust him with their safety. On top of that, the Minister's big rush to get the reactor operating ahead of schedule puts the public and the entire nation at risk." He shook his head, like maybe something just wasn't adding up.

Regardless, the news brought Allana's eyebrows closer together as she frowned, trying to mask her anxiety. "They wouldn't have cleared the facility if it were unsafe, would they?"

"It was operational a full year ahead of schedule, so if it's unsafe and he gained financially, when people across the river are struggling to feed their families, this is the type of financial proliferation that never sits well."

They walked the remaining two city blocks to Lenin Square in silence. Once they made it across the street, ul Kurchatova, they simply stared at the activity in the square, both of them lost in their own thoughts. There were families walking with children, lovers holding hands, a tight group of young athletes heading to the Energetik. There was a lot going on. With the temperature warming up, people wanted to get out and enjoy the pre-Spring warmth in their prospering little town.

If only they knew about the trouble brewing at the engine behind that prosperity, if they knew that major forces were conspiring to take away this freedom, class, and beauty of theirs…

Allana let out a long, sad breath at just how naïve these innocent, happy people were. She doubted that any of them had ever heard the voices that Alex had recorded, or that they'd ever discovered that their favorite record album had been modified, or that a man they'd enjoyed laughs and good times with was being accused of conspiring against the government.

Alex seemed to notice the shift in her mood, because he slid his arm around her waist and pulled her closer to him. The thought of someone seeing them, someone that might know Vasy made her a little uncomfortable. But then Alex took it another step farther kissed the side of her head. This time, she let him do it, but she also made sure she didn't fall into his trap and kiss him back. Not in public like this.

"Let's play a game," he whispered into her ear, and she felt the goose bumps spread down her ribcage, reaching all the way down her legs to her ankles. "Pick a couple. Or a person. Tell me which one you wish you were and why, and I'll tell you why your life is so much better."

"Sure," she said, using the game as a reason to roll out of his arm and study the crowds.

"Well?" he asked, giving her a nudge and directing her attention to a married couple with a young child holding each of their hands, running and swinging. "Will you go with married with a child, or…" He looked around then nudged her again toward a middle-aged couple that no longer held hands at all. "…or unhappily married to someone who has become distant and unfamiliar?"

She wanted to take a swing at him, but she didn't. Part of her felt like he was poking fun at her marriage to Vasy, but another part wondered if maybe he applauded it as well. Finally, as they reached the fence that bordered the amusement park, she made her choice.

"Let's hear it," Alex said, beaming.

"There's no one I'd rather be than me."

He laughed at her. "Boring. And cliché."

"Hear me out," she said. When Alex nodded, she went on. "A couple of years ago, when I first met Vasy, if you'd asked me that question, I'd have gone with the married couple with the kid acting like a monkey between them." She nodded. "But today, I'm happy to be me. That's my answer."

Alex grinned, staring off into the distance. Or maybe he was distracted by the Devil's Wheel, Allana thought. Did he remember the promise he'd made about kissing her on that ride once it opened in a couple of months? She imagined it would be a day like today. A day where Alex showed up while Vasy worked. A day they walked through the forest because she would have established her firm boundaries by then. A day where they strolled through Lenin Sqaure and ate food from a street vendor, and then rode the ride over and over, talking about the same bullshit they'd been rambling about today.

Maybe I'll make an exception that day, maybe I'll kiss him back and that will be our farewell because it won't be scary anymore, they'd be firmly established—strictly friends—and no more lines would get crossed.

She couldn't help but smile at such a romantic thought before setting it on fire in her mind, burning it to ashes because she would *never* make that exception. She couldn't. It was too risky, too dangerous when it came to Alex the American.

"Marriage is a piece of paper," Alex said, like he could read her mind. He nudged her to look another couple. "And that's exactly what that man over there is thinking. Go ahead, look at him. Watch how he never looks at his wife."

Allana turned her back to the fence as a big transport truck pulled onto the grounds behind her. She sought out the husband and wife in question. They had a kid swinging from their arms, but now the kid stopped and was holding only his mother's hand. The husband picked at his nails and when the wife said something, he shrugged. His unmistakable lack of interest disappointed Allana. Just a piece of paper, another detail for that husband to ignore.

Alex went on. "He thinks that his wife—who probably *appears* to love him more, but trust me, she doesn't—wanted marriage so that she could build a fence around him. Keep out the other Soviet-Ukrainian women."

"Has it worked?" Allana asked, watching how the family of three interacted on their way back to the Hotel Polissia. She noticed that when the child spoke, the father abandoned his nails and got down on one knee so that he could be at his level. She couldn't hear them, but she saw their lips moving as they spoke their foreign language.

"Doubtful," Alex answered, and the entire time he wasn't even looking at the husband. "And if it has, it won't last for long. You can tell by the shoes he's wearing—high end Pumas—and the plaid shirt. He lives his own life. He refuses to wear the Hush Puppies his wife would prefer or the softer colors that she picked out for him as a Christmas gift."

As Allana watched the husband stand straight again and continue walking, she finally got the impression that the man was the outsider, not the wife. "What's the point of all of this?" she asked, starting to feel uncomfortable because Vasy never wore the new t-shirts she gave him at Christmas either, preferring his semi-transparent ones with the stained armpits. *Was Alex suggesting that Vasy and his self-absorbed man didn't care for their wives?*

"Don't feel too sorry for the wife, though," Alex went on. "She plays her role well. Doting wife and mother in public, but at home when it's just her and their son, she can get angry, real quick. Short fuse. High standards, maybe a bit OCD. Just look at her leather jacket and the way she folded up her sleeves. Both sleeves are folded the same length."

Allana squinted because the family was getting farther away. Sure enough, the wife's sleeves were rolled up. And when her son started skipping and he reached for her hand but ended up pulling down on one of those sleeve instead, she snapped her arm free, her face turned red, and she folded up the sleeve so that it matched the other. Her husband said something that she would surely interpret as an insult, and when the wife saw that her sleeves were the same length, she took her son's hand.

Impressive call on Alex's part.

"She has a keen eye for the kind of man that will bring her the pleasure her husband has stopped providing."

"Alex!"

He shrugged, even as Allana slapped him gently on the shoulder. "Just keep watching," he said. "Next time a typical Ukrainian sleaze bucket walks by, watch their eye contact."

"Alex!" she repeated, but her eyes wandered across Lenin Square, searching to see if this bored and needy, OCD-wife would cross paths with such a male whore before she reached the hotel and was gone from Allana's line of sight entirely.

Stepping closer to her, Alex lowered his voice. "While you sit at home and silently loathe yourself for stepping outside the boundaries of your so-called marriage, you should understand that you're not the only woman who can love one man as a provider and another as her true soul mate."

"Oh, Jeez," she sighed, rolling her eyes. "I love one man, Alex, and that's Vasy. What happened between us was an accident." *Please, just let this go already.*

"Don't worry about my feelings," he said, chuckling but she could hear a ring to his words that revealed just how hurt he was. *Sometimes, the truth hurts.*

"I'm not." And just then, a man who spent way more time lifting weights than reading magazines like *Soviet Life* walked past the OCD wife. Allana watched her glance back at the man and check him out, and the man looked over his shoulder, too. He probably winked or gave her some other suggestive facial expression because the OCD wife smiled and blushed.

Very observant, Alex. "But you're wrong about me." She gulped. *He's wrong about me.*

"I doubt it," he said, and then whistled through the fence so loudly that Allana jumped.

When she turned around to see what was going on, Allana noticed that one of the workers had started toward them. He had broad shoulders and a moustache, the kind of eyes that feared nothing; the kind of man that the woman with OCD would have smiled and blushed for.

"What are you doing?" Allana asked.

Alex ignored her and began speaking to the man on the other side of the fence in Ukrainian. Once the man was close enough, Alex reached through the fence and held out his arm. The two of them shook hands, and then the other man pointed Alex toward the road where the transport truck had entered the amusement park grounds.

"Come with me," Alex said, grabbing her hand and tugging her toward that particular entrance.

"Did you just bribe that man?"

"I prefer the term 'tip,' Lana," he explained with a smirk. "I *tipped* him."

# # #

Chapter 30

As they came around the fence, Allana realized the transport truck had brought the carriages that would get fitted to the Ferris. While Alex still tugged her along, his face had become almost childlike with excitement. The closer they got to the Devil's Wheel, the more excited he appeared. Like one of those children that pointed and stared at the amusement park rides coming together like a puzzle with just the final pieces left to put in place.

"What did you say to that man?" Allana asked.

Alex refused to tell her and kept his grinning lips sealed. But his wide eyes essentially told her all that she needed to know—he'd bribed the worker so that he would allow them into one of those uninstalled, Ferris wheel carriages.

Sure enough, after the workers offloaded a few of the yellow carriages and lined them up on the ground next to the wheel, the worker that Alex had bribed said something to the others and they all had a mini-meeting about which carriage Alex and Allana could occupy. Sure, these things weren't installed on the actual Ferris wheel. Sure, they wouldn't be moving or anywhere near the top. But Alex clearly wanted to go for a ride, didn't want to wait until May Day for that kiss.

"Alex, this is stupid," Allana said as he guided her into one of the carriages. There were benches on either side, separated by a circular railing. She dreaded kissing him, didn't want to fall into that trap again, but she wasn't sure how she could avoid it now...

"Pick a side," Alex said, nudging her.

She chose the right side because that way she would be able to watch the workers make fun of them while Alex pretended they were rising and falling on the Ferris wheel, when in reality, they may as well have found a picnic table and played "let's pretend we're flying a spaceship."

"This is embarrassing," Allana admitted, covering her face as Alex slid onto the bench next to her. He placed a hand on her leg, which she quickly removed. "I'm not that married woman you were just talking about," she reminded him. *You're wrong about me, Alex.*

Shaking his head and smirking at the same time, Alex stared at her for a beat before asking: "Don't you think that if I could read a complete stranger so perfectly, I've already read you and figured you out?" He placed his hand on her knee again.

Once more, she removed it. Except this time, she slammed it onto his leg with a firmness that she hoped sent the right message. And if that didn't do the trick, she added, "Next time, I'll make your nose bleed again."

Alex's face dulled a little; she'd just reminded him that this wasn't all fun and games.

"What are we doing here, Alex?" she asked, still embarrassed and maybe a little exasperated as well. They'd started this journey talking about Gregor and conspiracies, but now they were fighting off a kiss that would only lead to disaster.

"We're riding the Devil's wheel before anyone else," he said. "Plus, I want my kiss."

"You're not getting a kiss." *Not if I can help it...* She swallowed her uncertainty.

"And I also want to remind you that I know how close Vasy and Gregor were."

Silence. It sounded like a veiled threat, linking her husband to a man who'd taken documents that could prove political corruption when it came to the construction of the newest reactor in operation.

"And I wonder if Vasy has any documents in his possession," Alex pondered with a quiet voice, faking a pensive stare as he playfully tapped a finger to his chin. "The kind that never should have left the power station. I mean, even a well-connected engineer like Vasy could have problems if an ambitious KGB agent ever got wind of documents that shouldn't be in your apartment."

Allana had heard enough. She punched him in the shoulder. "Alex, that's enough."

"What?" he asked, rubbing his shoulder and chuckling at her reaction.

It wasn't funny. "You're not going to scare me or blackmail me into kissing you," she told him. *Maybe my reaction was too much? Maybe I'd revealed something.* She rolled her eyes, trying to recover from her slip up and lighten the mood. "Besides, I don't kiss men who aren't my husband anymore."

Alex's eyes narrowed as he came to some sort of realization. "Which tells me that Vasy has documents in his possession," he said, shaking his head lightly. But something about the way he looked at her, she knew he was serious.

Allana chuckled nervously, rolled her eyes again. Still trying to recover. "He's a deputy chief engineer, I'm sure he's brought reports and other material home."

"And he's spent time in the United States getting educated. He fake-married an American woman. And right now, there's a lot of pressure at the Ministry level to get spending and waste under control, an initiative that wouldn't do well if someone like Vasy had documents in his apartment."

Allana turned her body so that she faced him and he could see she wasn't screwing around anymore. "Alex, my husband has done nothing wrong. Besides, you work with him. If anyone knows just how dedicated Vasy is, it's you. Don't play these games." Now it was her turn to make a threat. "Because you'll lose if you try to challenge him."

Alex's eyes shifted from the right side of her face to the left, and then back again. She could tell he was making some kind of calculation, weighing something in his mind. Like maybe he'd gone too far.

"Now," Allana went on, pasting a smile to her face, "why don't we close our eyes and imagine what this ride will be like on May Day, sitting up at the top of the wheel with the city lights beneath us?"

Alex's face lit up again, and Allana relaxed a little. It was working, she'd finally convinced him. She watched him smile and reach for her hand. This time, she allowed his fingers to slide between hers, enjoying it on many levels—some she refused to acknowledge, but also because he'd abandoned his accusations toward Vasy, which also kept her safe. She watched his eyes close, and then she closed her own.

In the blackness behind her eyelids, she saw a part of her youth. One of the first times she'd been out with her friends after she lost the baby. She'd gone to Boblo Island with Mitch, or was it Derek? Or Mike? She couldn't remember, so in her memory, it was just her all by herself on the Boblo Island train, a miniature ride that moved visitors from one end of the park to the other. And at one point, after waiting an eternity in the Sky Streak line and nibbling on candy floss—after riding the roller coaster, after playing the games and after convincing her date to avoid skinny dipping in the Detroit River—she'd taken a ride on the Boblo Island Ferris wheel, which was next to a line of trees like this one. Except once you rotated upward on the Boblo wheel, you climbed above the treetops and could see the water on the other side. And at night you could see the lights of Grosse Ile on one side and Amherstburg on the other.

It was heaven. And it had been a reminder to her that in the face of her losses—the baby and James—she was still *alive*. That night, after they drank the cheap beer that Mitch-Derek-Mike had bought for the twenty-minute ferry ride back to Detroit, hanging off the back railing and screaming at the top of their crazy young lungs, she'd let him take her back to his apartment and fuck her, any way he wanted. She'd taken it like a beating, too. Like she hated herself and her life, and despite the heaven she'd found at Boblo that night, the very next morning when she woke up in bed next to him, she'd taken her turn, she'd taken everything *she* wanted. And while Mitch-Derek-Mike claimed to enjoy the moment, he never called her again.

Today was very similar. Today was her heaven and her hell, her self-loathing and now her self-love.

When Allana felt his lips on hers, she returned the passion, reaching up and taking his face like she was back in that dorm room, like she was *taking* what she wanted again and it was the seventies again and she'd just lost everything that ever mattered to her, and this was her way to climb back out of that dark, depressing hole.

"Lana..." he murmured, his hand sliding up her shirt toward her breasts. "I want you. Right here."

Still with her eyes closed, she moved her hand between his legs and dismissed the alarms going off in her head about this being real-life, about this moment contradicting her previous resolution to end this. "Alex take me," she panted. "But not here."

Without opening her eyes, she felt his hand withdraw from inside her top and sliding into her hand again.

"I know just the place," he said.

Holding her eyes shut, Allana allowed him to draw her out of the Ferris wheel's carriage. She heard Alex say something to the workers, and nobody said anything back, so she imagined they waved.

By the time she opened her eyes and popped the bubble of her little moment, she wondered what she'd really gotten herself into.

"Alex, wait," she said, pulling her hand out of his and stopping in the middle of the lobby to the Hotel Polissia. "This isn't..."

She felt his hand on her lower back, guiding her past the concierge desk and toward the elevators.

"Alex..." she started again, shaking her head.

And then she realized, it didn't matter. He was going to take what he wanted, anyway.

Because he was like all the others.

And she would allow it, she would allow herself to go, to be with this man that suddenly didn't seem to care at all about her.

Because that was what she did. She was still that woman after all. Only now she accepted it.

# # #

Chapter 31

Alex had a third floor room at the Hotel Polissia, with a view that overlooked Lenin Square. It was a nice view, too. Allana should know because, after he'd stripped her, he'd bent her over the desk at that very window, his feet nudging her legs slightly farther apart. One hand was pushing down on the back of her neck so she had to angle her hips and give him access, while the other reached around her and traced a line from her navel up to her left breast. And, along the inside of her thigh, his hard, rigid—

"Oh, Alex," she moaned as he slid inside her. "Fuck me."

And he did. With the curtains wide open and all of those people in the town square, he fucked her like she'd been fucked as a teenager, in those hateful years after James but long before Vasy, in those all-important years that were meant to define a person.

And when she felt his tongue slide up her spine…

And when she reached that point of absolute release…

And when his thrusts accelerated to that point…

And when he seized her, hard… and never let go… and never… let… go…

Allana felt whole.

Sane.

"Thank you," she exhaled, her legs trembling as she collapsed onto the bed with her arms and legs spread. "Thank you."

Not *I love you.*

#

The shower spray brought her back to reality; the sounds of Alex in the bathroom with the door open, cleaning himself. Allana rose to her feet, her legs no longer trembling but a little sore. She looked around the hotel room and found photos of important Soviet people on the walls.

It was just a hotel room.

She rolled off the mattress and started opening the drawers in the tables next to the bed. With the exception of the Holy Bible, the drawers were empty. She searched the closet, the shelves, the open safe. Empty.

The sound of the shower spray continued, so she kept searching. Naked and frantic, she reached between the mattress and box spring, sliding her hand between the two.

Nothing.

She looked under the pillows, under the bed, behind the desk where she'd just been fucked.

Nothing.

The shower spray ended and she settled back onto the bed, crossing her legs.

And then she finally found something.

In the bathroom.

He stepped out of the tub and dried himself with one of the hotel's plush towels. She watched him toss the used towel into the tub and make his way to the main sleeping area of the room where she waited. Alex smiled when he saw her on the bed.

"What is this place?" she asked.

His smile melted away. "The Hotel Polissia?"

"No. Your room." She felt her heart racing. "Why do you have this room when you have an apartment just a few blocks away, Alex?" Like he owned it, because he hadn't checked in, he'd simply used a key on his key ring.

He walked to the spots where he'd thrown his clothes and started stepping and sliding back into them.

Her nostrils flared as it became clear. "Alex, you're a dangerous man, aren't you?"

He said nothing. He just stared at her with hard, cold eyes.

Allana wanted to cry. Her voice became dry and chapped. "How many other places do you have, Alex?" She'd seen other keys on his key ring, she'd had those keys in her hand that day when she borrowed his car to spy on Vasy when maybe she should have been spying on Alex.

He walked over to her and reached for her face. After a moment of inspection, he tilted his head to the side but she couldn't tell whether he was angry. "Lana, I know you're not married. Not here in the Soviet Ukraine and not there, in the United States. Not in Michigan, not in Massachusetts, not anywhere."

The first burning tear rolled across her cheek. *How...?*

"I know," he said softly but also without compassion, his eyes wide as his hand clamped onto her jaw. He forced her to look at him. "It was all for appearances," he went on, "it always is. You had your escape, and now he has his."

"I love Vasy," she sobbed.

Alex tilted his head to the other side and studied her. "But does he love you?"

She squeezed her eyes shut and tore her chin free of Alex's grip. "I don't know," she admitted as more tears ripped down her face.

She felt the mattress shift as Alex's hand rolled up her back and made big, supportive circles between her shoulder blades. "If he loved you," he said in a voice as soft as cotton balls, "he'd have told you on which side of the fence you could find him. He'd have told you why it was *truly* important that you come to the Soviet Union as a married couple. But he didn't, did he?"

Shaking her head, she thought back to some of the little details. Like the Billy Joel record. The 3am phone calls... The key to the mistress's apartment. There were other clues, she was sure of it, things she just hadn't been *paying attention to*. And now, she hated herself because *someone got hurt*.

The mattress trembled some more as Alex edged even closer to her. "I love you, Allana," he said, and the conviction in his voice left no doubt in her mind that he believed it, too. "Do you understand that? I love you in a way that no other man could ever love you. You hear what I'm telling you, right?"

She nodded. She was supposed to love Vasy, though. And she didn't think she could ever love Alex, especially now that she'd pieced together the full picture of Alex Petrokov. *Alex the American* everyone called him. *What a bloody joke!*

"Now, I need you to tell me something," he said, and the tone of his voice changed from the soft and docile *I love you in a way that no other man ever could* to firm and threatening and cold. The voice of a killer, she realized. "I need to know where else Vasy goes."

"Alex..." she said, shaking her head. "Don't—"

He cut her off. "We know he goes to Gregor's."

"The Energetik," she whispered, although the image in her head belonged to the door of his mistress's apartment.

"Uh huh. Already on my list."

She clenched her eyes shut again, and a couple more tears rolled down her cheeks.

"Lana, please," Alex pleaded in his cold voice. "When you open your eyes, I'll show you the cameras set up around this room, and maybe that will help you remember."

Her heart rate accelerated. *Cameras?* She felt sick.

"Tell me where else Vasy likes to spend his time, because…" he hesitated, but Allana didn't know whether to believe he had a heart or he needed to take a breath. "Because I don't want to show him what those cameras captured today."

She wept some more before giving up the names of people who had been at the party. They were just names, Alex would already know them, but she wanted to spare Vasy. She needed to spare him because she realized now that he was her only ticket home. "And Yuri," she added, still sobbing. "And his wife, Svetlana."

Even with her eyes closed, she knew that Alex was shaking his head at her. She felt the mattress bounce as he stood up. His scent moved in front of her. His hands fell onto her shoulders.

"Allana Harrison," he said with a voice so quiet she couldn't tell if it was still *I love you like no other man ever could* or the killer. "The girl who likes to party. Who wanted an escape and found her ticket to freedom by allowing her college sweetheart to convince her to falsify a marriage license and photos and whatever else. The girl who hunted down Jimmy, the young man that impregnated her, and found him living with another woman. The kind of who girl who could have done all kinds of damage, but instead walked away without Jimmy ever knowing you were there." Alex sighed. "Allana Harrison, you're calculating and smart and I know that you have more than just a handful of irrelevant names on your mind."

Shaking her head, she pleaded with him. "Alex, don't do this."

"I need *locations*, Allana."

"I don't know," she wept. "Outside of the Energetik, all he does is work."

Another sigh. She could tell Alex was starting to lose his patience because his grip of her shoulders tightened. And this scared her.

"Alex, I'm sorry, please let's just stop this and go home. Vasy will be worried about me if I'm not there," she rambled, trying to convince him, "and you know he likes to come home and surprise me for lunch some days, you know—"

Smack!

It happened so quickly that she felt the sting of his open-palmed slap before she realized what had happened.

"I'm sorry," he blurted with that *I love you more than any man ever could* tone. Definitely not the killer tone. "I'm so sorry, Allana. I don't want to hurt you. I really don't, but I fucking need your help here."

She felt his grip on her chin again, squeezing it and raising it.

"Open your eyes," he ordered with a cracking voice.

She did. And she saw the fear in Alex's face, the regret and the dread and the things that clearly tortured him. He pointed over his shoulder at the wall at a photo of Vladimir Lenin with his balding head, moustache, and goatee.

"The picture of Lenin," he said, gulping. "Do you see his left eye? The black oval? That's a camera shutter." Next, he pointed at another photo on the desk. "It captured what happened after I bent you over the edge of that desk, Lana. You remember what happened on the desk, right?" His face loosened and he wiped a hand across it. *Tortured, pained and self-loathing.* She understood those things too well from her youth.

She nodded. "I remember."

"There are five other cameras in this room that would have started capturing photos every two seconds since I opened the room door with my key."

With five cameras capturing her sin, she knew Alex could produce a textbook of photos for Vasy, and fake-marriage or not, it would destroy him;

she truly believed that because they'd been in love once and he'd promised a real wedding once they got settled and they'd been that couple for so long, and...

Alex's face crunched up, and he genuinely looked like a tortured soul. "Lana, please. Where's the apartment where you think he hosts his mistress? Please tell me where it is so I go and we can both get on with our lives."

She studied his face. He looked like he needed another shower. Although her cheek still stung from his open-handed slap, she knew that these kinds of situations could end a lot worse than this one had.

"I can do better than tell you," she said at last. "I can help you get in."

Alex frowned, apparently confused. "I need an address, Lana. Just the location. Please."

Studying his face once more, she recognized his dilemma. Maybe he'd never planned on falling in love with, but he had. He'd never thought he couldn't get rough with her, and he'd certainly tried just a few minutes ago, but a real jerk wouldn't have those new wrinkles around his eyes, or the sweat beading on his upper lip, or the quiver in his chin. A real jerk would have struck her harder. Taking a deep breath, she knew what needed to be done. So she told him.

"Gregor's building. Two units away," she confessed. "Or maybe it's three. I'm not sure. But if I saw it, I'd know."

The "two or three" seemed to work for Alex. His neck muscles relaxed, he closed his eyes and the world of tension seemed to flood out of his face.

"I can get the key," she promised. Anything to get him to relax even more because she didn't want him to try and hurt her again. "I just need a day or two, Alex. I need to wait for Vasy to be in the shower or away from his keys." Her eyes jumped all over Alex's face, the killer one, not the *I love you more than any other man ever could.* "Please, Alex. I want to see this place for myself." *I want to see who this woman really is—Mrs. Perfect or the blonde—and I want to destroy her.*

Alex seemed to think about it for a few seconds before standing up and ordering her to get dressed.

# # #

Chapter 32

It was Monday before Allana mustered the courage to slip out of bed in the middle of the night. Vasy was snoring next to her. He'd caught a cold at work, or from his mistress, and had fallen asleep by nine. Most days, he didn't get home until that hour or later, but today had been different because he was stuffed up and clammy, and she knew that if she wanted to keep Alex happy and quiet, she had better get the key like she'd promised.

Allana kept the lights out as she crept down the hallway toward the kitchen. She doubted that Vasy, who was normally a fairly light sleeper, would remain asleep if he the hall lights spilled onto his eyes, so she wanted to be safe.

Vasy kept his keys in one of two places. Normally when he arrived home, he would either toss them onto the counter right in front of the Mason jars with her baking supplies, or he would leave them in his jacket. When he'd arrived earlier that day, he'd tossed them onto the counter, so that was where she went instead of the closet.

Bingo!

With the keys in her hand, she filed past the familiar one that opened their apartment lock, then passed a few heavy duty keys for the power station, and finally settled on the unfamiliar deadbolt key, the one she assumed belonged to the mistress but which Alex felt belonged to someone else.

This was the one she would give Alex tomorrow morning after Vasy left for work, when he knocked on the door like he had been since last week. The last time he'd come, this morning, he looked like hell with dark bags underneath his eyes and a scratchy voice that promised to ruin her life if she didn't pull through with her promise. *One more day.* Whatever pressure Alex faced, Allana knew it wouldn't be good if she disappointed him.

As she slid the key in question off of the key ring, Allana heard something. It sounded like footsteps, which was impossible because this apartment was virtually soundproof with its concrete construction, thick carpeting, and high-density doors. All the same, Allana held her breath and waited, the key ring in her left hand and the mistress's key in her right.

"Vasy?" she asked, her voice quiet but not exactly a whisper. "Is that you?"

No response.

Shuffling to the end of the counter, she peeked around the corner of the wall and found Vasy shuffling toward her. The sight of him nearly caused her to scream; he looked like a zombie out of a horror movie.

"What's wrong?" she asked.

"You're out of bed," he mumbled, reaching out and taking hold of her shoulders. "It woke me."

"I'm thirsty," she lied.

"Everything okay?" he asked, his eyes foggy and big with concern. "You're not sick again, are you?"

She shook her head, surprised by his grip on her shoulders. Allana wasn't sick anymore. The past week with all of this pressure surrounding the key, she'd obviously become nauseous in the late-morning or early-afternoon, right around the time of day when she'd had sex with Alex at the Hotel Polissia. But she'd blamed that on a quiet and mild form of post-traumatic stress.

"Not, sick," she said, "I just need some cold water."

Finally, Vasy grunted, released her, and walked to the kitchen table where he sat down with a clumsy thud. "Me too."

With Vasy's back to her, Allana clanked two glasses from the overhead cupboard to mask the sound of her sliding the keys back in front of the Mason jars. And then she opened the refrigerator for the jug of cold water and started filling the first glass.

"Just half a glass for me, please," he said.

She noticed the mess her shaking hands were making, water spilling onto the countertop. After she poured their two glasses and replaced the jug, she sat next to Vasy at the table and watched him drink his water. He didn't look well.

"Did you get what you needed?" he asked.

Despite the dual meaning to his question, Allana nodded. "Yes."

Vasy finished his water before standing up. He swayed on his feet, so Allana quickly finished her water as well and joined him for the walk toward the bedroom, sliding her free hand into his while her other held on tight to the mistress's key. She wondered what would happen to the woman once Alex showed up at her apartment. Alex was expecting a spy, someone of substance, someone to interrogate and possibly hurt. The thought inspired a grin on Allana's lips—*hurt that bitch*.

"I love you," she said, steering Vasy into the master bedroom once they reached the end of the short hallway.

It wasn't until Vasy slipped back underneath the sheets that he said what he always said, "I love you more."

Except I don't believe you...

# # #

Chapter 33

The following morning, against her protests, Vasy grabbed his jacket and boots out of the closet and left for work. She watched him walk down the short hallway to the elevator, his face blotchy like he might be fighting a fever. Allana didn't understand how effective he would be at the power station and prayed today wasn't the day that some large, risky test would take place. Once he boarded and disappeared inside the elevator, Allana returned to her luxury apartment.

While tidying up from breakfast, she couldn't help but wonder why Nikolai Fomin hadn't arranged for this apartment right from the start. It surprised her that someone like Alex who needed to blend in and lie low—the real spy in her life—could get a place like this, while someone like Vasy who had all types of highly-placed political connections, had to live among the common people in their old building. It didn't make sense.

She didn't get to enjoy her solitude for long; by eight o'clock in the morning, there was a quiet knock at the door and she knew it had to be Alex. But when she opened the door, she saw Vasy standing there instead, his eyes red and puffy and a knowing smirk on his face.

He held out his hand and made a give-it-to-me gesture.

Gulping, Allana decided to pretend she didn't know what he meant.

"The key," he said with a coarse and sick voice.

She wasn't sure if he'd said keys *plural* or key *singular*. So she shrugged, freaking out a little because of how unclear he'd been.

Vasy stepped toward her. "I forgot them. Can't get far without those car keys," he said, and faked a chuckle.

Allana backed into the kitchen and grabbed the keys she'd left on the counter last night. How she'd not noticed that he forgot them earlier, she had no clue. She'd probably been too worried about seeing Alex this morning and what he would do to Vasy's mistress.

After she handed him the keys, he took her hand and pulled her into a hug. "This is going to be the longest day since I've arrived here," he told her.

"That's how I feel."

Vasy chuckled and then released her so he could leave. Again.

With her heart pounding in her chest, Allana closed the door behind him and watched him through the peephole. She wondered if he would notice the missing key, but he didn't even bother to glance down at the key ring in his hands. He was probably too sick to notice much of anything.

But what will I tell him once he's feeling better and asks about the missing key?

She didn't have much time to wonder because there was another knock at the door, this one less gentle and a lot more demanding. Allana knew before she opened the door that it belonged to Alex.

"Where's my key?" he asked, more forcefully that she'd expected.

Allana rolled her eyes and walked away, leaving him in the open door. As she walked through the kitchen toward the table, she could see her reflection in the glass of the sliding door. *Had Vasy been able to watch her replace his keys last night while he sat at the table and waited for the water? If he had, why didn't he say anything?*

"Nice to see you too, Alex," she said, trying to ignore the nagging suspicion that Vasy had seen what she did last night. *Would the glass be more or less of a mirror at nighttime?*

Allana bypassed the kitchen table and kept walking to the living room, expecting Alex to follow her.

And he did. He'd removed his boots, but not his jacket. His face looked tired. Not as beaten down as Vasy's this morning, but she could see Alex had lost a few hours of sleep last night.

"Lana, I'm sorry, but I'm not here to screw around," he said, stopping in front of her. Allana missed that version of Alex. "No pun intended."

She smiled back at him, reached out, and massaged the inside of his thigh. More to annoy him than anything else, because now she had key that he wanted. "You made time for me last week, Alex. What's changed since then?"

"The key," he said, stepping back and forcing distance between her hand and his thigh. It was nice for her to see him struggling with her advances the same way she struggled with all of his. "Give me the key, and then things can get back to normal." When he winked, it lacked its normal sleazeball arrogance.

She sat back into the sofa and considered his demands. "If I give you the key, I want to come with you to the apartment."

Alex shook his head. "I can get the key from you, or I can break down the apartment door," he said as an alternative. "And then Vasy will know for sure that you told me about this secret apartment."

Gulping, Allana wondered, "If I give you the key, he'll know it was me anyway. And if you break down the door, it could be anyone."

Still shaking his head, Alex abandoned his *I love you* tone. "Did Vasy tell you Gregor's gone?"

She frowned and the muscles in her back tensed. "What happened to him?"

"Most likely, he made his way to some remote airport, probably in

Belarus, and got on a private plane that flew him somewhere safe," he explained. "And far away from the Soviet Union."

Swallowing her relief that Gregor had gotten away, she pointed out, "You don't look well, Alex."

Alex didn't seem to care. He held out his hand for the key. "Please."

"You used to try so hard with me, Alex," she said, reaching out and squeezing his hand. She knew she was overdoing it. "You don't even have those fuck-me eyes anymore. What's happened to us?"

Finally, Alex realized what she was doing, and he managed to pull his hand free of hers.

"You want that key?" she asked, her tone switching from soft and loving to hard and cold. "Bring me along. We can go now if you want."

He sighed, shaking his head. Sitting down on the sofa next to her, he placed his hand on her knee. "I'm sorry, Lana. But that's a bad idea. Now, can I have the key? Please?"

"Come on," she purred. "You know how difficult it was for me to get the key. Where's the fun in it for me? What's my reward?"

He raised an eyebrow. "You know what your reward is. All of those pictures from the hotel room remain a secret. Vasy will never find out about us." He held his hand out again. "Now please give me the key and I'll be out of your hair."

She considered his offer, but she really wanted to see where Vasy spent so much of his time, the identity of his mistress, how she lived, what made her so special in the first place. "Alex," she nearly whined, "why can't I come with you?"

He sighed again. "I'm sorry, you can't be there."

"Why not?"

"Because!" Alex half-shouted. "If Vasy realizes the key is missing and he goes to the apartment, he'll see you!"

"He won't show up," Allana argued. If he realized the key went missing, he'd feel guilty about getting caught.

"That doesn't mean the apartment isn't equipped with the same kind of cameras that I showed you in the hotel room!" He crossed his arms. "And if that's not enough for you, what if the apartment is a safe house? What if there are people on the other side waiting for someone like me? What if they're armed?" He caught his breath, calming down and kneeling on the floor at her knees, his eyes pleading. "Allana, there are too many dangers. You need to trust me about this. Please."

She didn't care about dangers because she wasn't convinced that Vasy was the kind of man Alex suggested. And she was almost certain she'd find an apartment that belonged to either Mrs. Perfect or the blonde. "Why can't you compromise, Alex?"

He placed his forehead on her knees and made a frustrated chuckling sound. "Lana, please. Just give me the damn key. Let me do my job and I promise that if it's safe for you to come along, I'll bring you."

"You're lying."

"I'm not!"

"Then let me come and wait in the car while you run inside," she shot back.

Alex banged his head against her knee and made more of that frustrated chuckling sound. "No, you can't come with me and wait in the car, Lana. For the same reason why you can't come with me and enter the apartment. So, please. Please, please, please. Can you give me the damn key already?"

She waited a moment with his head on her knee, with the tingling climbing up her leg and the realization that what she'd done with Alex wasn't her sin, but Alex himself was the sin. She knew he was bad news, knew that handing over that key meant she might never see him again or have access to the apartment that belonged to Vasy's mistress. She had to surrender the key because if she didn't, he would share the photos that he'd taken during their last sexual encounter. And if that happened, then Vasy would leave her here to rot and die all alone...

"Please," he begged, and she felt his hand slide up her pants, rubbing against the back of her calf muscles. "You're killing me, Lana."

Closing her eyes, she felt a warmth spread up her thighs. Having Alex's hand on her leg and his head on her knee, so close to being right between her legs, she couldn't help but shudder and jump out of the sofa, snapping her eyes open.

"Lana!" he called after her as she walked back to the kitchen.

She knew he would follow her, so she reached under the sink, under the garbage bin where she'd hidden the key, and turned around just in time to offer it to Alex.

"Happy now?" she asked. To her own ears, her voice sounded panicked.

Alex's eyes shifted from the key to her face, and back again. When he reached for it, she snapped her hand behind her back.

"Don't forget your promise," she warned.

Tilting his head, Alex's eyes widened. "Never."

When she held the key out to him, he snatched it and then threw his arms around her, kissing her multiple times, all over her face and neck until his lips found hers and he held them there. It didn't take long for her legs to feel warm again.

"Go," she said, rolling out of his arms. She stared at the big balcony glass, watching her reflection and wondering, once more, whether Vasy had seen everything she'd done last night while pouring those glasses of water.

# # #

Chapter 34

For over two weeks, Allana didn't hear from Alex. As the snow melted, she went for walks and didn't see his car in its assigned parking space. A week ago, last Thursday, she rode the elevator to the fourth floor and knocked on Alex's door.

Three times. No answer.

He promised to come get me. And she'd believed him. *Maybe that was my mistake.*

She would never admit it in public, but she was a little worried about him. Alex had crazy ideas about spies and conspiracies, a private room at the Hotel Polissia where he took pictures of the women he screwed and then bribed them for information about their husbands—or fake husband in Allana's case.

As for Vasy, she worried about him, too. Though worrying about Vasy was something Allana couldn't hide in public or even in her own home. Ever since she'd taken the key, he had seemed withdrawn. Or maybe it was now that Gregor had left. Maybe Vasy missed his friend and hadn't even noticed the key being gone. If that was the case, she wondered why Vasy had never shared that little piece of information with her, the piece about Gregor being gone.

The past two Sundays, Vasy had stayed in bed until noon and skipped his workout. The first Sunday, he'd blamed it on his cold, and it seemed like a legitimate excuse to her. But this past weekend, he looked fine and said he felt fine. So when she asked him what was going on, why wasn't he going to swim his regular lengths at the Energetik, he blamed the warmer weather. So she ignored him and went out to the balcony for a smoke.

And when Vasy came out to join her, he leaned against the opposite railing and insisted they go for a hike through the forest instead. Allana was quick to get ready and had to hustle to keep up with Vasy as he navigated the path, and then he wandered off the regular trail. She followed him into a valley, not all that concerned about his weird behavior, and that was when he tried to have sex with her, pressing her up against a tree. But Vasy gave up— something was wrong, he didn't seem all that engaged—and claimed it was still too cold out and too physically awkward for him.

Although they laughed about it at the time, Allana knew he'd been distracted.

And then on Thursday, March 27, 1986, things really started to get weird.

Late that morning, Allana left the apartment to fetch the mail from the box in the lobby and she noticed the *Tribuna Energetika* newspaper that someone had left outside her door. Like a welcome mat. In fact, she nearly stepped on it and ruined its frail pages, but she managed to avoid that by dancing around it like a landmine. Once safely on the other side of the paper, she bent down and picked it up, noticing that two things fell out from somewhere within. One of those items was the key she'd removed from Vasy's key ring. The other was a Post-It note with a handwritten message on it.

Frowning, Allana picked up both items and turned the note over so she could read what it said. It wasn't Vasy's script, but it said: *Use the key, you know where.*

After reading the message a second and third time, her heartbeat echoed in her ears, pounding hard and fast, adrenaline pumping in her veins. After tossing the paper on the kitchen table inside the apartment, she grabbed her jacket, keys and enough rubles for round-trip bus fare to Gregor's old apartment building where she expected to have all of her questions answered.

Finally.

# # #

For the first time since stepping out of the elevator and onto the fifth floor of Gregor's building, Allana entertained a chilling thought. Maybe the entire floor was vacant now. Or worse, what if this was the floor where people like Alex and Vasy lived, each occupant a spy or conspirator watching her through their peephole. As Allana took the long trek through that tension-infused hall, she couldn't help but think of the movie *The Shining*, that part where the rivers of blood burst through the doors and rushed toward the camera.

This moment felt like that, as if some kind of ambush awaited her as she tiptoed down the hall with cold sweat dripping down her spine.

And when a door next to her snapped open, she jumped and spun around with her hands in a karate-chop position. Like showing her soft hands would scare off the attacker.

But there was no attacker, only a young Ukrainian man who stepped into the hall and used his key to lock up. He noticed her strange wannabe-karate stance and said, "*Dobroho dnia*," which meant *good afternoon* in Ukrainian.

Allana offered a guilty smile and a nod then finally lowered her hands and kept walking toward Vasy's mistress's apartment. She could hear the friendly, young Ukrainian's footsteps behind her, and she kept her ears tuned in that direction to make sure he didn't take a run at her from behind.

He didn't. Of course, he didn't; she was being paranoid, something she blamed on missing Alex more than she cared to admit and spending so much time with Vasy lately, who was acting all kinds of weird.

By the time she reached the unit, two doors down from Gregor's, the young man had already steered into the elevator enclave.

With a final breath, Allana reached into her pocket for the key that had fallen out of the newspaper. Once her fingers curled around it, she had to use both hands to get it inserted into the deadbolt.

She swallowed.

She said a quiet prayer.

She had no clue what she was about to do.

And then she turned the lock and pushed the door open.

# # #

The place was empty. All of the lights were out, and the furniture had been removed. Nobody lived here anymore.

Closing the door behind her, Allana made sure to engage the lock before pressing her back against the wall and taking a deep breath. *Calm down. Just calm down.*

If Vasy had entertained a mistress here, there was no evidence of it. Not here at the entrance, anyway. Maybe the bedrooms told a different story.

Keeping her boots on, Allana stepped deeper into the apartment. There was a large kitchen on the right, a bathroom on the left. A small bedroom straight ahead with nothing in it, and the master bedroom to the left, also empty. She searched the walls for signs of damage, as if Vasy might've rammed the bedframe or headboard into the wall, but there were no marks, no condom wrappers, no signs that anyone had rammed anything or anyone in either bedroom.

Back in the hall, she flared her nostrils, closed her eyes, and focused on detecting the scent of another woman in the abandoned air. As if Mrs.

Perfect's perfume, shampoo, or worse could be sniffed out of the plaster. At best, Allana detected stale cigar smoke and moisture, which made sense at this time of year. In fact, it had rained a lot in the past two days, with more precipitation on the way.

But no scent of another woman. No scent of sex.

Why would he have come here? To tell jokes and play dice with someone he didn't want me to know about? That makes no sense, it had *to be a mistress.*

Allana let out a long, relieved breath.

Though she heard no sound, she snapped her eyes open, half-expecting Alex to appear with a big smile on his face, his arms open in a typical, flirtatious gesture and his eyes glassed over with a knowing, *you-were-never-a-choice-for-me* wink in them. Just thinking about it made her want to punch him. But it also made her smile.

But instead of seeing Alex walking toward her, the place remained as quiet and vacant as ever.

"Oh, Vasy…" she sighed, backing out of the hall and heading to the living room. And that was when she saw it—the only thing that Alex or her note-writer had wanted her see was right there in the living room.

A record.

And an RCA record player, the kind that looked like a small suitcase with a speaker built right into its case-like frame.

Curious, Allana studied both items, wondering why they lay all by themselves on the floor, as if waiting for her. Like a host. As she stepped closer, she saw that the record player was an older model, something from the seventies. And—this was what stopped her in her tracks—the record had no label on it.

Just like the Billy Joel record.

Dropping to her knees, Allana picked up the record and ran her finger along its surface. She noticed that it had been broken into two dozen or so pieces, but her note-writer (it *had* to be Alex) had repaired it by melting those pieces back together and recreating the wire-thin wedges with some kind of device.

With a tenuous quake in her hands, Allana managed to lift the wobbly, label-free record onto the turntable. She slid the record player closer to the electrical outlet on the wall, plugged it in, and then flicked the unit's power switch. The speaker made a scratching noise before falling silent again, and then the turntable began to spin at a speed that was three or four times quicker than a commercial record player. It also spun counter-clockwise—*like the turntable in our apartment*—which wasn't something Allana noticed at first because the needle hand was on the right side like it would normally be.

And yet, when she moved the switch over to the AUT setting and the needle moved into place all by itself, reading the record *backwards*, the female voice on the speaker was as normal—*in plain American English*—as if the woman stood right here in the room with her.

Allana closed her eyes and prepared to listen.

# # #

Chapter 35

Allana sat cross-legged on the floor facing the wall, the backwards-spinning RCA mobile turntable within breathing distance. She turned the speaker volume down so that someone walking by in the hall couldn't hear it. She also kept the volume low because she didn't want to miss the sound of someone else entering the apartment and sneaking up on her. So it was a low volume listening experience for today.

The first thing she heard from the speaker was the date.

"February 9, 1986," a female voice said, and the needle skipped over the areas where the ridges in the vinyl had been melted back together. "Time is fourteen-thirty, Eastern European time. Present are agent G zero two four..."

At this point, three other men spoke up, each providing a combination of four or five letters and numbers. And then it was Vasy's turn; he spoke last with, "Seven L two three."

Allana's skin crawled at the sound of his voice and the name he used. She'd half-heartedly suspected he was an American spy, but hearing that he was Agent 7L23 really hammered that suspicion home. She felt the heat of embarrassment rising into her face, so she opened her jacket to let in the cooler air. *Deep breath.* She not only hated that she'd been so naïve, but how could a Soviet-born genius like Vasy turn like he had? He'd had every opportunity to make things better in Pripyat; he'd had the kind of ideals that could make a real difference. *Deep breath.*

The woman from earlier spoke up again, snapping Allana's attention back to the recording. "Regular scheduled meeting held at location fifty-one point four N, thirty point zero E, domicile thirty-eight E." The needle skipped, so Allana applied a little extra weight with her finger to get it moving forward again. Although she missed some of the earlier dialogue, she didn't bother going back. Someone had destroyed the vinyl record, so hearing any of it was something of a gift, she realized. Beggars can't be choosers, or something like that.

As it turned out, the voice coming from the speaker now belonged to Vasy. "...behaving in a way that's consistent with her character. This allows us to keep Alexei Petrokov under ongoing, albeit inconsistent and untrained observation."

Someone else spoke up: "Any reliability defects?"

"Plenty," Vasy sighed, and a few others chuckled. "However, Miss Harrison's behavior is both predictive and consistent, allowing us an angle we haven't enjoyed in the past."

Yet another agent asked: "The latest digital intelligence on Petrokov reveals that he has managed to intercept limited quantities of classified but relevant communications. Has Miss Harrison raised any of that with you, Seven L two three?"

Another sigh from Vasy, and a gurgling stomach from Allana. Now she knew that Alex had been right all along—the voices he'd captured on his closet-sized electronics equipment had really meant something. In fact, Alex's efforts made a little more sense now, but what he didn't realize was that the Americans—weren't they all on the same team?—had him doing exactly what they wanted and expected. Despite what Alex believed, these people on the record were still using him.

And they were also using her to keep an eye on him.

She felt sick and sad and worried and angry, all at once.

"Affirmative," Vasy went on. "Miss Harrison has been maintaining an ongoing relationship with Petrokov. As her only local contact, I suspect the relationship has had no option but to evolve in terms of depth, trust, and romance."

He knows? She felt her eyes burn as they filled with tears. *Did he say* romance?

"Petrokov has inquired about schedules for reactor tests," Vasy went on.

But I hadn't slept with Alex by then.

"While there's no question that Petrokov has instructed Harrison to 'pay attention,' nothing has been relayed to her about Gregor Onachenko, who has been assembling documentation for release to—"

At that point, the needle slipped on another melted groove.

Allana's heart raced underneath her jacket. And she felt hot. She even considered removing her jacket altogether so she wouldn't feel so warm and maybe the vacant apartment wouldn't to feel suffocating.

Another voice filtered through the built-in speaker once Allana settled the needle with her shaking hand.

"...leaves the matter of surveillance on Petrokov's apartment."

Vasy piped up. "March first, seven L two three will occupy the third-floor unit which is located directly below Petrokov's unit on the fourth."

"Noted," the voice from earlier interjected. "Once seven L two three has settled, our blueprints for the building in question indicate that we can run a hard wire through the ventilation system in the kitchen. It will require some drilling, which means seven L two three will need to distract Harrison."

Vasy added to the conversation yet again. "Petrokov has time off during the week of March fourth. He will agree to entertain her."

Closing her eyes, Allana thought back to that week of March fourth, almost three weeks ago by now, and her stomach clenched at the memory of Alex bringing her to his room at the Hotel Polissia and fucking her before he slapped her. Based on how these voices spoke about Alex, she couldn't imagine that they worked for the same team; these people spoke of Alex as if he were a nuisance, someone to watch and keep tabs on. Yet, he'd kept her distracted for an entire day, fucking her silly and capturing their sin with the use of multiple hidden cameras. That entire time, Vasy and his team of agents had managed to hardwire surveillance electronics that allowed them to see into Alex's apartment.

Allana didn't understand it. None of it. Vasy had never come here to escape, like she had. He'd come for a mission.

"Noted," the same voice said. "Agent G zero two four will offer an update on Fomin's schedu—"

Another ridge interrupted the narrative flow.

Allana placed some weight on the needle, and it picked up with yet another voice droning on about the Chief Engineer's daily agenda items.

"…mid-April with the weather warming up and settling provides optimal conditions for testing. By then, the subterranean chambers will have been dug out."

Vasy: "Fomin will approve testing based on the maintenance schedule in place for that time. I will recommend declining the engineering team's recommendations to proceed with a cooling system test, but Fomin will see it as opportunity. And I will continue to exert influence once Onachenko disappears."

"Noted," said the agent that Vasy had just cut off.

Vasy knew Gregor would be sent away? Was Vasy a part of why Gregor went? She felt sick to her stomach again. The reel in Gregor's bedroom the last time she'd seen him, she should have known. They'd all been lying to her.

"The theft campaign is finally seeing some traction. Most administrators at the power plant continue to place an excessive focus on reducing the petty thefts. We believe that distracts from—"

Another scratch, the needle skipping.

"Dammit," Allana huffed. She applied pressure on the needle again, but noticed how it wouldn't stick. She had to move the needle closer to the middle of the label-free record before it would settle down.

And that was when she noticed the change in tone. Like a sobering silence had settled over the group of agents that had congregated around whatever electronics device had captured this meeting and scratched into the vinyl. She heard Vasy speak first, Agent seven L two three.

"… magnitude on the same level as Hiroshima or Three Mile. But even then," he went on, pausing for effect, "we haven't received any kind of response from Alpha that either confirms or refutes the report I submitted in November, eighty-five. Sadly, this suggests nobody knows just how deep the consequences of our actions will be." A sigh. "At the risk of being accused of insubordination, I—Agent seven L two three—cannot condone proceeding until we have a better idea of the fallout."

Another agent, the female, cleared her throat. Allana jumped at the sound because the mood carried a heavy severity to it, all the way from the quickly spinning, broken vinyl, up the needle, and out of that crappy RCA speaker.

"Notwithstanding seven L two three's documented concerns, the weather patterns in April remain unstable. Without understanding the actual severity of our proposed actions, it's worth mentioning that a dust cloud can shift dramatically at that time of year. This implies that whatever unspeakable damage happens on this side of the world can potentially leave an impact on the other." The woman paused, sighed, and cleared her throat again. "It's imperative that we understand the magnitude of our actions, not only to plan for the collateral damage, but to plan for the long-term fallout of those actions. For that reason, I recommend delaying."

A few of the others in that room mumbled, "*aye-aye.*"

The woman cleared her throat again. "This concludes our report. The time is fourteen forty-nine." Then the needle slipped off the end of the vinyl, and its arm bounced off the turntable's center pole.

Angry, Allana yanked the wire from the wall and stared at the record player as it stopped spinning. She rubbed her eyes, her face, and stared for several more minutes before standing and picking up the RCA player and hurtling it at the opposite wall with a wild scream.

"Bastard!" She shrieked at the mess, the broken shards of vinyl, the cracked plaster, her broken heart. "Bastard!"

# # #

Chapter 36

Allana sobbed during the entire bus ride back home, trying to compute the data she'd heard in the vacant apartment. She didn't know whether to hate Alex for leaving that specific album for her to listen to, or Vasy for using her the way he had.

A pawn.

Outside the rattling bus windows, the countryside blurred.

I was a stepping stone.

She saw other buildings, entire complexes of them, and marveled at the absolute cluelessness of its tenants. Those people were living in Pripyat with their eyes closed, too focused on stupid little things like the Devil's Wheel and May Day celebrations. Living without any true understanding that, despite the yachts that visited in the summer, despite the expensive perfumes and furniture and clothes you could buy her and nowhere else in the Soviet Union, they were all going to suffer.

They knew I would form a relationship with Alex. It was planned.

A pawn. A player in their spy game.

Before we ever arrived in the Soviet Ukraine, my destiny had been written.

A deep, hot pressure built in her chest and it took all of her strength to not start hyperventilating while she sobbed. Through her blurry eyes, she noticed that a woman a couple of benches ahead of her picked up her things and moved farther away, closer to the driver.

He knew I'd cheat.

The bus stopped as close to her apartment as it would get. She had a short walk ahead of her, enough time to compose herself and wipe her face dry. She wondered what Vasy would say to her tonight when he arrived home. Because as much as she believed she'd been *paying attention*, she realized now that she was just another Pripyat dweller; she hadn't even opened her eyes.

Did he at least hope *I wouldn't sleep with Alex?*

As Allana reached the building and entered the lobby, the tears threatened to erupt again. The elevator carried her to the third floor, a silent reminder that even though she thought it had been her decision to move here, Vasy had wanted it far more. He'd *needed* it. To use her to get to Alex.

Clearly, the Americans wanted to halt the Soviets' advancement in nuclear energy. Because everyone knew about Chernobyl, the Americans were threatened by it. Maybe they didn't want Chernobyl to be the next Three Mile, which was still such a fresh wound. But more likely, the Americans— and half of the world, in fact—didn't trust the Soviets. Reagan and Gorbachev had an oil and vinegar type of relationship, except more poisonous and volatile. Regan's administration openly accused Chernobyl as a way for the Soviets to enrich their nuclear arms inventory.

Moving here had meant Vasy could proceed with his plan to decommission the Soviet's nuclear program. Shame them. Destroy them in the same horrific manner that Hitler had destroyed his enemies.

And this reality saddened her, because the people here deserved better.

As Allana slipped her key into the deadbolt and entered the apartment, she erupted into tears once again. She reached into her jacket for the Sobranies, but decided against them when she realized that the only way to drown her disgust with the so-called progress of humanity was through sleep. A deep, deep sleep.

Retreating to the large, luxurious bathroom at the end of the short hallway, Allana reached behind the vanity mirror for the sleeping pills. She cracked open the container and shook a couple of pills into her clammy palms before slamming them into the back of her mouth and washing them down with water from the faucet.

Still in tears, she retreated to the bedroom. As she crept closer to the bed, she stopped. The tears dried up, her emotional state switching gears—*fast*—and sending her into shock.

Her eyes widened as they locked onto the gift Vasy had left on her pillow.

It was a Dove chocolate, exactly like the one Alex had offered her on Valentine's Day, right before they'd made love for the first time.

She gulped and reached for it.

The sleepiness clouded her mind as she opened the wrapper and let the magical treat drop to the floor. It seemed like a sad waste to let such a delicious chocolate go uneaten. Still in shock, her knees gave out as she read the message inside the wrapper.

The message was part of the chocolate company's "Promises messages" meant to inspire romance. Even forbidden romance.

Allana blinked hard, focused on the wrapper and read the note again. The words spooked her.

"No," she mumbled, reading the message over and over.

She crumpled up the wrapper, pushed herself to her feet and hurried to the apartment door. The sleeping pills would kick in soon, if they hadn't started already. As she slipped her feet into her boots and grabbed her jacket, she considered forcing herself to vomit and expel the sleeping pills from her system.

Except she wasn't a graceful vomiter.

And she hated the aftertaste.

So no self-induced vomiting.

She left the apartment without locking the door or knowing what time it was, and rushed upstairs to Alex's. Rapping on the door with the same fist that held the Dove wrapper, Allana prayed that he would answer.

But he didn't.

He wasn't home.

Did Vasy expect me to come here? Was it planned like everything else?

She felt sick again and dry heaved.

I need to get out of here.

But where?

It didn't take long for her to figure out where she might find Alex, the only person she could legitimately trust right now. Yes, he'd threatened her. Yes, he'd turned on her. Yes, he'd even hit her, and anyone else would shake her until she realized how stupid she sounded.

But Alex had no interest in destroying the power station. Alex hadn't manipulated her into sleeping with another man—*or had he?* And, she couldn't think straight, but she knew she had no other option!

If she stayed, she couldn't even begin to imagine what Vasy would do with her. Would it make Alex's unconvincing slap across her face look like a tickle fight?

I don't feel well...

She dry-heaved at Alex's door again.

And Alex had been under pressure! Rightfully so, too! He'd been manipulated just like she had, and she wanted to do more than just slap someone right now, so Alex was forgiven for that.

Yes, because she had no other option!

Spinning away from Alex's apartment, Allana nearly fell over from dizziness—*the pills are kicking in*—and staggered to the elevator.

The wait wasn't long, and in the lazy, sleepy blink of an eye, she ended up in the lobby, stumbling through to the bright outdoors. The little snow that remained on the ground had a neon-blinding effect on her vision, and she raised a hand to block the light before she started toward the main road that would lead her into Lenin Square, the same path that she and Alex had walked not that long ago. But then she changed her mind, fearing Vasy might drive by on his way home and spot her. And then he would stop the car, convince her to let him take her home, and she would stumble into the car. And he would deny all of it.

All of it.

So instead of the safe and smart path along the road, Allana turned in the opposite direction and headed to the forest behind the building. The hiking path would keep her sheltered from the traffic on the road, from the man who had set her up from the very beginning.

He promised to help me escape from my past.

As the tears clouded her vision, she ran as hard as she could, careful to not trip in the mud or collide with a tree.

He used my past against me.

The surroundings began to blur even more, so she slowed down. Her legs felt like rubber. She couldn't trust them any more than she could trust Vasy. Tears poured down her face, mixing in with the sweat, burning away the numbness.

Alex is in danger.

She finally tripped over a rock, but when she glanced back at the offending obstacle, all she saw was a pebble. It made her laugh like a maniac, bringing her to knees. She laughed so hard that she feared she might lose control of her bladder—*I'm going to piss myself!*—rolling over onto her back staring up at the clouds through the confusion of interlaced branches and groping trees. She wondered what it had possibly meant when the female voice on the recording—*was she the mistress?*—had worried about the shifting winds.

At last, Allana couldn't think anymore. She closed her eyes and the words from the Dove chocolate came into clear focus as her grip opened and the shifting wind blew the wrapper out of her hand.

Through her blurry gaze, she saw those words get eaten by the breeze, yet she managed to find comfort in them now.

Temptation is fun... surrendering is even better.

# # #

Chapter 37

She woke in the dark hotel room of her nightmares, the one with the portraits of Lenin on the wall, the portraits with the miniature camera-shutter eyes. Groggy and confused, Allana searched her surroundings and noticed the dark mud on the bed sheets. As her eyes adjusted to the darkness, she spotted the figure in the chair in the corner, watching her.

"How did I get here?" she whispered, afraid but noticing that she wasn't tied or bound or hurt.

The figure didn't move.

The figure was asleep, she concluded. But she didn't know for how long. And she also didn't know whether she should trust the sleeping figure, regardless of whether it was Vasy or Alex (and she figured it was Alex).

"He knows," Allana said, her voice still raspy and quiet. She cleared her throat and the sleeping figure startled awake. "He knows everything."

"He knows what?" Alex asked, wiping his sleeve across his face as he leaned forward in his chair, into the rays of moonlight that cut through the darkness.

From her position on the bed, Allana saw that he had aged in the weeks since she'd given him that key. There was growth on his face, pockets around his red, bulging eyes, and a weary sound in his voice.

The key not only changed me, but it changed Alex as well.

"What did you find in his mistress's apartment, Alex?" she asked.

He stared back at her with a blank intensity that felt unfamiliar to her, the kind that belonged to hatred and confusion. To Allana's eyes, he looked lost.

"Do you know who she is?" she asked, her voice cracking.

Alex looked away before rubbing his hands down his face and standing up. He walked to the desk where he had fucked her from behind, the desk at the window where the curtains were pulled shut except for that three-inch gap through which the moon shone. Alex pulled the curtains open a little more so that the lights from Lenin Square illuminated the room, causing Allana to squint.

"Who is she, Alex?" she asked.

"Why do you care so damn much?" he asked, his back to her.

She didn't have an answer to that. *I don't know, but I do.*

"He's not your husband." He paused, staring out at whatever activity was going on in the town square at this time of night. "I want to know why you care so much about him, Allana."

She wanted to know, too. Vasy's betrayal hurt. And not just his betrayal of her, but to Soviet people. Even after all he'd done to her, Allana still cared for Vasy. Maybe she saw something hopeful in those soft eyes when he looked at her, maybe she cared because they'd been in love once, and she wanted to see that man again.

"Alex," she said, her voice a stern whisper, "who is the other woman?"

Alex hung his head and shook it slowly before turning around. He crossed his arms over his chest and leaned coolly against the edge of the desk, the edge she had gripped while he'd nudged her legs farther apart before taking her and capturing it all on film.

"Alex..."

Still shaking his head, he admitted, "There was no other woman,

Allana."

Her eyebrows furrowed.

"The apartment was nearly empty. There was furniture in the kitchen, a place where six people could eat a light meal. And a bigger table in the next room, something you'd buy upstairs at the supermarket for a farm house."

Gulping, she asked, "And the bedrooms?"

Alex shrugged, shaking his head as he seemed to struggle with his own confusion. "I think they knew I was coming, Lana. Somehow they knew, because the bedrooms were empty. All the furniture, or boxes or files or whatever occupied those rooms, had been moved out." His face darkened. "How is that possible, Lana? What did you tell Vasy?"

"I didn't tell him anything," she said, shaking her head. "Why would I? I thought it was his mistress's apartment, even after I showed up and saw it for myself."

He stared at her, his eyes narrowing. "Someone knew because there was a mess in the tub. Shards of plastic. Pieces of broken record albums," he went on. "He tried to burn them, and for the most part, he succeeded because none of them could be salvaged."

She swallowed the heavy lump in her throat. "Did you put that record together for me?"

He simply stared back at her, like maybe he hadn't heard what she said.

Gradually, the final fingers of fog from the sleeping pills drew away from her head and she came to a sick and crazy realization. She asked him the question she should have asked when she first saw him sitting in that chair. "Alex, did you leave the newspaper and key outside my apartment door this morning?"

Alex frowned and now he looked confused, too. "What key?"

"Did you, Alex?" she demanded, her voice a little higher pitched with panic.

Alex unfolded his arms and reached into his pants pocket, then pulled something out. "This key?"

# # #

After taking a shower to get the mud out of her hair and changing the sheets to get the mud out of the bed, Allana slid under the comforter and curled next to Alex, their butts almost touching. It was four in the morning on Good Friday, two days before Easter, and she couldn't help but wonder about the mess that had become her life. Look at her—in bed with this man, a man she barely knew (yes, just like ole times back in Detroit, those post-James, post-baby days) while the man that had saved her and helped her escape from that very same past turned out to be no better than any of the others.

Yes, Vasy had used her. She could acknowledge that now that the shock had settled and she could admit it to herself.

"Are you okay?" Alex grumbled, glancing back over his shoulder. "You're tossing and turning a lot."

"Sorry," she said, then rolled onto her back so she could stare straight at the ceiling. She'd already warned Alex to not try anything. She was in no mood, and when he made no argument and stuck to his side, she estimated that he was in no mood either.

After all, he knew that he'd been used, too. "When Vasy sent you to the apartment, it was because he knew I'd already been there," Alex mumbled.

Allana let out a deep, long breath. "Why did he bother sending me there? Why not confront me in person? Why not put an end to this whole charade? Instead he let me hear it on the record? It doesn't make sense to me." She felt her chest tighten at the memory of her and Vasy a couple of nights ago, cuddled up on the sofa with Vasy's arms around her. Despite what she'd done with Alex, Allana had loved him then, and Vasy had loved her back. Or so she thought, because all of this had already been in motion since February.

"Did you read the *Tribuna Energetika*?" Alex asked.

She punched him in the back, right between the shoulders. "I can't read it, it's not English!"

"Sorry, I forgot," he mumbled. He rolled his shoulders as if that might help with the pain, and then turned onto his other side so that he was facing her. "It published an article about the poor workmanship at the power station. The missing and defective materials. Does any of that sound familiar?"

"The reports Gregor took from the power station," she whispered.

"Yes. So now Vasy and his group have their outlet. A new reporter, a woman named Lyubov Kovalevska who now has a big target on her back. Lucky it's Easter weekend, she'd be dead already."

Allana's head spun. She wondered why Vasy would do this. And then it hit her… had he expected her to run to Alex once she heard the recording on the album? If so, then he knew she was spending the night with him now, didn't he? "How did he know any of this would unravel the way it did? How did he know that you and I would become friends like we did?"

Alex frowned. "Is that what you heard on the album?"

She nodded. "Yeah."

They lay in silence. Part of her wanted Alex to touch her, to pull her into his arms and make her feel safe again. She wanted him to promise he would pick up the pieces that Vasy had let fall. She wanted to be saved. Again.

"He knew you and I would have a romantic relationship even before we did," Allana said. "That's what I heard. It was all part of his plan."

Alex rolled over, putting his back to her. "I'm tired, Allana. I need some sleep before I meet my liaison in Kiev."

She couldn't help but wonder if that was such a good idea. Obviously Vasy and his other "agents" were keeping a watchful eye on Alex.

"They're setting you up."

Alex sighed. "Of course they are. It's the only thing that will keep them alive."

She thought about that until it made sense to her... by setting up Alex, they were expecting him to take the fall for what they were planning to do at the power station. But by the time she figured that out, Alex was asleep and she could barely open her own eyes.

# # #

Chapter 38

Allana spent Easter Sunday and the entire week that followed in Alex's private hotel room. Alone and scared. She would call room service when she needed to eat, and one of two hotel employees (depending on the time of day) would deliver the meals without question. When she needed exercise, she would run circles in the room, running around the chair, jumping up and over the bed, and repeating the little obstacle course until she broke a sweat and her muscles burned. Sometimes, she would do push-ups—not the cheating kind either—with her feet up on the desk chair and her arms pushing her off the edge of the bed. She didn't know if it was the isolation or some other physical *need* that inspired the exercise, but it always felt good.

Sometimes, when things got really boring and she'd already gone through the obstacle course a few times, she would watch the propaganda channel on the television; it showed beautiful, scenic images of the Soviet Ukraine, even though she never understood what they were saying.

And then there was the one English television channel. Every night at dinnertime, she would watch the *Young and the Restless* from three years ago while eating room service. She needed to hear voices to stay sane.

By the time she reached the end of that week, Allana was stunned into boredom with the looping images on the propaganda channel. So she would stand at the desk where she'd last had sex, and pull open the curtains to watch the activity in Lenin Square. She'd play the game that Alex had prompted that sunny day not so long ago—*if you could be anyone in the square, who would you be?* Particularly the children entertained her the most. The kids were always pointing at the amusement park, and she swore she could hear them begging their parents to make May Day come quicker. Like it was Christmas and they'd never seen a Ferris wheel before.

She'd managed to completely quit smoking too, and the daily sickness and stress ended. She believed it was her little obstacle course that had made that happen.

Her period ended as well.

But she didn't blame that on the new exercise routine. She would tell Alex about it once he came back, tonight or tomorrow.

#

By April 6th, Allana had run so many laps in the room, watched so many loops of the propaganda channel, and heard so many whiny children in the hallway and in Lenin Square below that she began to lose her mind. It had been ten days, and Alex still hadn't returned from Kiev. He was two days late now, and this bothered her.

After so long in solitary confinement, she began speaking to the hidden cameras in Lenin's eye, or the one on the desk, or the one above the bed. Just in case Alex was watching from some other room.

But he never came back.

She began to wonder if he might be dead.

So on Sunday, Allana made a decision. She felt brave enough to venture out of the room, so she walked down the hall to the luxury elevator and down to the extravagant lobby with its marble floors and brass accents. She stopped at the front desk and asked if they could produce another room key, but they refused. They said she wasn't listed as a guest on Mr. Petrokov's registration form, so she wasn't entitled to a key.

With no way to get back into the room, Allana left the hotel anyway. She didn't care, she needed out. She nodded at one of the bellhops, a guy she recognized from serving her meals through room service, and he smiled and nodded back.

"I'll be back," she promised.

He continued to smile and nod, as if he didn't understand English or want to acknowledge her as Alex's dirty little secret.

Out in Lenin Square, she walked to the fence and squeezed in between a few of those over-excited kids she'd been watching from her room window. The kids seemed to idolize the workers as they tested the Devil's Wheel, replacing damaged lights in the bumper cars and setting up and testing other rides. Back home in the States, a celebration this big would happen on July 4th.

When she turned around, she thought she saw Alex's face in a crowd of people walking toward the Energetik. Smiling, Allana spun away from the fence and started toward that crowd, running ahead onto the front steps of the Energetik and searching the men's faces as they walked past her. But she didn't find Alex among them. She held herself back from shouting his name.

Discouraged, she followed the rest of the people inside and climbed upstairs to the second level where it was a little quieter, less busy. She was bummed that she hadn't found Alex, but then she remembered that today was Vasy's exercise day. From this angle, she should be able to see him enter the building.

But no, she had a better idea. She walked through to the back door, the one that led to the rear parking lot where Vasy always parked their blue car. *Does he miss me?* Interestingly, it wasn't there.

"Where, oh where might you be, Mr. Vasy?" she whispered under her breath. Then again, maybe he couldn't think of exercising while she was absent.

But then she spotted Vasy's car turning into the back lot.

Curious, she stepped back inside the building and nearly trampled over a teen and his girlfriend. The girl said *"vy idiot,"* which wasn't too difficult for Allana to translate.

Feeling the adrenaline pumping, she ran to the second floor and watched Vasy enter the building with his gym bag slung over his shoulder. He looked around as he strutted toward the men's change room. Part of her felt disappointed that he could maintain his routine, but what had she been expecting?

A minute later, just before Allana was ready to turn and head to the swimming pool's viewing deck, she noticed Mrs. Perfect. She entered the building through the same door as Vasy and there was an older man with her. Both of them carried gym bags that looked a lot like Vasy's, except with one difference.

They had red handles.

Or maybe that wasn't the difference. She groaned, unable to remember whether Vasy had just entered the Energetik with a red-handled bag or not. Maybe it didn't matter, but she found it strange that all three of them had similar bags. And it no longer felt like a lovers thing, where they have the same bag to look cute. It felt... bigger than that, especially as she watched them all disappear into their respective change rooms.

Allana knew that watching from the pool's wide-open observation deck might result in Vasy seeing her. But she didn't care at that point. She wanted to confront him. She had a few questions for him anyway. Like why he always said he loved her more. How could he say that, only to turn around and do what he did.

Disgusted, she suddenly changed her mind about sticking around.

Bolting from her seat, Allana headed straight for the exits when she noticed Vasy stepping out from the men's change room. The old man, the one that had accompanied Mrs. Perfect, exited the change room with him. Even though he was considerably older, the old man carried on a conversation with Vasy like they brothers, all familiar smiles and back-handed shoulder slaps. Yet, despite both of them owning similar gym bags and wearing black Speedos, they looked nothing alike.

But they do *know each other.* She could see it in their body language, their close proximity, the banter as they slipped into the water.

When Mrs. Perfect entered the pool area, she joined the two men at the corner, easing her too-perfectly curved ass into the water backwards like she had last time. And like last time, Vasy didn't seem to notice.

Quickly, Allana searched the other swimmers for the blonde, but she wasn't there.

Frowning, Allana realized that Vasy and Mrs. Perfect knew each another, but they certainly weren't having an affair. If they were, why would Vasy have not even acknowledged her? It seemed too convenient, too contrived.

As Vasy and the old man finished their conversation and began their stretches and warm-ups in their respective lanes, Allana finally pushed open the observation deck door and slipped out where the air was less stuffy and warm. But she didn't stick around to enjoy it; she left the Energetik at a light jog and ran home, back to the apartment she shared with Vasy.

# # #

Allana knew that Vasy was only twenty or so minutes into his lengths, but she was still careful about unlocking her apartment door and easing it open. Like he might leap out at her. Poking her head inside, she listened for signs of him. Or someone else. When she heard nothing but silence, she finally stepped in and, slowly and carefully, closed and locked the door.

The kitchen appeared exactly as she remembered it, except with more dishes stacked in the sink, waiting for her to come home and clean them. Vasy had always claimed to be allergic to doing the dishes manually, maybe he hadn't been lying about that. *Jerk.* The living area also seemed unoccupied. She wandered down the short hallway to the master bedroom and found that the bed was unmade, and the Dove chocolate was no longer on the floor where she'd dropped it on her side of the bed.

Walking around to Vasy's side, she saw the bottle of vodka on the floor, along with an open pack of Sobranies next to one of their better crystal drinking glasses with ashes and cigarette filters in it.

"Jesus, Vasy," she hissed, a little disgusted. She couldn't decide whether he was falling apart because of her absence, or he'd always been a natural bachelor.

Disgusted, she left the master bedroom and headed to the second bedroom at the other end of the apartment, grabbing one of the chairs from the kitchen table on her way. She wanted to get into that box of record albums again, but when she entered the walk-in closet she stopped short at the sight of the gym bag.

It had red handles.

Why did Vasy need two gym bags all of a sudden? She knew this one didn't belong to the other woman from the pool—she'd seen Mrs. Perfect carrying her own version of this bag—so, what did this mean?

Forgetting about the chair, Allana dropped to her knees to open the gym bag. Inside, she found an album, along with three audio reels like the ones she'd seen in Alex's closet upstairs, or the one she'd spotted on Gregor's dresser. The album belonged to *The Captain and Tennille*, the one where they sit in a sauna, half-naked with Tennille showing off her long, freshly waxed legs. Her father had owned that same album.

When Allana slid the vinyl out of the sleeve, she noticed that its label was missing. Just like Billy Joel's was. Which reminded her…

Pocketing the smaller audio reels from the bag, Allana positioned the chair underneath the shelf, in such a way that she could reach the box of albums. When she pulled the box down, she reached inside and studied each of the albums. She expected to find at least one of those sleeves to be holding another blank album.

But they all had labels.

What the hell is going on here? she wondered.

And then she heard the door opening and a voice calling out, "Honey! I'm home!"

# # #

Chapter 39

Allana listened past the pounding in her ears, and tried to locate where the female intruder might be. But the apartment was so incredibly quiet that even under the other woman's weight, the floors offered no hints as to her whereabouts. It didn't make sense that someone would be here while Vasy was out swimming lengths. And, based on the time, he should still be in the pool for at least twenty more minutes.

And then Allana heard the woman whistling.

Kitchen. She's in the kitchen.

A cupboard door opened and closed. Then the refrigerator door opened and closed. Like maybe this woman had been here before because she knew exactly where to look to pour herself a glass of water or milk.

Maybe she'd even been here the entire time Allana hid out at the Hotel Polissia in Alex's room.

Maybe even before...

Who is this bitch in my apartment?

Taking a deep, frustrated breath, Allana crept to the closet's open door and peeked out into the second bedroom. She couldn't see into the apartment's main area from this angle, but it gave her a better vantage point to listen in. Whatever she was doing here, she hadn't come to rob them. She'd come because she'd been before.

Now Allana wanted to hurt her. Make her bleed. If she could give

Alex a bloody nose, she could certainly break the other woman's face.

The sound of a cup slipping into the kitchen sink told her that the intruder had finished drinking whatever it was she'd poured from the refrigerator. So Allana eased back into the closet, like one of those fish cowering back into the anemone where they live. Just in case this woman decided to come snooping around.

And she listened.

When she heard the bathroom door at the end of the short hall on the other side of the apartment, she felt relieved and also a little insulted—*who is this woman who thinks she lives here?*

Allana started to plan for an escape. She closed her eyes and listened a little harder, and when the shower water started, she tiptoed out of the closet and into the bedroom. At the next doorway, she could see into the vacant living room and spotted another gym bag on the edge of the sofa. It also had red handles—*which meant the whistling either came from the old guy from the pool, or from Mrs. Perfect... Jesus, that wasn't too obvious!* Now she really wanted to break that bitch's face and make her bleed.

Allana didn't waste too much time analyzing the bag's design qualities.

With Mrs. Perfect in the shower, Allana decided to bolt from the apartment and hurried through the kitchen, passing the kitchen sink—*let that bitch clean the fucking dishes*—and that was when she noticed that none of the other glasses had lipstick on the rim.

And another thing: Allana's own boots were on the welcome mat.

Mrs. Perfect hadn't noticed them?

What about the bedroom, the unmade bed, the smokes and bottle of vodka on the floor next to it?

Allana started to ease her feet into her boots, half confused by the whole scene when she sensed movement in the corner of her eye. Snapping her head to the left, she glanced toward the bathroom where Mrs. Perfect was showering. The door was closed and Allana heard whistling again.

Except Allana wasn't *paying attention.*

Because while she stared down that hall, she couldn't see Vasy creeping up behind her. With a gag in his hand. A gag soaked in chloroform that he promptly placed over her face as he restrained her with those big, hard arms that had previously made her feel like the safest woman in the world.

"I always knew you'd come back," he grunted as Allana's eyes rolled back and the rest of the world faded to black.

# # #

When she regained consciousness, Allana realized she was at the kitchen table. Her hands were bound behind her back, through the rails of the wooden chair. Lifting her head, she opened her eyes and discovered that Vasy was sitting across from her with one of their sharpest cutting knives placed before him. His eyes studied her the way they always had, which made her sad because she finally understood that all of this time, she'd misunderstood that look in them. She'd thought that was the look of compassion and love but this was nowhere near those things. This was torture. Cold, calculating and evil.

When Vasy saw that her eyes kept jumping to the knife, he chuckled like a psychopath. For some reason, she remembered the vodka next to the bed and the cigarette filters and ashes in the cup right next to it. *He's lost his mind. And now I'm going to die.*

"Allana, Allana, Allana," he practically sang, shaking his head. "You still don't know me, what I'm capable of and how far I will go, do you?"

Her chin quivered, but the tears she barely noticed. She'd cried so much over what she'd discovered about Vasy that this hardly counted. And combined with the comments and the woman that had distracted her earlier, the knife aroused a tinge of worry about Alex. Allana wondered what Vasy had done with him.

"Who is she?" Allana asked.

"'She?'" He smiled, his eyes growing wide. "There's nobody else, Allana."

Lies. She didn't believe him. How could she believe anything he said anymore? "All you've ever done is lie to me."

Grabbing the knife, Vasy waved it at her. "This? I'm not going to hurt you, Allana. No matter how much you broke my heart." He shook his head at her, and she noticed the broken spirit behind those eyes of his. "The knife was for the peach." He leaned over and reached under the table to pick up the pit, shrugging.

"Fuck you," she spat. "You killed me when you brought me here!"

"Coming here was what you wanted," he answered in a calm voice that could only belong to a calculated, heartless liar and killer.

"You used me, you played me, you lied and cheated and…" Allana wept some more. "Why, Vasy?"

He stared back with his cold, broken eyes for a fraction of a second before glancing away and shaking his head. "Cheated? I've already told you, there's nobody else. Just you. It's always been you."

"You're lying to me!" she screamed, thrashing in the chair and pulling at the plastic ties that bound her hands together. "I saw her! I heard her!"

Vasy shook his head. "I wish I were lying. There's never been anyone else."

Allana calmed down as the ties cut into her wrists. They hurt. The chair hurt, too. And her head hurt. "Where's Alex?"

With that same stone-cold face, he stared back at her. Despite that poker party in January where Vasy couldn't bluff his way out of a box, his poker face stunned her now. He gave no clues. So she assumed the worst.

"Why?" she asked, her eyes spilling tears once again. "Why would you do this to me? Of all the people, why would you..." She surrendered to the tears.

"Was he good in bed, Allana?" Vasy asked at last, tilting his head to the side.

"I hate you," she cried. "You're a monster."

Vasy didn't speak again until she finally calmed down, which felt like an eternity. The sun, which stayed out later these days, began to fade outside the window behind her back. She couldn't see it, but she knew the power station's lights were on, the red blink on the reactor towers, the bright white ones just over the tree line. She'd watched those lights many times, wondering if Vasy could see her standing at the balcony door, watching and waiting for him to come home and drown out her boredom after his twelve-hour workday.

"I didn't force you to spread your legs," Vasy said, still with that same calmness in his voice.

Allana wept some more. "You don't know what you're talking about."

"Yes, I do. I have photos from your visits to his hotel room."

She blinked, shocked. Alex...? Why would he have given them to Vasy?

He offered a sick grin. "So I *do* know what I'm talking about. I *do* know what you've done."

She gulped, then she cried for a long time. Not from being caught, but because she never wanted to hurt this man.

"You put me in that room," she snarled, but the venom in her voice had diluted. "Everything, from forcing us together to making him befriend me, you pushed me there, Vasy. Why would you do that to me? Why would you pretend you were saving me, only to abandon me once we got here and push me onto Alex?"

At that, he snapped his hand down on the table, causing her to jump and the color in his eyes to cloud into a shade of rage. "I never asked you to sleep with him! You're a whore! You cheating whore! And you whine about me breaking your heart?"

Staring back at him with her puffy, red eyes, it was now Allana's turn to shake her head and use a soft voice that made her sound like a psychopath. "You partnered me with the only man who paid attention to me. While you were out sneaking into secret apartments and smoking cigars with Gregor and who knows what else you did—"

"For you! It was all for you!" he shouted, shoving back from the table so hard that it skidded into her ribs and his chair toppled over. Vasy grabbed the knife and threw it at the wall in the living room before letting out a roar and ripping at his hair. Once he stopped acting like a monkey, Vasy looked lost. Angry and lost as he rushed to her side of the table and grabbed her by the collar, lifting both her and the chair off the ground.

Allana held her breath, worrying she might piss her pants.

"I loved you." His words seethed past his white, tight lips. "I did everything I promised."

Releasing his grip, the chair toppled sideways onto the floor. Allana landed on her side, pain roaring through her shoulder, down her arm and across her ribs. From her sideways perspective, she watched Vasy pacing in the living room. And she cried some more.

She'd never cried so much. Even after James, even after her stillborn baby, even after everyone else in her life had abandoned her. Now this was no different, she'd been fooled once again.

"Who are you?" she sobbed.

He stopped pacing and pointed a stern finger at her, admitting, "I'm the one man that loved you more."

"Vasy, you have some horrible secrets," she said, ignoring the bullshit out of his mouth because she knew he'd never cared for her. Ever. "You worked so many hours. That's not how people love one another. And this stupid thing, with you making me keep an eye on Alex, it's your faul—"

He roared as he rushed back into the kitchen area, grabbing the edge of the table and turning it over before dropping to his knees right beside her. She could tell he wanted to hurt her. "Those secrets kept you the safest you'll ever be in your life," he hissed through his clenched teeth. "And Alex... next you'll tell me I was the one that bent you over that desk for him to fuck you!"

She closed her eyes against his rage.

Vasy reached out, seized her shirt and pulled her upright, back into a seated position. Still with her eyes clamped shut, she heard the scraping of the overturned table against the floor, and then another chair getting pulled up in front of her.

"Look at me," he demanded.

"Not when you're like this," she told him, a whine to her tone.

"Look at me!" he repeated, more forcefully this time.

Allana opened her eyes and saw just how angry he was. She'd never seen him like this. She was scared; he'd already toppled the chair, what else could he do in this state?

Maybe he wanted to pause before launching into his next rampage, or maybe her tears slowed him down, talked him off that ledge a little. Because when he spoke next, his voice had taken on a strange calm. He was a different man, not only onto a new chapter but a new book altogether it seemed. This wasn't the Vasy she'd met in college.

"You have a choice to make, Allana. You can go home, which causes some degree of problems for me at work and with some of my colleagues at the power station."

"Problems?" she asked, letting out a humorless laugh. She made a show of looking over her shoulders at her arms that were tied behind her back, through the chair.

He nodded. "They'll want to know what happened to you, of course, and I'll have to explain why you went back to America. Except nobody can just pack up and get on a plane to the States here. So that's a problem, a big problem."

She laughed again, more maniacal this time. "Let's talk about problems, Vasy. Or…let's talk about what I heard on the album in your secret apartment. Or…how about those secrets themselves? Why can't we talk about *those* problems?"

As if he might be considering her suggestion, he frowned. But after a few seconds of deliberation, he sat back in his chair and ran his hands through his hair.

"I can't trust you," he said, groaning. "You know enough to get a lot of people killed, and I don't believe that you won't shoot your mouth off to the wrong person. Like Alex." He paused, and the sound of Alex's name made her nervous. "So," he continued with a knowing smirk, "maybe going home is the best option for you."

"Vasy…" she started with a whine to her voice. "You knew from the start that I would go to Alex."

"And now Alex is gone." Again, he mentioned Alex. But this time, she bit.

"Gone?" she asked, her voice pitched high with worry. "What happened to him?"

Vasy shrugged. "I don't know. I don't care." He sighed next, and then he leaned forward, placing his elbows on his knees and holding his head up with his hands. "But what I do know is that he left the Hotel Polissia and ran to Kiev. Most likely, he's talked to Vitali Sklyarov or someone else on his staff, probably just about anyone who'll show the patience to listen to him." Vasy shrugged again, raising both elbows like it was anyone's guess. "And this time, he'll have evidence. With the *Literaturna* article last week, it's likely someone has listened to him. But who?" Another two-shoulder shrug. "Alex is a freelancer, a hobbyist, and if he talked to the wrong person about everything that he saw, heard, knows… it's difficult to say if he'll ever be back for you, Allana." He gave a sad facial expression, as authentic as their marriage license.

Allana knew she'd had a difficult relationship with Alex. Notwithstanding the seduction, bribery, abuse, revenge sex, and everything else, Allana couldn't help but acknowledge that, unlike Vasy, Alex was most likely telling the truth when he'd claimed to love her. She hadn't been a choice, not to Alex. And he always opened his arms to her, always took her back, always kept *trying*. Allana wanted to close her eyes and cry again, but she came up dry.

"*That's* why I paired you with Alex," he said. "So you could keep him here. Keep him within reach. Keep him out of harm's way with whatever he happened to find, *including* the things you might have told him and the things I wanted him to know."

"You used me," she said, her voice cracking. It hurt because if she had known about Vasy's plans, she would have done a better job. She'd believed he loved her this whole time. She would have assassinated Gorbachev if he'd asked nicely enough. "You used me, and I would have done anything for you."

His eyes widened in disbelief. "Yeah?"

She nodded, insistent. "Absolutely."

"You would have helped me figure out a way to decommission the power station and risk the lives of fifty thousand people, maybe even several *million* people? Innocent people who might not understand why they're all dying of radiation poisoning which, I'm told, is a painful and horrible way to die? You'd have done that?"

Allana couldn't help but wonder how serious he was. "What are you talking about? The power station is everything to these people, and when you start talking like this, I don't know if I should be afraid of you, or proud of you." She shook her head, trying to get rid of the ringing that was screaming between her ears. "Tell me what you're planning do, Vasy."

His lips curled upward. "I can't. Because, like I said two minutes ago, I can't trust you."

Suddenly, there was a knock at the door. Vasy allowed his glare to linger for a moment before heading back through the kitchen to answer it. Allana waited in the kitchen for their guest to arrive, and if she hadn't been tied to the chair, she would have fallen out of it as Vasy appeared with his guest.

"Nice to finally meet you," Mrs. Perfect said with a guilty but wide smirk. And her voice… Allana recognized it, but couldn't remember where. "Vasy has told me so much about you, and your friend Alex, and he's shown me—"

"Go to hell," Allana spat. *It's you, you're the one that made herself feel at home and then distracted me with that shower.*

Mrs. Perfect glanced over at Vasy, still smiling. "Please don't tell me you'll be long."

He said something back to her in Ukrainian so that Allana couldn't understand, and judging by the vicious sneer on Mrs. Perfect's face, it probably wasn't very flattering.

And that was when Allana realized where she knew that voice: the recording she played on the RCA record player.

#

Allana said she needed to go to the bathroom, hoping Mrs. Perfect might cut the ties around her wrist. But all that psycho bitch did was lean her back in the chair, drag her to the bathroom, and lift her into the luxury shower, positioning the chair directly over the drain.

"You can piss yourself in here," Mrs. Perfect said and then left.

"That won't be very comfortable," Allana shouted back at her.

Mrs. Perfect returned, leaning one arm against the doorframe and staring her down. "You really have to pee?"

Allana shrugged. "Could be something else, too."

Rolling her eyes, the other woman re-entered the bathroom, made sure Allana's ties were still tightly secured behind the chair, and then came around the front. She reached forward and unbuttoned Allana's jeans before hooking her fingers around the waist of the pants.

"What are you doing?" Allana asked. "Stripping me?"

Mrs. Perfect gave a curt nod. "Yeah, to make things more comfortable for you."

"No!" Allana screamed back. "No, no, no!"

"I've seen you completely naked in those photos," Mrs. Perfect confessed. "So how about you help me get you out of these pants before you soil them?"

Allana considered the offer, then admitted, "I don't have to go anymore."

Releasing the waist of her pants, Mrs. Perfect walked to the sink and washed her hands; Allana interpreted that as an insult.

"What's your relationship with Vasy?"

With an emotionless stare, she gave Allana an uncaring shrug. "Should I bring you out to the main area, or leave you in here?"

"Bring me out," Allana said.

Mrs. Perfect dragged her back out to the living area.

"About Vasy…" Allana continued after a pause.

Mrs. Perfect turned on the television to a Soviet channel before dropping back onto the sofa. Like she'd been here before. *Or called at 3am and talked to Vasy while he sat on that very same sofa.*

"You know, I figured out the two of you knew each other at the pool," Allana admitted. "The way you both worked hard at ignoring each other that day, I figured you were acquainted."

Mrs. Perfect whistled; she'd surely won whistling contests as a child. "That's impressive."

"How long?"

Her eyebrows rose. "Pardon me?"

"How long have you been sleeping together?"

Mrs. Perfect chuckled for a heartbeat before frowning at the television. "Shhh," she said. "This is getting good."

Allana focused on the television and saw that it was a commercial for Obolon, the Ukrainian beer. *Yeah, you bet this is getting good.*

"So, G zero two four," Allana started, hoping she remembered her agent number correctly, "when are we going to blow up the power station?"

Mrs. Perfect laughed, unfazed at Allana's comment. She pointed at the television. "That was hilarious! Did you see that?"

"Oscar-worthy." Allana rolled her eyes.

"So," the other woman said, turning her calculating, steel-cold stare onto Allana, "tell me something, Allana Harrison from Detroit, Michigan, who grew up in a little townhouse complex off of Lafayette Street, if my memory serves correctly."

Allana looked away.

"Your father, Gerry, worked at one of the automotive paint factories in town. Bit of a drinker, I believe?"

Allana shrugged. *How did she know?*

"Had a tough time making it through the week without spending some of the rent money on cheap beer. And your mother—Betty, wasn't it?"

"Elizabeth," Allana mumbled.

"Yes, well she couldn't hold down a job any easier than you could hold down James, even after you delivered his dead baby."

Allana's face burned with the same kind of rage that she'd seen on Vasy's face earlier. *Vasy had shared all of her secrets with this bitch, hadn't he?*

Mrs. Perfect sat up and stared at Allana with eyes as hard and cold as the marble floors in the lobby of the Hotel Polissia. "You think you're good at reading people, huh? Because Vasy and I avoided eye contact at the Energetik? And now you think you're smart enough to step into the middle of this? Really?" She added a condescending huff, something out of a high school cafeteria.

"It's Detroit," Allana half-mumbled. Detroit had been the hub of the industrial world; at some point, it couldn't feed the world's demand for cars. "This is Pripyat, and it has a chance."

"And it's dying, Allana. Just like Detroit is dying. Twenty years from now, you won't recognize either place." Mrs. Perfect raised a single eyebrow. "You have the foresight of a mole and the intellect of a rat. And that, my dear, makes you extremely predictable."

Her stomach tightened, her throat constricted, her eyes welled up. She hated to admit it, but this bitch was right; she'd been extremely predictable. It was what attracted Vasy to her, right from the onset.

"Let me help you," Mrs. Perfect offered. "After you went missing, Vasy knew you would eventually track him down. We all did. We saw you at the pool. We saw you in Lenin Square. We saw you in Alex's hotel room, staring out the window and wishing you could run around, free like the rest of the people."

"And the bags," Allana pointed out. She suddenly remembered Vasy at Gregor's, that time in February when she'd followed him to the apartment and watched him bring one bag back to his car before returning to the building with another. *He'd always had two bags.* "I know about the bags."

Mrs. Perfect clapped without the slightest hint of enthusiasm. "Wow, that's amazing. I'm glad I'm sitting down for this. Just blown away that you figured out our convenient and efficient courier system in this restrictive and highly corrupt environment." She nodded toward the kitchen. "You ever wonder how Vasy knew so much about your relationship with Alex?"

Allana stared toward the kitchen, but realized that she hadn't been to Alex's apartment since the American spies had hard-wired the surveillance equipment using the exhaust vent above the stove.

Mrs. Perfect chuckled. "Oh, dear. I know you haven't visited his apartment since you moved in, but that doesn't mean your amateur sleuth didn't create a shrine to you." She chuckled some more, leaning even closer to Allana in her chair as she narrowed her eyes. "Vasy's a good man, Allana. Better than you ever realized. Better than you'll ever see again."

"He's a cheater. A liar. A selfish manipulator. The worst kind of person to exist." He was worse than all of those things if he intended on destroying the power station and poisoning all of the people in Pripyat.

"No," Mrs. Perfect insisted. "No, you're confused. You're the cheater. Vasy loved you the same way he would have if you were his real wife. He was devoted to you in a way that you could never commit to any single man. That's Vasy, he gives one hundred percent, even when it's something he might not fully believe." She sighed before reclining back in the sofa. "So go ahead and give yourself a pat on the back for figuring out the very things that Vasy and the rest of us wanted you to figure out. But you also need to take responsibility for being blind to the most obvious thing in all of this."

"Vasy's twisted view on monogamy?" Allana spat.

Mrs. Perfect shook her head, annoyed. "Even more obvious than that."

At last, Allana knew what she was talking about. And she was right; so right, in fact, that Allana couldn't hold it in any longer. The bile forced its way up, and Allana vomited all over the floor, sick with the thought that she'd never changed after all, that in her big escape from her past, all she'd managed was to change the scenery.

"Jesus," Mrs. Perfect scorned. "Get yourself together, dear. It's not like it's a huge surprise. You've always been a whore."

# # #

Chapter 40

It was the following morning when Vasy returned home, a gym bag with red handles over his shoulder. Allana had fallen asleep in the hard, uncomfortable kitchen chair, her legs and ass had gone numb and her neck kinked from hanging her head. When she glanced over at Mrs. Perfect on the sofa, she saw that her prison guard had also fallen asleep. Allana shook her head. But when the other woman heard the main door open, she rolled off the cushions and stood up like she hadn't even blinked once.

Bitch.

"Don't move," Mrs. Perfect warned as she left the room and followed Vasy to the second bedroom.

From the living room, Allana heard them speaking in Ukrainian, most likely so Allana couldn't understand what they were saying. As if she might cause trouble. In her head, she heard Mrs. Perfect whistle at her for making that deduction.

But Vasy was always a dozen or so steps ahead of her. He'd known how she would get along with Alex, known she would develop a soft spot for him. He'd known she would eventually come home after running off like she had—he'd obviously known to look for her at the Energetik yesterday, too, which led Allana to conclude that whatever they were talking about, they couldn't allow her to know about it because then she might be on the same level as them. In other words, it was important stuff.

Vasy was the first to appear in the living room. He looked tired, big bags underneath his eyes, with shadows, and lines in areas of his face that had never been there before, and his ratty t-shirt looking worse than normal. When he stopped in front of her chair, he crossed his arms and frowned down at her.

"I need your help, Allana," he said, keeping his voice quiet and calm. "Either I send you home and we never see one another again, or I keep you around and we figure this out." The way his face lit up a little, she wanted to believe he wanted to figure this out with her. But...

She stared back at him, and then noticed Mrs. Perfect hovering at the foyer, now wearing her jacket and boots and ready to leave. Allana wanted to blow her a kiss, followed by her middle finger, but she bit down on her lip.

"I'm leaving," Mrs. Perfect said.

Good riddance.

Without glancing back at her, Vasy said goodbye. "See you in a few hours." Once Mrs. Perfect left, Vasy lowered himself to his knees. He didn't seem to care that he was close enough for her to kick him, but then again he would have predicted long ago that she wouldn't. "If I had a say in your decision," he said with big, hopeful eyes, and this moment reminded her of how she'd once hoped he might propose to her, "I'd like you to stay, Allana."

She swallowed. She wanted to believe she knew better, and maybe his hope that she might stay was nothing more than a nudge for her to leave. "Why?"

Vasy seemed to think about his response before answering her.

"The truth, Vasy. What's really going on here?" But if he wanted her to leave, why would he even give her the option in the first place?

"The truth?" he asked, his tone coming out small and a little tortured, like he felt guilt about all that he'd done. At last, Allana felt a sliver of hope. "If you leave, I don't know what will happen to you. I'm not ready for that." He gave a nod, still with his big eyes, but now he looked sad rather than hopeful.

She swallowed the lump in her throat. She believed him, and what he said frightened her. If she left and they hurt her, what would happen to Vasy?

"Plus I don't have time to come up with a believable reason to give people for why you left. You have no family or friends here, so they'll know you returned to the States. That will set off alarms because nobody can get a visa that quickly."

"But I'm an American," she argued.

Vasy's face tightened. "With that fake marriage certificate in the system, you've had to renounce your citizenship," he explained.

Allana's eyes nearly popped out of their sockets.

Sighing, Vasy placed a gentle hand on her knee. "And... if you stay..." He seemed hesitant.

"How did I renounce my citizenship?" she asked, barely able to breathe.

"Because I needed to stay," he said. "I'm sorry." He shook his head, but she didn't buy his fake, bullshit regret for one minute. "I couldn't have you leaving. And I still can't. Because if you stay...."

She hoped that he would say something sweet, something with the kind of hopeful promise he'd had when they first met.

Instead, he went on with, "If you stay, Alex might come back."

So there it was. The truth about what she now meant to the man she'd fallen so hard for, the one that had presented himself as her salvation all of those years ago. And, more than anything, she wanted to tell him off and leave. Her instinct wanted her to take her risks and flee, as far away as possible.

Don't be so predictable, don't give him what he wants. Give him the opposite.

With a tightness in her chest, throat and head, she gritted her teeth and allowed a nod. "I understand," she croaked, choking on hurt and tiredness. *Be strong. Be titanium.* Besides, just yesterday, she'd told Vasy that she would have helped him all along if she had known the truth. Now that she knew it, she had better follow through. It wasn't all about being less predictable, about doing the opposite of what he wanted, it was about staying true to her own word. Right? "I'll stay."

At last, Vasy heaved a deep breath and put his forehead down on her other knee. It used to drive her wild when his face came that close to her legs, but then again, if Allana believed what Mrs. Perfect had said, that type of arousal was something Vasy had used against her. *You're a whore.*

Allana no longer wanted to feel anything when he touched her. He'd betrayed her, ruined her, and now she had no choice.

"Can I have these ties removed?" she asked, staring down at his head. It surprised her that her voice came out smoother than she'd expected.

Vasy raised his head off her knee, and Allana detected a shred of hope in his eyes. "I can trust you?"

She bit her tongue before responding in a calm, level voice. "Yesterday, when I said I'd have helped you if I knew the truth, I meant it."

His eyes bore into hers, like he was a human lie detector.

"Besides, Vasy. What if I'd said I wanted to leave?" she asked, making a big show of rolling her eyes because she knew he'd have never been able to send her back. How could he?

"You'd have boarded a plane—"

"Like Gregor?" she asked before biting her tongue again. *Stay strong.*

"—and you'd have ended up somewhere in the States. With a house, probably on a military base somewhere. And a new name, probably something belonging to a new recruit with no hope in ever coming back. Maybe even a job, the kind of position they'd given a war hero's widow." He shrugged, sighed. "You'd have the kind of identity you've earned as an ally to this mission of mine."

She didn't know what that meant. An *ally* to *what* mission? She also didn't have the stomach to ask.

"And maybe someday, you'd see Gregor again," he added, grinning. It seemed like a genuine, nostalgic grin, too. "At some school where he'd surely be teaching nuclear engineering to young, gifted kids in a high-risk neighborhood. And maybe you'd see Yuri and his wife, Svetlana, too, who will likely find new careers as Slavic language instructors on that same military base." He grinned at his fantasy, like maybe he missed Gregor and would miss Yuri and Svetlana once they were on their way home.

"And what about you, Vasy?" Allana asked because maybe now was the time to get some answers of her own. "Once this is all over, then what? Some new name, a new job as a workaholic courier for the CIA or something?" She chuckled at the suggestion, trying to lighten the mood but Vasy simply stared back. And now it was her turn to pretend to be a human lie detector.

"I'm all in, Allana. After this?" he sighed, shaking his head as the severity weighed in. "I don't know where I'll end up, but it won't be in the States. That's too easy, and despite what you think, I will have done some good work here in Pripyat."

She shook her head. "No, Vasy. No good will come of this, and you know that."

He grinned. "But you're wrong. Saving the world from the Soviets will be hailed as an act of heroism."

"You mean 'terrorism?'" she asked.

Vasy chuckled, shaking his head. "I'll get promoted. But soon, I'll have another mission. At the very least, I'll get a deputy ambassador job at some foreign office. They're saying the Middle East is our next threat, so I don't know."

Next threat... Her eyes narrowed, and the tension climbed into her neck and spread like fire across the back of her head. Her voice came out as a whisper. "You really are an American spy?" Of course, she'd known it, but she hadn't wanted to believe it. As an American, Allana would never turn on her country; Vasy wasn't only doing that, he was exposing his comrades to possible, massive execution. *The worst, most painful and horrible kind of death*, if what he'd said about radiation poisoning were true.

Without breaking eye contact, Vasy nodded. He was proud of it, too. "These people in the Soviet-Ukraine deserve better than what they've got. I'm the one who will make that happen," he vowed.

"By blowing up their nuclear power station?"

"No. By decommissioning it," he said. And he sounded a little offended, too.

Allana shook her head. "You talked about people losing their lives last night," she reminded him.

"If I don't step in, there will be *widespread* death," he explained. "The reactor design is flawed. They need a separate cooling chamber."

"Like Three Mile?" she asked.

He ignored the comment. "The materials in the RBMK reactor don't moderate properly. The construction was rushed and incomplete. It's all over the news, Allana."

"And it's based on information you fed the media," she said. *Unbelievable.*

"The engineers doing the actual work are untrained." At last, he reached up and took her face with his hands, like there was an urgency to what he wanted to tell her. "Listen, I don't know what Alex has told you, but

Chernobyl is a piece of shit. It's unsafe, and it's political, and if we can't destroy it in a controlled manner, the untrained staff will blow it up and potentially contaminate the rest of the planet. And then we all die."

Allana tried to tear her face free, but his grip had tightened. "You're hurting me," she whined.

"I'm going to save all of these people," he explained, his intense stare latched on to her. "You believe me, don't you? You believe me?"

Allana nodded as much as she could while he squeezed her face with his hands. "Yes," she said. And she did believe him, too. The way he explained it, the Americans weren't just advancing their own interests, they were helping avoid what could be the world's worst nuclear disaster. And Vasy was right at the core of that operation, a man who had never come across as someone who wanted to hurt anyone else. Despite how he'd hurt her through his manipulation, Vasy always had big ideas for the world, his life... they all involved safety and happiness. "Yes, I believe you," she repeated. *But it doesn't mean I'm not scared of you.*

He stared at her for what felt like a few minutes, and then nodded. Letting go of her face, Vasy reached into his pants for a pocketknife. He walked behind the chair and cut the plastic ties off of her wrists.

Allana sucked in a lungful of air, as if the ties had been suffocating her, and then she massaged the lines in her skin. She looked back to thank Vasy, but he'd already disappeared.

A moment later, she heard the bedroom door ease shut.

Point taken, she stepped away from the chair and settled on the accommodations in the second bedroom, which was located at the opposite end of the apartment.

# # #

Chapter 41

Allana played nice for the rest of that week. She woke early every morning and prepared a full breakfast for Vasy. Like old times, before he started leaving at six in the morning, before they'd ever moved to Pripyat, before she knew the truth about why they were there in the first place, and before things got complicated. Before it had become a matter of life or death, and not just for her or for Vasy, but for so many other people who truly had no clue.

Most mornings, she only shared a few cordial words with him. She would ask trivial things, like "Has Alex returned from Kiev?" Or "Will Agent G zero two four be coming by for afternoon tea?"

For the most part, Vasy would shrug (he didn't know where Alex was). Sometimes, he would chuckle and shake his head (no, Agent G zero two wasn't coming for tea).

But every morning before he left for work, Allana would send him off with the usual, "I love you, Vasy." *Why not, it hadn't meant anything to him anyway.*

A part of her waited for him to say he loved her more, but he never did.

Because there never was 'more.' It was all a big lie.

And that hurt.

On Friday, April 11, 1986, Allana finally managed to crack Vasy's protective shell. A little, anyway. That morning, after walking him into the hallway and saying she loved him, he turned back.

Her heart skipped; she didn't know whether to expect him to ask her to stop saying that, or for him to respond with something sweet, something from the Vasy she'd fallen in love with, the forgiving one from their college days.

Instead of blurting a quick response, he reached out with his free hand and touched her stomach. "I know you're pregnant, Allana," he said, his face twisting into all sorts of emotion.

Allana choked. Pregnant? No.

But wait... She supposed it was possible; she hadn't had her period in over two months, but she also didn't have morning sickness. Looking down at his hand on her slightly bulging belly, she wondered if Vasy suspected Alex as the father.

"I don't think so," she admitted quietly, shaking her head. She stepped back so his hand fell away. Part of her believed that, too; she'd been pregnant before, she knew that morning sickness lasted a lot longer than the first couple of weeks.

He raised an eyebrow with an expression that asked if she was serious. "I thought you'd learned by now that I'm always one or twenty steps ahead of you."

She punched him in the arm, playfully. Cautiously and flirtatiously, even. But she wasn't stupid enough to let her guard down, to let him in after everything he'd done. She took another step back.

"Hey, I'm a federal agent, and that's a class D felony," he said, looking around like one of the other agents might jump out and take her down for assaulting him.

Allana smiled. Although he'd tried to be funny and lighthearted, the reality of his mission in Pripyat meant there was no room for humor.

When she didn't laugh, Vasy nodded and frowned again. Back to being serious. "I know. I'm not funny," he admitted. "And you're pregnant, Allana."

She rolled her eyes. "I think I'd know if I'm pregnant. Besides, I think that's just your asshole way of saying I'm getting fat."

Shaking his head, Vasy admitted, "After what we're going through, do you seriously think I'm worried about your feelings if I thought you were getting chubby? Not a chance."

She punched him in the arm again, harder this time. "You *are* an asshole. And I blame you for—"

"Would love to chat, Allana," he laughed, cutting her off and hitting the call button for the elevator, "but I've got lots of work to do."

"Ugh," she groaned, pivoting on her heels and starting back toward the apartment.

"Oh, one last thing, Allana?"

She stopped, her heart skipping again because maybe this was it, maybe he would say it now.

"If you're worried about packing on a few pounds, you're free to take a stroll while the weather's still nice."

"Thanks," she said, flipping him the middle finger without turning around. She heard the elevator doors open, followed by Vasy's laughter and footfalls as he boarded.

Returning to the apartment, she considered his suggestion. A walk. The temperature was hitting the sixties now, and it would feel good to taste the fresh air. Maybe take a stroll into town and see the family doctor…because maybe Vasy was right about the pregnancy.

She shook her head at that idea. No, ignoring Vasy's suspicions was probably easier. *He's manipulating me. Again.*

But what if she went for that walk and then swung by the Hotel

Polissia? What if she managed to access Alex's room and lock herself safely inside, away from Vasy and his clan of letter-and-number CIA agents, or whatever they were? And what if Alex had returned, and she told him every little detail she knew about her husband and his purpose here in Pripyat?

Would Vasy have expected *that*? Would he still be a couple of steps ahead of her?

But then again, Alex already knew everything and anything she could tell him, so why would it even matter?

Why me?

She groaned at the spray from the showerhead.

I don't know anymore. I just don't know.

#

The workers at the amusement park were testing the Devil's Wheel. Allana watched while standing at the fence. On either side of her, families with excited kids pointing through the fence at the big Ferris wheel, and rambling about May Day, *Pershotravneva* as they called it. While the families and people talked, Allana wondered if she would ever see Alex again. Was he dead? How had he died? Had he seen it coming?

Was that why he'd bribed one of those workers to let them sit in one of the carriages before installing them on the wheel? Because he knew he was in trouble?

Even though she hoped he was okay, part of her didn't know whether it would be a good thing or a bad thing to see him again. Alex had also caused trouble for her, and he'd hurt her and used her just like Vasy had. And now, if she truly were pregnant like Vasy suspected, she might have to blame him for that as well because she and Vasy hadn't been able to conceive in almost a year.

"*Zvidky vy?*" one of the kids asked her.

She shrugged because she didn't know what it meant. The child's mother gave her a disgusted look, but it didn't change things so Allana shrugged again before hurrying off.

Glancing back to see if any of Vasy's spy friends were following her, she made a wide turn toward the Hotel Polissia. Trouble or not, she had to know if Alex had returned. And she also wanted to know if anyone would follow her.

As she entered the hotel's lobby, she slowed down. The man that had brought the room service to Alex's room was busy with another couple, and he didn't even notice her slip past the crowd to the elevators.

She rode up to the second floor and headed down the hall to Alex's room. She raised her hand to knock, but held back. *Pay attention.* She thought about it, remembering the time she'd followed Vasy to Gregor's building and how he had knocked on the apartment door where she'd found the RCA record player and the pieced-together spy album. It only took a moment's hesitation before she remembered the pattern. *Because maybe this will make a difference.* Maybe it would result in Alex answering the door, or maybe even someone else that could provide a clue.

Knock knock pause *knock.*

Part of her didn't believe anyone would answer. If Alex had returned, Vasy probably would have known. And, she guessed, he would not have given her the freedom to take a walk today.

So when nobody answered, she wasn't really surprised.

Turning away from the door, she returned to the elevators, rode back down to the lobby, and then walked home where she waited for Vasy to return from work.

Like before.

Always waiting.

And waiting.

And losing her mind.

#

Chapter 42

Sunday, April 13, 1986 arrived quickly. Allana didn't know it, but it would be the last full day she would ever spend with Vasy. Even if she had known, it was doubtful that it would have made a difference. That Sunday, the last full day she would spend with him, she made her usual Sunday breakfast— scrambled eggs with potatoes, ham and toast—and served Vasy the moment he left the bedroom and made his way to the kitchen. He looked groggy, tired from the long week of work and maybe even a little worn down because of the looming, dangerous task ahead of him.

Placing a plate of food before him, she asked: "Are you swimming lengths today?"

"I don't think so," he admitted. "I don't feel like I fully recovered from that cold a few weeks ago. I'm wiped."

She made a plate for herself and settled in the chair across from him. Allana ate her breakfast, allowing a mild silence to settle between them.

"Maybe we can walk to the Energetik," she suggested. "I enjoyed swimming with you the last time we did it together. And that might be a way to reinforce our, um, solidarity as a couple."

Vasy didn't even raise his attention to her. He obviously wasn't buying it.

Half giving up on making suggestions about how they should spend their time together, Allana focused on her food. Maybe Vasy detected her disappointment, because halfway through his plate, he finally looked up and told her that he had already made plans for the day.

"Just the two of us," he added, and although the words sounded romantic by themselves—*just the two of us*—they meant to be more of a disarming promise. Vasy shrugged. "If we go swimming, we'll see people." He meant his fellow CIA friends, like Mrs. Perfect and the old guy, no doubt.

Allana smiled, nodded, and kept her head down as she finished her meal. *Good, now we can talk.* Once she finished her food, she started clearing the table.

Vasy remained seated, though, reclining back and taking a deep breath while he stared out the balcony door at the weather outside. "I heard it's going to get cold today. You'll want to dress warm."

"I will," she said from her position at the sink.

"Also, I got my hands on one of those pregnancy tests."

Allana flinched and started the water. She didn't want to think too much about the pregnancy test. Not now. She needed to be strong.

"I know they're not a hundred percent accurate, but this one came from back home. They're the next generation, not even on the market yet. I put it in the bathroom for you."

Not knowing what to say, she allowed a quiet, "Thank you."

Vasy grunted, pushing his chair out from the table and disappearing into the short hall. She heard the bedroom door click shut while she sped through the rest of the dishes and let them air dry on the rack.

With her "date" with Vasy approaching, Allana raced down the hall toward the bathroom at the end. She spotted the pregnancy test on the counter as if it had a siren attached to it.

Ugh.

Dropping her panties, Allana sat on the toilet and pissed on the stick—*think nasty thoughts to confuse this test*—and by the time she finished in the shower, she had an answer to Vasy's pregnancy theory.

This time, no names.

# # #

If Allana had known that Vasy wanted to have coffee at the Pripyat Café, she might have put up a bit of a fuss. The Café was the first place Alex had brought her, where she had first let her guard down. That had been the same day she'd given Alex a bloody nose, but from that moment onward, she'd softened toward him, let him in a little each time thereafter, just enough that he'd managed to wiggle his way in deeper and convince her that it was okay to betray her fake vows to her fake husband.

Closing her eyes, she shook her head. *I was so stupid...*

"Are you coming?" Vasy asked, half chuckling as he poked his head back into the car.

Allana nodded, unbuckling her seatbelt and slipping out of her seat to join him. His lighthearted nature bothered her; with such a big task ahead of him, only a psychopath wouldn't lose sleep at night, especially since he didn't know just how deep his actions would resonate throughout the world. *Unless he's faking it.*

"It's a latté you like to drink, isn't it?" he asked as they entered the café.

Nodding, Allana offered, "I'll find a table." She was surprised he'd even known her favorite drink; he always seemed too absorbed in his own life to write notes in the margins about hers.

The Pripyat Café was a lot busier than the last time she'd been here. She passed a teenaged couple holding hands over a plate of biscuits and two cups of coffee, a family of four with kiddie cups of hot chocolate for the two young girls in their spring jackets, and also a couple her age, each of them quietly reading—*Soviet Life* for her and a newspaper for him. Eventually, she settled on a small table for two close to the windows. Removing her jacket, she wiped the surface clean of crumbs and then sat down. And waited.

She wondered if any of the people here belonged to the other voice she'd heard on that recording in the apartment. But none of those people paid much attention to her, much less Vasy when he stepped up to the table and handed her the large latté cup. Vasy had opted for a latté as well, but once he settled into his chair, he revealed a small sampler of vodka and poured the clear liquid into his cup.

"Better than sugar," he said as he replaced the cap on the empty miniature bottle, sliding it back into his jacket pocket.

They sipped their drinks in silence and every few seconds or so, Allana glanced out the big windows at the calm lake water. She remembered the summer barbecue when she'd first met Alex. Vasy had introduced them.

Alex had been sober at the barbecue. Maybe that was why he'd lacked the hunger and sexual appetite that had been present during the poker night.

"I never want to go back home," she admitted, shaking the memory of that summer barbecue out of her memory. "I was never happy in the States."

Vasy looked up from his cup, his gaze betraying that lightheartedness from before. "You'll be fine this time."

She raised her attention, matching his stare. "If I have to go back, I'd like you to be there with me."

He stared back at her before shaking his head and taking another swig of spiked latté.

Allana swore that she spotted hatred in his eyes. She couldn't tell if it was hatred toward her, or something or someone else. At last, she couldn't hold it in any longer. She reached across the table and seized his hand. "These are good people, Vasy," she insisted, her voice a whisper—a *powerful* whisper, but still. "They don't deserve this."

Vasy leaned halfway across the table. "You don't know these people. You don't speak their language. You don't know what life is like for them, the fear they live in."

"Then don't make it worse," she suggested.

Vasy rolled his eyes. "I changed my mind." He huffed. "You need to go."

She stared back at him. "Look around you. Look at these people. They're here because of that power station. I listened to that record, Vasy, and nobody knows just how bad it will be once that power station is decommissioned. Or, most likely, *destroyed*," she hissed, narrowing her eyes into slits. "You wanted me to take a pregnancy test, but what for? At least with James, my daughter was dead before she ever knew what life was." She ripped her eyes away, feeling them burn with tears. A sip of her latté and she noticed the people around them again before facing Vasy and finding him waiting for her to continue. "You're nobody's hero if you go through with this. You've already betrayed your country, Vasy. Don't destroy it and the rest of the planet along with it."

Vasy laughed at her, drawing glances from the others in the café. *What a jerk.*

Shaking her head at him, Allana decided to give up as Vasy finished the rest of his latté in a single sip and nodded at her cup. "Drink up. I want to walk the shore."

# # #

The lake still had a thin layer of ice on it, but by this time of year the ice-fishing shacks had been removed and people weren't skating anymore. It wouldn't be long before the warm weather melted the rest of the ice and turned the lake into bath water, with barbecues and Frisbees and all types of activities cluttering the shore.

This morning, it was just the two of them walking the brisk shoreline. The bare trees and grey skies made the place look abandoned.

"You weren't always like this, Vasy," Allana said, keeping up with his pace as they came around the path at the top of the lake. "I know you loved me at one point."

"Allana," he sighed, "let's just forget about it for today."

She grinned, ignoring his comment. "Remember that party? The night we met? It was that rooftop place in Boston—"

"Mickey's." Not even a small smile. Like he knew what she was doing, saw it a mile away.

She snapped her fingers. "Yeah, Mickey's, and you gave me a drink and pretended you were looking for someone else. You lied to me and said the drink was for her." She chuckled at the memory. *He'd have been on the hunt for someone like me, he saw a stupid girl with lots of boyfriends that never went home on holidays or long weekends, and he'd chosen Mickey's to make his move. Asshole.*

"It honestly was meant for someone else," he admitted with his same monotonously serious voice. "It was so busy that night," he went on, "and I was a little drunk."

She felt sad that he kept lying to her, but she shrugged and forced a fake laugh anyway. She had to keep trying. "Well, you gave me the drink. And I wasn't giving it back."

"I should have seen that as a sign. I should've run," he said, a little playful now because they both knew Allana should have been the one running.

Smacking him on the shoulder, she gave a whiny, "Hey!"

At last, Vasy chuckled. Like maybe he'd finally let his guard down and would start listening to her. So she kept at it.

"You worked hard at trying to get to know me, Vasy. So you see, I know you have it in you to believe. To believe in people and believe in a purpose." She cozied up to him, matching his footsteps as they started down the backside of the lake. When Vasy refused to comment, she went on. "I'm not suggesting you'll want to walk away and run out on the US government."

"Then what are you suggesting?" he asked, back to stern and serious.

She gulped. Here goes. "Mercy."

She glanced over at him and found that his face had set in a stone-hard frown.

He sighed. "Impossible. Can we talk about something else already?"

Allana felt the smile fade from her lips, and she turned her attention back to nature. She admired the lake and the domestic buildings of the town beyond it.

"It's beautiful here," she admitted. "If this kind of town existed back home, you'd have people begging to come here. No matter how poorly it was built and how under-qualified the engineers are, there's the technological advancement of the power station, which is how I imagine Detroit would've been when Ford showed up on the scene, with its big factories and prosperity, and all the promise of what it was doing. They changed the world in that city, Vasy. And that's exactly what we have here. These people know that they're changing the way the world works. In a dozen years, I bet you'll have nuclear power stations in every country on this planet."

"That's why we need it to stop," he muttered, more to himself. To Allana's ears, it was the first time she detected doubt in his words. "Because there are too many uncertainties, Allana. Between the safety of these buildings, the handling and disposal of these highly radioactive power rods…" He shook his head. "We need to put this to an end, it's already out of control."

"Don't you see, Vasy?" she pleaded. "If you do that, it will impact the American program, too. I'm not a spy or political scientist, but even I can see that a fallout of this magnitude ruins nuclear energy for everyone."

Vasy nodded. "Yes, you're right. And I know it, too. Because, as we speak, we're building more and more nuclear power stations back home, and as much as I love my country—my *adopted* country—I just don't have the faith in anyone. And neither do our leaders. We've seen it with our own radiation leaks at Three Mile. A valve?" He shook his head. "It's dangerous, and even the world's most respected scientist confirm that this kind of power can never be controlled." More head shaking followed by a frustrated groan. "And we all know it, too."

With her heart pounding at the progress she was making with Vasy, Allana digested his admission for a few seconds and stared out at the apartment buildings across from them. "What's the average age here, Vasy?"

He shrugged, keeping quiet. "Thirty?"

"The oldest person here, I swear, is that guy I saw with agent G zero two four the day you two ambushed me at the apartment."

He chuckled. "Nik? He's in his late-forties, that's not exactly old."

"Exactly!" she roared, but she swore he'd been in his sixties. *Bad career choice after all, eh, Vasy?* "So at under-fifty he's the oldest guy I've seen around. This place works because we're all so young, we're all at the same stages in our life. And we all want the same thing: Prosperity."

"Yeah, it's just like your average post-college town," he said, rolling his eyes.

"So if you pull through with what you're saying you need to do, it all falls apart."

"Allana," he sighed. "You need to let this go and let me do my job."

She glanced over at him and marveled at how drawn his face appeared. They'd been talking about the youth of Pripyat, and it seemed that

Nik's advanced aging was contagious where Vasy was concerned.

She took a deep breath. "But if you do your job, you'll destroy the promise of any kind of prosperity. Not just for Pripyat, and all of these young people who want the same things you want, or I want, or anyone else our age wants. But for the rest of the planet. For everyone just getting started with their lives, their families and their dreams…you'll ruin it because they'll all be dead." Maybe that was a little too much. "And if they're not dead, they'll at least be ruined." She felt her heart sink at that realization. "So you're not just decommissioning a power station, but you'll be ending a generation of hope and prosperity."

Another sigh. "People adapt. They'll figure out another way, because that's what people do."

"Mass destruction, ruined crops for *hundreds* and maybe even *thousands* of years, and a new generation built on severe… birth defects," she exclaimed, rubbing her tummy and turning just slightly so he could see it out of the corner of his eye.

They walked in silence before Vasy sighed, shaking his head. "And, just for your own knowledge," he said, but it sounded like a childish afterthought, "you should know that the Soviet Union is running out of money. It's got its share of problems, and what I'm doing is helping to give people a new start, quicker."

Allana tried not to laugh. "I don't know if I believe that," she admitted before turning her attention back to his face. "And you know what? I don't think you believe it, either. Because this isn't an economics sabotage, it's entirely political and… I don't know, biological?"

"Then what do you believe, Allana?" He shook his head at her. This also felt like a childish afterthought, the part in a toddler argument where the one losing the debate said "you're stupid," and walked away. "Keep in mind," he added, "that my statements and actions are driven by facts uncovered by the finest intelligence reports available, I'm curious what you think the real consequences are if we allow this power station to survive."

She didn't miss a beat. She'd been cursed with a lot of time—*waiting and waiting and driving herself insane*—to think about these things. Between hiding out in the Hotel Polissia and just recently her own apartment, she'd thought about a lot of things. "Maybe you're right and the world goes on. But maybe you're wrong and power stations continue to get built cheaply and poorly, and they'll continue to produce the energy they need at the hands of even more-unqualified men and woman. And in that case, what you're doing here is completely inconsequential."

Vasy dropped his head back and stared at the low clouds. Next to him, Allana spied the internal war surfacing on his tired face.

"Vasy, no matter what happened between us, please don't get involved with something that will put the next Hiroshima on your resume." She tried to slide her hand into his, but he refused it—*too much, she should have just kept her hands to herself.* "This is your chance to be a real hero. You've got to stand up and choose between life and death, not just for Pripyat but for the generations that will be affected by this."

"It won't have a big fallout," he admitted with a sigh, keeping his voice low. "Not like Hiroshima. What we're doing is shutting down the reactor, keeping the rods safe to avoid a leak. We're just shutting it down," he repeated, and now Allana began to understand the weight of his pressure because Vasy never repeated himself. "And when the rods cool…" he trailed off. "No, there won't be any social damage, there won't be contamination, there won't be civilian deaths."

Maybe he believed his own words, or maybe he was trying hard to. "And Nikolai Fomin?" she asked.

"He knows it's a risk. He knows there are structural flaws, safety flaws, and he knows the government is corrupt and looking for ways to save money."

"And your family?" she asked. "What will they think when they find out you've betrayed your native country and sabotaged the power station on behalf of an American spy agency?"

Vasy's jaw muscles flexed.

"Will they hurt your family, Vasy?"

He stopped walking and gripped her shoulders so hard that there would be bruises later. "Whatever you're trying to do," he said between his gritted teeth, "it's not working. It's already in motion. And that's not my doing, it's Alex's."

She couldn't help but flinch at Vasy's mention of Alex's name.

Release her, Vasy stepped back, his eyes bulging. "That's where your worries should li. With Alex. Because he's the one sharing the truth about this magical power station. He's the one who will tell them about the flaws we discovered and how we're going to put it out of business. He's the one that will talk about American spies in the same town as their coveted masterpiece." He paused, gulping. "And he's the one that will suffer the consequences because he can't deliver the facts as they are. He'll point to me, the highly respected deputy engineer, and he'll point to Yuri, one of the most highly regarded nuclear physicists in the entire Soviet Union, and they'll think he's crazy. Even if they went looking and they found those chambers under the reactor core, even if they discovered the explosives or devices that will interrupt the command station's directions... who do you think they'll listen to? An *American* freelancing for a KGB that they don't trust? Or homegrown natives with impressive political connections?"

"Vasy," she started, but then she saw his face, his eyes full of fear and hate and... "You know this won't end the way you think it will," she argued, and he increased his pace. "I see it in your eyes and hear it in your voice. This will spiral out of control, it will be worse than anything you've ever imagined, and you know it, too. You know there's only one way to avoid it and—"

At last, Vasy made a sudden halt. "Stop!"

Tilting her head, Allana made a wide-eyed plea. "Let these people live!"

His eyes bore into hers with the wild rage of a madman, and for the first time since meeting him at that rooftop bar during her junior year at college, she saw the possibility that maybe Vasy wasn't quite as put-together as she'd always assumed. Because unlike the planning and manipulating he'd done with her—she was *predictable*—no amount of planning and manipulation could offer the promise of survival after he destroyed the power station. Everyone knew that!

"Vasy," she said, her voice sober and soft as she made one final plea. "Please don't hurt these people. Please don't—"

"It's done," he told her, his eyes growing wide with a plea of their own, "it's all done. The Soviets are done, regardless of what happens with this dangerous and deteriorating power station. Their hope for prosperity is done, it's already sliding out of their reach, they just don't see or know it yet. No matter what I do. And that place," he pointed down the lake toward the stacks in the distance with their red and white stripes, "it's done, too, it's a risk to the rest of the world. No matter what I do." He gulped.

She reached out for him, but he stepped back. "Then let it end on its own. Let's get out of here and let these people ruin their own lives."

"It's a weapon, you know that, right? Because, like a vehicle in the hands of a toddler, it can't be controlled. That child needs a parent to take the wheel. And I'm here to not only take the wheel, but to take the keys out of that toddler's hands." His face crunched. "You understand that, don't you?"

What she understood was his fear. The way his worry materialized as beaded perspiration at the edge of his hairline, she also understood that this was a new side of Vasy, one she had never known because he'd always been so confident. But not anymore. That old Vasy could make promises, and he could deliver. But standing at the side of the lake, Allana saw a true and genuine fear in him because he couldn't deliver anymore. In his own words, *it's done.*

# # #

Chapter 43

When Allana's alarm clock chimed the following Sunday, something felt off. Different. The previous Sunday had a goodbye feel to it, and it had left her sad and anxious. Rolling over in the spare bed (which had become *her* bed), she freed herself of the blankets and noticed that the collar of her pajama shirt felt damp, like she'd had a nightmare at some point in the night.

Maybe it was the seven o'clock waking hour. Or the four hours of sleep.

The only time Allana had waited up for Vasy this week had been last night. And when he came home at two in the morning, they'd spent a good hour talking. Mostly, Vasy had talked; Allana had barely managed to keep her eyes open. And mostly, he spoke about what life would look like for Allana once she returned to the States—the new friends, new routines. The promise of starting a family with her baby and establishing a career. In *English*, he'd chuckled. All of it in *English*.

It had sounded so perfect, the way he explained it, but in typical Vasy fashion, he'd fooled her into believing it. Because all of it had been a distraction of some sort, she knew that now as she rubbed her eyes and sat up on the edge of the bed.

Allana tried to focus on what she believed would be one of her final Sundays with Vasy. She thought about the Ferris wheel in Lenin Square. She knew that no matter where Vasy and the U.S. Government sent her for her pristine "new life" back in the States, there would always be carnivals and amusement parks nearby, and the sight of a Ferris wheel would always remind her of her time here. She'd miss Pripyat and yearn to come back.

Get up, she urged herself.

Sliding into her slippers, she wandered to the kitchen and assembled the ingredients she needed for Vasy's Sunday morning breakfast. It was important that she continued to do this, *especially* after everything that had happened between them; if she'd stopped, he would never listen to her. She placed two frying pans (one for the eggs, the other for the potatoes) on their respective elements, but she kept the stove turned off, and then retreated to the sofa in the living area where she could stare out the window and watch the early morning clouds roll past. She would just sit here until Vasy woke.

At least, that's what she told herself. At some point, she passed out. She dreamed about her childhood, the last time she'd gone back home to the townhouse on Lawrence. She was sitting on the front porch, waiting for her parents to come home from work. It was a Friday, which meant pay day, which also meant Dad would have a case of twenty-four Molson that might last midway through Saturday, and Mom would have a bucket of KFC that would last through dinner that night and breakfast the following morning.

That day, even in her dream, her parents came home with a new car. It was the new Ford Taurus with its rounded corners, plastic bumpers, and alien-looking headlights. It was something straight out of Europe, her father had bragged, as if saying it lent him an edge of sophistication.

That had been the last summer she'd ever gone home; the following summer—last summer—she'd moved away with Vasy. And while she missed her parents and missed knowing that they were surviving and living and happy in their own dysfunctional way, she also enjoyed the autonomy of being on the other side of the world, far away from them and all of the bad things they'd allowed to happen to her, particularly where James and the baby were concerned. They'd been the first people to introduce her to the concept of manipulation when they teamed up with James' family.

When Vasy's bedroom door opened, followed by the bathroom door clicking shut, Allana snapped awake and realized that the dream had served as something of an answer to one of her questions. And it wasn't a happy answer.

Pushing herself out of the sofa, Allana went to work in the kitchen. Same routine as always, and by the time Vasy came out, the electric kettle was boiling and ready for tea.

"Why do you keep doing this for me?" he asked in a groggy voice that suggested his morning had begun the same way hers had—full of confusion and anxiety. Still, he blew on the steaming tea and took a quick, slurping sip.

"Because, Vasy," she said, walking over to where he sat at the table. "We fell in love once, and I like to think that despite everything, you're still that man I fell in love with." She smiled, hopeful. "The kind, merciful and generous man I met at Mickey's, the one who promised to take me away and delivered on that promise."

Vasy said nothing, kept his neck bent forward, his head hanging over the tea.

She sat at her regular spot and watched for a while before asking, innocently: "How will my parents know I'm okay?"

"They'll know," he answered without looking up.

"And when will I see them again—"

"You won't," he snapped with the same tired voice. "Are the eggs almost ready?"

She swallowed her sadness. Despite Vasy delivering on his promise and rescuing her from her past, he'd ruined her life in bringing her here, but she kept quiet about that. It saddened her that she would live the rest of her life without hearing from or seeing her parents again. Even though she'd always thought she'd never miss them and their idiotic ways, Allana wanted nothing more than to give her mother one more hug and have a final beer with her father.

Taking a deep breath, Allana retreated to the stove and ran the spatula through the eggs, breaking the yokes and further scrambling them in the pan. Same thing with the potatoes, except there was nothing to break there. None of the food showed signs of black, not even a hint of brown, so she increased the temperature on both elements.

"It smelled like something might be burning," Vasy added.

"Nothing's burning," she said, although she could tell he was bothered about her never having a chance to say goodbye to her family. *He should be bothered, it's his fault.* When a choked sob erupted from her, she clamped her eyes shut and forced herself to pull her act together.

"I'm sorry," he sighed at last. "I know it's unfair. But your life will be at risk if you go back home. The first place the Soviets will look for you is in your past. They'll track you down to the States and your parents' shitty little townhouse, and they'll kill you for your affiliation with me."

She took a deep breath, sniffled and wiped her eyes with her sleeve.

"I'm sorry," he repeated, his voice groggy and laced with guilt. "I needed an American wife. A strong woman who wouldn't look back. Someone I wouldn't care for, even though I ended up caring for you, Allana." He paused while she stood at the stove, trying to absorb every word. "No, it was more than that. Because I fell in love with you, but..." He groaned before continuing. "The US Government did a lot for me and my family, and I love the country. It welcomed me, trained me, and showed me how much they care for peace and order in the rest of the world. If any country could be love—no matter what anyone says or believes—it's the States. I believe that, and my role here proves it." He sat in silence for a few seconds. "And I needed an American wife to make this work. Someone who could distract people, shift the attention from what I was doing with Alex and the power station and bring that attention onto herself."

After a deep breath, she asked, "why are you telling me this?"

His chair scratched the floor as he turned around. "Because you're important in all of this. I needed someone special, and that's you."

It was all bullshit, she knew. *Manipulating me, yet again.* "No. You needed someone whose family wouldn't miss her," she concluded, because she'd strung together those pieces long ago. "Whether I died here with you, or got shipped back under some kind of protection program, I needed to be the kind of girl that nobody would miss."

Vasy looked tired, the same way anyone spending hundreds of hours a week at work should. Forget about the pressure. Forget the fact that if he did anything to the power station, the fallout from such a disaster would be on his shoulders for the rest of his life. Vasy looked old and worn down and ready to crack.

"I loved you," she said, staring him down. "You did this to me."

"Hey, I fell in love with you just like you fell in love with me," he said, like that made things all better.

Allana shook her head. "You knew what you were doing. Right from the start when we met at Mickey's."

Vasy was the first to break their stare and turned back around in his seat. "I'm sorry."

Using her spatula to sweep two servings of eggs onto two plates, she did the same with the potatoes, her brain racing. And then she served the breakfast, sat across from Vasy and watched him shove a mouthful of eggs into his mouth. After swallowing her first bite, she asked him, "you said I was special?"

He grunted an affirmative, or something that sounded like an affirmative. Still eating like he hadn't seen food in a week.

"I was just a babybsitter for Alex," she confessed, her voice pitched a little higher. *How special was that?*

Vasy laughed, a tired and cranky sound. "More than that, Allana. You gave him everything we needed him to have. And then you confirmed it. And it wasn't just those six or so things you told him about me and my work. It was the time you spent with him, the way you would have answered his questions. Just like me, Alex fell for you, another American just like him, someone who fell in love with the Soviet Ukrainian culture and lifestyle."

"And now he's dead," she said, surprised by the punch in her own voice. She tried to eat, but the food tasted bland.

Raising his eyebrows, Vasy shrugged. "It's possible."

"And that's why I'm still here," she went on, staring at him again to see how he responded. "Just in case he's not."

Vasy stopped eating and stared into her eyes, reading her for signs of a bluff. And then he shrugged and stabbed at his plate. "If anyone can bring him back, it's you, Allana." He kept eating. "You're special."

She'd heard enough. Shoving her half-eaten breakfast plate across the table, she got up and retreated to her bedroom where she dropped back onto the mattress and cried into her pillow until she fell asleep once again.

# # #

It wasn't long before Vasy let himself into her room. She heard the door and opened one of her eyes—just a slit so he wouldn't see—to watch him cross the small space before her in his workout gear. He sat down on the mattress, still smelling like breakfast. Wasn't even delicate about it either; he sat like he did everything else, without a care in the world about anyone else except himself. And then rubbed her back. It was the first time since March that he'd shown any kind of affection toward her. Yes, she'd been keeping track.

"Allana?" he asked with a soft voice that came out like he didn't want to startle her. "I know you're awake. I saw you open your left eye when I walked in. I didn't even need my spy training to notice that."

"What do you want?" she grumbled, but kept her eyes closed so she wouldn't have to look at him.

"I need you to keep fighting," he admitted with the same soft voice. "For us. For the people. I can't have you giving up like this. Because you're not a quitter."

She knew it was all bullshit. She knew there was only one motive behind his words, and it wasn't so he could change his mind about his task.

"You're a survivor," he went on. "You're a fighter, and that's inspiring, and I need inspiration right now." He rubbed her back some more.

Her cheeks flushed red with pride, but then she reminded herself not to get her hopes up. Vasy had come here to destroy the power station. And he was a master manipulator. If he wanted her to fight for anything, it was to help him achieve his own objectives.

"Allana, things might never be the same between us, but please don't think I never cared," he said. "I never thought I'd be able to look at you again after we intercepted those photos from Alex's hotel room."

Wait...*Intercepted? Alex hadn't volunteered them?* She kept her eyes clamped shut, thinking his plan was to provoke her into opening them.

"But I've come around, and now I look at you all the time. And even though I never thought it would hurt me to see you with another man, it killed me." He sighed, another show of just how exhausted he was. "For what it's worth, those pictures hurt. And deep down, I'd believed maybe you wouldn't have done anything with him, maybe you'd have managed to stay faithful to a fake husband who manipulated you and abandoned you and pushed you into another man's bed. I take full responsibility, Allana. I'm sorry, and I know it doesn't count for a whole lot in the big scheme of things."

He was right, it didn't count. But more importantly, *why was he saying these things?*

"On the other hand, if you hadn't developed a relationship with Alex, what would that say about you as a human being?" He chuckled, shaking his head and cause the bed to shake again. "All I'm trying to say is, whatever happens from here on out, it will be for the best."

She said nothing, believing he would give up and go away. It was just another Sunday for him—breakfast, then swimming at the Energetic with Mrs. Perfect and Nik, the old guy, and then who knows what. But Vasy didn't leave. He kept rubbing her back.

"Go," she said at last.

He withdrew his hand. "Ha! I knew you weren't asleep." Like he'd just won the lottery.

"You woke me up when you jumped onto the mattress," she explained without moving from her position. And then she felt his lips on the top of her head. A condescending type of kiss, not the forgiving type.

"I'm off to the Energetik," he told her. "And then I have to swing by the power station to review the proposed testing schedule for this week."

She kept her eyes closed and tried to listen past the sudden ringing in her ears. If he was talking about a testing schedule this week, it meant...

"Goodbye, Allana," he said, and then she opened her left eye again—just a slit—and watched him walk out on her.

# # #

Once she heard the apartment door close and the lock engage, Allana jumped out of bed and hurried to the balcony. Staring down at the parking lot, she waited for Vasy to exit the building and get into the car before hurrying back indoors. Grabbing her keys from her bedroom, she ran out of the apartment to the elevators, knowing that Vasy had told her about the test schedule for this very purpose—so she would run upstairs, or anywhere else, looking for Alex so she could tell him all about it.

Except, like the last few weeks, her frantic pounding on his apartment door went unanswered.

Placing her ear to the door, Allana listened for sounds of movement or anything else.

Silence.

After a final knock went unanswered, she left the fourth floor and returned to her unit. She grabbed her jacket and boots and hurried out of the building. She wanted to try the room at the Hotel Polissia again, the only other place she knew to look, even though she remembered seeing more than just two keys on Alex's key ring at one point.

Instead of running like a madwoman along the sidewalk that led to Lenin Square, Allana resorted to the shortcut through the forest. The last time she'd taken that route, she'd passed out from the sleeping pills and awakened in the same room where she was headed. She prayed the end result would be the same this time around.

But when she reached the crowded, busy square, she reminded herself to not get too excited. Because she'd been to the Hotel Polissia already and Alex hadn't been there that time. The odds were against her.

She didn't have to think too much about Vasy's true intentions when he'd told her about the tests. Of course, he'd expected her to run to Alex. But why? If Alex knew about the test, he could complicate Vasy's mission.

Or could he?

Was this all part of Vasy's manipulative ways?

Suddenly, instead of pushing through the crowds and heading to the Hotel Polissia, Allana changed direction and headed to the Energetik. The warm weather meant it was busier than ever; between the last-minute, pre-Spring warriors looking to improve their shape for May Day, as well as the higher volumes of tourists and regular fitness freaks, Allana almost had to shove her way into the otherwise busy building.

Hurrying up the stairs to the second level, she marveled at the crowds. The observation deck overlooking the pool was also busier than normal, allowing Allana a narrow degree of anonymity while she surveyed the water below. Despite having her doubts about whether Vasy had indeed come for a swim, she found him three-quarters of the way through a lap. Trailing behind him, Mrs. Perfect swam with the same precision and grace, her arms and legs moving in tandem to propel her through the water.

Sliding back out to the second floor hallway, Allana was a little surprised to find that Vasy had indeed come to the Energetik like he said he would. She'd expected that to be a big lie, and the confession about his caring for her and the upcoming week's tests nothing more than a way to manipulate her. But he'd come here...

Back outdoors, she decided again to visit Alex's hotel room. There was no harm in checking; she'd already made the trip to Lenin Square.

When in Rome...

But after knocking a couple of times on the hotel room door, Allana heard the same absent silence from back at Alex's apartment.

Maybe he is *dead.*

But then why would Vasy tell me about the testing schedule in the first place?

Stepping back from the door, Allana wondered if maybe she was knocking on the wrong room. Again, she'd seen multiple keys on Alex's key ring during that first visit to the apartment building. And after her week-long stay, she had been confused and half-crazy from the isolation, so maybe she was mistaken about the room.

So…where else?

There'd been other keys on his key ring, too, she remembered from that first visit to his apartment. She clearly didn't know where those keys led, couldn't even think of another location where Alex might be hiding from her, Vasy, and whomever else.

Disappointed and deflated, she left the Hotel Polissia and looked around at the crowd outside, and then beyond at the buildings poking up over the treeline. There were hundreds of apartments in Pripyat, probably even thousands. Too many to count, but the point was simply that if Alex were alive, he could be hiding in *any* of those units.

That was when her fingers slipped across the teeth of an unfamiliar object in her coat pocket.

Frowning, she closed her fingers around the cold surface and withdrew it from her jacket.

A key.

Of course, it was *the* key!

Now she knew exactly where she needed to go next.

# # #

As Allana headed from the bus stop to Gregor's apartment building—one block north—she kept reminding herself to walk. Not run. Not jog. Not even speed-walk. Just *walk*. And no matter what, don't look back, even if you feel eyes following you.

She entered the lobby and could almost *taste* the apartment where she was headed. A smile surfaced on her lips, broadening as she boarded the elevator that grinded up to the fifth floor.

Why hadn't I thought of coming back here sooner?

Although she'd managed to rein in her excitement during the walk from the bus stop, she couldn't help but skip to the second last apartment on the floor. She reached inside her jacket for the key, slid it into the lock, and took a deep breath.

She fully expected to find Alex hiding out inside that unit or, at the very least, more information about Vasy's big plan.

But when she tried to turn the key, the lock didn't budge. The key didn't work? She frowned and removed the key before trying again.

And, again, the lock didn't turn.

Curious, she pocketed the key and stepped back from the door, staring at it like it might speak up and offer an explanation for why it didn't like her key. And just when she was ready to turn and walk away from the mute door, she heard something.

A knock. A feeble, quiet knock.

Craning her neck forward, she scrutinized the door. "Are you talking to me?" she asked, like she was going crazy.

But there was another knock. And not from the door in front of her.

It came from the end of the hall. Gregor's old apartment.

When Allana started toward Gregor's door, she stared straight at the peephole. It started out dark but as she got closer, she watched it light up.

Someone is inside that apartment.

Trying the knob, she wasn't all that surprised that the door didn't open for her. That would have been too simple. So she withdrew the key and tried it in the deadbolt.

It turned.

Swallowing, Allana pushed the door open. She glanced back down the hall, curious about why the other apartment's key worked in Gregor's lock. Had the key always worked in Gregor's lock? Or had someone swapped the locks? If so, who?

Allana poked her head inside, making sure that nobody was waiting before she entered. And once she did, she discovered that the place was completely empty except for the nails on the wall that once held up paintings and photos.

Maybe this wasn't such a good idea. But just as soon as she entertained the thought, she heard a voice.

"Close the door."

Startled, she stumbled back and closed the door.

"I thought you'd never find me," Alex said, stepping out of the hallway and coming toward her. He looked sick, skinny, and scared, and when he spread his bony arms, she slipped into his embrace with ease.

"How did you get this key to me?" she asked, her heart pounding. She expected to hear that he hadn't, and then she would know that Vasy had masterminded yet another thing that had put Alex's life in jeopardy.

"You always had it," he said, bringing his lips closer to her ears. She heard him inhale the scent of her hair. "I switched Gregor's lock with the one two doors down, that's all I could do," he explained. "God, I missed you."

"I actually…" she gulped, squeezing her eyes shut and feeling the tears slip out through the cracks as she refused to admit to missing him as well, "I actually thought you were dead."

"I know," he whispered, then bit down on her ear lobe.

"Hey!" she said, shoving him back and waving her fist at him.

Alex smirked in that flirtatious, relentless way of his, and then they stared at each other like old friends. For Allana, it was easy to stare because he needed to cut his hair, eat a meal, put some weight back on.

"I thought you were dead," she repeated softly.

With a straight face, Alex said, "Good."

"But they'll know you're alive now."

He frowned.

"Vasy will know. Somehow, he will."

Alex nodded. "Have you been paying attention, Lana?"

She swallowed, nodding. "They're scheduling some sort of tests for this week. Can you stop them?"

Alex frowned. "This week?" Like he was busy with some sort of other plans.

"Alex," she begged, her heart sinking. "They can't do these tests. They can't even predict how bad this will be. People will *die*, we need to do something!"

Walking toward the balcony window, Alex sighed. "You need to leave."

"Not a chance," she said. It might not even matter if she left, this thing could have global consequences! She stepped up behind him, noticing how his pants hung loosely off his hips. "Alex…"

"By now, he's offered that option to you. You need to take it."

"I'm staying." Her voice was firm. "We need to do something."

"You'll die if you stay."

"Then I guess I'll die," she insisted. She wouldn't leave without a fight—even Vasy had said she was a fighter—and even if nothing ever came of the sabotage attempt at the power station, staying was better than going home alone, to nothing except some fabricated life and fake identity. "But I'm not letting Vasy do this."

She could hear Alex's heavy breathing, and she still didn't know how she felt about him. But she absolutely loved how *he* loved *her*. He made her feel more valuable than she was, yes. He made her feel more desired than any man ever had, yes. But he also made her realize that love is a messed up thing. *Love makes us think it's about* who *we love, but that's backwards. Love should be about* who *loves* us.

And Allana admitted that everyone else would love him a whole hell of a lot more if he could do something to stop Vasy and his team.

"It's messed up," she said.

"You don't know what we're dealing with here, Lana." He shook his head, his voice timid and faraway. "Or what *they* are dealing with. What we're up against is substantial."

"I know," she admitted, happy that he was finally talking like they might do something, no matter how futile he thought it might be.

Alex turned around and pulled her into his arms, bringing his face within half an inch of hers.

"Don't even try to kiss me," she warned him, grinning. She punched his shoulder lightly. "Alex, what are we going to do?"

"If I promise to do something, will you promise me you'll leave and we'll kiss on the other side of this?" He raised his eyebrows, his eyes comforting her. There was something about this man… she couldn't quite identify it. Or maybe she refused to.

But knowing Alex for these few short months, she'd come to realize was that promises are easily broken. Just as Vasy had broken his promises to her, she had broken hers to him. And just as easily as Alex could break his promise here, she could break hers to him as well. Promises were words, malleable and insignificant words, tools in the manipulation trade, nothing more.

"Deal," she stated, releasing him and stepping away. "But first, I want to know what you're going to do."

Alex walked her to the door. "I'm going to fight," he said, his face firm.

"Fight?"

"Yes," he insisted. "I'm going to fight. Because I'm a fighter. A survivor."

She grinned inwardly. "Apparently, so am I."

He smiled back at her, like she might kidding. "I'm serious, Lana. I'm going to contact my liaisons in Kiev and Moscow and let them know what's being planned this week." He frowned, thinking about it. "These people will know Nikolai, they'll convince him to stop whatever tests are underway. They'll know..." he sighed, sliding his fingers through his longer hair. "They'll make sure this is all stopped."

"How will I know it's done?" she asked. "Before I leave..."

Alex raised an eyebrow. "You need to leave," he said, keeping his voice low but firm. "I promised I would do this. Now you need to make sure to leave."

She nodded. She had no reason to doubt him. But something didn't feel right, still. She swallowed the lump in her throat. "How will you escape?" If he planned on sticking around to see this through to the end, what kind of assurances did he have that he would survive at all? She felt her chin quiver and her stomach cramped, which reminded her of the pregnancy she'd denied ever existed. "Alex, how will you collect your kiss?" she asked, her voice cracking.

"Shhh," he hushed, hugging her again. "I'll find you. I promise I'll find you."

It was a lie. Alex couldn't bluff his way out of a confessional, no matter what he thought, no matter what kind of luck he'd had at the poker tables that night in January. But Allana nodded anyway, holding back her tears.

Finally, as she calmed down, she pulled back.

"I will find you," he promised.

# # #

Chapter 44

From the second bedroom window, Allana watched the Devil's Wheel light up the night as the workers at the amusement park ran their tests, making sure the ride was safe and ready for the May Day celebrations, one week and one day away. After watching the large wheel make a couple of lazy rotations, Allana moved to the balcony where she turned her attention to the power station. The facility had a calmness about it, the lights flickering silently like an airport runway before the real chaos started. By midnight, she retreated indoors and went to bed.

Like always, she set her alarm for the following morning, allowing herself a good buffer so she could prepare breakfast for Vasy. The routine allowed her to bury her anxiety over everything that was happening in her life, which felt like a Jack-in-the-box as she went round and round and round, expecting something bad to jump out at her any minute. The next morning, she watched Vasy while he ate, searching his face or demeanor for hints of what might happen that day. And when he gave a sign—a nervous cough, erratic eye movement, a word he wouldn't normally use—that today might be *the* day, she asked him a simple question: "When will I see you again?"

Vasy returned his regular smile—faked, of course—and promised to see her at dinner. Every morning, he promised the same damn thing.

Thursday night, as she sat at the dinner table alone for the fourth time that week, Allana wondered why Vasy kept breaking those same promises. He never showed up for dinner and tonight was no exception. And each night, she was surprised that he still hadn't sent a mushroom cloud into the sky. Was it *all* lies? Just some ploy to bring Alex out of hiding?

If so, why had Alex not surfaced? She'd done her part, she'd shared the test plans—because was what Vasy had wanted her to do, wasn't it? Find Alex and tell him about the tests they would use as a decoy to destroy the power station, right?

Grabbing her hair, she tried to pull the confusion out of her skull. She didn't even understand why they cared so much about Alex, a freelance spy who obviously had some kind of connection to the KGB and political heavyweighters throughout the Soviet Union. But even so, all he'd done was intercept and receive communications that the Americans had allowed him to. Was the test news another one of those things they'd wanted him to know so he could make their job easier?

She pushed her dinner away and lay down on the sofa to indulge in a quick, two-hour power nap. By the time she awoke, Vasy still hadn't arrived home so Allana strolled to her bedroom window, watched a few rotations of the Devil's Wheel in the distance, and then walked to the balcony and watched the quiet power station. She noticed a light flash at her—a quick *SOS* type of flash—and wondered if that was some kind of sign.

"I'm losing my mind," she moaned, shaking her head and turning away.

When Allana settled into bed that Thursday night, she felt pretty hopeful about life in general and the future of the world in particular. The May Day celebrations were right around the corner and she doubted Vasy would proceed with anything that could risk that holiday.

Yes, despite everything else going on, Allana felt pretty good. Stressed, but good.

That was all about to change.

#

Friday, April 25, 1986.

Allana awoke with the alarm like she normally did and made breakfast for Vasy, watching his face for signs of a tell. The first giveaway that something preoccupied his mind was the twitchy eye. The second was the way he'd glance at her with each bite, something he didn't normally do. The third thing Allana noticed was that he seemed to be eating quicker than normal. And the fourth thing was that he wasn't talking, and even first thing in the morning on the worst of days, Vasy would say *something*.

But not today.

"What's going on?" she asked, leaning back in her chair and crossing her arms.

He ignored her and kept twitching his eyes and eating quickly. Like he was famished.

"The test aren't going to happen, are they?" she asked.

Vasy shook his head, no, and kept eating. *No as in they weren't going to happen, or no as in she was wrong.* She opted for the former.

"Was that all part of your bullshit plan to see if Alex would show up again?" she asked, tilting her head.

At last, Vasy stopped eating. He placed his fork next to the plate and wiped his mouth with a napkin. "Bad weather delayed last night's test," he explained. So it was a *no as in she was wrong.* "As long as the weather stays good, the first part of the test will start before I get home tonight."

Allana felt the color drain from her face as she shook her head. She imagined the children at the Devil's Wheel, staring and pointing and excited for the May Day festivities, their parents urging them that it was time to go home for dinner and… and then *what?*

"Why now?" she managed to choke out. "Do you even know what the fallout will be, how many people will die because of you?"

Vasy shrugged, his eyes glued to her. "New reports show the damage will be a very small fraction of anything we've ever seen."

She raised an eyebrow. "Vasy, you've seen the kids in the square. Please don't do this. At least..." she shook her head, her voice cracking. "Can you delay it?"

"It's a *small fraction*," he repeated, his voice stern. "It's tiny. Tinier than tiny, Allana. I'm fine with those numbers." He shrugged like he didn't care that even a tinier than tiny small fraction of anything they'd ever seen was still big enough to cause widespread damage and death.

She felt like she might be sick. "You're a monster."

"I have to get to work," he said, ignoring her. "I'll be home for a quick dinner before heading back for the start of the tests."

# # #

Shortly after six, Vasy came home just like he'd promised. It was the first time he'd honored those words that week. He looked tired and, after removing his shoes and jacket, he went straight to the table without saying anything to Allana. Maybe he was still annoyed with all of her kickback at breakfast.

Taking his cue, Allana went to the kitchen and heated up the pierogis she'd already cooked; Vasy's favorite, plus she knew that if he was wrong and the destruction at the power station produced more than a tinier than tiny small fraction of what they'd ever seen, then... She couldn't help but swallow the reality that if Vasy were wrong, this could be one of their last meals. *I should have prepared something better than perogies.*

While the food heated up, she poured him a glass of wine and brought it to the table.

"They're on track to proceed with the tests," he said before taking a sip of wine. "We're piggybacking off of the scheduled maintenance routine, and using the cooling system's down time to test the core."

Allana made fists, hoping to control the trembling that rocked through her own core. "When…" she took a few deep breaths, good practice for when she delivered her baby. "When will people start… dying?"

Gulping, Vasy shook his head. "I don't know. People might not die at all," he offered.

"Vasy, that's completely inaccurate and you know it."

He closed his eyes and seemed to focus on something in his head. "Once the core temperature is low enough and there's stability, I'll be coming home." At that point, he returned his attention to her eyes. "But I think you should pack a few things, Allana."

"Where are we going?" she asked, biting back her anger. Deep down, she wanted to leave. She'd tried to fight this moment, this disaster waiting to happen, and she'd failed. Now it was time to leave… time to *run*.

"Yuri's wife will be joining you for the trip back to the States," he explaiend, his firm tone leaving no room for negotiation.

Allana frowned. "Where will you be?"

"Here. Making sure we achieve our objectives."

"From the apartment? Or at the power station?" she asked, wondering if this would be a permanent goodbye.

He nodded past her at the balcony. "That's why we moved here."

Pursing her lips, Allana nodded and walked back to the stove to test the warmth of the pierogis. Satisfied that Vasy would eat them at their current temperature, she filled two plates, grabbed the tub of sour cream from the refrigerator, and served their—possibly last—dinner, taking the seat opposite him.

"So…" she started, "you're going to sit on the balcony and make sure the right number of people die."

"No, not like that," he snapped back. "I'm going to make sure there's no chance that the Soviets continue to operate this facility. Civilian death isn't a priority, and our research supports that the danger will be contained to the power station."

Allana didn't believe him, not one bit. But then, how could a man facing the promise of death—his own as well as the potential for the entire town—sit down and eat perogies? Maybe there was a bit of legitimacy to his research and statements.

"But at what cost do you determine that the power station is inoperable?" she asked, accepting that maybe he was telling the truth. She sighed. For once, maybe this was the truth.

Vasy nodded. "Yes, that's a good question. From here, I'll be able to direct the team on the ground and make sure the leak is contained."

He ate in silence, but Allana kept staring at him. She had no appetite, too worried about how things would unfold in the coming hours. Because it's great to know that maybe Vasy was telling the truth about containing the radiation, but if that were the case, why send her away with Svetlana? Why couldn't she stick around?

"I'm saving your life," Vasy said like he could read her thoughts. "You realize that, don't you? If you stay here, you'll die."

She felt her eyes shoot wide open and her shoulder drop. "You just finished saying there'd be no deaths!"

"Yuri will be here before midnight," Vasy continued, ignoring her protests, and there was something in his voice, something that made her skin crawl—rising panic. "He'll have Svetlana with him, probably waiting in the car, and he'll drive the two of you out of town to a place where a private plane will be waiting to take you out of here."

Allana heard him, but she said nothing.

"It's cautionary. Just in case I'm wrong and something goes bad." Despite his reassurance, the panic was still there.

"You asked me to fight," she said at last. "Remember that?"

"Yeah. Fight for your life."

"Help me, Vasy. I've done what you wanted, now help me go back on my terms, not on the back of some nuclear disaster that may or may have global implications."

He frowned like he might be entertaining her plea, but not long enough to convince her that he actually cared. He shook his head after less than ten seconds of consideration. "I loved you, I swear I did."

At last, it hit her. "Vasy, what's really going to happen tonight?"

He sighed, closed his eyes and rubbed his hands down his face. She'd never seen him under this much pressure before. "You have to leave with Yuri tonight, Allana. If not for yourself, please do it for our child."

She gulped, and her hand dropped automatically to her stomach. *Our child?* "Vasy—"

"I saw the test in the garbage, and I know it's mine," he interrupted her, his eyes showing a determination and conviction that didn't quite belong there.

"Nooooo," she moaned, shaking her head. She knew what he was doing. "Vasy—"

"It's already done." He stood up from the table and made his way to the door. "So pack your things."

She didn't cry. Not for Vasy or herself or anyone else. She felt sad about his decision, and she hated that he was sending her back to the States, that he didn't know just how bad tonight would be, but felt it would be bad enough that he needed to send her back. No, Allana didn't cry because she wasn't sad. She was angry.

"Vasy!"

Once he had his boots and jacket on, he walked to the elevator. Allana chased after him and before he boarded, she grabbed his sleeve and held him back.

"Vasy, listen," she begged, her eyes wide and pleading. "For god sake, I'm sorry, too. I... I didn't want things to be like this, and I'll go. Okay, I'll go."

He nodded, pulled his arm free of her grip before leaning forward and kissing her forehead. Allana hated when he kissed her like that, it was condescending and emotionless.

"Please make the right decision tonight," she begged, still begging as he stepped backward onto the elevator.

"You too," he answered as the doors shut.

# # #

The knock at the apartment door came slightly after nine o'clock. Not even close to midnight, Allana complained as she woke in the dark bedroom and considered ignoring Yuri altogether. As she dragged herself out of the bedroom, she cast a glance out to the balcony and noticed the clear, night sky and the blinking lights on the reactor towers in the distance. She wondered how much progress Vasy was making with the tests, half expecting another *SOS* flash of light.

More knocking.

With the apartment so dark, she wondered why Yuri was so persistent. Maybe Vasy had told him to not leave without her, to drag her kicking and screaming if she resisted.

Maybe something horribly wrong had already happened and they needed to evacuate.

But by the time Allana reached the door and peeked through the peephole into the hall, she noticed that it wasn't Yuri. A smile curled her lips upward and she quickly unlocked and tore the door open.

"Alex!" she nearly shouted.

"Shhh," he warned her, slipping into the dark apartment. "I'm not supposed to be here."

Locking the door, she followed him into the living room. "No kidding. What's going on?"

Even in the dark, Allana could see the terror in his face. He seemed shifty, too; bouncing from one leg to the other like he needed to relieve his bladder or was high on some kind of stimulant.

"Alex, talk to me!"

"Nikolai Fomin approved tonight's tests," he said, shaking his head. "And he's purposely staying away."

Allana's stomach sank, she suddenly felt ill. "Vasy's there now," she mumbled. *Why would Nikolai stay away when Vasy insisted on being there? Vasy wanted to destroy the place.*

Pacing, Alex slid his hands through his hair. "My contact at the KGB told me that Fomin knows that the outcome of the tests will be catastrophic. Even though it looks like the same tests they ran a year ago, they're going to change things up a little and lower pressure, kill the power and rely on the backup."

"It's routine?" Allana asked, wondering what she was missing. And then she had it, something they'd mentioned on the record album. She snapped her fingers. "Explosives," she said. "Under the reactor. Look for explosives."

Alex shook his head, placed his hands on her shoulders, and lowered his voice. "There's no time for that. Now listen to me, Allana."

"What do you meant there's no time?" Allana blinked back her fears.

"Listen to me." His grip tightened on her shoulder, hurting her a little. "I met Fomin when I was in Kiev. I told him and the committee everything I'd been hired to find out about Chernobyl. You know what Fomin said? A lot of it pointed at Vasy, or at least the job that Vasy has. So of course, with his name attached to Vasy, he was curious to hear me out."

Her chest pounded, she could barely breathe. She nodded at Alex to continue.

"Here's the thing," Alex continued, speaking quickly. "Nikolai didn't receive the test proposal from Vasy. Not even Vasy's group at the power station. That's why he approved it. In fact, despite everything I had, Fomin says Vasy has been doing a great job. Everything I delivered—the recordings, the information that only Vasy would know—Fomin questioned its legitimacy because it all contradicted his practical experience with Vasy." Alex took a deep breath. "Your husband—your *fake* husband is a golden child at the power station."

"But it was all Vasy's doing," she told him, half mumbling. "He must have manipulated others into doing his dirty work. The same way he manipulated me! And you!" She had to take a deep breath of her own. "Vasy isn't a *golden child*. If anything, he's a demon child!"

Alex nodded, motioning for her to calm down. "I know, Lana. But you should know that Vasy delivers." His wide eyes were more of a threat. "And he's promised the American government that he would deliver a decommissioned nuclear reactor."

"I know," she admitted, blinking hard again.

"Nikolai considered him a brilliant engineer. Even I consider him to be a genius, because none of his actions *appear* to be a threat. He's isolated himself quite nicely." He shook his head like he couldn't believe it.

"Vasy is *not* innocent in all of this," she insisted. "He's asked me to pack my things and leave. *Tonight*. This is going to happen soon, and it'll be too late to argue over his innocence or genius or anything!"

Alex nodded and motioned his hands again for her to calm down. "Is it possible someone else is calling the shots, Allana?"

Shaking her head, Allana just couldn't believe what she was hearing. "Are you listening to me? Tonight, Alex. Vasy set it all up! Vasy! Whatever those tests are, they're going to result in the destruction of Pripyat! Tonight!"

He frowned. "Why would he want you or me or anyone to know about that he's planning to use the tests as his vehicle to destroying the reactor?"

"I don't know." *Was Nikolai Fomin involved with this? Who else was corrupt enough to let this happen?*

While she struggled with her own thoughts, it seemed Alex wrestled with his own. "Do you think he wanted me to talk to Nikolai?"

Allana nodded. "Of course he did."

"But why?"

An hysterical laugh erupted from her tight throat. "I'm not the freelance spy, Alex! You tell *me*!"

"That's the thing. I believe something's going to happen, there's enough evidence of that. But it doesn't make sense why Vasy would have me inform the Soviets of the time, date, and method of attack."

Allana shrugged. "I'm at this level," she explained, holding one hand at breast-level, "and Vasy is at this level." She held her other hand well above her head. "Maybe he wants you to make sure the government evacuates the town?"

"Nikolai already knew about the routine maintenance schedule," Alex went on, his eyes jumping all over the place, searching the shadows and every little corner of the apartment like the answer might jump out at him. "He approved tonight's tests because there will be the right amount of emergency personnel on hand to handle any kind of deviation. And security levels will be at their highest. Everyone's expecting this."

They stared at each other for a good thirty seconds before it struck Allana. "He said the damage would be contained at the power station. With all of these people there, if they all die, nobody will be left to run the program."

The way Alex frowned and half-shrugged his shoulder, he didn't seem convinced.

"Then maybe this is just a huge distraction for something else," she suggested as an alternative.

"If they started the maintenance, then the test is already underway as well," Alex said, walking to the second bedroom. "I need to get out of here."

Allana followed him to the window. "Where are you going?"

Donning a pair of gloves, Alex opened the window and started to climb through.

"You're going to jump?"

He shook his head. "I'm going to *slide* down the side of the building. Three floors is the highest I'll go, but some of the guys I know will go as high as ten." He chuckled and shook his head, all of it in the face of the power station blowing up any minute now.

She tilted her head, eying him with bewilderment. "Um, what's wrong with the elevator?"

Although Alex laughed at her question, Allana wanted an answer. "Oh," he said, frowning. "You're serious. Well… They're probably watching the elevator. This is Vasy Gurin's apartment, someone will always be watching it."

She nodded, unable to say anything because she was sure he'd fall.

Grunting, he started to lower himself out of the window but paused. "Lana?"

"Be careful," she begged, leaning forward as if to kiss him, but stopping short because she didn't want to be the one responsible for pushing him to his death.

"You need to get out of Pripyat." Alex's face twisted with worry, and while she thought it might be the discomfort from holding himself up like that, the undeniable reality was that he simply wanted her to be safe. "Your life depends on it. Okay?"

"What about you? Are you going back to the power station?"

He grunted before answering: "No. I'm supposed to be dead." And with that, he released his hold on the window frame and disappeared.

Releasing a frightened yelp before snapping a hand over her lips, Allana leaned out the open window in time to watch him slide all the way to the ground. *He's alive.* She waved, but he didn't even look up before sprinting through the dark and disappearing into the forest.

A second later, she heard a car door open and close, followed by a shadow running in the same direction Alex had just gone.

# # #

Chapter 45

After packing her getaway bag like Vasy had asked her to, Allana retreated to the living room and dropped into the sofa. Exhausted from the day's events, she stared at the shadows, and then decided to pack the wedding photo, too. She grabbed it from the television and returned to the sofa.

The day she and Vasy had taken the fake wedding photographs had been clear and warm. Early May. They'd taken a ferry to Nantucket Island. She remembered enjoying the feeling of the wedding dress clinging to her body, the way Vasy hadn't stopped smiling, how they'd fit so perfectly together that day.

It was a fake wedding!

Fake or not, she'd believed the look in his face when he'd told that he would love her forever. And now look at them. He wanted to get rid of her. He refused to listen to her and never wanted to see her again. He'd discarded her, left her after pushing her into Alex's arms. And she hated to think that it was truly over between them. A year ago, she never would have believed that love like theirs could ever be over. They'd made so many plans.

It can't be over if it never began.

That was the truth of it, wasn't it? Unlike Alex, Vasy's sole purpose had always seemed to revolve around meeting his own needs. Whether that meant faking a marriage or using her to manage Alex and the information he received and redistributed to the KGB, her relationship with the man who had apparently saved her life was one that had concerned him only.

Even the way he makes love...

And Alex... he was the polar opposite. He existed purely for her. He'd come to her tonight, not to push his own needs and agenda upon her, but to save her and possibly everyone in the town—the planet, even—and to reinforce Vasy's message that she needed to flee.

Tonight.

So when Yuri finally arrived at a little past eleven o'clock, it seemed logical that she would join him for the walk down the hall, out to the waiting Skoda where his wife would be seated in the passenger seat, waiting with her own getaway bag in her lap.

Knock knock.

Allana rose from the sofa and glanced into the peephole.

Sure enough, Yuri was standing on the other side of that door, his face somber with a suspicious glean to his eyes. But there was someone else with him.

Mrs. Perfect. She leaned toward the door and knocked again. She looked impatient.

Sighing, Allana unlocked the door and opened it. She put a cordial smile on her face, overdoing it in the fakeness department on purpose.

"Hi."

Yuri grinned. Mrs. Perfect, aka Agent G zero two four, offered a fake smile. "You ready?"

"I changed my mind. I'm not coming with you."

Still grinning, Mrs. Perfect said it wasn't an option. "Vasy gave us strict instructions."

"Well, you can tell Seven L two three he can kiss my ass." Knowing she had to move quickly, Allana simultaneously slammed the door shut and said, "Sorry!" She snapped the lock shut as the knob rattled and the door banged against Yuri and Mrs. Perfect's attempt to break it down.

Grabbing her bag, Allana ran outside to the balcony.

What the hell am I doing?

Looking up, she realized she could never climb to Alex's apartment. And even if she could, what then? Since *up* wasn't an option, that left *down*, and despite being weak from fatigue, she leaned over the railing and swung her bag onto the second-floor balcony before climbing over the edge. Lowering herself, her toes barely touched the railing below before she released her grip and somehow landed on that next level.

That was a miracle.

Picking up her getaway bag, Allana pounded on the second-floor balcony door incessantly until the lights came on inside. A man yielding a baseball bat appeared, opening the door and shouting something at her in Ukrainian, which she didn't understand.

"Shhh," she told him, placing a finger over her mouth as she let herself into his apartment and just as quickly walked through its kitchen and left via the main door.

The man continued shouting at her in Ukrainian, but she placed a finger over her lips once more and repeated her original warning, "Shhh," which she thought was universally accepted as meaning *shut up before you get me killed.*

Apparently not getting that message, the man slammed his door and locked it as Allana slipped into the emergency stairwell and hurried down to the ground-level exit. Rushing outside, she scanned the parking lot for Yuri's Skoda, spotted it, and then decided to head in the opposite direction.

Which meant the forest.

In the middle of the night.

Taking a deep breath, she ran off with her getaway bag over her shoulder.

There was only one other place she could go, and it would take her until after midnight to reach it.

# # #

Using the apartment key she'd found in her pocket less than a week ago, Allana unlocked the door to Gregor's apartment and slipped inside. Her heart raced as she entered the darkness and slid her hand along the wall in search of a light switch. When she finally flicked on the lights, she was a little surprised that the electricity still worked.

The power station hasn't been destroyed—um, decommissioned *yet.*

She turned the lights off and called out, "Alex?" and after a few seconds, "Alex, are you here?"

When she heard nothing, she walked through the dim apartment and slipped outside onto the balcony. Pressing her sore back against the glass door, she lowered herself to the concrete surface and stared through the iron railing at the lights of the power station in the distance.

She didn't want to leave like this. Like Vasy, she wanted to be present for what would happen next. If she had her way, she would help to save lives in the morning when chaos reigned.

If there will be any chaos at all.

And if all that happened was a few people at the power station got hurt, then fine. With the town people safe, she might get on the plane after all.

She hoped that would be the case. No casualties, ideally. Just a broken nuclear reactor that would get the appropriate authorities involved to shut down the Soviet nuclear program once and for all.

Yes, that would work best, Allana realized, pressing her hands together and closing her eyes. She began praying for the safety of the town, an uninterrupted May Day weekend, but it didn't last long.

Within minutes, she fell asleep.

# # #

It wasn't the rumbling that made the floors, walls, balcony, and entire building shake, but the explosion that awakened her.

Allana's eyes snapped open and she realized how cold she was, having fallen asleep on Gregor's fifth-floor balcony with a perfect view of the power station.

She didn't know what time it was—*sometime after one o'clock*—or how long she'd been asleep, but she heard the crack of an explosion rip through the town, followed by the echoing clap that seemed to blow through the trees and across her face, and then, finally, the flash of bright light that erupted like the sun at the power station.

Right away, she felt sick.

A second later, the sky turned blue from the flames shooting toward the stars.

Rising to her numb feet, Allana stared off at the power station and the wild blaze licking at the black sky and her first worry was Vasy.

Not Alex.

Not the innocent people of Pripyat.

But Vasy.

Her fake husband who had lied to her yet again about just how "contained" this disaster would be.

# # #

Allana's lungs burned by the time she made it all the way back home—*he'd said he would supervise everything from their balcony.* Sprinting across the parking lot, she hadn't bothered to look for Yuri's Skoda, but if she had, she would have noticed that it had left. They'd abandoned her, just like she'd wanted, and now she dug through her getaway bag for the keys she'd stashed there. She came out with two and tried them both in her moment of panic. Of course, it was the second one that opened the lock.

Inside the apartment, she hurried to the sliding glass door that led to the balcony and her heart sank at what she saw.

It was vacant.

Spinning around, she called for Vasy. "Where are you?" she demanded, running down the short hallway and slamming the door to his bedroom open.

Empty.

And that was when she noticed the dresser drawers, pulled open and left empty. As if he'd grabbed all of his things and left in a hurry.

With the blue fire raging out of control at the power station, Allana began to panic.

Vasy's gone. My chance at escaping is gone, too. Now I'm going to die with the rest of the people here.

Walking around to the opposite side of the bed, she noticed the same bottle of vodka on the floor, the same cup with cigarette ashes and filters in it.

But then less than a few minutes later, she heard the apartment door crash open.

"Allana!" Vasy roared. He sounded ripe with rage.

She bolted out of the bedroom, ran down the darkened hall to his hulking shadow at the door and wrapped her arms around him. Fiercely.

He groaned under the pressure, and she smiled. *If he's alive, things can't be all that bad. He'd made a good decision after all!*

And she smiled because he'd come back. Because he was in her arms again. Because he was safe and alive, and he'd acknowledged her. He was merciful after all.

He groaned louder as she squeezed harder, and then she released him.

A light flicked on, illuminating Vasy. And she saw the burns and scratches and blood on his face. Her eyes widened in horror as she let out a scream.

# # #

For half an hour, Allana pressed ice to Vasy's face, hands, and neck, and every piece of exposed flesh. His skin had a burnt tint to it, crusted and black in patches, and his voice was coarse, worn, broken.

"There was power loss," Vasy explained without prompting. He sounded distant, a little lost like he wanted someone to know the truth. "But then power ramped up. We ordered water to cool it down. We had all kinds of water pouring into the reactor, but it didn't matter. It was already set. It was done. There was an explosion, and they'll deny that, they'll deny the explosion, Allana. They'll deny it."

"Okay," she agreed.

"But it was us. It was our explosion."

"Shhh. I know. I felt it."

"No," he said, his brows rising. She noticed the red blood vessels in his eyes, bursting and filling the whiteness. "It happened right before the buildup of steam in the core, right before the cover blew off."

She watched him try to cry, watched him struggle with the pain of the tears that refused to come.

"You should have left, Allana," he said, his voice breaking and his eyes rolling backward into his head. "You should have gone with Yuri."

She wanted to argue, wanted to tell him she couldn't have left until she knew he'd done what he said, and now that she knew it, she would go, yes she would leave because she was a lot like him, she *delivered*, but there was a pounding at the door, loud and violent and unforgiving.

"Don't answer it," he ordered, a gurgling sound in his throat.

"I won't." She brushed her hand through his hair and noticed how so many strands clung to her fingers. She knew he'd been exposed to high doses of radiation from the burn marks. Even the bursting blood vessels in his eyes confirmed that. But she hadn't expected his hair—his long, dark, lush hair—to come out in clumps between her fingers.

Suddenly, a *craaaaack!* shattered the stillness inside their silent apartment and a trio of men burst through the door. They had guns and flashlights and started shouting at her and at Vasy and at each other, all of it in Ukrainian. It happened so fast, the way two of the men picked up her fighting husband with an incredible ease and left the apartment with him. The last man to leave, he tried to shut the door, but it was no use because the frame had been broken, so he just left it, the door swinging back open and letting the hallway's emergency lighting spill into the foyer.

Allana ran after the men to stop them from taking Vasy, but the last one who left the apartment, swung around on his heel and punched her, just once, between her eyes.

Just once. But it knocked her out.

#

Chapter 46

Allana woke in a dark, damp cellar. Or it felt like that. She could tell a bandage had been placed over her face where she'd been clocked, and when she tried to wiggle her nose, the pain spread like tentacles, all the way back to her ears. Tears poured from her eyes, but they had no meaning until she remembered what had happened. Once that memory sharpened in her mind, she bolted upright in the bed, surprised that she could move at all.

Turning her head, Allana noticed two things.

The first was that her bed and the medical equipment surrounding it were encased in a semi-transparent, plastic dome of sorts. There was an opening above her bed where filtered air was fed through a hose into what she could only describe as a bubble.

The second thing was she had been cuffed to the bed.

Panic rose inside her, and she screamed as loud and as hard as she possibly could, ignoring the increasing *beep-beep-beep*-ing from the machines around her.

Within the span of a couple of minutes, as she started to feel light-headed from all the screaming, a man in a white gown, mask, and gloves came in. She knew those eyes, and then she recognized that they didn't belong to a man.

They belonged to a woman.

Mrs. Perfect.

Removing Allana's mask, she offered a studious glare. "You're lucky to be alive," she said, bitterly. "You've been exposed to twenty times more radiation than people are meant to experience in their entire lifetime."

"Where is he?" Allana spat.

Mrs. Perfect raised her hands. "Just relax. Vasy won't be with us long."

"*Where is he!*" she screamed with a voice so shrill that it curled the hair on her own arms and forced Agent G zero two four to take a step back. She'd never seemed to like Allana, but after that scream, her face soured; she clearly disliked Allana even more now.

"Relax," she ordered again, her voice stern. "You'll see him once we confirm your levels."

Allana frowned. *Levels?*

"You've been exposed, Miss Harrison. Yet your readings are abnormally... normal. It doesn't make sense." She frowned, as if she could never be wrong.

But they've been wrong all along. The power station... the radiation...

Baring her teeth and yanking on the restraints, Allana demanded, "I want to see Vasy. Now!"

# # #

Vasy's bubble was larger than Allana's. He had a larger bed, too, and oxygen tubes feeding into his bloody, mucus-crusted nostrils. But he was also in horrible shape, she saw as she pulled a plastic door aside and walked closer. His skin was charred, pulled tight against the bones in his face, and it was covered in a clear lubricant, possibly as a way to keep him comfortable. Stopping at the side of his bed, Allana saw that his eyes were closed and his chest was heaving in sporadic bursts.

It spooked her to see him like that. In fact, no matter how things had turned out for them, it broke her heart, ripped through her with a sadness she never knew existed as the entire history of their pre-Pripyat romance rushed at her. Their dates, their kisses, their love-making and the broken promises of a real marriage and lots of kids… her hand dropped to her belly and her lips trembled, and she wondered if she should be placing anything so close to where the baby grew. Vasy's baby? Or Alex's? She didn't know, and it didn't matter at this point.

Don't touch him, she'd been warned by Mrs. Perfect. *And don't speak too loud because it will make his ears bleed.*

"Vasy?" she whispered once she was close enough. "Can you hear me?"

She watched his eyes flutter open. It was a slow process, and she could tell from the acceleration of his heartbeat monitor that it was also a painful one. The whites of his eyes had gone completely red and the irises had blanched out.

He's dying. That was another warning Mrs. Perfect had given her: *Vasy has been exposed to extreme levels of radiation poisoning.*

"It's okay," she said, putting a smile to her face. "You don't have to speak."

He seemed to take a deep breath and then hold it for a few seconds before releasing it.

"I'm not here to yell at you," she said, trying to lighten the mood. "But I wanted to see you."

Another deep breath. A pause. Then release.

"I wanted to tell you that I loved you, too. I believed in you."

Another breath. A pause. Release.

"And…" she felt a tear roll down her cheek and watched it drop onto his arm. A beat later, he flinched from the pain and the heart monitor accelerated. "And Yuri is coming to get me. I'll go with him this time. I'll do what you asked me to. Happy now?" Allana smiled, still trying to keep the mood light, trying to keep herself together.

At last, Vasy closed his eyes. His breathing seemed to have stopped, too.

She leaned in a little closer, watching him and trying to remember the last time they'd danced. It was at the poker party, right in the middle of their living room floor after the turntable played Cyndi Lauper in reverse. She'd have loved to dance with him and see that same smile on his face again, one last time.

At last, Vasy inhaled a deep, long breath.

"You tried to put the fire out," she said.

He shook his head, no.

Allana choked on her laughter. "I don't believe you, Vasy." She leaned in close to kiss him, but when her nose touched his cheekbone, she held back. Not because she changed her mind about kissing the man that had dragged her through so much, but because Mrs. Perfect's voice ruined the mood.

"Maintain your distance, Miss Harrison!"

Vasy's skin felt surreal. Not like real skin, not pliant or alive at all. She also noticed that the flesh of his cheekbone clung to her nose and ripped away from his face when she pulled away.

I can't kiss him without killing him.

She wiped the torn cheek flesh from the tip of her nose. "They told me, Vasy. They told me what you did to stop that fire from getting into the atmosphere. So, I'm sorry I don't believe that you weren't the one trying to save those people."

He shook his head again, no.

"It's okay," she assured him, still smiling, still proud of his efforts. He'd made a good decision after all. It would kill him, but her faith in humanity was restored, at least a little. "Your secret is safe with me. And if it makes you feel any better, you're right; you probably didn't save anyone."

She watched his parched, split, and bleeding lips try to curl upwards.

"And I'm told by G zero two four that they started the evacuation exercise yesterday. You should know that even though it's taken this long and a lot of people have been exposed, the Soviets aren't leaving their people to die here. Reactor four has been decommissioned."

Vasy didn't even try to speak, and Allana was okay with that. She feared what sounds he might make.

"You did well by your standards," she told him with a sad nod. "And you did even better by mine when you fought the fire to save the town."

A male voice chirped up behind her, interrupting her little monologue. "You need to leave now, Miss Harrison."

Allana glanced back at a young man in full medical gear, standing outside the yellow circle painted around Vasy's hospital bed. "A minute."

"You've been exposed," the young man said, his voice stern.

Allana considered him and his advice. At last, she nodded before facing Vasy again. She leaned in closer. "I'll miss you, Vasy. And like I said, I always loved you."

They stared into each other's eyes long enough that it felt like he was urging her to get lost. So Allana smiled and nodded at his unspoken request.

All Vasy seemed able to do was close his eyes. She watched him to see if he was going to reopen them, but he didn't. He kept them closed.

As she turned away from his bed, she felt his finger tap her sleeve.

Spinning back around, Allana noticed that his eyes remained closed, but his lips were moving. Like he was trying to suck in air, trying to breathe. But that wasn't it. She leaned in closer. It wasn't that he was trying to breathe, but that he was trying to tell her something.

"More," he said in such a low volume that it barely sounded like more than breathing.

I love you more.

# # #

Epilogue

All of Allana Harrison's stories started with a party.

Thirty years later, the party looked a little different. Today, it was just a quartet of women in their mid-fifties drinking Coors out of the bottle at a comedy club in Chicago's West End. And her name was different, too. Her friends called her Nora Davis and, unlike the people that barely understood English at the poker party back in '86 Pripyat, these women were a lot more like her: single, for starters. Two of them (Denise and Tammy) had never been married, but Janet had lost her two children and husband in a small plane crash off Meigs Field in the nineties. In many ways, Janet and Allana were a lot more alike because Allana had lost her children, too. The only difference was that Allana's children had both died to save her life—the first one, her daughter, had kept her out of James' life and led her to Vasy, and the second child, her son, had absorbed all of the radiation she'd been exposed to and led to the discovery that pregnant women at the time of the Chernobyl disaster had been spared permanent damage by their fetus.

Allana had never married, never attempted to have another child. Two stillborn babies could do that to a woman.

"How do you know this guy?" Janet asked, leaning in close as the lights dimmed.

"Hmm?"

"The comedian," Janet chuckled, smacking her across the shoulder. "You never told us *how* you met."

The truth was that Allana hadn't seen Alex in three decades. When she'd noticed the ad from the *Tribune* taped to her apartment door, she'd known Alex had found her. Finally. It had taken him long enough!

"Nora!" Janet insisted. "There's a story here that you're not telling me!"

She smiled. "Another time," she promised.

"At least a teaser?" Janet begged, flapping her long lashes at her.

Rolling her eyes, Allana smiled and watched the stage as the seating area lights dimmed. "Remember how I told you about the man I married? And the other man that filled in the gaps?"

Janet's eyes widened.

"This is the one that filled in the gaps."

# # #

Acknowledgments

As cliché as it sounds, this novel would not have been possible without the help of a lot of people. I'll start with the readers who buy my books and keep pushing me to write, write more, write better, and just write. You provide a tremendous amount of direction when it comes to the stories I write, and while I write for me, I publish for you.

I couldn't write an "acknowledgments" section without making a special mention of Kelly (KM) Golland (fake name to protect the innocent, obviously) who really pushed and pushed and pushed for something new after a year and a half of absence. Your belief in me and so many other indie authors is why I write.

The fine folks who throw their hands up and offer to read through the earliest versions of my novels… you are invaluable and save me from a ton of mistakes and humiliation (which I'm good at achieving on my own). This time around, Rhonda Koppenhaver, MJ Fryer, Denise Tung, Laveda Kasch, Patricia Green, and Helen Williams were quick to offer assistance on a later draft. I can't thank you enough for putting aside your reading pleasure in favor of reading for the mistakes.

Lisa Seich for helping turn an earlier draft into something readable, so a huge thanks to you for believing in me and this story and taking the time to read through *1986* back when it was a rough, gravel road… I think it's a lot smoother now (maybe with a few potholes, but those are my doing).

Amy Clark who read through the earliest pieces of the story, 5,000 words at a time, believed in it from the start (even though you're a tough reader), and kept encouraging me to write, write, write, even when 45,000 words in a week's time seemed impossible... Anyway, it's easy to write when I know you've got the hard work looked after; you keep so much of the behind-the-scenes stuff in order for the books, websites, newsletters, social media accounts, and other projects that I don't know how any other author can ever get anything done.

And of course, my editor, Megan Hand who turned this ugly, jagged rock of a story into the gem it's become (in my eyes anyway). Turning in the first draft of *1986* took a tremendous amount of trust. Megan offered so much insight into the story and where it needed to turn that I sometimes wonder why she didn't just write the whole darn thing for me. A good question, I think... Megan is a literary guardian angel.

Hang Le of byhangle.com always takes my ideas and concepts, and she builds a book cover around it. There's true magic and genius in what she does. Hang, I appreciate how accommodating you always are with me. Thank you!

Kendell Rea who took on the truly thankless task of publicizing *1986* to the masses. Each time we chatted or messaged about an idea or concept, she renewed my faith and excitement in what *1986* was meant to be and do. A huge thank you to Kendell and the folks at Smith Publicity for turning this project into the success it was.

Lastly, my wife, Heidi, who tolerates the insanity of these tight deadlines and has a strange faith in me. I often feel like pinching myself because you are the exact opposite of the crazy spouses I write about. I obviously find my inspiration for "crazy" in the kids.

# # #

Want More From Morgan Parker?

Sign up for sample chapters from my next novel at

www.officialmorganparker.com

Scheduled for publication in September 2016, my next novel tackles the concepts of memory and love. It follows Niles Kneade as he struggles with his flawed memory, as he holds on to the belief that the love he has with his soul mate—a love unlike any other, stronger than the world's finest titanium, unbound by anything—can never be taken away… not even by a damaged memory like his. But as Niles senses the impending incident that will rob him of his memory, he decides on taking drastic measures that will allow him and his soul mate to exist together forever, holding hands and walking along the beach every night at sunset for an eternity.

Personally, I find our relationship with memory interesting. How we create and store one good (or bad) memory for a lifetime, yet manage to completely forget or supress or burn an equally good memory is something I'll never understand. This mystery struck home one spring while my family was moving and I came across a notebook I'd written during my oldest child's first year. Inside that notebook (like the ones Niles keeps), I wrote things like "we had an argument about vegetables today, and he's right, broccoli sucks," or "second day this week that he filled his diaper with the equivalent of his body weight." But I also wrote something that no parent should ever forget: "Today, he crawled up my chest at nap time and kissed me on the forehead…

greatest day ever, I didn't even wipe away the teething drool!"

I read that entry a dozen times, showed my wife, my son, anyone who would listen because my memory had somehow allowed me to forget all about that moment. When I read about that first kiss, all of those years later, I shed a tear. Not because I'd forgotten it, but because I never would have remembered it if I hadn't found my notebook.

Yes, memory is a funny thing because I don't need notebooks to remember the hospital trip for a concussion after a weekend at his grandparents, or the time I watched him win a running race, or the time he rubbed my back when I had a tummy ache.

And with my grandfather, I witnessed an incredible struggle with the cruellest memory disease, Alzheimer's. My grandfather was good at faking things, keeping his act together. During one of our last visits, he told me stories about how, at the tired aged of 89, he'd spent the entire day rowing his boat across a lake. He even faked the sore arms and apologized for not being very talkative, blaming his fatigue on the physical exertion.

Yes, memory is a ghost—you don't know if it will be kind or cruel.

That's Niles' struggle, too. He has notebooks. He has fear. He has a few made-up stories. He fakes it. But the one memory that's kind to him is the one about his love for the woman he considers his soul mate.

Well, maybe that's the cruel part.

You'll have to read the novel to come to your own conclusions about Niles and his memory and the Santa Claus of all emotions known as love.

When you sign up for my mailing list at *www.officialmorganparker.com,* I'll send you the first few chapters well ahead of the official publication date in September.